THE SARDONYX NET

"One of the best-plotted stories she's written, with a delightfully complicated story line. THE SARDONYX NET is, I think, the first evidence of Elizabeth A. Lynn as a mature writer. It's an excellent novel, and mature science fiction."

—Jeff Frane, *LOCUS*

Elizabeth A. Lynn

"HER WOMEN HAVE DIGNITY AND STRENGTH!"

—*Marge Piercy*

"A FINE EAR FOR THE RIGHT WORD AND A FINE EYE FOR ACTION!"

—*Vonda McIntyre*

The SARDONYX NET

ELIZABETH A. LYNN

BERKLEY BOOKS, NEW YORK

*For Marta, who read it first, and
for Debbie, who read it twice.*

This Berkley book contains the complete
text of the original hardcover edition.
It has been completely reset in a type face
designed for easy reading, and was printed
from new film.

THE SARDONYX NET

A Berkley Book / published by arrangement with
the author

PRINTING HISTORY
Berkley-Putnam edition / December 1981
Berkley edition / June 1982

ISBN: 0-425-05326-1

The assistance of the following people is gratefully acknowledged: Dr. Jane Robinson, Dr. Seelye Martin, Sonni Efron, Lyndall MacCowan, Martha McCabe, Fran Krauss, Ellen Jacobs, Robert W. Shurtleff, Marion Zimmer Bradley, Gordon R. Dickson, Chelsea Quinn Yarbro, David G. Hartwell, and Yvon Chouinard.

"History is not romantic."
—Nakamura Kenji, *History of Chabad*

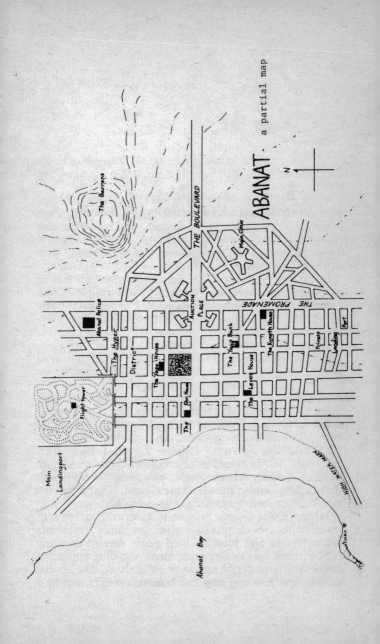

Chapter One

Dana Ikoro, smuggler, stood facing Monk the drug courier across the floor of the starship *Treasure*. He was furious.

Monk had ebony skin and a sleek, shaven skull. She wore silver leggings and ruby earrings, and between her breasts dangled a shiny gold medallion, sister to the one Dana Ikoro wore around his neck. She was well known on the dorazine circuit. She was two meters tall and Dana had to look up to her.

It was not a position he liked. He clenched his fists in his pocket and swore under his breath in Pellish. Monk gazed at him, eyelids drooping evilly, ostenstatiously bored. He repeated what she had just told him. "The drugs have already gone?"

She nodded, slouching. "That's right."

He could see she enjoyed his discomfort, and it enraged him. "You want to tell me how you managed to lose three thousand unit doses of dorazine?"

She shrugged. "I follow instructions. Instructions said, Wait for a ship carrying this code, hitting these coordinates, at this time. I pick up the stuff from the robo, Jump here, wait. Twenty minutes ago, *Lamia* Jumps in, matches codes with me. I know *Lamia*. I know Tori Lamonica. We've done business before. Codes match, we transfer. Twenty minutes later, you Jump through with the identical code, the dorazine's gone. That's not my fault." She gazed over his head as she talked.

Jacked, Dana thought. Damn it, Lamonica jacked me!

He'd never been jacked before. Dorazine was prime cargo. Damn and blast it, he'd never *carried* dorazine before! He'd had to buy equipment: the drug spoiled at temperatures under 6° and over 14° Celsius. The special cooling unit had cost him five hundred credits, but he'd expected to realize at least three thousand upon sale of the drug on Chabad. He was not only out his own money, but he'd been made a fool of, and in the smugglers' canon, ridicule presaged poverty. He might never get a second chance to run the drug.

It did not make him feel any better to know that he'd been taken by an expert. Tori Lamonica boasted of her skill in jacking cargoes in every sector, planet, and port of the Living Worlds. He controlled his anger with an effort. This was Monk's ship; he could hardly tear it to bits as he wanted to—and Monk didn't care if he went bust as vacuum.

"Great," he said. "That was my cargo. Now what do I do? Got any suggestions?"

She smiled, showing perfect teeth. "Jack someone else."

Dana bristled. "That's not my style. I'm no thief."

The tall woman yawned. "I wouldn't call Tori Lamonica a thief—not to her face, anyway. Who suckered you into this business?"

The question was rhetorical and insulting but Dana decided to answer it anyway; he might learn something. "I've been running comine," he said. "I thought I might make more credits working for The Pharmacy."

"Sure," said Monk. "If you don't land in a cell." She took two steps to the pilot's chair, sat in it, touched a button negligently. The screens came on. "Don't know why Tori wants your cargo, anyway. Dorazine's not safe."

"What?"

"You haven't heard?" Monk tilted her head to one side. Even her eyebrows were shaved. "That new top drug cop, A-Rae. He's snake-mean about the dorazine trade. Obsessed. The cops have left off haunting drop points—not that it ever did them any good. They're clustered down in Sardonyx Sector off Chabad, picking runners up when they try to land, playing leapfrog along the spaceways."

"I hadn't heard about that," Dana admitted.

"The regulars are looking for other work," said Monk. She chuckled, and stretched her legs halfway across the starship's floor. "The Pharmacy's *real* unhappy."

All the regulars except Lamonica, Dana thought. He glanced at the starship's vision screen. It showed the darkness of spacetime normal, mitigated by the pulsing light from a nearby Cepheid. The yellow star had no planets, and that made it a convenient place for a drop point. There were hundreds of such points scattered through the eight Federation sectors.

"Lamonica's going to Chabad," Dana said. It was not a question. Hypers did not ask each other about other Hypers.

Monk yawned again. "She's got nowhere else to go. She's carrying dorazine." Her tone was weary—an expert, explaining something to a slightly stupid novice. Dana's temper flared. He turned and strode to the lock which connected Monk's ship with his own. He slithered through it, graceful as all Hypers were, balancing without thought as the floor rippled under his feet. Palming the hatchway plate, he waited for the door to open, then grabbed the bar and swung within his starship's curving walls. The door slid shut. He checked the seal. . . . "Disengage," he said over the audio link.

Zipper jogged as the other ship sucked back the lock tube. Dana watched in his screen as *Treasure* Jumped, going from silver-gray to blue, to green, to orange, to blazing red. . . . After the ship vanished into the Hype, the rainbow emissions lingered in normal space.

The Cepheid pulsed, half a light-year away. Dana swore at it in Pellish. The day he'd been accosted in Liathera's, the Hyper bar on Nexus, he'd thought the luck was at last turning to smile his way. Now it seemed as if she were only playing with him. . . . He'd probably never get a chance to run dorazine again. Now he could go back to the gamblers' runs—running nightshade for the Verdians—picking up two hundred credits here, five hundred credits there, always watching his back for the Hype cops. Damn! He'd lived like that for six standard months, loathing every insecure minute of it. It was a cheap, chancy way to survive.

Or—he loathed the thought—he could sell his ship, and work for some damn corporate fleet, no longer Starcaptain but a simple pilot, taking the orders of some fish-brained, planetbound administrator.

He'd be damned and pickled before he'd live like that. Fingering the medallion round his neck, he wondered which of Liathera's regular customers had overheard his conversation with The Pharmacy's agent. It might have been anybody with good ears, catching a word here, a code there, waiting until the deal was set, then trotting off to sell the information to Tori Lamonica. He'd never know. He wondered how much she'd paid for the information. Savagely, he hoped it had been a lot.

Now he had nothing: no money—well, very damn little, just enough to survive—no dorazine to sell, not even the name of a contact in Sardonyx Sector. He blanked the vision screen to help himself think, and sat in the navigator's chair. It creaked. Everything on *Zipper* creaked or whined or rattled, except the Drive. But she was *his,* his ship, his home, his ticket to the Hype. No one who was not a Hyper could quite understand what it felt like to have your own ship. He'd picked her out of the Nexus yards, with Russell O'Neill's help. . . . He wondered if, by some lucky chance, Russell might be working Sardonyx Sector. Russell the Pirate; Russell the thief. Russell might know someone on Chabad.

But Russell did not run drugs. Indeed, the redhead had warned him sharply that if he was planning to turn drug courier, he should stay well away from Sardonyx Sector.

"I won't argue morals," Russell had said. "But consider some facts—the Yago Family owns the Net, and the Net runs on dorazine. So, when you transport dorazine to Chabad, you can figure that most of it is destined for the Net. But it's as illegal to transport dorazine to Sardonyx Sector as it is in any other sector of the Federation, and if the Hype cops catch you with it anywhere in the sector, they'll try you and convict you and toss you into prison, and from prison you'll go to the Net, where they'll shoot you full of dorazine and turn you into a slave on Chabad, and serve you right. You want to run drugs, that's your business, not mine. You make your own ethical choices. But you'd better get some more experience on the circuits, Dana, before you try to run dorazine."

Dana grinned, remembering. . . . That conversation, like many others during the six months he'd been pilot on the *Morgana,* had ended up in bed. He'd never made love with a man before, but he learned soon enough that it was hard to say no to Russell. The loving had been fun. But he'd kept the lecture in mind over the last eight months. For the first two of them, he had even looked for legal work. Russell, had he heard of *that,* would have surely laughed. Finding nothing that sparked his interest, Dana had turned to the drug trade. Gamblers' runs had seemed exciting, at first, but the excitement quickly palled. And then, in Liathera's, the agent said, "You've got quite a reputation. Aren't you getting a bit tired of gamblers' runs?"

Dana admitted that he was.

"You're young, tough. Maybe you'd like to pick up some bigger credits?"

"Sure."

"Want to work with The Pharmacy? You'd need some supply money—nothing much, maybe eight hundred credits—and a contact in Sector Sardonyx. But you've got that, I'm sure."

"Sure," Dana said again.

He'd lied. He didn't know one single soul on Chabad. But the agent hadn't known he'd lied, and why should he? With a cooler full of dorazine, Dana had figured, he'd find a dealer after two hours on Chabad. The agent's instructions were simple. They liked two-courier runs in the dorazine trade. Dana, as the second runner, would be responsible for making pickup and paying the transfer fee. He would then proceed from the drop point through the Hype to just off Chabad. He would land *Zipper* illegally, fly his bubblecraft to Abanat, the planet's only city, and meet—find, Dana had thought—a dealer.

Half an hour ahead of him, with his dorazine in *Lamia's* cooler and six years of experience in Sardonyx Sector, Tori Lamonica was thinking about him, and laughing.

He scowled at *Zipper's* walls. Then he punched instructions to the ship's computer, putting the starship at half-gee gravity. Shedding his clothes, he jumped for the monkey bars. The smooth metal bars, each a meter long and half a meter out from the wall, ran up one curving wall at intervals, like ladder rungs, over *Zipper's* ceiling and back down in a regular track to the other "side" of the continuous wall. Hand over hand, Dana pulled himself along until his shoulder muscles ached and his ivory-yellow skin felt oiled. He dropped lightly down, breathing hard. Climbing the bars was good exercise, and they were remarkably useful when the ship went into null-grav. Better than magnets in free-fall.

Now—what to do? He could return to Nexus. He was not *entirely* without funds, and in a cache in the wall he had a small stash of comine which it would not be hard for him to sell. Or—he grinned—he could go on to Chabad and try to run a doublejack on Tori Lamonica. He'd have to be crazy to attempt it, inexperienced as he was and without a single contact in Abanat. The only thing that might make it work was that Lamonica would not be expecting it. . . .

And why not? His grin widened. He could try it. He'd never been to Chabad; he might as well see it. It could be fun. He pulled his jumpsuit back on. The comine, still wrapped, sat snugly in its hole in a wall panel. Grabbing it, Dana palmed the inner door of the lock, pushed the bagged powder through, closed the door, and punched the button which released the outer lock door. He turned on the vision screen to watch the comine go: transparent bags bursting, comine floating, granule by granule, into vacuum, wreathing the ship. With no drugs onboard, he should have no trouble landing on Chabad's moon and passing the inspection which he knew they would subject him to in Port. Clean as a cop or a tourist, he would ride a shuttleship to Abanat, well ahead of Tori Lamonica taking the tortuous overland route from her concealed ship in her bubblecraft. When she arrived in Abanat, looking for her dealer, he, Dana, would be waiting for her.

He wondered if he should jettison the dorazine cooler. Its very presence on the ship would tell a cop what he had really come to Chabad for. But, damn it, he'd paid five hundred credits for it, and besides, he would need it if—when—the doublejack worked. They would suspect him, but they might do that anyway, and so what if they did? Intent to commit a crime was not by itself criminal.

He touched a button on the computer console. Clear music lilted through the ship, obliterating the hum of machinery. It was old music. It had been written by a man named Stratta during the strange and joyful time after the Verdian ships touched on Terra. Dana had heard it on a street corner in Nexus. He had practically had to shake the composer's name out of the startled street artist. He had never paid much attention to music before, but this music was—different: clear as a theorem, stirring and haunting. He carried with him in *Zipper* a collection—perhaps the best collection that existed—of Stratta's pieces, on musictapes. They perfectly complemented his solitude.

He told the computer to find him the fastest course to Chabad. It blinked figures at him. The course took three standard days: two in the Hype, a Jump from this into another hyperspace current, another half a day in hyperspace, half a day through spacetime normal to Chabad's only moon. He told the ship to use the course. He settled into the pilot's chair; the Drive came on. Spacetime normal went away. Dana cleared the vision screen; from rainbow it darkened into the brutal, mind-capturing blackness of the Hype. At an unimaginable distance, red dust glittered, the dust of dying stars, or of stars not yet born.

Ikoro smiled as the music wove its melody around him. His young, rather stern face relaxed. His dark eyes lost their angry gleam. Lamonica had a start on him, but it would take her at least a day to fly from the wilds of Chabad to Abanat. He tapped his fingers to the complex, familiar tune. Even if the Hype cops boarded him, which they might not do, since he had only a minor reputation, even if they did, they would have only a shred of evidence on which to hold him.

"To Domna Rhani Yago, from . . ."

Rhani Yago sat in the alcove of her bedroom, sifting through her mail. The hot, bright light of Chabad's sun drove through the panes of glass, reflecting sharply off the papers and lightening the color of the deep blue walls. A few elegantly calligraphed missives dignified the day's scattering of computer-printed reports. The topmost letter was from the manager of the Yago-owned kerit farm in Sovka. Respectfully hysterical, he informed her that kits from the last four litters of Prime Strain kerits had been found dead in their cages, apparently from massive internal hemorrhage. He enclosed the post-mortem analyses from the Sovka laboratory. Rhani examined them: translated from their jargon, they said: *"Sorry, we don't know what this is."*

The next letter was from Sherrix Esbah, Family Yago's principal drug dealer in Abanat. Apologizing, Sherrix stated firmly that she could not possibly supply her usual quarterly shipment of dorazine. The drug runners were bringing in comine, nightshade, tabac, zimweed, but the pressure was on in Sector Sardonyx, and no one was carrying dorazine.

The next letter was grimy. Rhani opened it with care, read the ugly threat within, and put it away. Beneath it was her house steward's report. She laid that aside too, for later. She had no doubt that it would be accurate; Cara Morro had run the Yago estate for twelve years, since before the death of Rhani's mother Isobel, and her reports were unfailingly accurate. The last letter lay sealed. It bore the Dur crest: a stone axe, raised to strike. *"From Ferris Dur,"* read the superscription, *"to Domna Rhani Yago."* Rhani touched the beautifully textured paper with her fingertips. Paper was one of the few things that could be manufactured out of the tough, orange, thumbsized grass of Chabad. A month ago the lettering would have read, *"From Domna Samantha Dur."* But Domna Sam was dead. Half of Abanat, it had seemed, had joined the twilight procession that had taken her coffin to its grave. It would be hard for Ferris to succeed her. He was waiting out the forty days of respect before he took the title Domni. Family Dur was the First Family of Chabad and they never let you forget it; everything they did or said or owned had style. At least, it had been so when Domna Sam was alive.

Rhani broke the seal on the letter. She read it in growing puzzlement. ". . . Demand to speak to you on business of import to Chabad . . . reply without fail . . . hope this will be convenient for you. . . ." Such phrases did not belong in a letter from the head of one Family to another. This was how she might write to the manager of the kerit farm. She controlled her annoyance and laid this communication, too, aside. She turned in her chair to look at Binkie, her secretary. "Do I have to go on?"

"You might want to look at the PIN reports."

PIN stood for Public Information and News, Chabad's wonderfully redundant news system. It catered mostly to the tourists. Rhani glanced at the headlines. "WHAT TO DO AND SEE AT THE AUCTION." "Feh," she said disdainfully. "THE LIFE-CYCLE OF A KERIT." "They only print what we give them." She touched the threatening letter.

"There have been more of these lately than usual, haven't there? Some steps should be taken to find their source."

"I'll see to it."

"Tell Cara I'll see her here this afternoon. And one last thing. Send a communigram to my brother."

Binkie's training held, his face and voice did not change, but his long pale hands fisted at his sides. "What message?"

"Send a précis of these letters. Let me see it first. Include the report from Sovka, the letter from Sherrix, and the one from Ferris Dur. And you'd better include the threat. The Net should be off Enchanter. Send a message capsule with a 'For-Your-Eyes-Only' seal. The whole sector doesn't need to know our business, so leave the Yago crest off the capsule, and omit the place of origin. Zed will know."

"As you wish, Rhani-ka." He took the letters from her, and went to the compscreen to draft the précis. Rhani gazed out her window. The familiar image of the breedery in Sovka—white buildings, orange grass broken by the bleak wire fencing of the kerit runs—superimposed itself upon the even more familiar green. The death of eighteen Prime Strain kerits was going to hurt the breeding program. The manager sounded badly flustered. At least he had been able to keep the news of the deaths from leaking out to PIN. He had been her mother's appointment to the position; Rhani had been planning to suggest to him that he should retire.

And something was wrong with Ferris Dur, if he thought he could order her to meet him, as if she were his employee or his slave, and not in fact his equal, and head herself of the Third Family of Chabad. She remembered him vaguely from the last few months when Domna Sam had been so sick, giving orders to the house slaves; he had struck her then as an arrogant, impatient man. She wondered what he thought was so important that she would drop her work to see him, and why he didn't simply tell her what it was. Eventually he would.

The veins in the polished marble of her desk gleamed in the sunlight. That was something else Chabad produced: stone. But there were few quarries on the planet: workers and machines could not endure the glare of Chabad's sun, and the breakdown rate for both was ridiculously high.

Rhani traced the patterns with one finger. The marble was lovely and cool. The drying up of the drug supply worried her badly, and she hoped it would not go on long. It had never happened this severely before.

Chabad had to have dorazine. It was the glue that held the slave system together; without it, the men and women who did most of the labor on Chabad would grow sullen and angry, resentful of their penitential status; they would plan and scheme and ultimately rebel. Without dorazine, Chabad would need an army to keep them at their jobs; with dorazine, all it needed was the drug. It often struck her, the irony of the Federation statutes that made transport of dorazine to the sector illegal. The law was a sop thrown to those who felt that slavery (unlike prisons, brain-wipe, forced therapy, etc.) was immoral, and yet the moralists could not see that dorazine was the one element that made slavery endurable for most of the slaves, that kept them docile and sane, most of the time. It was the moralists who had created The Pharmacy and the drug runners, not Chabad.

Rhani contemplated, for a few moments, making the formal request of the Federation of Living Worlds that the sale of dorazine to Chabad be made legal. Legalization would slash the black market price. It might even force The Pharmacy, whoever and wherever it was, to sell her the dorazine formula. For five years, Sherrix—and Domino four years before her—had sent a message through the drug network to The Pharmacy: *"Name a price. Family Yago will buy."* They had never answered; Rhani did not even know if the offer had reached them. There *was* precedent for a Yago to approach the Federation. But she shook her head; only for an emergency would she consider bringing Chabad to the attention of the Federation. It was easier for them all to buy the euphoric/tranquilizer on the illegal market than to subject Chabad to the presence of and problems created by outsiders.

Pushing back her chair, she walked the few steps to the glass doors that led onto the terrace garden. She slid the doors open and walked out onto the balcony. Amri knelt there, watering the fragile dawn plants that nestled in the brickwork. Seeing Rhani, she stopped work. Rhani smiled at her and gestured at the pale blue blossoms.

They looked random, stuck in the cracks of brick. She
remembered Timithos digging around the bricks with a
trowel, setting each tiny plant into a crack by hand.
Nothing green grew accidentally on Chabad. "Go on,
Amri," she said. Amri picked up the watering can.

The lawns lay below the balcony, green and lush,
pretending to be a countryside. The estate was eighty
years old. It had been built by Orrin Yago, Rhani's
grandmother. Rhani dimly remembered Orrin: an old,
bent woman with silver hair who leaned on a black cane.
Beyond the estate wall lay orange hills. West of the Yago
estate by ninety-seven kilometers lay Abanat, Chabad's
capital and only city, set like a bright jewel by the shore of
a warm and sluggish sea. North of Abanat lay Sovka;
south of it, Gemit, site of the Dur mines. White-and-black
roofs and bits of green marked where the colonists of
Chabad lived. Elsewhere on land it was hot, red-brown,
and dry. Nobody lived there now.

Once someone had. Rhani leaned on the balcony wall,
looking over the green of the estate to Chabad's terra-
cotta hills. She knew her planet's history rather better
than the tourists who swarmed the streets of Abanat. At
the end of the twentieth century, Old Earth reckoning,
the Verdian ships had landed on that planet, bringing the
hyperdrive equations and access to the galaxy to the
human race. Repossessed of a frontier, humans set out
with great energy to colonize the stars. They founded
New Terra, and New Terrain, and Enchanter and Ley and
Galahad and Summer and colonies on planets all over the
Milky Way. The center of their universe became Nexus
Compcenter, where the starship fleet was based. A colony
might be no more than several thousand people. Some
were less. They survived, fighting heat and cold and
disease and famine and the venalities of humankind.

In most colonies, criminals, however the colony defined
them, were either killed or ostracized. In one sector of
space, the colonies—who were light-years away from
each other in spacetime normal but a few days' flight from
each other in Hype time—decided to create a prison
planet, on which criminals could be dumped to work out
their salvation or damnation apart from those they had
harmed.

They chose an uncolonized, largely lifeless world circling an AO dwarf star, and named it Chabad. Its seas were salty and warm, its land masses regular and dry and covered with orange plants whose stalks were thick as an average human thumb. It had no birds, no bears or seals or tigers or horses or trees, no maize growing wild. It had beetles and snakes and clawed vicious, furry predators named *kerits*. The colonies in Sardonyx Sector sent their criminals there, with tents and tools and packets of seed.

Most died. More arrived every year, to burrow and thirst and mostly die. At the end of the first century after the opening of space, a group of investors came to Chabad from Nexus. There were four of them: one of them was Lisa Yago, Rhani's great-great-grandmother. They mined and tested and scanned. They discovered huge cores of silver and gold. They developed techniques to breed the truculent kerits for their incredibly beautiful fur. They realized that Chabad's inhospitableness itself could be exploited, and they built Abanat on the seashore. They watered it with towed icebergs from Chabad's small poles. They turned it into paradise, a feast of color and light and music, and beyond paradise lay the barren rusty hills of Chabad.

The rich of Sardonyx Sector came to Abanat to play. Tourists on Chabad bought kerit pelts and handblown glass and tapestries and golden chains and silver rings, and slaves.

Rhani gazed at Amri, still watering the flowers. The young slave's eyes were focused and clear, pupils normal, and she had none of the symptoms of the dorazine addict about her. It was a point of pride with Family Yago that their house slaves were never kept on dorazine. The dorazine that the Yagos bought went to the kerit farm in Sovka, or to the Net. Most of it went to the Net. Rhani rubbed the top of the brick wall. It was powdery with dust. It had seemed a logical transition to the investors, to make the criminals who came to Chabad each year into slaves. Surely, it was easier to be a slave than a prisoner in a cell, or an exile condemned to swelter and starve in the shadeless valleys of Chabad's hills. She recalled the text of the threatening letter. It was the fourth in three months. "WE WILL KILL YOU, SLAVER. Signed, The Free Folk of Chabad."

At least the Free Folk of Chabad are terse, she thought.

A dragoncat, its coat flame-red, long tail waving, came silently onto the terrace and poked its head under her hand to be stroked. It rubbed its shoulder against her thigh. She petted it absently. It went to sniff at Amri, who scratched its ears. It purred. Rhani smiled; she loved the graceful beasts. They had full freedom of the house and grounds. They were imports from Enchanter, whose labs had given them their fanciful name. They had sharp claws and great speed and were rather more intelligent than the great Earth cats whose genes they had been bred from. They fretted, sometimes, at the heat, and the sameness of the smells, at the lack of hunting, and especially at the walls that edged the greenery and kept them in, unable to run. But in the burning, waterless plains, they would only die.

She went back to the house, and touched the intercom. "Binkie." It sounded through every room. Silent as one of the dragoncats, he came to the door. "Get me the files on the personnel at the kerit farm," she said. "Someone has to be promoted to the cretin manager's place."

He bent over the computer. "Yes, Rhani-ka."

Sitting at the desk, she dug out a piece of paper and her favorite pen. She wrote to Sherrix in their private code, offering to pay double the quoted price for dorazine if that would unblock the market, although she did not think it would. Then she spread out her steward's accounts, and was soon absorbed in them. The rise and fall of her household, for an hour, was as important to her as the rise and fall of her financial hegemony. When Binkie brought the stack of printouts to her, she said, without lifting her head, "Leave them here."

The fair-haired secretary/slave laid the files down on one corner of the big marble desk, and went away.

Zed Yago, commander of the Net, paced along the curving corridor of his kingdom toward his cabin. His eyes stung. He had been wakeful for nearly two shifts, supervising the transfer of slaves from the Enchanter prison ships to the Net cells, and he was very tired. The Net rotated in spacetime normal off Enchanter while the third shift checked out the systems before the final, long-awaited Jump to Chabad, to home.

Two crew members passed him; they were suitless, as

he was, looking forward no doubt to well-deserved sleep. They murmured greetings, and he nodded back, friendly but aloof, for on the Yago Net he was king, master, overseer, senior medic, and controller. He touched the pouchpocket on his chest, feeling the slight stiffness of the scrap of microfiche. A message capsule had brought it through the Hype to Enchanter, and Enchanter had 'grammed it to the great, graceful, silver torus.

In his cabin, Zed slid the microfiche into the viewer's slot. Words marched across the creamy background. Zed recognized his sister's secretary's style, and smiled.

But as he read the message, his smile vanished. When it ended, he tossed the plastic strip into the disposal, and brushed the switch of the communicator that put him in touch with the bridge.

"This is Zed."

"Clear, Zed-ka." That was deep-voiced Jo Leiakanawa, his second-in-command, the Net's chief navigator.

"Double-time the checkout. Get us home."

"Yes, Zed-ka." The communicator pinged once and was silent. Zed sat on the hard bunk. His hair was red-brown, like his sister's, and he wore it to the shoulders, and almost always tied. He stretched his legs out, staring without seeing at the bulkhead in front of him.

Three out of ten Chabadese months he lived in the Net, not luxuriously. The great craft consisted mainly of the Drive Core and two kinds of storage space: holds for food, water, and drugs; and cells in which people could stand, sit, and lie. They could not walk more than a few steps; where on the Net would slaves need to walk to? The crew cabins were little bigger than the slave cells. Each year the Net traveled to Sabado, Belle, Ley, and Enchanter, the other four worlds of Sardonyx Sector, to choose prisoners from their prisons to fill the Net cells. The sector worlds paid the Net for this service. The Net had particular standards; some criminals were too brutal to make useful slaves; others, too stupid. The Net medics, including Zed, spot-checked prisoners and reports before allowing the prisoners to be loaded. This, Enchanter, was the end of that circuit. Now the Net returned to Chabad, where the Auction would be held.

Non-Chabadese swarmed to the planet at this time,

willing to live in Abanat and pay exorbitant residence taxes so that they might own one, two, a household of slaves. Wealthy Chabadese bought house slaves. The city bought maintenance slaves. Slaves came with their owner's credit disks in their hands to buy garden or factory or workshop slaves. Ex-slaves, now with skills and businesses to run, came to pick out slaves. Net crew members spent their credits in the Hyper bar in Abanat. In seven months a shuttleship would take them, broke and bored, from Abanat to Port on the moon, and they would ready the Net to Jump once more.

"Attention, third shift crew. Attention, third shift crew." That was Jo's voice. Zed heard the sound of running feet outside his closed door. The crew would be angry at the new orders; they were tired of working hard. Zed shrugged. They would not show their irritation to him. Complaints would go to Jo; she handled the crew. She was good at it. Though he was its commander, Zed knew very well that he could not have run the Net without her. That knowledge did not trouble him at all.

For one swift, sybaritic moment, Zed permitted himself to think of Rhani standing in the moonlight on the green lawn of the Yago estate, or smiling under the Chabad sun, waiting for him. That vision had succored him for five years on Nexus, while he learned to be a pilot and then a medic; even now it eased his heart. With practiced discipline, he turned away from it to think of something else: the message, particularly that enigmatic communiqué from Ferris Dur. Till the building of the Net—begun by Orrin, finished by Isobel Yago—Family Dur had been richer than Family Yago. Now, without seeing the balance sheets, Zed guessed that Family Yago's profits exceeded Family Dur's, and had for ten years. Samantha Dur had not been a woman to see money flowing past without trying to tap it. She had made a formal offer to buy into the kerit farm. The offer had been refused. In the Chabad Council, her deputy had moved to raise the hefty fee the Yagos paid yearly for license to operate the Net. The Council defeated the bill. He wondered if, in pique and in senility, she had initiated a bit of sabotage at the kerit farm. Rhani would know better than he; she knew the old woman as well as anyone. But Zed knew that at ninety-three Samantha Dur had never learned to listen when someone else said, "No."

Was Ferris Dur trying to follow those implacable footsteps? Zed tried to remember what the Dur heir looked like. Dark, he thought. They didn't meet more than once or twice within a year. Zed ignored the social whirl, preferring the solitude of the Yago estate to tourist-laden Abanat. He hated parties.

His wrist communicator let out a tone. "Yes, Jo," he said.

"Zed-ka, the checkout is proceeding as ordered, no problems, but we have a medical query on Level 6, Block A, Cell 170, and I can't get response from Nivas." Nivas Camilleri was the on-shift senior medic.

"She's probably asleep," said Zed. "She worked two shifts, like everybody else. What's the situation?"

"Permission is asked to increase dorazine dosage."

"I'll look."

On Level 6, Block A, outside the door of Cell 170, a worried junior medic stood, peering through the door of one-directional glass, keys jangling in her hand. The occupant of the cell was a brown fat man. He was sitting on the bunk, huffing; there was a purpling bruise on his forehead. As Zed watched, he gathered himself up, hunched his shoulders, and threw himself into the bare wall, keeping his hands at his sides. His head and one shoulder hit the wall; he fell, gasping, to the floor. He crawled back to the bunk again and faced the wall. "Senior, don't you think—" said the junior medic.

"Yes," said Zed. He brushed a hand over his head, freeing his hair from its tie so that it fell to his shoulders. Taking the key from the junior hand, he opened the cell door and went inside.

The fat man looked up. He had split open the bruise on his forehead. Blood trickled down the left side of his face. Zed glanced at the wall screen on which the prisoner's name, age, crime, planet of origin, planet of imprison-ment, dorazine dose, and length of slave contract were noted. "What are you doing?" The man did not answer. Zed repeated it. "What are you doing, Bekka?"

Bekka's gaze fixed on him. His pupils were moderately dilated. "D-d-damaging the merchandise."

"Why are you doing that?"

"You think I'm going to go and be a slave?" He

staggered upright. "Get out of my way."

He took a deep breath, preparing to launch himself forward again. Zed took a step and caught the man's left arm, fingers finding the nerve just above the elbow. Bekka's feet went out from under him at the unexpected pain. He landed hard, his face screwed into a grimace. "For a man who managed to embezzle credits from two fairly astute companies, you're not very bright," Zed said. He put the pressure on. "Are you listening?"

"Ah—don't—yes!"

Zed let go. Bekka curled the fingers of his right hand around his left elbow. "You're an accountant and a programmer. A slave with talent can go far on Chabad. You're on a five-year contract. At the end of five years, you'll step into the streets of Abanat a free man, with credits enough to buy passage offplanet, a house, a business, even your own slaves. You'd be surprised at how many ex-slaves stay on Chabad when their contracts expire. Make trouble and you'll spend the next five years in a dorazine daze, grinning like a dog, with no sense of who or where you are. Behave, and you might get to keep your senses and do the work you like. You understand?"

"Yes," said the rebel.

"Then stop acting the fool. Will you behave?" Zed touched the man's left arm again.

He jumped, and stammered, "Yes. Yes."

"Good. Clean him up." Zed left the cell to let the junior medic work. He was almost disappointed in how swiftly the man had capitulated, but not, he reflected, disappointed enough to have prolonged the incident. Bekka was not, physically or emotionally, an especially interesting type. The medic worked swiftly. When she finished, she came into the corridor, locking the door behind her. Bekka sat quietly in his cell, a gel bandage over the cut. "Tell the guards to check on him every two hours," Zed said. "And increase his dorazine dosage for the next three days to one-point-five-five, until we get to Port."

He went back to his cabin. The encounter with Bekka had made him sweat. He stripped, and stepped for a few minutes under the warm spray of the shower. A visitor to the room might have been surprised. It contained no ornaments, no pictures except a small holocube of Rhani

Yago, no pillows or rugs, nothing to soften the utilitarian
severity of walls and floor. In comparison, the technicians'
quarters in the Net were hedonistic. But no one knowing
Zed Yago would have been surprised. He was not that
kind of a sensualist.

He lay down on the bunk. The ship's walls hummed
softly. Zed Yago lived three months out of his year within
that sound; he no longer heard it.

It changed. The equipment check was complete. In the
Core of the Net, the Drive came on. The ship Jumped.
Zed curled his knees almost to his chest, and closed his
eyes.

Chapter Two

Coming into Port on Chabad's moon, the sky was
thick with ships, if, Dana thought, you could pretend that
an airless planetoid possessed a sky.

The ships were invisible but extremely audible. "Flight
Tower calling *Seminole* . . ."

"*Seminole* here, Juno on the stick. Hello, Control. Will
you tell Ramirez to please get his nose out of my ass!"

"Control to Ramirez, back off. Calling *Mirabelle*.
Come in, *Mirabelle*."

"*Mirabelle* here, Control. Ramirez on the stick. I'm
backing off; two hours I've been backing off. My passengers are sick of staring at the shiny side of a rock."

"Tough shit, Ramirez. Calling *Cholla*, Hello,
Cholla . . ."

Lying on his bunk, half-asleep, Dana grinned as the
pilots bickered and snapped at each other across the
spaceways. He rubbed his eyes. He'd slept since the Jump
out of hyperspace into spacetime normal. Crossing the
ship to the control console, he pulled a food bar from the
unit and sat in the pilot's chair to add his own voice to the
chatter. "*Zipper* calling Flight Tower. *Zipper* calling
Flight Tower."

There was a lag, then a voice crackled, "Flight Tower
to *Zipper*. Identify, please."

Dana pursed his lips. Of course they did not know him,
as they knew Juno and Ramirez and the pilots of the

passenger lines. He said, *"Zipper,* MPL-48 Class, home registry Nexus, pilot and owner Starcaptain Dana Ikoro. Request permission to birth."

Control's impersonal voice softened, momentarily respectful. "Permission granted, Starcaptain. Welcome to Chabad."

"Welcome," said a woman's voice. "Juno in *Seminole* here."

"Thank you, Juno," Dana said.

The other pilots echoed her, offering him welcome. Control broke in: "Starcaptain, please lock your computer in for descent."

Dana snorted. Pointedly, he said, "Wipe your own ass, Control." But Control was already bitching at someone else.

His ship's computer yapped silent numbers to itself. They flowed across the compscreen. There was no need for him to be awake; nothing ever happened during descent that a ship's computer could not handle. Nevertheless, Dana watched compscreen and vision screen, listening with one ear to the reports from the other approaching ships. All pilots did that; it was automatic. He wondered: Why the crush? The din of voices reminded him strongly of the landing approach to Nexus. Then he remembered, as Ramirez said sarcastically, "Control, if you keep us out here much longer, I'll have to tell my passengers they're going to miss the Auction."

"The Auction's not for another twenty-seven standard days," snapped Control. "Tell them to go to sleep."

"Oh, sorry, Control," said Ramirez sweetly, "didn't mean to upset you." The other pilots chuckled.

"Mirabelle," Control grated, "inform your passengers that you'll be landing in one standard hour."

"Control," Dana said, "this is *Zipper.* Request landing ETA."

"Zipper, this is Control. Your landing ETA is approximately six hours."

"Thanks, Control," Dana said. Sighing, he switched the audio to off/alert. If anything changed, Control could signal the ship's computer and a warning light would flash on. He hunted through his tapes for something quick, light, and distracting; he was beginning to feel anxious about going planetside.

He found Stratta's "Two-Part Invention in C Major." With music making background to thought, he told the computer to show onscreen everything it had stored about Chabad.

He scanned the marching array of facts. He was not trying to learn any of it; rather, he wanted to get a feel for this place he was descending toward. *Chabad had been a member of the Federation of Living Worlds since Year 72 AF.* Fine. *Abanat was its capital and its only city.* Great. *There was a Hyper bar in Abanat called The Green Dancer.* That was good to know; he would undoubtedly stop there in his efforts to line up a dealer and intercept Lamonica. *Politically, Chabad was a representational oligarchy, run by a Council. . . .* Dana skipped the political stuff. *The temperature in the temperate latitudes often rose as high as 62° Celsius.* Sweet mother, it was hot. *Products for export included gold, silver, platinum, glass, paper, kerit fur, seaweed, apton—a kind of cloth—and Osub RNsub (small p), which the computer identified as a rare blood-type.*

Enough. Dana turned the compscreen off, wondering what kind of music they listened to, and if anyone there had heard of Vittorio Stratta. The computer could not tell him that. He doubted it: the only places he knew of which had tapes of Stratta's compositions were Nexus and Old Earth. Someday, he wanted to go to Terra, to Florence, the city in which Stratta had lived. Indeed, he thought, for all he knew he was near it, insofar as any place in spacetime normal was close to any other place. On the Hype map, it was not close at all; Terra was in Sector Alizarine, and though it might be only ten or twelve light-years distant, by non-hyperdrive speeds that was very far away. But Hype routes and the distances of spacetime normal were seldom congruent. To get from Chabad to Old Earth, Dana would have to return to Nexus Comp-center and map a route from Nexus through Alizarine Sector to Terra.

It was strange to gaze at the sky and know that the stars you saw might have worlds you would never go to. The pathways to the Living Worlds flowed through an inside out, topsy-turvy universe where there were no suns or planets or inhabitants at all, only shipbound pilgrims who could not stop.

The theme of the music changed, interrupting his musings. Dana glanced at the vision screen. He was still quite far from Chabad's moon, but for a frightening moment he thought *Zipper* had somehow tumbled into a collision course with another ship. A wheel of silver loomed across the screen. A space station, he thought, and realized that no, it couldn't be a space station; Chabad had no need for one. Few worlds did—and anyway, this was clearly a ship, he could see the fusion thrusters bulging from a segment of the rim. He stretched a hand to the audio control to hear what the pilots' chatter might tell him—and drew it back as he realized what the wheel-like ship had to be. It was Chabad's property, the Sardonyx Net, returning to the planet, he guessed, after its journey through the sector.

He suppressed a tremor of distaste. The contract-slave system into which Sector Sardonyx impressed its criminals was no better or worse than methods in other places. There were worlds where criminals were brain-wiped. And anyway, dorazine runners could not afford scruples. The slaves on Chabad were his market, so to speak; the system which created them had created him. He'd better approve of it.

He listened to Stratta's "Invention" until it ended, and then slept again, after setting a four-hour alarm. When it woke him, he checked the screens and then turned on the audio link. So far he'd seen no sign of the Hype cops, and it made him wonder if Monk could have been mistaken. The pilots bickered with Control. He was close enough to the moon's surface to see the domes of LandingPort Station. There was nothing for him to do but watch and listen. It was only in the shifts and changes of hyperspace that the course of a ship could not be directed by a machine. The swirling currents of ruby dust were unpredictable, unfathomable, inaccessible, some said, to any but an organic intelligence.

Shut in his round, metal canister, Dana hurtled toward LandingPort Station like a thrown stone.

The Flight Field, where he landed, was outside the living domes. Before leaving the ship, Dana touched his dark, straight hair with silver glitter and put his ruby earrings in his ears. He was damned if he was going to be mistaken for some gawking, tranquilized tourist. He called a bubble from Port and inserted his Starcaptain's medallion in its control slot, intending to tell it to go straight to the shuttleship port.

But as it rose from the surface, it changed directions, detouring, and deposited him at the lock of an inspection portal. Dana scowled, and stepped through. A hard-faced official greeted him. "Welcome to Chabad, Starcaptain Ikoro."

"Thanks," Dana said.

"What's your purpose in coming to Chabad?" the official inquired.

"Who wants to know?" Dana said.

The man pulled out a certificate I.D. NARCOTICS CONTROL, it said.

"I see," said Dana. The man repeated his question. Blandly, Dana responded, "Tourism. I've berthed my ship; I'm going planetside. I've never been to Chabad before, as I'm sure your records will tell you. I came to see the Auction."

The official looked skeptical. "Are you carrying cargo?"

"No."

"If you're carrying cargo, we need a cargo roster. Chabad interdicts certain substances: glass, paper, silver, platinum, living cargo of any kind, unless previously cleared . . ."

"I'm not carrying cargo. I'm just a tourist."

"We'd like to do a check."

"On what grounds?" Dana demanded, putting up the fuss a tourist would make.

"Section D, Article 49307 of the Federation Code: 'When any vessel or owner of said vessel is suspected or has previously been suspected of being or having been in violation of the Illegal Substances Ordinance—'"

Dana held a hand up. "All right."

The official opened a panel in the wall. "Key us in, please."

Dana inserted his I-disc into the unit's slot. This unit was specifically designed to make contact with the Flight Field, and could, if necessary, direct individually or en masse every berthed ship. Dana tapped out the code which would permit the Port inspectors to enter *Zipper*.

The official nodded primly. "Thank you."

Grimly, Dana said, "If your inspectors damage my ship, I'll personally wring your neck."

The official sniffed. He then inserted a second disc and punched out a code which registered the Port's guarantee that the inspection would be orderly and nothing on *Zipper* would be disturbed.

Hell, Dana thought, this is silly. No one smuggles drugs to Chabad this way. Besides, if the Chabadese ever decide to uphold Section D, Article 49307 of the Federation Code, the economy of the whole damn planet'll fall apart.

"Are you finished?" he said. "May I go?"

The official said coldly, "LandingPort Station takes responsibility for the safety of your ship until released by you, except in cases of uncontrollable accident, malice, fraud, insurrection, or act of god. Directions within Port are available from any Port employee and from the wall panels. Corridors are color-coded; please follow the arrows and do not pass beyond designated points. The blue stripe will lead you to the shuttleship loading port."

"Thanks," said Dana. He thought, His mother probably runs dorazine on the side.

"You're welcome. Enjoy your stay on Chabad."

"Up yours, too."

Glaring, the man slapped the wall plate, releasing the door lock. Dana smiled at him. At the corridor's end he turned right, following the pathway traced by the blue stripe.

The Yago Net arrived at Chabad's moon on time.

In Abanat the clocks were striking five. Zed Yago stood by a pilot's vision screen, looking—his eyes said *down* but his training said: *No, not down*—at his planet, itself in phase relative to the position of its moon, a white and blue and orange quarter. Abanat lay in shadow. If it were daylight, he would even now be talking with Rhani. In the corridors he heard voices, orders, the shuffle of feet. The transport of nearly four thousand slaves from the Net to the Barracks in Abanat, by shuttleship, had begun. It would take five days. At the end of those days, he and Jo and Genji Kiyohara, the chief pilot, would leave the Net, and a cleaning crew would board her. Zed disliked these days of transition; the functions of Port, the arrival of the tourists, had long ceased to interest him. He wanted to get home.

He gazed at the bright, thick crescent of his world, irritatedly willing it to turn.

"Zed-ka." Jo had come up behind him. Of all the Net crew, she alone called him by his first name. To everyone he was "Commander;" to the other medics he was "Senior Yago." She had been his second for nine years, as long as he had been the Net's commander.

"Yes."

"There is a direct-line call for the commander of the Yago Net from a police officer by the name of Michel A-Rae."

"The—" Jo was nodding.

"The very same."

Zed scowled. Every five years or so the Federation gave the job of head of drug control to someone else. This was the latest holder of the job. "What does he want?"

"I don't know," Jo said.

Zed stepped to the com-unit, touching a button to blank the distracting vision screen. He tried to recall what he knew of the man, but came up with nothing except the memory of a blurred image from a PIN transmission. None of A-Rae's predecessors had ever called the Net. "I'll take it."

Maybe, he thought, A-Rae was about to tell him where all the dorazine had gone. The compscreen image cleared. Zed felt Jo move to gaze over his shoulder. There was a soft whisper through the room as the pilots heard what was going on. Zed said to the image, "I'm Zed Yago, Net commander."

The man on the screen said, "I'm Michel A-Rae."

Zed thought, I know that voice. He replayed the sentence in his mind—but nothing about it stood out, and even as he struggled to identify it, it lost its familiarity. A-Rae's face was unremarkable: he had the smooth brown complexion common to many Enchanteans. From the minute transmission lag, Zed knew his ship had to be quite close by. "Did you want to tell me something?" he said.

"Not precisely," A-Rae said. He stepped back, so that Zed saw him enframed. His uniform was plain, black without trim, and he wore the silver insignia of his rank on his chest. Behind him shadows moved, his ship's crew and staff hovering at his elbows as Jo loomed at Zed's, not in focus and barely seen. "You do know who I am."

Does he think me a fool? Zed thought. "You are head of the drug detail of the police arm of the Federation of Living Worlds," he said.

A-Rae tucked his hands into his black hide belt. "With jurisdiction over all inter-sector transport and sale of prohibited drugs in the galaxy."

Zed said, "The Yago Net respects the directive of the Federation. The Yago Net transports dorazine to the prisons of Sector Sardonyx, and nowhere else." By now he was sure he did not know A-Rae. Beside him, Jo was scowling.

"I know that, Commander," A-Rae said. "But let's not play with each other, if you please. Family Yago does not produce dorazine on Chabad, or even elsewhere in the sector. The Yago Net obtains dorazine from its dealers, and they from runners, and the runners get it from The Pharmacy, being thus linked in a vicious and illegal chain." His voice acquired a fanatic's ring. "As you must be aware, my people are watching the spacelanes for known runners. I persuaded the Federation to increase my staff, and it has done so. We intend to break that chain, Commander. I doubt that those who profit off such evils as drugs and slaves will be able to stop us."

Zed said, "I think you mean me. I appreciate the warning, I assure you. But why give it? I'm not frightened by threats."

"I know that," said the man in black. "I know a lot about you, about Family Yago, and about Chabad. You must know I am an Enchantean. No, Commander, I didn't expect to scare you. I just wanted to meet an enemy." The screen grayed.

"He has a taste for melodrama," Zed said. The man's afterimage lingered in his mind for a moment. "That *was* interesting." He had a flair. It was unfortunate that he had been able to sway the Federation to his way of thinking. This explained where all the runners had gone: A-Rae's people in their fast little ships had scared them away. He could tell Rhani that, though she would not be pleased.

In a few hours it would be dawn on Chabad. He could call her then.

Again, Jo said, "Zed-ka."

"Yes, Jo." The last few days on the Net tended to be full of trivia, all of which seemed to demand his personal intervention.

"It has been brought to my attention by an inspector here: a type-MPL starship just landed in Port, owned and piloted by one Starcaptain Dana Ikoro. Records show that Ikoro is a drug runner who usually works Sector Cinnabar, running comine, tabac, and Verdian nightshade. He bought shuttleship passage to Abanat; claims he's a tourist. His ship contains an empty dorazine cooler."

"How odd." Occasionally, dorazine addicts in other sectors (of which there were a wealthy few) sent runners to Abanat to buy one load of dorazine. But if A-Rae's people were picking up the runners, surely a smuggler would know that there wasn't any dorazine for sale or even theft. . . . "Jo?" He swung around. "Did you view that microfiche before you gave it to me?"

"Yes, Zed-ka."

"It said 'F-Y-E-O.'"

Jo shrugged.

Zed shook his head at her. "I could order you not to do that again, I suppose, but I know you won't obey me. Talk to that Starcaptain. I can't believe he's just a tourist. Find out what he's doing. He's an anomaly. I don't like anomalies."

"Clear, Zed-ka."

"And feed the conversation through to my room. I want to hear it."

Jo inclined her grizzled head. Zed stepped away from the bank of vision screens, returning them once more to the pilots.

The Net made Dana Ikoro claustrophobic.

He was used to curving walls; all MPL starships had them. In *Zipper* he was as much at home as a nesting bird. But the long Net corridors curved before and behind him, endless as a treadmill. Sometimes they met. He felt as if geometry had somehow been abrogated, as if the great silver structure existed in another dimension, as if he were walking inside a hollow Möbius strip.

He glanced at the crew members beside him, wondering

where they were taking him. They had met him at the shuttleship loading port. "Starcaptain Ikoro?" the woman said.

"That's me," he agreed.

"Will you follow us, please? Your presence is requested aboard the Yago Net."

He could, he supposed, have refused. But their manner, so imperious, made him hesitate, and the errand they had come on made him curious. They had put him on a private shuttle and brought him to the Net. At the lock of the silver wheel they had passed prisoners, waiting for the shuttleships which would carry them to Port. None of them looked at him. They were dressed alike, in blue coveralls. Even their expressions seemed the same, as if the Net, or the dorazine, had leached away their individuality and replaced it with—he didn't know what.

He was cold. He rubbed his arms, wondering where the hell he was being led to. He was sure it would do no good to ask his escorts. The corridor gave no clues: it was featureless, lined with red, blue, green, and yellow doors. The crew member ahead of him stopped. Dana nearly bumped into him; embarrassed, he caught himself in midstep. A blue door slid aside. "Go in," said the crewman.

As he stepped through, Dana heard the door hiss behind him. He looked swiftly around for another exit— and his attention was riveted by the presence of the largest Hyper he'd ever seen.

She was much taller than he, and massively boned, but she was all in proportion—as a mountain is in proportion to itself. She seated herself at a table, and gestured for him to do the same. Her joints appeared to move on steel bearings. Dana had seen Skellians before, but never this close. It was rare to find them in space. They worked Port cities all over the Living Worlds, but almost never trained as Hypers: frequent exposure to null-grav weakened them. It drove the calcium from their bones, turning them brittle.

This woman seemed unaged, or ageless. "My name is Jehosophat Leiakanawa," she said. Her voice was melodic and deep. "I am second-in-command of the Yago Net. You, I know, are Starcaptain Dana Ikoro." She pressed controls in the tabletop, and a pitcher and glasses rose from a hidden compartment. "It was gracious of you to agree to interrupt your flight to Abanat. Please accept the Net's thanks for your help."

She spoke as formally as a Federation diplomat. Dana said, deliberately ingracious, "It doesn't matter. There are always shuttleships."

"Of course," she agreed. "And you're not in a hurry." She had the Hyper skill at making questions sound like statements. "The Auction is three weeks away. The hotels are very crowded; I hope you have friends in Abanat."

"I'll manage," Dana said shortly. All this courtesy was beginning to frighten him. The palms of his hands started to sweat.

What was he doing on this—this jail? Despite the filtered air, he could smell the characteristic prison scent, made of equal parts of boredom, hopelessness, and fear. "How may I help the Yago Net, Commander?"

"Navigator," Leiakanawa corrected. "The commander aboard this ship is Zed Yago." She laid massive forearms on the table. "This is embarrassing." She did not sound the least embarrassed. "You said, at Port, you are a tourist, Starcaptain. But your activities—let's say, your reputation—in other sectors has preceded you to Chabad."

That damned son-of-a-bitch inspector, Dana thought.

"Let me say, it would surprise no one on Chabad if, while you are in Abanat, you decide to mix business with your pleasure."

I hope to, Dana thought. "Navigator, I plan to watch the Auction," he said.

"Of course," she said approvingly. "Everyone on Chabad goes to the Auction." She leaned back a little in the chair. It groaned. "Let me come to the point."

Do, Dana thought.

"You are known to our Port police as a drug runner, Starcaptain. I am prepared to pay for any information that you can give me about the current state of the drug market."

Dana's heart made a funny little jump in his chest. His mouth grew dry. He pulled the pitcher to him, poured himself a glass of the clear liquid in it, and drank. It was cold water, as he had hoped.

"Is this conversation being recorded?" he said.

"Of course," the Skellian said. "But you are in no danger, Starcaptain. There are no Hype cops on the Net."

Dana nodded. He wanted to help; the trouble was, he didn't know very much. "Who wants this information, really?" he said.

"Family Yago."

Dana wondered what they wanted to know. "What are they prepared to pay me?" he said. It was always a sensible question.

"Five hundred credits," Leiakanawa said promptly.

Five hundred credits would repay him for what he'd spent on that damn cooling unit, at least. Dana licked his lips. Damn, his mouth was dry. He drank more water, wishing Tori Lamonica were sitting in his place. "Suppose I say I don't want to talk to you?" he said.

Leiakanawa folded her hands in her lap. She reminded Dana of Terran bears he'd seen in a zoo on Pellin: possessed even in repose of a fluid and terrifying strength. "It's not wise to offend Family Yago," she said.

Dana knew very little about Family Yago. Four families ran Chabad: the Yago Family was one of them. But they ran the Auction; they owned the Net. They bought dorazine.

It wouldn't do to seem too eager to talk.

"Six hundred credits," he suggested.

"Is your information worth that much?" she said dryly.

"In the business I'm in, it's bad practice to be buyable."

"So you want to set a high price. All right. Six hundred credits."

Dana said, "I'm going to Chabad to pick up a shipment of nightshade."

"I need to know your buyer's name and the name of your contact in Abanat."

"You don't need to know my buyer's name. My buyer isn't even in Sector Sardonyx. I don't know my contact's name. I've never met him. I'm supposed to meet him in a bar. A friend of mine—I won't say who—gave me a set of recognition signals that he always uses." He went on interlacing nonsense with truth about a run he'd made in Sector Cinnabar half a year ago. "How the hell do I know this'll stay private?" he said suddenly.

"Why shouldn't it?" said Leiakanawa.

"Listen, I know it's all going down on tape, every word

I'm saying. How do I know you won't just sell me to the cops?"

"You forget," said Leiakanawa, "our offer of money for information makes the Net an accessory to everything you're saying."

"Well, I don't know." He clasped and unclasped his hands, pretending nervousness. It was only part pretense. It's this damn ship, he thought. Built like a metal sausage.

The door opened without warning. A man walked in. Leiakanawa, who had started to say something soothing, fell instantly silent. The man moved like a Hyper, all grace and strut. He was lean, not very tall, with russet hair held in a silver clip at the back of his head. He had tremendous, top-heavy, muscular shoulders, and striking amber eyes. He said, "Starcaptain, you missed your vocation. You should have been an actor."

Dana stared at him blankly, held the stare, and then decided to get angry. Theatrically he clenched his fists, pushed the chair back, and stood. He was slightly taller than the other man. "Are you calling me a liar?"

"Yes," said the intruder. "Verdian nightshade comes from a plant that can't be grown on Chabad, Starcaptain. You aren't buying it here. There's a cooling unit for dorazine sitting in your ship."

"I was getting to that—"

"Never mind. If you're trying to buy dorazine on Chabad, you'll be disappointed. The supply is scarce. You came from Nexus? I don't suppose you'd like to tell me who you're buying for on Nexus. Some one-shot user? It won't pay much, but that name might be worth, oh, two hundred credits."

"Go to hell," Dana said. "If you don't like what I told you, make the rest of it up. I don't sell out my customers. I'm shinnying. Get out of my way."

He started for the door. Seated as she was, the Skellian could not move fast enough to stop him. But the russet-haired man stayed smack in his path. Dana slashed at him with the edge of his hand. It was a good blow, a trained blow, and it might have done some damage if it had landed. But the man closed one hand around his wrist as it reached him, and twisted downwards with inexplicable and frightening power. Pain arced up Dana's arm to the elbow. The grip forced him to his knees. A fist like a hammer hit the side of his head from behind. He fell, half conscious, and the Skellian lifted him in her huge arms.

She put him back in the chair, holding his shoulders so that he couldn't move. The russet-haired man looked at his head, flashed a light twice into his eyes, and probed at the muscles of his neck with gentle authority. "You'll have a headache," he said. "Didn't your mother ever tell you not to skop with Skellians?"

Dana said nothing. His ribs hurt, his elbow ached, and his brain felt jellied from the Skellian's blow.

The russet-haired man said, "Thank you, Jo. That's all." The Skellian left. Dana swallowed back the blood in his mouth.

"Well?" he said.

The russet-haired man said, "I'm Zed Yago, commander of the Net."

Dana said, "I'm not pleased to meet you." But despite the bravado behind his words, he was afraid. Chills shook the base of his spine.

The Net commander smiled, a corner of his mouth quirked. In an odd, almost affectionate gesture, he ran two fingers along the line of Dana's jaw, and then stepped back. "Would you like to tell me, Starcaptain, what your true business is in Abanat?"

Dana said, "No. I'd be cutting my own throat. I could never work Sardonyx Sector again, and when word got around—and it would—no other sector either. Forget it." He took a deep breath, trying to ease the pain in his side, and straightened slowly.

Zed Yago said gravely, "You don't yet understand your situation." He walked to the table, and leaned from Dana's view. When he came back, he was holding something in his hand: a printout. Dana took it in his left hand. His headache made it hard for him to focus. Finally, he puzzled out the meaning of the legal terminology. He was looking at a slave contract for ten years, from Chabad.

His name was on it.

He went cold. Zed Yago took it from him. "You are a drug smuggler, Starcaptain, though you've not yet been tried or convicted. The cooler in your ship proves you traffic in dorazine, which is a Federation crime. Transporting dorazine inter-sector is illegal, punishable by a high fine and a prison term, which in Sector Sardonyx translates to—this." He held up the contract. "This is an actual contract; it even has your retinal pattern on it. I made a record of the pattern when I checked your eyes. I can tear it up, take it off the computer, return your ship to you, and let you go to Abanat to watch the Auction . . . if you talk to me. *If.*"

Dana flexed the fingers of his right hand, trying to work feeling back into them. "I don't believe you," he said. "Having a cooler isn't legal proof of anything. Transporting dorazine inter-sector is illegal, sure, but you can't prove I did it. You can't even get a conviction on the charge unless your evidence is cleared by the Hype cops. I'm damned if I'll tell you anything. You're bluffing." He put both hands to the arms of the chair and tried, uselessly, to rise.

Zed Yago said gently, "You're wrong, you know. You didn't look closely enough. This contract was made up by LandingPort Narcotics Control, and it's already signed." Before Dana could speak, he reached forward and pressed a gel capsule against Dana's neck. It was cool. Dana felt it dissolve. "You're going to sleep, now, Starcaptain," said Zed Yago in that gentle voice. With one hand he freed his hair from its clip. Loose, it brushed his shoulders. "When you wake, we'll talk."

Wait! Dana Ikoro tried to say. Wait, let's talk now. . . . But his mouth was numb; his lips wouldn't work. He couldn't even blink. The door opened. He sat paralyzed as tears dripped to his cheeks. He couldn't even lower his eyelids. Zed gave some orders. Two crew members appeared and lifted him between them, not roughly. He felt their hands pick him up. They asked Zed where he was to go, and Zed answered, "A holding cell." But I didn't—I wasn't—he tried to speak and could not. He could barely feel his own breathing; he listened, and was infinitely reassured to hear the steady huff-huff of his lungs.

The walls danced past him; he was being moved. "Careful," said Zed Yago's voice. As the crew carted him from the room, Dana felt fingers brush against his face. With a look as tender as a lover's, the Net commander stroked Dana's eyelids down over his smarting eyes.

· · ·

He lay in a room on a bed.

The room had curving walls. He tried to turn his head to follow the curve, but his head would not move. With great effort, he could open and close his mouth and his eyes. Maybe the paralysis was wearing off. He was naked, slightly chilly but not unbearably so. His bare feet looked distorted and very far away. He could move nothing below his waist. He sensed, without seeing them, that his wrists were strapped down near his sides.

He heard a hum. He heard voices; in a hallway, he guessed, outside the room door. He heard his heartbeat, regular, strong; he heard his breathing. He thought he could hear the blood washing through his veins.

He heard footsteps.

The room door opened.

Zed Yago walked in. He sat down on the edge of the bed. Dana felt it dip. He looked intent and happy. Lightly, he cupped one hand under Dana's chin, holding it rigid, his thumb lying under the ear against the soft flesh below the jaw. "Do you feel that?" he said. "Don't try to speak. I can see you do."

He took his hand away. "The drug I gave you is a variant of dorazine. It was originally developed to treat catatonics. It increases the nervous system's receptivity to sensation. Theoretically, it shocked catatonics from their delusional state by forcing them to experience the world around them. But it caused a deep withdrawal in a significant number of patients, and its use was discontinued. There's a large, illegal traffic in it; you may even have carried it yourself. Don't let the paralytic effect scare you. It wears off."

Dana worked his lips. They felt numb still. He bit the lower one. He tried to cough.

"Uh," he said. "Wuh?" Zed laid a hand on his mouth to silence him.

Then again he took Dana's chin in his hand. He moved his thumb along the jawline. He pressed inward. Hard.

Pain drove through Dana's face and head. His left eye went dark. He strained to jerk his head away from the pain. He tried to scream. He could only grunt. Tears rolled down his face.

The pain went away. Zed Yago wiped the tears from his face with a cloth. "There's a nerve plexus there," he said.

He touched Dana's shoulder, and then slid his hand down Dana's bare arm to the elbow. Dana cried out as pain blossomed and spread through the elbow like flame. Zed released the pressure, but kept his fingers near the spot where he'd hit the nerve. "There, too," he said.

Dana fought to steady his breath. It sounded in his ears like a thunderstorm. "Why?" he gasped, tasting the salt of tears in the corner of his mouth.

Again, Zed smiled a happy smile. "I don't like people to lie to me," he said. "That's one reason. A better reason is that the information you have about the drug market could be important to Family Yago. A third reason is that you're going to be a slave, and slaves don't need reasons. You'll get used to that. But the fourth reason, and the only real one, is that I want to do it." He slid his hand up Dana's arm to the shoulder, and from the shoulder slowly up to the line of the jaw.

Dana shut his eyes involuntarily, and tried to contain his scream.

The horizons of the world shrank. Morning was when he woke to hear Zed's footsteps in the corridor. He learned to pick their rhythm out of fifty others. Night was when Zed left him. During the night other people, not Zed, bathed him, fed him, gave him water, and then let him sleep. He had no idea how long day lasted, how long night was, or even, after a while, where he was. The boundaries of his world shrank to a small island, and the name of it was Pain.

By the end of the second day, he told his soft-voiced tormentor everything Yago might have wanted to know about the drug traffic, about Dana Ikoro's life. Writhing in the straps, he learned to interpret every nuance of Zed Yago's voice, the cock of his head, the set of his mouth, the movement of his hands. On the third day, the questions stopped. Information was not what Yago wanted from him. The awful care with which the hurt was administered helped him to understand it as a sexual act, as intense and blinding as orgasm. Zed let him ration his own rest. "Five minutes," he gasped. He lay untouched, blessedly free from pain, for five minutes. Then the hands returned. But if he asked too often for mercy, he got none.

By the fourth day, he no longer had the strength to beg

for release. He lay voiceless. Zed said to him, with approval, "You're very strong." He smiled. "But if you think you've reached the end of your endurance—you're wrong."

The morning of the fifth day, when he heard the familiar, terrible steps in the corridor, his muscles knotted. He began to shake. Zed opened the door. Dana waited for him to walk to the bed. But Zed only looked at him. He nodded once, like a man who has finished something, and stepped back outside, and slid the door closed.

Dana did not know how many hours it was before his convulsing muscles relaxed. It was a long time before he could cry.

When Zed came in again, he closed the door and came to stand by the bed. He watched Dana shake. At last, he reached out and smoothed Dana's hair. "All right," he said. "It's all right. It's over."

Dana's throat ached. The light dreadful stroking went on. After a while, he perceived it as comfort. He stopped trembling. Zed held a cup in front of his eyes. "Water," he said. "Drink it; I'll hold your head." He supported Dana's head with one arm as Dana drank. Then Zed rested him again on the pillow and put the cup aside.

Zed said, "In the morning, you'll go with me on the last shuttle to leave the Net. It bypasses the moon and goes directly to the Abanat LandingPort. There you'll be tried for drug smuggling: the LandingPort Narcotics Control has already filed its evidence, and your confession to me is evidence too." He smiled. "Normally, after conviction, an ombudsman would explain to you your rights and duties as a slave, and then you'd go to the pens to be prepared for the Auction. But you won't be auctioned, Dana. I intend to buy you. Not for myself—I don't own slaves. But you're uncommon, a Starcaptain, a smuggler, and Family Yago can use your skills and knowledge. You'll be for my sister, Rhani. She'll decide what to do with you. You'll serve her well. If you serve her very well, she may even decide to free you early. She's sentimental about such things. I'm not. Remember that, Dana, if while you serve my sister you're tempted to escape, or steal from her, or lie to her, or even to make mistakes. Remember this." He ran a fingertip along the line under

Dana's jaw. Dana shivered. Zed touched him elsewhere, light reminders of past sensations that made him whimper. Then the Net commander walked softly from the room, and left him lying alone.

Chapter Three

Curled in her favorite wing chair with papers scattered around her, isolated from the rest of the house, Rhani Yago did not hear her secretary's soft sentence until he repeated it. "Rhani-ka, your brother's home." She jumped from the chair; the papers flew in all directions. A dragoncat dozing on the kerit fur rug lifted an inquiring head.

"Here, now? Where?"

"In the garden," Binkie said.

Rhani hastened to the glass door, slid it back, and stepped onto her terrace. Zed was not in sight. "Zed-ka!" she called.

"Coming, Rhani-ka," Zed called from somewhere below her.

In the bedroom Binkie had picked up the scattered papers and piled them neatly on the tapestried footstool. His face was whiter than usual and there was something wrong with his eyes. Rhani knew what it was. "Binkie."

He turned to face her, a sheet of paper in one hand.

"Put that down, find Amri, tell her to come and wait on us, and then go to your room and stay there."

He swallowed. "That isn't necessary, Rhani-ka—"

"It is," she said. "Don't argue with me." He bowed his head in acquiescence and left. In a moment Zed entered the room, arms wide. Rhani flung herself at him. He smelled of grease and antiseptic. His hair had grown long and straggly in three months. Straining, she hugged him hard.

"Rhani-ka," he said in her ear, "you look very well."

She pulled out of his embrace to look at him. "So do you. Pale, though." She thought, I always say that.

"There's no sunlight on the Net."

"You were walking in the garden."

"There's a heat-lightning storm over Abanat. We flew

around it to get here. I wanted to look at it from the ground."

"Just like a tourist," she teased him. Amri tapped hesitantly at the door. "Wine," Rhani said. "Have you eaten, Zed? Do you want food?"

"Chobi seeds?" he said. Rhani nodded at Amri. He put out a hand and drew her closer to him. "It's good to be home." He drew his fingers in a lover's gesture, old between them, along the line of her jaw. He cupped her cheek in one hand. "I'm sorry I wasn't home to be with you through Domna Sam's death."

She let her head rest in his cupped hand. "Yes. I missed you."

"You and she were close."

"She was a wonderful woman." Rhani moved restlessly. Zed dropped his hand. "Tough and strong. She teased me about being too soft. *'You have to be mean,'* she said. *'It's the only way you'll get along.'* I used to tell her the Durs could never be as mean as the Yagos. She laughed at that. This last year, she was—difficult. Calling me at strange times. I suppose she'd grown senile. But she never made scenes in public. She was a great lady."

Zed said, "Ferris will find it hard to follow her."

Rhani sniffed. "Ferris will learn. I did."

Zed grinned at her. "Ferris Dur isn't you, Rhani-ka."

Amri entered with a laden tray. Zed picked up a glass. He held it to the light as Amri poured. "Too bad we can't grow decent grapes on Chabad," he said. "It's the one thing we lack."

"The one thing?" Rhani took the second glass of wine. It was an import from Enchanter. She sipped. The ruby liquid was sweet. "I can think of something else we lack. Dorazine." She sat in the wing chair. Brushing the printouts from the footstool, Zed sat, legs outstretched, dirty bootheels soiling the white fur rug. He scooped up a handful of chobi seeds.

"Yes," he said. "I forgot about the dorazine."

Rhani grinned. He was teasing her, of course. No Yago would ever forget dorazine. He had called her from the Net to tell her that he was back and that all was well, and had described to her the encounter with Michel A-Rae. She had at once sent a communication to all Family Yago associates throughout Sector Sardonyx, requesting information about the man. The noun "associate" meant, in the Yago lexicon, someone paid covertly by Family Yago for information or influence. "I've sent out a call for all information available on Michel A-Rae."

Zed nodded. "Good. But I'm not worried about an Enchantean fanatic."

"He could be dangerous," Rhani said. "If, indeed, he is responsible for the dorazine shortage—"

"He may be," Zed said. "If he is, I'm sure you can deal with him."

"You don't think it's important?"

Zed frowned. "I'm concerned for *you*."

Rhani could not think what he was talking about. "For me?"

"Yes. The Net crew would tell you how quickly we came home. We should still be in space. What did you do about that threatening letter from the Free Folk of Chabad?"

"Oh, them," Rhani said, relieved. "I told Binkie to find out where they were coming from."

"They?" Zed sat up. "There were more? You didn't tell me."

Rhani smiled at him. "There are always letters like that, Zed-ka. Isobel kept them in a drawer. When I grew haughty about being heir to the Third Family of Chabad, she would sit me down beside it and make me read them."

Zed's tone grew exasperated. "Rhani, those are threats against your life! The least you could do is take them seriously!"

"How should I take them seriously?" she demanded, irritated in turn. She bit down hard on a chobi seed. The shell cracked between her teeth. "I should never have bothered mentioning it to you. Do I stay in the house all the time? Hide inside like a craven with guards at every turn of the hall?"

"Did I say that?" he countered. "Did I?"

"You were thinking it!"

"You thought it too!" Brother and sister glared at each other, and then burst out laughing. Rhani laid a hand on Zed's arm. Under the light shirt he wore, she felt the ropy stretch of his muscles. When very small they had pretended to be twins, to make a reason, even a false one, for the likeness between them.

They still looked alike. But we are different, too, Rhani thought. We grew apart in the years we lived apart.

"It's good to have you home," she said.

He grinned. "Absence makes the spice. I brought you a present."

"A star to hang on my wall," Rhani teased. Zed often brought her trinkets made on the other sector worlds.

"Not a star. A Starcaptain."

Rhani rubbed her chin. She had no Starcaptain friends, but perhaps Zed had, a friendship formed during his pilot's training on Nexus: someone he'd liked, and met by chance, and invited home. But Zed never invited strangers to their home. "Who?"

"No one you know. He was on his way to Abanat to make contact with a drug smuggler. It's a complicated story; he's a smuggler himself, new to the dorazine market, and another smuggler got in ahead of him and jacked his cargo."

"And with the Hype cops blanketing the sector, he chose to come to Abanat anyway?" Rhani said.

"Yes." Zed stretched, arms reaching for the ceiling. "It was that—audacity—that drew him to my attention."

Rhani scratched her chin. "He sounds interesting," she said. "I don't suppose he knows the location of The Pharmacy."

"No," Zed said regretfully. "Runners don't know that."

"Dealers don't. And we poor buyers don't." She rose, pacing a little. "I thought Hypers didn't talk to strangers."

Zed half-smiled. "We aren't precisely strangers."

"Is he a friend of yours? Someone you knew on Nexus?" Rhani turned to face her brother. She was intrigued: the only Hyper Zed ever brought home—besides the Skellian, Jo Leiakanawa—was Tam Orion, chief pilot of Abanat's Main Landingport. But though she loved to hear discussion of other worlds, other systems, the Hype, she hadn't from him, because Tam Orion never talked. "I've never met a Starcaptain. What's his name?"

"Dana Ikoro." Zed smiled oddly. "He's not a Starcaptain precisely, either, Rhani-ka, not now. He's a slave."

"What?"

"I bought him for you."

"Bought me a slave? Zed-ka, what am I going to do with him?" Rhani scowled at her brother. "There's nothing for him to do here, and Hyper slaves are more trouble than they're worth. You have to put them on dorazine, and I hate that."

"You won't have to put this one on dorazine."

"Then he'll always be trying to escape."

Zed said, "This one won't." He sounded certain. The drowsing dragoncat rolled over on the rug. Zed leaned to rub the soft snowy fur on its belly. Upsidedown, it licked his hand. "Last time I was gone you complained when I came back because you had had to hire a pilot. He'll be your pilot. Or you can find him other work to do. He'll do what you tell him. He's a helpful man."

Rhani looked down into her wine glass. For an instant she saw, framed within it, Binkie's whitened face.

Zed said, "What did you write to Ferris Dur?"

"Huh," said Rhani. "I wrote nothing to Ferris Dur. He wrote again. I have the letter here. Why did you push all my papers on the floor?" She knelt on the rug, shuffling through the papers. The cat decided this was a game, and batted at her fingers. "Isis, stop that. Here." She read the letter aloud. It was much like the first but with more imperatives. It finished with a second demand for a meeting. "It arrived this morning. I haven't answered it. In two weeks I'll be in Abanat. If Ferris Dur wants to talk with me, he can come to my house."

"He has no manners," said Zed, amused. Rhani crumpled the letter and threw it at him. He batted it away. The cat leaped after it, forepaws extended, pretending it was prey.

"Maybe he wants to buy into the kerit farm again."

"It might be nice to know," said Zed.

"You think I should go?" asked Rhani.

Zed shrugged. He ate a cracker. "I just think it might be nice to know what he thinks is so damned urgent." He finished his wine. "Come downstairs with me, Rhani-ka. I'll introduce your new slave to you."

Dana Ikoro sat in a chair against a wall, trying to stay awake.

Zed had said, "Sit here and don't sleep." They had

ridden together in a two-person bubble from a small
landingport in Abanat to a place that Zed said was the
Yago estate. Zed flew the craft around a lightning storm.
He small-talked: about the weather, the city, the estate;
things of no consequence. He was easy and light-handed
on the controls. Dana thought it, and as he did Zed
glanced at him and said, "Say what you're thinking."

"I was thinking you're good at that."

"I was trained on Nexus. Thank you. You're probably
better."

Dana's fingers went again to the plain blue letter "Y"
tattooed on his left upper arm. It was the Yago crest: a
badge of servitude. They'd put it on him after the trial,
without hurting him. The ombudsman, a brisk woman,
had talked to him about money, his legal status, and so
on. He would be compensated, she told him, for time
spent as a chattel. Money would be held in trust for him
until his release. He could not be damaged, she said. This
had made him smile. He could not, except in certain
circumstances, be killed.

The words made sense but the information did not: it
seemed irrelevant. When he walked from the room, the
first thing he saw was Zed. They'd walked to a hangar and
climbed into the bubble to come here. The house was
white, with a flat roof covered with solar panels; he'd seen
that from the air. The chair was wooden; its edge hurt the
back of his knees. Zed had put him in it, and told him to
stay awake, and then had drawn his finger along the line
of Dana's jaw, saying, "Remember." He had walked into
the garden.

Dana sat and shook on the embroidered cushion of the
chair.

Zed and Rhani Yago came downstairs side by side.

Dana had expected something else in Rhani Yago:
someone very old or very young, a freak, a monster.
Rhani was her brother's height, and looked in the dim hall
so like him that Dana wondered if they were twins. At
Zed's gesture he stood up, swaying with weakness, and
put out a hand to buttress himself against the wall.

Zed said, "Rhani, this is Dana." He put an arm around
her shoulders. "I'm going upstairs; I'll see you in the
morning." They hugged; Zed went up the broad staircase
without looking at Dana. His absence made it easier to

breathe. Rhani Yago wore black pants and a red shirt; her eyes, like Zed's, were amber.

Dana bowed to her, awkwardly. He had never bowed before. She did not look monstrous. Wealth could buy longevity in the form of drugs; she could be any age, thirty or ninety or two hundred, but she looked ten years Dana's senior, no more.

"When did you eat last?" she said. She had a low voice, not unlike Zed's.

Dana tried to remember when he had last had a meal. "I don't know," he said.

"Stay here," she ordered, and vanished through a swinging door. Dana leaned on the wall, wondering how long he could stand before he fell over. All his bones hurt, and his knees wobbled.

Suddenly she was back with a tray: on it were a plate, a glass, and food. He smelled meat and cheese and the aroma of fresh bread. "Sit down, man!" she said. "Here." He sat, and she laid the plate on his knees. His stomach rumbled. He took a piece of meat. "Eat slowly, or you'll get sick," she warned him. He made himself take small bites. He ate two pieces of meat, a hunk of bread, a slab of cheese. Abruptly he could not eat any more.

She watched him eat, standing.

"Thank you," he said, adding, "I don't know what to call you, I'm sorry."

"You're welcome. My title is Domna. But the folk of the house call me Rhani-ka. You may, too." She rubbed her chin. Her hair was longer and finer than her brother's, and she wore it pulled back from her face in a thick braid. He wondered if she were like her brother in other ways.

"How old are you?" she said.

"Twenty-four," he answered.

Surprise crossed her face. "Young to be a Starcaptain. How long have you had your medallion?"

The phrase hurt. "Eight months Standard," he said. And added, "I trained to be a pilot first."

"How long is your contract for?"

"Ten years," he said, What had Zed told her about him?

She glanced toward the swinging door. Dana looked, too. A shadowy figure stood there. "Amri—if Binkie's awake, ask him to come here." The figure disappeared.

Dana wondered who Binkie was, and if she/he were a
slave, and if so, why Rhani Yago said "ask" of a slave.
She had brought the food for him herself, too.

The door swung aside for a slender, fair-haired man.
He looked curiously at Dana Ikoro.

"Binkie's my secretary. I couldn't do a thing without
him. Bink, this is Dana. Zed brought him from the Net.
Find him a bed and some clothes, and take some time
tomorrow to show him the house."

"Yes, Rhani-ka," said Binkie. He beckoned to Dana.
"Come with me." Dana stood up. His legs felt leaden. He
bowed to Rhani Yago again. They went through the
swinging door, into a metal-and-wood kitchen, and into a
hall flanked with paneled doors. Dana was reminded of
the Net.

"Cara," said Binkie. "Immeld. Me. Amri. Timithos
sleeps in the garden. You." He opened the fifth door.

Behind it was a room, small and warm, wood-paneled,
lit by a line of soft paper lanterns strung across the ceiling.
There was a narrow bed in a wooden frame, and a round
mirror on the wall. Dana stared at himself. He looked
older than his memory of himself, thinner, with lines on
his face that he did not recall, and wary eyes.

Binkie said, "You sleep here. Amri will wake you in
the morning. I'll tell her to call you late." He turned to
leave.

"Wait—please," said Dana. He felt lost. Binkie turned
around. He gazed at Dana with sympathy mixed with a
strange, tight defensiveness. "I don't—are you a slave?"

Wordlessly Binkie pushed up his sleeve to exhibit the
tattooed crest, the blue "Y," on his left upper arm.

"What did you do?"

Binkie said, "We don't ask. Slaves don't have pasts, or
homes, or property. Or even their proper names."

"They say that, but you don't have to."

"What difference does it make? I could be an arsonist
or an axe-murderer. I'm here. I don't want to know what
you are." He turned again to leave. Dana's legs would no
longer keep him up. He sat on the bed. "Good night,"
said Binkie.

"Good night," Dana said to the other man's back.

He was alone.

He kicked off his shoes and pulled his feet up under

him. The bed creaked as he shifted on it. He caught himself listening for footsteps.

It's over. It's all right.

He leaned into the softness of the pillow and stroked his hand on the rich glowing grain of the headboard. He felt the soft fabric of the blanket. The hall outside was silent. He got off the bed and explored the room. It had a closet, empty, and a bathroom with a shower. He opened the door and looked out into the empty hall.

Night was the safe time, and Rhani had said he could sleep. He closed the door. He started to pull off his shirt, and stopped. He did not want to sleep naked. He took the blanket in both hands and wrapped it like a cocoon around him. The light control was on the headboard. He thumbed it. He curled on his side in the gracious darkness, listening to the steady music of his breath.

He waited for sleep.

Zed Yago spent his usual dreamless, untroubled night.

Waking, he lay motionless in the warm bed, watching the bright bands of sunlight climb the walls. The first few days off the Net everything on Chabad seemed transient, as if it might disappear when he took his eyes off it. He found himself staring at things and people, willing them to stay there. This room had been his place since childhood. His booktapes lined one wall. One closet held his clothes, and the other his ice climbing equipment: suit, hammers, axes, pitons. In one corner of the room was the wired human skeleton that he had used in medical school on Nexus; its skull was twisted to look sightlessly over one shoulder in a grotesque and impossible position. Zed guessed Amri had been cleaning it. His medic's case sat at its dangling, bony feet.

He swung out of bed and went naked to the doors of the terrace. He could see the blooming garden, misty with water arcing over it in hissing rainbows of spray. A dragoncat loped across a creeper. By a flower bed, Timithos coiled a hose. Zed pulled the glass door open. Heat poured through at him. The air was molten. Sweat prickled on his shoulders and down his sides. After three months away from it, even for someone born and bred on Chabad, the heat took getting used to. Zed breathed deeply. He wondered if it would be a waste of time to mention the threatening letters to Rhani yet again. Perhaps he was being an alarmist. She would laugh at him. Finally, stepping back into the cool, quiet house, he slid the terrace doors closed. It was an hour after dawn.

He dressed. He could hear voices downstairs: Cara and Immeld, chatting in the kitchen. He started down the stairs and met Amri on her way up, tray with breakfast fruits in hand. "I'll take it," he said. Balancing it on one palm, he returned up the stairway and tapped at Rhani's door. "It's me," he said.

"Come in!"

She sat in the wing chair. He put the tray on the footstool. She wore a jumpsuit of deep metallic blue, the Yago crest color, the color of Chabad's sky. It darkened the amber of her eyes to hazel. "Good morning, Rhani-ka."

She lifted her face up for his kiss. "Good morning, Zed-ka."

There were three printout sheets, covered with figures, at her feet. "What are you working on?"

She took a piece of fruit from the tray. "Dorazine. Binkie computed for me this morning our storage figures and our demand figures: what we will need to supply the Net, the prisons of Sector Sardonyx, and our own workers at the kerit farm for one more year. We do not have enough. Look." Zed took the sheet she handed him. "I wrote to Sherrix days ago, the same day I sent you the communigram. I offered to pay double the current market price for dorazine, hoping to loosen the market."

"You told me that when I called you from the moon," said Zed. "That was also days ago."

"And I expected to have an answer from Sherrix by this time."

"You haven't."

She shook her head. "She's never not answered me before." Her shoulders hunched.

"Write again," said Zed.

"Yes," she said almost absently. "I can do that."

Zed said, "What else is happening on Chabad besides a dorazine shortage?"

"Huh?"

"Marriages, births, deaths?"

She focused on him. "I'm sorry, Zed-ka. I was thinking

. . . and no matter how badly I've missed you, an hour after you came back from the Net, it feels as if you'd never been away. Deaths—Domna Sam. And one of Imre and Aliza Kyneth's children almost married, but it didn't come off. I forget which one. Imre was re-elected head of the Council. He suggested I do it but I said I wouldn't if it meant I had to live in Abanat. Imre and I had a fight about water rates. I won. Tuli opened a second shop." Zed nodded. Tuli had been cook on the Yago estate for three years: a silent, clever woman. When her contract expired, she took her money and bought a shop in Abanat.

"Were things well for you?" Zed asked.

"I missed you," she said. "I was busy. I went back and forth to Abanat a lot." She rubbed her chin. "I could have used a pilot. Domna Sam kept sending a bubble for me. I think I spent more time with her than Ferris."

Zed said, "I don't even know what Ferris looks like." Rhani made a face. "I'm sorry I wasn't here to pilot you." *Were you happy?* he wanted to ask. *Did you take a lover?* If he asked her the first question, she would only smile, and say, *"Of course."*

He never asked about her lovers.

She said, "I have to go to Sovka."

"Why?"

"I retired the old manager, and appointed a new one, Erith Allogonga. She was head of the birthing section. I want to see how she's getting along. And I'm concerned about those litter deaths."

"Are you feeling nostalgic?" he teased.

She laughed. "For Sovka? Zed, one *couldn't* feel nostalgic for Sovka."

Unable to restrain himself, he said, "You went there eagerly enough."

It was an old sore between them. Rhani touched his arm with her palm. "Zed-ka. I was seventeen, and I was not asked if I wanted to go. I was told to go. I was frightened. I couldn't talk back to Isobel."

"I know. I'm sorry I said it."

"Shall I tell you more gossip? I can't think of anything more to tell. You'll have to ask Charity Diamos. Or I could have Binkie make printouts of the old copies of PIN."

Charity Diamos was related to the Yagos: she was a vicious, malicious harridan and the worst gossip in Abanat. Zed choked.

Rhani laughed. "You talk to me," she said. "Tell me about the trip. You've not yet given me the Net report."

"It's on the computer, you can read it there."

"No. I'd rather hear it from you."

She sat with her head cocked slightly to one side, fingers clasped together loosely in her lap: it was her listening look. Zed picked up a piece of fruit. "All right," he said. "The trip was uneventful until the end. . . ."

Downstairs, in the quarters set apart for slaves, Dana Ikoro dreamed the sound of footsteps in a hall.

He came awake, sweating and cold. The room was very bright; the dappled brilliance of sunlight, not the desolate glare of artificial lighting. Someone was knocking on his door. A woman called his name; her voice soft through the heavy wood. He sat up. He was sticky. "Come in," he called. A small blond girl came in.

"Hello," she said. "I'm Amri." She wore a soft light shift of red-and-yellow; she reminded Dana of a butterfly. She carried a pair of straw sandals in one hand, and a gray jumpsuit over her arm. "These are for you. Binkie says they should fit."

Dana sat on the edge of the bed. "What time of day is it?" he asked.

"Two hours after dawn." She had pale fine hair that fell to her waist and equally pale, near-translucent skin, an infant's skin. The shift was sleeveless; Dana saw the tattooed "Y" on her left arm. That meant she was a slave. He blinked, shocked. She looked barely fourteen; he couldn't imagine what possible criminal act she had committed. But she was here.

He took the clothing from her. "After you're dressed," she said, "come have breakfast. The kitchen's at the other end of this hall."

"Yes, I remember. Thank you," he said.

Walking down the hall to the kitchen Dana experienced that unmistakable twinge in the head that says: *You have seen, done, smelled, tasted, been here before.* He puzzled out the *déjà vu.* He was sixteen, walking from the sleeping space to the eating hall in the Pilot's Academy on Nexus, wearing a uniform, a hundred unfamiliar terms and customs crowding his mind, his hair brushing the tops of his shoulders, shorter than it had ever been on Pellin. He hadn't wanted them to cut it. He liked his hair long. He closed his eyes abruptly, remembering *Zipper,* Russell O'Neill, Monk, Tori Lamonica, Nexus, the forest-crested hills of Pellin, the faces of his family—freedom, he thought. He wondered where his musictapes were now. He pictured some Net crew member riffling through them, listening to one, frowning in boredom, tossing them aside. *"Nothing of value, Commander."* Inside his head he heard, like birdsong, a few swift, improbable notes of Vittorio Stratta's "Fugue No. 2 in C." The gay ancient music drew tears.

He rubbed them out with the heel of his hand and went inside the kitchen. The walls were red wood; the floor was squares of brown tile. Binkie, Amri, and two women he hadn't met sat at a counter on high metal stools, eating.

Their faces did not change as they turned to look him over. Binkie said, "This is Dana. This is Cara Morro, steward of the Yago estate, and Immeld, the cook." Cara was angular and brown, with silver hair that trickled down her back in asymmetrical ringlets. She had a pale scar on her left upper arm. Immeld was younger, jaunty, and talkative.

"I saw you come in last night," she said. She pushed a platter towards him. "Have some food. There's a stool over there." Dana turned, to find Amri bringing it to him. His feet dangled to the bottom rung. He picked fruit and cheese from the plate. "Are they awake?" said Immeld.

Amri said, "Zed took the tray from me to bring in himself."

"Someone was in here last night."

"That was Rhani," said Amri. "She brought *him* something to eat." She pointed at Dana.

"What time was that?"

"About three hours after sunset," said Binkie. He said, ostensibly to Dana, "Immeld likes to know everything."

"So do you," said Cara tartly.

"Does anyone want more cheese?" asked the cook. No one did. She put the platter in a cooler. Casually she said, "What's new this morning?" She looked at Binkie.

"Nothing's new," he said. "Rhani's working."

"On what?" asked the cook.

"I don't talk about Rhani's work," said Binkie. "You know that."

Immeld chuckled, unabashed at her prying. "I just wondered."

"How many more days before they go to Abanat?" asked Amri.

"Ten," said Binkie.

"I want to go with them," Amri said. She kicked the rungs of her stool. "I like Abanat."

"I don't," said Binkie.

Diffidently, Dana said, "What's the Chabad calendar?"

Binkie said, "Nine days to a week, five weeks to a month, ten months to the year. Every fifth year they add two days to the last month of the year."

Immeld said, "And they don't celebrate birthdays at all on Chabad. I miss not having a birthday. I used to get two: Standard birthday and—"

"Immey!" said Cara. She frowned at the younger woman. "We don't discuss the past."

Immeld shrugged. "I do miss it," she said stubbornly.

Dana nodded. Most colony planets used two time standards: the year/month/day as it was measured on the planet, and Standard, which was the old calendar of Earth. On some planets this meant that people had two birthdays to celebrate, since maturity was defined on most worlds by the Standard age of fourteen. Some colonies did away with all birthdays: you were simply informed when you reached fourteen Standard. On Pellin, there was a small ceremony.

Immeld said, "Rhani and Zed always go to Abanat for the Auction. Rhani always takes one of the house slaves with her to the city. One besides Binkie, that is; he goes every year. Timithos won't go; he hates to leave his garden."

"How many people live here?" Dana asked.

"We four," said Immeld, "and Timithos. And them, of course, and now you. What were you bought for?"

"I don't know," said Dana. "They didn't tell me."

A bell rang, two-toned, *ping-pong*. Binkie stepped to a speaker grid in the wall. "Yes, Rhani-ka." The others fell silent. Rhani's voice was a jumble, too low to hear. Binkie murmured, "Yes, Rhani-ka." He turned from the speaker to look at Dana. "She wants you."

Dana swallowed hastily. "Where do I go?"

Amri said, "I'll take you. I have to get the tray." He followed her up the marble staircase. Along the second-story landing, Dana counted seven doors. Amri stopped at the third one. She tapped, and grinned up at Dana. "You don't have to be scared of her," she said encouragingly. "She's very nice."

"Come in," called Rhani. Dana obeyed. The room was light and airy. The rug was white, the curtains were white, the walls were blue. Rhani wore blue. She sat in a cream-colored chair whose rounded back and arms flowed about her like a mantle. Zed stood behind her, one hand brushing Rhani's hair. Dana faced them. His heart began to pound.

Amri took the tray off the footstool. "Do you want more, Rhani-ka?" she asked.

"Thank you, no," said Rhani. She smiled at the child, then turned to gaze at her Starcaptain. He looked steadily back at her. After a moment, she recognized the thing that was wrong with his eyes. She twisted in her chair to look at Zed. "Zed-ka—"

Zed nodded. "When you want me, call. I'm in my room." He went out the terrace doors. As if pulled by a magnet, Dana Ikoro's head turned to watch him go.

She said, "Zed says you are a drug runner."

His attention snapped back to her. "I was," he said.

"A dorazine smuggler."

He said, "That's not quite right. I was attempting to smuggle dorazine. My cargo was jacked. I'm not a dorazine smuggler."

"But you made a deal to do it."

"Yes."

He was stiff, and overpolite. Part of that was fear, she knew, and part shame, and part uncertainty, and a good part pride. She understood all those, and approved of them all, except the first. Pride made a slave work, and shame and uncertainty kept him obedient. Unlike Zed, she saw very little value in fear.

And if pride turned to rebellion, and shame to sullenness, well, there was always dorazine.

"Come here," she said. She pointed to the footstool. Stiffbacked but still graceful, he sat on it. "Binkie will have told you that on Chabad, the past is past. But you know, I think, that there is a dorazine shortage on Chabad. This is of major concern to Family Yago. We buy most of the dorazine that runners sell to the dealers in Abanat. It goes to the Net, and also to the prisons of Belle, Enchanter, Sabado, and Ley. We use it also at our kerit farm in Sovka. The other Families and industries on Chabad that are not controlled by the Four Families buy their dorazine separately." He was relaxing; all the words were putting him at ease. He had a mobile, expressive face; as he listened to her, his dark eyebrows drew together. "I want to ask you some questions about the dorazine trade. I know from my dealer that dorazine is made and processed out of sector, by a concern that everyone calls The Pharmacy."

"That's right," he said.

"Is it true that no one knows the location of The Pharmacy?"

"I've never heard anyone name a sector," he said, hesitantly. "They send their shipments out in roborockets which go to drop points in all eight sectors. They have agents who contact the runners for them. I don't know how the agents get their instructions, but I've heard they come without a sector designation. That's what the agents say."

She could see that he was unsure of what he could tell her, and was trying to be precise. "Is dorazine sold elsewhere, besides Chabad?"

"Buyers from other sectors send runners to Chabad for one or two loads, sometimes. But comine's cheaper. It's expensive to be addicted to dorazine." His face tightened. "That's what your brother thought I was, at first: a runner picking up a one-shot load."

Rhani said gently, "That doesn't matter." She touched his hand lightly. "You know, you're mine now. You're not Zed's property. Dorazine comes to Chabad. How does it come in? The officials in Port city check incoming ships, and they're supposed to turn you over to the Hype cops if they catch you with contraband." She smiled as she said it. She knew the Port officials had trouble taking the Code seriously.

"Runners don't come to Port, or to the moon at all. We—they—Jump from the Hype to spacetime normal near the planet. They landed on Chabad—or if there's, say, a captain and crew, the captain takes the bubble and the crew keeps the ship in orbit—and fly a bubble to Abanat."

"Who was your dealer in Abanat?"

He half-grinned. It changed his rather severe face attractively. "I never had one. I was bluffing." His yellow-ivory skin was not very ruddy, but it grew perceptibly whiter. "I tried a bluff on the wrong person," he said painfully.

She said, "Do you know anything about Michel A-Rae?"

"No, Rhani-ka. I'm sorry."

"Did you eat?"

"Yes, Rhani-ka."

"Is your room comfortable?"

"Yes, Rhani-ka."

"Have you had a chance to see the estate?"

He shook his head.

"Come." She beckoned him to follow her. She opened the glass doors and stepped out to the terrace. "Don't look at the sun!" But he was already shading his eyes, focusing away from that brutal pinpoint to the green lawn. The shadows looked like cut-outs in the brilliant light. She beckoned him to the wall. He laid both hands on the brick.

"It reminds me of a place I lived when I was a child," he said.

"What world was that on?" she asked.

"Pellin." He gazed at the rolling westward slope of hills. "This is beautiful."

"I think so. It was built by my grandmother Orrin. Family Yago was the first Family to live away from Abanat. Now all the Families have private estates in the hills, but this is the oldest. I try to keep it green."

"I'd heard Chabad was a dry world."

"It is," said Rhani. She pointed at the trees. "This estate is tiny. It's a pocket of green on a hill. The water to keep it green is piped here from Abanat. The green ends at a wall. You can't see the wall through the trees, but it's there. Outside the wall, the land is waterless. The gate is that way." She jerked her thumb back toward the front of the house. "No one will stop you from walking through it, but if you do, you'll either return or die. The heat will kill you in half a day, and it's a three-day walk to Abanat."

"Has anyone tried it?"

Rhani said, "Everyone tries." It wasn't really true. But she hoped he believed her; she hoped he would not try it. Unhappily, she remembered the time two years back when Binkie *had* tried it. She wanted to warn Dana. But if she said Zed's name aloud, his face would go tight. She was sure of it.

The mother dragoncat wandered onto the terrace. Scenting a stranger, it froze, growling its odd musical growl. The fur on its back and tail rose. "Stop that!" commanded Rhani. She held out a hand. "Come here, Isis." The cat glided to her. Dana stood very still. "Friend, Isis. Friend." She stroked the cat until its fluffed fur went down. "Hold out your hand." Dana held his hand out, palm up. The cat sniffed it. "This is Isis. She's the oldest. I let her stay in the house a lot; she's stiff, and partially blind. But she can still smell. She's mother to Thoth, Horus, and Typhon."

Isis's tail switched lazily back and forth. She rubbed her head on Dana's thigh. "What is she?" he said.

"A dragoncat. *Felis draco;* bred in the Enchanter labs. Dragoncats are twice as smart as the best guard dogs. Now that she knows you, she'll tell the other three how you smell so that when they meet you they won't tear you into little bits and pieces."

"How can she do that?"

"The labs breed them with rudimentary, species-selective telepathy. They're expensive."

"I'll bet," he said, stroking Isis's triangular head.

Rhani said, "When my brother told me about you last night, he suggested you become my pilot. Can you do that?"

He said, "I was trained for it."

"Good. I don't spend my life in constant travel, though. I may ask you to do other things."

He smiled. He had a good smile. "I'll make a poor cook or secretary, Rhani-ka."

"I'll remember that," she promised.

A door slid open from the other bedroom. Zed stepped onto the terrace. Rhani felt Dana stiffen beside her. The dragoncat stopped purring. Her tail twitched. Slowly she backed away from him, fur rising. "Isis, no," Rhani said. He must smell of fear, she thought.

Zed said, "Did you get answers to your questions, Rhani-ka?" He looked at Dana. Reassuringly, Rhani laid a hand on Dana's bare arm.

He started from her touch as if her hand were made of ice, or acid.

"Yes," she said. "Dana was very useful. I agree with you. He'll make a good pilot."

"I'm glad you think so," Zed said. "Go downstairs," he said to Dana.

With a constrained, almost clumsy bow, Dana left the terrace. Rhani heard the sound of the sliding bedroom door. She gazed at the lovely patterns of the cool falling water, hands bunched in her pockets, back to her brother.

"Rhani-ka."

She would not turn.

"Rhani, I'm sorry." Now she turned. "I said he was yours, yours he shall be." He made a face, a small-boy look, rueful and contrite. She reached to take his hand.

She could not stay angry with him. She never could. Her anger hurt him too much. "Let me tell you what he said," she offered.

Chapter Four

It soon became apparent to Rhani that there was nothing about Dana Ikoro she could say that her brother did not already know. Nevertheless, he listened patiently to her summary of the conversation. At the end of it, he said, "What are you looking for, Rhani-ka?"

She paced slowly around the bedroom. "I'm not sure," she said. "Chabad has to have dorazine, Zed-ka. I can't believe that *nothing's* coming in. If I could just reach Sherrix. . . . Maybe she's gone underground."

"Too bad you can't use a direct line," said Zed. The problem with direct-line calls, of course, was that the computer kept records of them. They could be traced; with the right equipment, they could be overheard. "She might have had to leave Chabad unexpectedly."

"Frightened off by the Hype cops!" Rhani said. She scowled. "I wish I could think of something that would frigthen off Michel A-Rae."

Zed said, "I suspect he's well protected, Rhani. Do you know what district Sherrix works from?"

"Hyper district," Rhani said. "How about some nasty accident? A broken leg?"

"I might be able to help."

"What?" Rhani said. "Break Michel A-Rae's leg?"

Zed frowned. "Rhani-ka—"

Quickly, she said, "I'm teasing you, Zed-ka. You can help me reach Sherrix?"

He nodded. "Or find out where she is. You need someone who can walk through the Hyper district and not be out of place, someone who can ask questions without seeming to, someone who knows Hyper custom—"

"My Starcaptain!" Rhani said.

But Zed shook his head. "I think not, Rhani-ka. He's newly a slave; he's not used to it yet. If he met a runner or some Hyper he knew, he might try to escape."

"I wouldn't want that," Rhani said. I *should* tell him what happened to Binkie, she thought. He needs the warning. "You can't do it, Zed-ka?"

"No." He perched on the arm of her chair. "I'm not an outsider, but I'm too well known to be of use. No runner or dealer would discuss drug business with the Net commander. But there's Jo Leiakanawa, my second. Remember the year the Net had a pilferage problem? Some crew member was stealing dorazine—"

"From the Net supplies," Rhani said, "and bringing it back to Abanat, where it was sold to dealers who turned around and resold it to Gemit or to the city, making a double profit. I remember. You sent me a 'gram from Enchanter."

"That was it. We never found out the identity of the thief. But Jo talked to the dealers, and the stealing stopped."

Rhani said, "I could write to her." She frowned. "But even if I call the mail service to send a special bubble for the letter, it will sit in Abanat a day before it's delivered."

Zed said, "Even if you wrote to her, she might say no."

Rhani raised her eyebrows. "If *I* asked her?"

Zed spread his hands; his voice grew apologetic. "I know, you're her employer. But she and I have worked together for so long, I think she thinks she's working for me."

"But you said she might help."

"If *I* asked her. I could fly back to Abanat and find her, request her to find Sherrix."

Something in his voice warned her. She walked to him and touched his thigh. "If you don't want to do it, Zed-ka, then don't."

He looked up at her, and then rested his hand lightly on hers. "No, I'll do it. Not today, though. I'd like two more days with you."

The simple words reverberated in both their minds. Rhani looked away from his face. *Give us two more days!* he had pleaded with their mother, the afternoon that Isobel had realized how truly close they had become and decided to separate them, and send Zed to Nexus, and Rhani to Sovka. He had been fifteen; Rhani, seventeen. I should have told her no, Rhani thought, tormented by an ancient guilt. I was older. We *should* have stayed together. I *could* have said I wouldn't go.

But she had not, and now it was long past, and Isobel was dead. If we had not separated, Zed would not have gone to Nexus, studied medicine, become a pilot, be what he is. She remembered him as he had been; gentle, loving, focus of her heart, as she was of his. So what if they had—as Isobel feared they might—gone to bed together? Who would it have hurt? While now. . . . But Rhani did not want to think about now. Zed was no longer gentle, and no longer the focus of her love.

"Two more days," she agreed. "And hurry back."

He smiled. "I won't linger in Abanat." He rose. "And now I'll let you be. Your work doesn't stop just because I come home, and I know it."

"I wish it could," she said.

He walked to the door and turned back. "I don't suppose you ever heard from The Pharmacy about your offer to buy the dorazine formula."

She shook her head. "I don't see why they would want to sell. As long as it keeps making money—"

"What if it were legal to transport dorazine inter-sector?" he said. "Perhaps it's time to approach the Federation with that proposal."

"Not if Michel A-Rae is typical of current Federation attitudes," Rhani said.

Zed said, "Do you think he is?"

Rhani shrugged. "How can we tell? They appointed him to the job." She sat in the wing chair. "I'm sick of him, Zed-ka. Go away, let me read that report you spent the morning telling me about."

He laughed, and went. For a moment, she was tempted to call him back, tell him to wait a week, a month, before leaving. But she told herself not to be silly, that the errand had to be done, and that he would come home soon.

She curled into the big wing chair. It was true that she had to work: she wanted to read the Net report, to review the minutes of the last Council meeting, to review the Federation directives on drug trade. And the latest mail delivery had contained five pages of closely handwritten material from the Yago Family spy at Gemit. Her mother, she thought, would never have wasted half a morning talking to a good-looking slave. Thinking of her mother suddenly made her think about her long-dead grandmother, Orrin Yago. Isobel had been a strong but cold woman, unyielding as the Abanat ice. Orrin had been passionate, about Chabad at least. Isobel used distance to threaten and protect as other folk use force, ruling the Yago interests from the haven of the estate.

But Orrin had built the estate to remind her daughter and her daughter's children that there were other places in the universe. She had seen them. Isobel had not.

Domna Orrin Yago had fought the Federation of Living Worlds and won. Before the construction of the Net, ships from Belle, Sabado, Ley, and Enchanter had brought their prison populations to the Chabad slave pens, where the Chabadese drugged them and readied them for Auction. Then, as now, off-world tourists came to watch, titillated by a condition that their own laws would not permit. Some of them even purchased slaves, and took them back to those home worlds. They were shocked to discover that, on their worlds, their slaves were slaves no more.

Cries of fraud and double-dealing rose all the way to Nexus Compcenter, seat of the Assembly of the Federation. By its own rules, the Assembly was bound not to interfere with local regulations. But export of slaves from Chabad was a non-local concern. A bill was proposed in the Assembly to ban slavery on Chabad, and the Chabad Council was invited to send a representative. They sent Orrin Yago. Rhani imagined her as she must then have been: a lean, small woman, deep-voiced, amber-eyed, her thick, short hair prematurely white. She would not, then, have needed her cane. She rode a starship to Nexus—she had never been offplanet before—to listen to the heated debate. Finally, she rose to address the gathered representatives of fifty-six inhabited worlds.

Outside, in the trees, the birds were singing. Orrin Yago had never heard live birds.

"I propose this," she said. "Sector Sardonyx will retain the practice of slavery. However, we will severely limit the participation of non-Chabadese. Any non-Chabadese wishing to own a slave must agree to remain on Chabad for the duration of any slave contracts held by her/him. Slave contracts shall be null and void off Chabad. No slave may be removed from Chabadese soil. Only beings arrested and convicted of criminal activities within Sardonyx Sector may be subject to slavery, and only the worlds of Sardonyx Sector may offer prisoners to the slave auction, understanding that when they do so, these criminals, whatever their crimes, talents, and places of origin, may serve out their sentences to become citizens of Chabad with all due rights, privileges, and responsibilities."

Children in Abanat schools learned that speech by heart. So had Rhani. She heard it now in her head. The debate had broken out again, still hot. Slavery itself was illegal, considered immoral on many Federation worlds.

But the Federation had bound itself not to interfere with local custom, and the other worlds in Sardonyx Sector supported Chabad. They looked for Orrin Yago to tell her that she had won, and found her sitting on a bench in a dusty park, listening to the birds.

I'm like my mother, Rhani thought. I hide here; I hate to travel. I even hate Abanat.

But she was like Orrin Yago, too. Domna Sam had said

so. "You learned to be a Yago from your mother," she whispered, leaning up on one elbow to stare at the younger woman out of her huge silken bed. "But you're not like Isobel. You're like your grandmother, you even look like her, small and tough. You're like the shell of a nut, and inside the shell there's fire. Don't stare at me, girl! I know it's there, even if you don't. Someday you'll know it, and when you do, Rhani Yago, you'll be twice as hard and twice as dangerous as your mother ever was. Twice as dangerous as you are now, and now you're very dangerous. But not as much as I am. You remember that: the Dur crest is the axe, lifted to strike, and if you oppose the axe, it cuts."

She had rambled on, mumbling threats and promises, and Rhani had ceased to listen. Poor Domna Sam, she thought. She stretched. *I wonder if she was right. If Michel A-Rae continues in his hostilities, I shall need to have the toughness of Orrin Yago.*

She pictured herself in the Assembly of Living Worlds on Nexus, requesting that the Federation legalize the sale of dorazine. She did not think they would agree to do it. There were too many people in the eight sectors who agreed with Michel A-Rae.

She glanced toward the secretary. "Binkie?"

He turned to her, attentive as always. "Yes, Rhani-ka."

"Have any reports about Michel A-Rae come in yet?"

"Not yet, Rhani-ka."

"Please tell me when they do. What have you done about tracing the Free Folk of Chabad?" She made a face at the name.

"I wrote a letter of inquiry about them to the Abanat police."

"Thank you." She smiled her gratitude at him. "You know, Bink, I think Family Yago would fall apart without you here."

He bowed his head, coughed, stammered something, and looked away.

"Let me have the Gemit report," she said. He fished among the papers and brought it to her. *"To Domna Rhani Yago. . . ."* The handwriting was abominable. She scowled at it; wishing the Gemit spy could have taped his report. But the Gemit security forces undoubtedly would have discovered any tape.

She sighed, and drew her legs up in the chair. "Tell Cara I'll want lunch here," she said.

"Yes, Rhani-ka," said Binkie.

Sweet mother, Rhani thought, he's written on the back as well! "Binkie!" she said. "Dinner too, probably."

But by dinnertime, she had finished deciphering the report. She ate with Zed in the small dining alcove on the first floor. It looked into the garden. The moon was gibbous, and brilliant overhead; by its light, the dragon-cats moved silently, weaving feral patterns among the shadows and beneath the trees.

"There's something going on at Gemit," she said.

"They ran out of gold," suggested Zed.

"No. I wouldn't want that—I think. No, it's internal. One of their researchers has come up with a new twist in the refining process. It will halve the time it takes to separate the pure metal from the ore, but the initial outlay of money to equip is enormous. The Dur accountants think it's a waste of money and refused to authorize the funds. The head of the research department resigned in protest. They're fighting."

"How nice for them," said Zed.

"Maybe," Rhani said, "that's what Ferris Dur wants to talk with me about."

"To ask your advice?"

Rhani grinned. "Not likely, no."

"What possible interest would *you* have in the Gemit mines? Open interest, that is."

"Maybe he wants to trade," Rhani said. "I get an executive power struggle; he gets a cageful of dead kerits."

"You think he knows about that?" Zed separated the last bits of meat from his plate and pushed it from him. Amri took it.

"He must. I'm sure he has spies in Sovka, just as I do in Gemit. Not good ones," she added, "I hope." She turned in the chair. "Amri, tell Immeld to make egg tarts for tomorrow's breakfast."

"Yes, Rhani-ka," called the girl, and Zed smiled. He was a glutton for Immeld's egg custard tarts.

"You know," Rhani went on, "if the Hype cops do chase all the runners out of Sector Sardonyx, we'll have to make arrangements to use another drug, one of the dorazine derivatives, for the Net. We might even be able to buy the patent from whoever owns it."

"None of them works very well," said Zed.

"But they're better than nothing."

Zed managed to look both thoughtful and doubtful. "The best of them is pentathine."

"I'll tell Binkie to find out who owns the patent."

"But I think you overestimate Michel A-Rae."

Rhani brandished her fork at him. "You said he was a fanatic, dedicated!"

"He is. But the Hype drug cops have to cover eight sectors, and there are a lot of illegal drugs in the Living Worlds. He can't spend all his time and funds concentrating on dorazine. He's been at his job a few months, and while he may have shut down traffic here, it's got to be thriving elsewhere. The other sector worlds aren't going to like that, and pretty soon one or more of them is going to complain."

Rhani shook her head. "Obsessives don't think like that, Zed-ka. He'll keep on until he's circumvented or stopped."

"He's being paid to do a job. Eventually he'll have to do it," Zed argued.

Rhani spread her hands. She was not going to argue about obsessions with her brother: the only ones he understood were his own. "Maybe," she temporized. "I will certainly think about what you say."

Dana Ikoro sat in the kitchen, wondering what they were talking about, and—he thought—going a little mad.

After Zed had sent him from the terrace, it had taken him half an hour to stop shaking. During that time, he hid in his room. When he felt strong enough to move, he went into the garden, like a dog seeking a hole to hide in. He met Timithos, a sturdy, dark man with dirt under his nails and hair burned pale as straw by the sun. When Dana spoke with him, he simply smiled and did not speak. The dragoncats came by to sniff at him; Dana found a string and dragged it for them, and they consented to some regal play, but they grew bored before he did. The inactivity made him itch. He wanted to ask permission to visit the hangar behind the house, but to do that he would have to seek out Zed. He also started to walk through the front gate, just for the hell of it, but a vestige of sense held him back.

Finally Cara took pity on him. "Come," she said and brought him to the kitchen. Cutting vegetables did not make him feel better, but at least it gave him something to do. He had begun to comprehend Immeld's constant curiosity about Zed and Rhani's talk. During their meal, the slaves gathered in the kitchen to eat. Amri ate first, since she served the meal. Dana wondered what would happen if, in the middle of the meal, he screamed.

He decided he was not yet crazy enough to want to find out.

"Here," said Immeld, thrusting a dish between his hands. His fingers closed automatically. He glanced down; it was sherbet topped with nuts.

"Why are you giving me this?" he said.

"Because I'm sick of you hanging around," she said. "Go spoon it into those glass bowls over there."

He did as he was told. Binkie, seated on a stool, smiled a private, ironic smile.

"Now what?" Dana said.

"Now take it into the alcove," said Cara. "What are you, a moron? That's dessert."

"Oh," Dana said. "Right." He wondered what Rhani would say to see him march out with the dishes. He wondered if Zed would comment. Sweet mother, he told himself, it's nothing, you're simply going to serve a meal! He walked from kitchen to alcove and set the first dish in front of Rhani, the second in front of Zed. The Net commander didn't bother to look up. Relieved, Dana returned to the kitchen. Timithos had come in, a dragon-cat at his heels. Immeld gave him food in a brown, covered pot. He smiled at them all, murmured something incomprehensible, and left.

Binkie said, "That man's a fool. He can barely talk. He won't even sleep in the house."

Amri said, "The garden's nice at night."

"Would you sleep there?"

"I can't. I have my work to do."

"Yes. Well, Timithos likes his work too much."

Amri said, "What's wrong with that? I like my work."

"You would."

"Don't torment the child," said Cara. Immeld banged the lid on a cook-pot, frowning.

"Don't you like your work?" asked Amri.

Binkie said, "It has its advantages."

Immeld said, "What are they talking about tonight?"

"About the mines at Gemit," said Amri, "and about dorazine."

"The shortage," said Immeld.

Cara said, "It won't affect us."

Binkie said, "It wouldn't affect you anyway, Cara."

Cara said, "Don't snip at me." She glanced at the white scar on her own arm. "It did once."

"Yes, I know," said the secretary. "You were lucky." He looked at Dana. "Cara was so devoted to the Yagos she stayed on as steward after her contract ended."

Cara said, "It's a good job."

"So's my job," said Binkie. His tone was ironic, brittle as glass. "But when my contract runs out, Chabad will never see me again, and Sector Sardonyx and Family Yago can go to hell!"

Cara said softly, "You'll get into trouble talking like that."

Binkie's lips tightened. He swung around and left the kitchen for the dark slaves' hall.

"Poor Binkie," said Amri. She trotted from the room, and returned with the plates. "They're going upstairs."

Immeld put the leftovers into containers, and the containers into a cooler. "That's done till tomorrow," she said, sighing. She and Cara walked toward the slaves' hall, their arms around each other.

Amri cleaned the table, and wiped the kitchen counters. Dana wiped the pots and dishes clean. It only took a few moments. "What Binkie said—" he hesitated.

"About what?"

"About Cara—did he mean she's not a slave?"

"Yes," said Amri. "Immey told me. She was a slave when Isobel Yago, Rhani-ka's mother, died. Then her contract was canceled. That's the law. You go free if your owner dies. Her contract had three more years to run. But she stayed. She's been here all this time."

"If Rhani died, would you stay?"

Amri looked shocked. "Don't talk like that," she said. "It's bad luck to talk about somebody dying."

"I'm sorry," said Dana. "Do you want me to stop talking?"

"No." She sat on a stool. "I like it. Cara and Immey don't talk to me much."

"How long have you worked for the Yagos?"

"Three years," said the girl. "They bought me to help Immeld." Reaching out, she dimmed the kitchen lights.

"What do you do?"

"I do the housekeeping. I straighten the rooms, I do the laundry. I water the plants inside. Wash the windows. I'll show you. You can come with me tomorrow."

"I'd like that," Dana said. "Can I ask you something else?"

"Sure."

"What happened to Binkie?"

Amri bowed her head. Her hands twisted in her lap. Dana was not sure she had understood him. Finally, she said, "It was Zed."

"Oh." I should have known, he thought.

"He tried to run away. Out the front gate. It was stupid, you can't live out there, it's too hot. He left at night. In the morning, Zed took the bubble and brought him back. His lips were all bloody where he had bitten them for moisture, and he was sick, because he tried to eat the plants. Zed took care of him until he was stronger and then—"

"You don't have to tell me," Dana said.

"—punished him," finished Amri. "Rhani was angry. She and Zed had an awful fight."

"Good," said Dana grimly.

"It wasn't," protested Amri. "It's horrible when they fight. But then Zed went to Abanat, ice climbing, and when he came back it was all right. He leaves Binkie alone, but Binkie hates him."

Dana said, "I can see why. When was that?"

"About a year ago, I think." Amri frowned. "I can't remember. It was sometime before the last Auction. When there isn't any weather, all the times seem alike."

In the dim kitchen, the sentence, spoken in Amri's high child's voice, was poignant as a cry. "Where are you from?" Dana asked.

She twisted her hands. "We're not supposed to talk about that." Her huge gray eyes, pupils wide in the darkened room, stared past him. "Belle," she whispered. "It rains there, all the time. I miss it."

He put his arm around her. "Don't cry."

She stiffened. "I'm *not* crying!" She sounded very much like one of Dana's younger brothers. She yawned, a great jaw-cracking shuddering yawn. She put a belated palm up to hide it.

"You should go to sleep." He walked her to her door. She clung to him a moment in the hushed hall.

"I like you," she said. He kissed the top of her head lightly. Her hair smelled of cinnamon. "Good night."

"Good night." Silent as a ghost, she slid inside her room. Again Dana wondered what she had done to come to Chabad. What sort of system made slaves of children?

There were lights on in Binkie's room, none in Immeld's, a flicker of a candle in Cara's. Dana went to his room. He sat on the bed. He didn't think he could endure ten years of this: kicking around a lonely house, doing nothing, piloting Rhani Yago once in a while, fighting off shudders whenever Zed came near him. He would go mad. Nobody could live like that.

Tears of rage and despair swelled into his throat. He stood up violently. The bed rocked. "Don't cry!" he ordered himself, as he had Amri. He had no use for tears; he had cried enough.

The panic—that was what it was—halted.

Through the jitter of misery in his head, Dana heard music.

He heard it clearly; Stratta's "Concerto in A Minor." It grew in strength: a soft, precise, intransigent construct of song. It stopped the tears. His head and his bowed spirits lifted of their own accord. He listened until it stuttered in his mind, and was lost. Walking to the washroom, he scrubbed his face. A somber reflection looked at him from the mirror. He made it grin. You won't go mad, he told himself.

The next day Rhani was aware of an oddity in the house: whenever Amri appeared to make a bed, straighten a room, replace a towel, Dana came with her.

The girl chattered to him blithely, mostly about Abanat. He listened, smiling. He seemed almost happy. Rhani had not expected him to adjust that fast. He was young, of course, and flexible—but his docility surprised her, and it made her watch him. Once he was in the bedroom when Zed came in; he froze, and she saw his shoulders hunch. Amri looked at him in puzzlement. Zed said, "Go on with what you're doing." After a moment Dana's hands moved again. Zed turned away from him. "You had something to show me, Rhani-ka?"

"To ask you." She hunted through the printed Net report. "I see that we lost a technician again. Can you think of anything to stop that? They disappear in the sector—I don't like the idea of just anyone being able to learn all about the Net. I don't understand it. Where do they go?"

"Enchanter, or Ley, or Sabado. They see green, water, rain—and they just jump ship." The discussion engrossed her.

But when it was done, and Zed gone from the room, Rhani retained her awareness of Dana bending over the bed: an afterimage. He was gone. He had been a Starcaptain; did he like making beds?

Before lunch she went into the garden, half to take a walk, half looking for Cara, to tell her Zed was leaving the next day at dawn and would be back that night. She could hear Amri singing off-key in the slaves' quarters. She passed through the kitchen. Dana sat there, on a stool, hands on his thighs. His face was intent, shuttered. He looked as if he were listening to something. She listened for it but all she heard was the hum of the aircooling system, and Amri's discordant voice. "Dana?"

It took him several seconds to respond. "Yes, Rhani-ka."

"What are you doing?"

"I was listening."

"To what?"

"'Concerto in A Minor for Electric Flute,' by Stratta."

"I've never heard of it," Rhani said.

"Not many people have."

"It doesn't sound contemporary."

"It isn't. Stratta wrote about four hundred years ago. He's obscure . . . I like his music. I had a lot of tapes of it in *Zipper*. I don't know what happened to them." He looked away from her. "They're probably destroyed by now."

"Zipper?"

"My starship."

She wondered if he knew that Zed had bought the ship for Family Yago. Property taken from slaves belonged to the world their crime was committed on. "You hear this music in your head?"

"Not very well. I was trying. Is there something I can do for you, Rhani-ka?"

Rhani bit her lip. He was warning her off the subject, as deferentially and adroitly as Binkie might. "I was looking for Cara."

"She and Immeld are walking in the garden."

His face had taken on that look of patient waiting shared, Rhani thought, by slaves and children. She had worn it as a child. He had not looked like that smiling at Amri. She wanted to see him relax. With a twinge of disloyalty, she said, "Zed's going to Abanat tomorrow."

His dark eyes came alive.

"Just for a day. He's going to talk with Jo Leiakanawa, the Net second. We need someone with contacts in the Abanat drug market to—" She heard herself sharing Family Yago's business with a stranger, a slave, not even a secretary. Astounded, she stopped.

But Dana's head was cocked to one side. He was listening. Rhani started to speak. He held up a hand. She listened—and heard, over the sounds made by the house, a high-pitched whine. "What is it?" she asked, and then answered herself. "It's a bubble. But the mail bubble comes at dawn, and it isn't due for two days yet."

They went out the kitchen door. Shading their eyes, they stared at the sky. Dana pointed west. Rhani gazed up. The drone continued. Light flashed: sunlight glinting off metal. She glanced back at the house; Zed had come out to the terrace. He was wearing sunshades on his eyes.

An hour before noon it was hot even under the shade trees. Timithos had turned the water off. By noon, taking a breath felt like you were filling your lungs with sand, and sweat evaporated from the skin at once. The most indefatigable tourists napped. Who would fly a bubble so close to noon, so near the estate? All the Abanat pilots knew how strongly the Four Families valued their solitude.

Now she could see the little craft clearly. At the last

instant, it changed course. Making a wide swerve, it skirted the wall of the estate, and circled back toward Abanat.

Rhani said, "Maybe a pilot lost the way. It's dangerous, Zed says, to fly in the noon sun."

"Maybe the pilot's new to Chabad," Dana said.

"Or some tourist offered a pilot a bribe to fly as close to the Yago estate as she dared," Rhani said. "It's happened before."

He said, "I was wondering—" and stopped.

"Yes?" Rhani said.

"I was wondering about the mail bubble."

"What about it?"

"On Pellin, and Nexus, too, mail goes through the computer network."

Rhani smiled. "Custom on Chabad is different. Public mail, trivia, news: this goes through the computer. But Family matters, business dealings, private communications we write on paper, with ink."

He said, "Some people might call that archaic."

"It is archaic. Though we prefer the word 'traditional' on Chabad. The Founders, the folk of the Four Families who turned Chabad from a prison planet to a successful mining colony, were very traditional people."

"But what is the point to avoiding the com-net?"

"To keep private information inaccessible to unauthorized persons who might try to see it."

He looked doubtful. "Paper and ink—aren't you afraid that someone might steal the letters? It's physically easier than cracking the computer network. Or"—he sounded serious—"if you have to make some data inaccessible, why not just file everything under a 'Restricted' code?"

"I said we were traditional!" Rhani exclaimed. "Not paranoiac. Actually"—she rubbed her chin—"I think we write so many letters on Chabad because one of the few things the planet produces, besides precious metals and kerits, is paper."

He sighed. "It's different," he said.

"You'll get used to it," she said, but gently, so that he would not feel that she was dwelling upon his state of servitude.

Cara and Immeld walked toward them, arm in arm. Rhani said, "Did you see the bubble, just now?"

Cara nodded. Immeld said, "It came very close. They never come that close."

Cara said thoughtfully, "They're not supposed to do that."

"No," Rhani agreed. "I'll tell Binkie to call Main Landingport and remind them. Cara, Zed is going to Abanat tomorrow, just for one day. He'll be back in the evening."

Suddenly, Dana began to laugh.

All three women turned to look at him. "What are you laughing at?" Rhani said.

Controlling the laughter, he hiccoughed. "Sorry, Rhani-ka. It occurred to me that the pilot of the bubble might be someone I know."

"Who?" asked Immeld, Cara frowned at her, and pressed her arm.

"It doesn't matter," Dana said, "because it can't be her. The timing's all off."

"I thought you didn't know anyone on Chabad," Rhani said. But she remembered as she said it that he had not exactly stated that.

"I don't."

"Then who were you thinking of?" she pressed.

His face closed like a fist. "A Starcaptain," he answered, "named Tori Lamonica."

Zed Yago left the estate in the dark before sunrise.

Rhani walked with him to the bubble hangar. In the west, the stars made a frosty diadem on Chabad's horizon. "Good hunting in Abanat," she said. "I'll miss you."

"I won't be gone long. Jo drinks at The Green Dancer. I'll talk with her about Sherrix and I'll be back. I want to stop at the Main Landingport and talk to Tam Orion about that overflight."

"I was going to have Bink write."

"Let me complain. It was probably a newly hired pilot, but that's no excuse."

Rhani said, "That's what Dana said. I thought some tourist offered a pilot a bribe."

Zed palmed the bubble door. "They're paid on Nexus' scale. They don't need bribes."

She caught his sleeve as he reached for the ceiling bar to swing inside the bubblecraft. "Zed-ka—where's Dana's ship? You told me you bought it from the Council."

"*Zipper?*" He dropped back to earth lightly. "At Port, on the Field, with the Yago seal on it. He should know better than to bother you about it."

"He didn't. But yesterday I found him listening to the air, to music in his mind." Zed was nodding. "You know about his music, Zed-ka?"

"I know about it," said Zed.

"He's adjusting well to the change in his life."

"He'd better."

"But I think he would be more content, less inclined to run, if he had his music. He thought the tapes were destroyed."

Zed said, "They weren't. I gave orders that nothing in *Zipper* was to be touched. If you want, Rhani-ka, I'll call up to Port and have them send the tapes to Abanat on a shuttleship. If I call this morning I should have them by tonight."

"I'd like that, Zed-ka." She smiled, picturing Dana's surprise and joy.

Zed said, "Don't coddle him, Rhani-ka."

"Happy slaves work better."

He smiled at her. "We've had this discussion before." He ran his fingers along the edge of her cheek. "I'll bring the tapes."

"Thank you, Zed-ka. Don't stay all day at the Landingport, exchanging lies with the chief pilot."

"I will not," he said with dignity. He reached again for the ceiling bar. He disappeared into the bubble. Rhani stepped back as the two halves of the hangar roof began to slide apart. The bubble hummed. She clapped her hands over her ears. Zed transpared the skin, waved briefly, and then opaqued it over. The bubble shivered, and lifted straight up.

Dana, awake in his bed, heard the familiar drone.

It swelled, and then died, till all that he could hear of it was a dry arthropodal whine.

Zed was gone. In his head a chord sounded. He got out of bed smiling. He washed and then dressed. The straw sandals were already conforming to his feet. He went to the kitchen and helped himself to fruit. The house was quiet. The kitchen door was unlocked. Pushing it open, he strolled outside.

The shadowless light was pleasant. The cool air seemed softer. Dana picked his way to the rear of the house, where the bubble hangar sat. A slight figure rested on a hangar strut, arms folded. Dana hesitated. Rhani saw him. She leaned away from the hangar. Shoulders hunched, hands in her pockets, she came to join him. She looked thoughtful.

Delicately as a dragoncat, she lifted her chin, sniffing the air. "Smell the moisture?"

Dana said, "I thought it seemed less dry."

"In the valleys at sunrise, sometimes you can feel dew on the grass. In winter it even rains: three storms a season. When it rains in Abanat the shops close. People leave houses and stores to walk in the rain."

"Amri said there were no seasons here."

"She wasn't born here."

"She was remembering Belle."

"She seems taken with you," Rhani said.

"She reminds me of one of my little brothers."

"You have more than one?"

Dana smiled. "I have seven."

"Seven!" Rhani marveled. "All eight sons of one mother?"

"Oh, no." He chuckled. "No. We go in for extended parenting on Pellin. There are actually nine sons, ten daughters, eight mothers, five fathers."

"Do they all live together?" Rhani asked.

"No. But they get together all the time, to party, or to sing and dance, or to go on caravans. They get into three wagons and travel for months around the countryside."

Rhani said, "So many people—I don't think I'd like it."

"Not everyone on Pellin likes it," he assured her. "People go what we call *bersk*. They get very grumpy and have to be alone for a time. I spent two years alone, off and on, in a cabin, gone *bersk*."

They strolled slowly toward the garden. "I gather," Dana said, "that family customs are different on Chabad."

"Rather," said Rhani dryly.

"You don't have children early."

"Nor in such quantities." She chuckled. "Ah, I lie. Imre and Aliza Kyneth have a brood of children, enough to fill a wagon. But they have been together thirty-five years, they are married, and their daughter, Margarite, the Kyneth heir, is only three years younger than I."

He wondered who these people were. Friends? Relatives? It made him curious about her life. She seemed gentle, decent, no monster. They came to a bare patch of earth, and Rhani knelt to touch the dusty ground. On the top of her head, her hair was more red than brown. She said, "This spot just soaks up water, and nothing ever grows." Standing, she brushed the grit from her fingers. Dana saw again how much she looked like her brother. Like Zed, she was fair. Fine blond hairs glinted on the backs of her hands and along her arms. Zed had bought him for her. Did she know? he wondered. Did she know what her brother was? He chanced a personal question. "Don't Yagos marry?"

"No. We never have. My mother, Isobel, is the only Yago to bear more than one child. I never knew my father, not even his name." She smiled. "Does that shock you?"

"Yes," he said.

"It's our custom. We bear late, too: my mother had me when she was fifty-five. Zed's my heir, until I have a child. If something were to happen to us both, the line reverts to cousins: the Diamos family. Lisa Yago had a brother. It's a parallel line. There are scores of them. *We* stay solitary: we give our strongest years to Chabad. Isobel was eighty when she died." For a moment she seemed to have forgotten Dana. Then she said, "I know your age. How old am I?"

"Thirty-five?"

"Thirty-six." Sunlight touched her; a cluster of small lines radiated from the outer corners of her eyes toward her hairline. "You guess well. Zed's two years younger." She cocked her head to one side. "Do you hear something?"

Dana listened. "It's a bubble," he said, focusing on the sound. He shaded his eyes and found it. "There it is."

"That's odd." It winked across the western sky, a traveling point of light.

"Could it be the mail bubble?"

"I suppose. It isn't due till tomorrow."

"It sounds like the one that overflew us yesterday."

Rhani looked surprised. "Can you tell that just from

the sound?" The bubble was hurrying closer. As it neared the estate, it slowed almost to landing speed. It crossed the wall. Rhani waved. The bubble seemed to hover. A door slid open. An arm poked out. Something small and dark fell from the arm toward them. It struck the grass-carpeted earth.

The bubble shot away at top speed.

"What—"

Dana reacted on reflex. He seized Rhani around the waist. Yanking her off her feet, he threw her toward a clump of nearby trees. He saw her face, frightened and enraged. "Stay down!" She landed, rolling. He dove after her, and fell on top of her. She squirmed beneath him, fighting to be free. Her hand whipped his cheek. "I'm not—" he started to say, but his voice was lost as the explosion slapped the earth. He clung to the grass, keeping Rhani beneath him. His ears blazed with noise. Something hit his head from behind. Rhani cried out. His head whirled, riotous with pain. He tried to warn her not to rise, to stay down, and then felt darkness wrap about him, incombatable as death.

Chapter Five

Thirteen days before the Auction, Abanat was *en fête*. Main Landingport was busy and noisy, jammed with gaily dressed tourists fighting their way off the shuttle-ships. As Zed brought the Yago bubble down to the landing strip, he wished with all his heart that he did not need to talk to Tam Orion. Without that need, he could have landed at Landingport East, which the city maintained for the exclusive use of the Four Families and their guests. But he did not want to speak with Tam on a comline.

He avoided the tourists by entering the Flight Tower through the pilots' door. Inside Communications, his way was barred by a harassed young operator. "I'm sorry," he said, with weary courtesy, "but only Landingport personnel are authorized to enter the Tower."

Zed smiled at him, liking the youngster's looks. "You're new, aren't you?" Behind him, the other communications operators were chuckling.

"He can use anything he wants in the place," said one. "Asshole, that's Zed Yago."

The new man gulped and stepped aside. "Sorry, Commander."

Zed shrugged. "No harm done. Seen the chief?"

"In his office," someone called.

"Thanks. See you later."

As Zed left the room, he heard the new man saying, "I didn't even know the chief had an office."

The chief pilot's "office" was in the nose-cone-like cubbyhole at the top of the Flight Tower. All landingports, except the smallest, had Flight Towers. In this one, the little space was reachable on a private elevator. Zed used his I-disc to bring the elevator to him. In a moment, he was whisked up the spire. He knocked on the only door. Tam Orion opened it himself. He beamed at Zed and stepped to one side to allow the Net commander into his hole. Zed slid in.

"Mind if I admire your view for awhile?"

Tam gestured at the scene below. It was truly breathtaking: Zed could see in all directions across Abanat; west to the ocean and the twin peaks of ice, east, north, and south to the city streets and the brown, bleak hills beyond.

"Got a bit of a complaint to make," Zed said casually. He glanced at Tam, who nodded. Zed often wondered how many years it had taken Tam to learn to signal when other people spoke to him, and if he had any idea how unnerving strangers found his silence.

"Yesterday, around noon, a two-person bubble overflew the estate. It was too bright to see registration markings. I thought I'd better mention it to you. I figured it was probably a new pilot who doesn't know how foolhardy it is to fly at noon on this rock."

Tam nodded; tugging at an earlobe, he made a great effort. "Right." He drew a spiral in the air with an index finger. Zed knew from long association that the gesture referred to the Net.

"The trip was fine," he said. "No problems."

But Tam had ceased to notice him. He was leaning forward, watching a large, overladen bubble begin a wobbly descent. Zed wondered what he was telling the pilot. Tam Orion was a one-way telepath: he could send but not receive. It did not interfere with—indeed, it helped—his job, but it made him a freak among telepaths and non-telepaths alike. When Zed had first met him, he had been drinking himself to death in a Nexus bar. Zed had learned his story and, knowing himself what it was to be a freak, had decided to rescue him.

The bubble's path smoothed, and became a circle. Tam relaxed.

"Needs some work on that," Zed said. Tam nodded, tapping his fingers in brisk march time. The beat reminded Zed of the promise he'd given Rhani about Dana Ikoro's music.

"Tam," he said, "may I use your com-line link?"

Tam swept a hand toward the com-unit keyboard. Zed edged in front of it and sent instructions up to LandingPort Station to have Dana Ikoro's musictapes placed aboard the next Abanat-bound shuttle. "Thanks," he said. Tam grinned, bouncing lightly on his toes. Zed sidled away from the com-unit and gave the chief back his seat.

In the elevator, he wondered if his sister knew about Tam's talent. He could not remember telling her. All the Hypers knew, of course. The elevator halted at the foot of the spire. He crossed the Port. At the Gate, a crowd of tourists had made a knot around a tired-looking guard.

"But we have to have someone to carry our bags!" said one of them, waving at a pile of luggage.

"Carry them yourselves," the guard said.

The tourists all stared at him. "I thought this planet had people who did that for you," someone said.

"Carry bags? I think that's ridiculous."

"Sorry," said the guard, not sounding sorry at all. "That's the rule. Slaves are not admitted to any portion of the Abanat Landingport."

"But what are we to do?" said a plaintive woman.

The guard gazed at her, infinitely bored. "You can hire porters." He indicated the line of porters resting against a wall. The tourists moved away, grumbling and talking among themselves. Zed brushed passed them. Outside the Landingport, he walked a few blocks, then stepped onto a movalong which would carry him to the Hyper district.

As the slideway traveled south and east, he tried to ignore the tourists. But it was difficult not to notice them; they were everywhere around him. They jammed the movalongs, chattering about Chabad, about the Auction, about the Four Families, of which they knew very little, and about each other. Some of them were naked; most, coming as they did from worlds with G-type suns, wore the skimpiest clothes they owned. Many of them would end up in the Abanat clinics, where the medics would treat them for sunstroke, sunburn, acute dehydration, and melanomas.

Zed reached the Hyper district with relief. Here there were no tourists; Hypers were notoriously intolerant of being gawked at. Quietly, he threaded his way through winding streets to The Green Dancer. At the door, he paused. The bar buzzed softly with talk. A few faces slanted to look at him, and the rhythm of the talk dipped and steadied. He recognized some of them: they were from the Net. He wondered if they had been talking about him.

Jo Leiakanawa rose out of a clump of people. He walked to her. She nodded at him. "Zed-ka."

"Jo." He jerked his thumb toward an empty table. "Sit with me." She followed him and sat. "Are you surprised to see me?"

"I am," she said, imperturbably. "I thought you were going home." Her smooth, heavy face showed no surprise.

Amber MacLean, the bartender and part-owner of the bar, strolled over. "Whaddya want?"

"Dry wine," Zed said. He did not bother to reach for his credit disc: by custom, the first drink of the day in The Dancer was free. The sunlit room was restful. Over the bar hung a badly painted portrait of a Verdian dancing; the dance was supposed to be a ritual in their religion. It was called, Zed remembered, the *K'm'ta*. Amber brought his drink and he ordered one for Jo. Amber brought it, took his credit disc, and sauntered back behind the bar.

Zed said, "I came to ask for your help, Jo."

Jo sipped her wine; her great hand dwarfed the glass. "How may I help you, Zed-ka?"

"You may not be able to. The situation is rather delicate. I don't know if you are acquainted with Sherrix Esbah."

"I've heard the name."

"She seems to have dropped out of sight, or at least, out of reach of Family Yago." He explained briefly. "My sister, I think, fears that Sherrix has been arrested by the Hype cops. I think it more likely that she decided to take an indefinite vacation. She may even have left Chabad. I'd like to know."

Jo folded her hands around her glass. "I can inquire," she said. "When I need to, how may I reach you?"

Zed smiled. He had expected her to say yes, but still . . . "Write a letter. We'll be in Abanat, at the house on Founders' Green, in about eight days."

Jo nodded. "Clear, Zed-ka."

Amber came to the table. "You want to eat," she said. It was not a question.

Zed nodded. "Put it on my credit disc." Amber went behind the bar. A meal in The Green Dancer consisted of broiled fish and seaweed, nothing else. She brought the navigator triple portions.

The bar grew more crowded toward noon. The rhythm of conversation grew more complex. Two Verdians came in, arms around each other. Zed wondered idly what sex they were. Some porters arrived from Port, half-drunk and looking for a fight; Amber drove them out vituperatively before one could start.

Just after noon Zed returned to the Landingport. Automatically, he checked the displays; the shuttleship traffic was moving normally. Suddenly, he caught sight of his own name on the pilots' message board. *"ZED YAGO,"* said the blinking lights, *"CONTACT COMMUNICATIONS, INFO URGENT SOONEST."*

He went quickly to Communications. The back of his neck felt chilled. He had to raise his voice to be heard over the babble. "You have a message for me?" The new operator handed him a piece of paper. It said, *"ESTATE BOMBED, R. Y. UNHURT, ONE SLAVE HURT, A.P. CALLED."* The signature at the foot of the paper was that of Tam Orion.

Zed swallowed. His fingers closed hard on the paper. When he looked up, he realized that the operators were staring at him. The new one, who hadn't known him, was backing away, and Zed wondered what his face looked like. He took a deep breath and brought himself around.

"I'm taking the bubble out," he said. "Clear the flight." The operator jumped. Zed whirled and pushed to the door, not even waiting for them to answer.

As he ran toward his bubble, someone moved to intercept him, calling his name. Ignoring it, he palmed the door open, swung into his seat, and punched the craft to life. Someone hammered on the bubble's skin. Realizing that it might be a further message from the estate, he opened the door. A woman stood there, wearing the uniform of a shuttleship crew member. She held out a box. "Commander, you asked for this," she said. "We brought it."

Zed took it and tossed it on the seat beside him. "Thanks," he said. The door slammed shut; the woman barely had time to yank back her hand. She skipped out of the way as Zed sent the bubblecraft hurtling up.

As he brought the bubble in, low over the estate, Zed saw a dark rift cutting through the green, like a wound in the earth. Rage rose in his chest; a hand seemed to squeeze his heart. He forced it back, telling it, *Later, later,* and, with steady hands, dropped the bubble through the hangar's open roof to its place.

Leaping from it, he hurried to the house. Rhani met him at the kitchen door. There were gel bandages on both her arms. He put his hands lightly on her shoulders, afraid to touch her. "I'm all right," she said. She laid her lips against his. "I told Binkie to put it in the message. I'm all right."

Indeed, she looked fine, except for the bandages. He touched them. "What's this?"

"Grazes," she said cheerfully. "No worse than the times I fell out of trees as a child."

"What happened?"

"That bubble came back. At least, Dana said it was the same one. They flew in close and"—she shrugged—"dropped a bomb. That's all."

"A slave was hurt?"

"Dana. He was protecting me, and something hit his head. I thought at first it was a stone, but if a stone had hit him, he'd be dead, wouldn't he? It must have been a clod of earth."

She was talking too much, Zed thought; a reaction from

the shock. "You called the Abanat police?"

"They'd be right here, they said." She glanced around. "I told Timithos not to touch the garden. Of all of us, I think he's most upset."

Zed's heartbeat was almost back to normal. *If I had been here* . . . he thought, and suppressed the thought, because if he'd been present, there would have been nothing he could do. "Let me see Dana," he said. "Where is he?"

"Timithos carried him to his room," Rhani said. "Amri's with him." They went inside. Zed watched her walk down the hall. She *was* unhurt. She could have been killed, he thought, if she had been closer to the blast, if Dana had not protected her, if a stone had hit her, if, if. . . . He caught his breath. Fury moved like a living thing through his bones. He wanted to break something.

Dana lay on his right side in the bed, loosely covered by a sheet. The left rear quadrant of his skull was bandaged. Amri sat beside him, holding paper and a pen. She held it out to Zed mutely. She had been taking his pulse and counting his respirations every half hour. The figures were normal. Dana's forehead—Zed touched it—was cool and dry. "Has he wakened at all?" he said to Amri.

"He opened his eyes once. He saw me. He said my name and then went back to sleep. He sounded afraid, or angry, I couldn't tell." She rubbed her eyes. "Will he be all right?"

"Don't cry," Zed told her. "Let me get near him, Amri." She scurried back from the bed. "Was the head wound bleeding, Rhani-ka?"

"No," she said. "It was just a discolored lump."

Zed touched the bandages. "I want to take this off," he said. "Amri, get me warm water and a scissors and a sterile cloth."

"I don't know what that is, Zed-ka."

"Go into my room, look in my closet, and bring me my medic's kit."

She brought it instantly, carrying it in both hands. Zed took the clumsy bandage off. The swelling beneath it was purple. He cleaned the area, using the scissors to cut Dana's hair, looking for blood. There was none. "It should have been iced, not bandaged," he said, "but no harm done."

Rhani stared at the swelling. "It looks terrible."

"It's not. What about the rest of him?" Zed drew the sheet away.

"Is it a concussion?" Rhani said.

"It may be one."

Amri said, tearfully, "Why won't he wake up?"

On Dana's back there were welts and abrasions where debris from the explosion had torn the skin away. Zed resisted the urge to lay his fingers, ever so lightly, against those places of pain. Dana breathed evenly, his fine eyelashes trembling. "He will," Zed said. "Dana." He pitched his voice. "Dana." The long body stirred. "See, he hears me. Wake up."

Dana heard Zed calling. *Wake up.* He resisted the command, wanting only rest. But he had been harshly schooled to listen to that voice. He surfaced into consciousness blinking. The daylight was blinding. His eyes teared involuntarily; he could not make out a face.

A cloth wiped his eyes. He saw clearly: Amri, Rhani, Zed. Zed held the cloth. Dana remembered: an arm, waving from the bubble. Something falling. Noise. Yes.

Rhani said tremulously, "Dana!"

He focused on her.

"I would be dead, if not for you."

"Who?" he asked.

Zed said, "We don't know. Yet."

His lips felt thick and sore. "Was anyone else hurt?"

Rhani said, "A dragoncat was killed. And Timithos is furious because the bomb tore a huge hole in his beautiful garden."

Dana tried to swallow. His mouth was dry as bone. Zed said, "Thirsty?"

"Yes."

"You can have water. No food yet. Sleep as much as you like. Don't get up. Here." He put a hand into his pocket and drew out a small box. He held it over the bed. Small hard pellets—musictapes—cascaded out. "These should keep you still. Don't get a headache. There's an auditor in the library. Amri can bring it to you."

Dana touched the musictapes, unbelieving. His fingers shook.

Zed touched his shoulder to draw his attention. "You did well," he said.

Dana struggled. "Thank you, Zed-ka."

Rhani leaned over the bed. "Don't tire yourself," she said. Self-possession had returned to her voice. She linked her arm with Zed's. "Zed-ka."

"I am with you," he said. They left; Dana heard their footsteps, matched, recede along the hall. Amri pattered in, carrying the auditor. She put it where Dana could reach it. His hands felt stiff; his fingers fat, unwieldy as clubs. He fumbled among the tapes for the "Concerto in A Minor."

"I can do it," Amri said.

"I want to," said Dana. He inserted the tape. Stratta filled the room.

"That's pretty," Amri said.

Dana closed his eyes.

An hour after Zed's return and some four hours after Binkie's call to them, two members of the Abanat police arrived at the estate.

The officer in charge of the case was named Sachiko Tsurada. Her companion's last name was Ron. Rhani never heard his first name; later she decided that perhaps he didn't have one. Tsurada was small and dark and clearly the worker of the duo. When the bubble landed by the hangar, she emerged first, hand outstretched in greeting. "Domna," she said briskly. She held out her hand to Zed. "Commander." She surveyed them. "I am glad you were not hurt. I apologize for the length of time it took us to respond to your call." She permitted herself to smile. "No one in the department wanted this assignment, you see."

"I can understand that," Zed said grimly.

"I would like to see all communications you have received from the Free Folk of Chabad, all other threats from anyone, the bomb crater, and, if you retrieved them, any pieces of the bomb."

"There were none," said Zed. He had spent an hour searching through the shrubbery. "At least, none that we could recognize."

"I would also like to tour the estate grounds."

Rhani said, "I'll take you."

The policewoman looked disconcerted. "That isn't necessary, Domna, a slave can do it."

Rhani put her hands on her hips. "I'll take you, I said. They're *my* grounds." The scrapes on her arms and legs stung. She led the way to the house. On the assumption that the police would want to see them, she had told Binkie to sort out the various ugly letters and threats. From the downstairs hall, she called him on the intercom.

"Binkie, please bring the threatening letters downstairs," she said.

"Yes, Rhani-ka," he answered. In a moment, he came down the stairs and handed them to her. She passed them to Tsurada, who glanced through them with a look of contemptuous distaste.

"May we keep these, Domna?"

"If you think it will help."

"It may," she said, passing the neat pile to Officer Ron. "I should tell you, Domna, the Abanat police have never heard of the Free Folk of Chabad. They haven't surfaced before. There are groups like them scattered all about the city, of course; but those we know—most of them are infiltrated—and none of them are organized enough to plan an attack which includes a dry run, or, indeed, sober enough to build a bomb."

Zed said, "I'm not convinced that the attackers are the Free Folk of Chabad."

Rhani said, "But if the Abanat police don't know them, it's more likely to be they than a group that is well known."

Officer Tsurada said, "We'll find out."

"How?" said Zed.

Tsurada smiled. "Brilliant police work, naturally. Probably one of them will get frightened, and turn informer. That's how we get most of our information about these groups. I assume you don't want this event made public, Domna?"

Rhani frowned. "I do not. Has PIN heard about it already?"

"They monitor the police com-lines," Tsurada said. "But I've already told them that whatever they hear, they may not use. They're used to being told not to print things."

"Thank you," Rhani said.

"I would like to see the bomb site, now."

Rhani escorted them to it. Timithos sat on his haunches

nearby, staring disconsolately at the ugly scar. Tsurada walked around it. "From what distance was the bomb thrown?" she asked.

Rhani shook her head. "I don't know. It happened very fast."

"Dana might be able to say," murmured Zed.

"When he wakes up, I'll ask him," said Rhani. "Dana is one of my slaves," she explained. "He was with me when it happened. He was hurt."

Tsurada glanced at Timithos. "Your gardener?"

"Yes."

"Have you seen anything around this hole of metal or plastic, anything unfamiliar that might have come from the bomb?"

Timithos looked frightened. "I found stones," he said timidly.

"I don't think Timithos would recognize a piece of a bomb if it hit him," Rhani interposed.

She and Zed led the police officers around the entire estate. They examined the walls, admired the dragoncats, and walked through and around the gate. As they walked back to the house, Tsurada said, "I don't think there's any way for you to be completely safe here, Domna, short of building a Cage-field over the grounds, or quartering an army on your lawn."

Rhani said, "There is no army on Chabad, and I don't think I could live inside a cage."

Tsurada nodded. "Nor could I." She frowned. "I wish I had a piece of that bomb. With your permission, I'd like to send a team out to examine the grounds."

"You have it," Rhani said. "But why is it important?"

"A piece would tell me where it came from, for starters; if it was made on Chabad, or smuggled in from the outside." She glanced at Timithos, who was now talking softly to the dragoncats. "Domna, have you thought at all that your attackers might be slaves?"

"Ex-slaves, you mean," said Zed. "I assumed that."

"I don't mean that," Tsurada said. "I mean slaves, the slaves who live in our houses, run our computers, arrange our lives. Slaves can use their owners' prestige, their owners' wealth, to get almost anything done. Until and unless one of them made a mistake, proof would be almost impossible to find."

Rhani swallowed. She could not believe . . . "Not my slaves," she said.

Tsurada shrugged. "You know them. It need not be your slaves." She hesitated, and then said, "Domna, you must know that if any Family on Chabad is responsible for slavery, in the slaves' minds, it's Family Yago."

In the hangar, Tsurada shook hands again with Rhani, and then with Zed. "The team will fly out tomorrow morning," she promised. She mounted the bubble, then leaned down to say, "Do you intend to keep to your usual custom, Domna, and go to Abanat for the Auction?"

Rhani had not even considered canceling the trip. "Of course," she said firmly.

"While you are in Abanat," Tsurada said, "you might think about hiring a bodyguard."

Walking back to the house, Zed said, "That's not a bad idea."

"A bodyguard?" Rhani scowled. She hated Abanat; she was never happy there; but she didn't want to be trailed around the streets by some galumphing hired guard. "Ugh."

"Jo could do it. Skellians make excellent bodyguards."

"Jo can't be in two places at once, and she's supposed to be finding Sherrix."

"That's true," said Zed. "But it's still a good idea."

Rhani put her hands in her pockets. Mutinously she thought, I *won't* have a bodyguard. She chuckled suddenly, remembering that wonderful Pellish word Dana had taught her. *Bersk.* I'll get very grumpy and have to be alone for a long while.

Zed said, "Will you at least think about it, Rhani?"

She sighed. "I'll think about it, Zed-ka."

With the discipline that years of practice had taught her, she put Tsurada from her mind. In her bedroom she took out the letter from the Gemit spy. Using pen and paper, she drafted what she wanted to tell him, which was, to listen, report, and when he could discreetly, to foment trouble. Life was going ill with Family Yago; why should it go well with Family Dur? Binkie was at the computer, using the display screen. He was very pale, and she wondered if Zed had been at him for some imagined or trivial wrong.

"Binkie," she said. He turned around to face her. "What's the matter?"

His hands were shaking. "Rhani-ka, I—I seem to have made an error. Days ago you instructed me to take steps to find the source of the threats. I drafted a letter to the police, with details. I thought I'd sent it—but it's still here, on display mode, which means I never sent it at all. If I had, the attack, the bomb—none of that might have happened!" His tone lifted shrilly.

"Stop that," Rhani said, sharply. "You didn't drop the bomb. You simply made a mistake."

"But—"

"No, that's enough. What's done is done." Coldly, she watched him as he fought himself under control.

"You—you won't—" He gulped for air.

"Tell my brother? No, why should I?" she said. Weak with relief, he sagged against the bedroom wall.

She picked up the Gemit report, heartsick. Damn Zed! She had never told him, but she had guessed the night before it happened that Binkie was going to run.

I should never have let Zed do what he did, she thought, and then sighed, knowing that the compulsion driving her brother was too strong for him to break and that under certain circumstances she, even she, could not control him. Again she glanced at Binkie. Fear was effective, but it destroyed all trust. She needed her slaves to trust her. She would use dorazine if she wanted to be served by a houseful of automatons.

"WE CAN DO IT, TOO."

The mail bubble, arriving as scheduled the next morning, brought amid the mail a dirty envelope with a piece of paper sealed inside it. It was signed, "The Free Folk of Chabad."

Rhani, reading the ugly scrawl, grew angrier and angrier, until she could no longer sit in her chair. She thrust the scrap at Binkie. "Here. Give it to the police when they are done." She went onto the terrace. Below her, the police hunted through the bushes for evidence. She made herself lean, relax. The dawn plants, she noticed, were wilting into the brick. Amri had neglected them to sit with Dana.

One of the police officers was coming toward the house. She went inside. "Give me that thing," she said to Binkie. Holding it at a corner, she took it downstairs. The policeman had just entered the house.

"Domna," he said, "we're done. Sorry to have troubled you."

"Did you find anything?" she asked.

He shook his head. "Not a thing."

"Here." She gave him the letter. "It came in this morning's mail. You'd better give it to Officer Tsurada."

"Yes, ma'am." He produced a plastic bag from somewhere and thrust the letter inside. "Thank you." He nodded to Immeld, who was smiling at him from a kitchen stool. "Thank you for the lemonade." As he stepped across the threshold, he turned back. "Domna, I just want to say—you sure have a lovely house."

Rhani smiled. "Thank you, Officer." She followed him outside, wondering idly where her brother was.

She found him by the crater, bare-chested, leaning on a shovel and talking to Timithos. As she walked toward them, she found herself admiring his smooth skin and the play of the muscles in his shoulders. "What are you doing, Zed-ka?" she said.

He grinned. "Working off anger," he said. Bending, he shoveled a load of earth back into the crater. "It doesn't help to be angry."

"Yes," Rhani said, "I noticed. I got a letter this morning from the Free Folk of Chabad. It said: "We can do it, too.""

Sweat ran down Zed's sides. "What did you do with it?"

"Gave it to the police, told them to give it to Officer Tsurada."

Zed scowled. "Nice of them to sign their handiwork. They might just as well have taken an ad-spot in PIN."

Rhani scratched her chin. "You think they mean it," she said.

"Of course they mean it! Look at it!" He pointed with his chin at the scorched and broken earth.

"Why didn't they do it, then?" Rhani said.

"What?"

"They blew up a piece of the lawn, when they could easily have dropped that bomb right on my head." Rhani stretched her arms out. "They don't want to kill me, Zed-ka. They want something else."

Zed's face was thoughtful. "Hmm. What do you think it is?"

"To frighten me, perhaps?" Rhani picked up a clod of dirt. She squeezed it tightly, feeling the rich soil compress. It smelled good. "I don't know." Letting it fall, she dusted her palms.

"Romantics," said Zed. "Fools." He chopped shortly at the earth with his shovel. "Rhani-ka, you should get a spade and join me, it's good exercise."

"I hate exercise."

"I know. You used to promise to go ice climbing with me sometime. Have you noticed that I no longer ask?"

"I meant to," she said sadly, knowing that it was too late, she would never go ice climbing with her brother on the slopes of the Abanat icebergs. She hunched her shoulders.

Zed's motion stopped. "That damn fool!" Rhani looked swiftly up. One arm around Amri, Dana Ikoro was maneuvering his way through the kitchen door. Zed swore, and let the shovel fall. "I'll be right back." He strode toward the house. Rhani opened her mouth to call him, and then shut it.

Dana's weight was too much for Amri to support. As Zed reached his side, he groped for the wall and, knees wobbling, began to fall. Zed caught him under the armpits. "What do you think you're doing?" he said.

Dana folded to the ground. He squinted at Zed's face. "Walking."

"Who told you walking would be good for you? You're concussed, do you know that? How many fingers am I holding up?" Zed did not try to keep the irritation from his voice. Dana concentrated on the splayed fingers.

"Three."

"Humph." He had not expected the answer to be right. "Let me look at your head." Dana bent his neck. Zed probed gently around the purple lump. Dana winced. "How does it feel?"

"It feels as big as my fist."

"It isn't. Do you have a headache?"

"No."

"Good. Look straight ahead. Follow my finger. Don't turn your head. Follow my finger as it moves. Right." Dana's eyes turned as Zed moved one finger up, down, in a circle, and sideways. Zed cupped a hand under Dana's chin. The grip, precursor of pain, made Dana's muscles tighten. Softly, Zed said, "Did I tell you to get out of bed?"

Dana mumbled, "No, Zed-ka."

"Say it clearly." Dana repeated it. "Don't get up again until I say that you can. My sister wants you healthy. You understand?"

"Yes, Zed-ka."

Satisfied, Zed rose. By the crater, Rhani was watching him. Dana spoke from the ground. "Zed-ka?"

"Yes?"

"Thank you for my music."

Zed half-smiled, thinking of the challenge Dana had presented to him, and the pleasure his subjugation had been. "Thank Rhani," he said. "She asked me to get them."

The following morning, Rhani and Zed ate breakfast on the terrace.

Below them on the lawn, Timithos was planting vines in the crater, which was now a flower bed. Behind them in the bedroom, Amri was whipping bedsheets about. Cara had had to order her to leave Dana's room to get her work done. She had argued. Rhani tried to picture sunny little Amri arguing, and couldn't. She lifted the bowl and drank her egg broth. "Zed-ka, how is Dana this morning?"

"Getting better," said Zed. "He wants to get up."

"Should he?"

"Not if he gets dizzy when he stands." Zed smiled. "Don't look so gloomy, Rhani-ka; he'll be all right."

"I was thinking about Amri."

"What's the matter with Amri?"

He hadn't noticed. Rhani decided that for an astute man, Zed could sometimes be oddly blind. "She's head over heels in love with Dana."

"Amri?" Zed raised his eyebrows. "I shouldn't think she'd ever had a sexual thought in her short life."

"Not body love. The kind of feeling we used to call spun-cotton love."

Zed said, "I wonder what Dana thinks of it."

"Dana says she reminds him of one of his younger brothers."

Zed said, "He's more concussed than I thought, if Amri

looks to him like anybody's brother."

"I think," said Rhani, "that he meant his feelings for her are purely affectional."

"How touching," said Zed sardonically. He said, to the wall, "Last night, and the night before, I lay awake wondering what it would be like if you had died. I decided it would make life insupportable. But then, my feelings for you have never been purely affectional."

"Zed-ka." She reached for him, across the table. He turned his head. His mouth was a line. Love and desolation mingled in his eyes. "I have no intention of dying, not for fifty or sixty years. I plan a long life. Last night I, too, lay awake. I was thinking about taking a bodyguard."

"What do you think?"

"I think you and Officer Tsurada are right."

Zed smiled. The set look left his face.

"But you know how I feel about privacy. I hate to add a stranger to the household." She picked up a piece of fruit and used her teeth to scrape the pulp from the rind. "This morning it occurred to me: I don't have to. I already have a bodyguard."

Zed looked troubled. "I can guard you when I'm with you, Rhani-ka, but—"

"I didn't mean you." She laid the rind on her plate. "I meant Dana. He saved my life once, and he's going to need something to keep him busy while we're in Abanat. He's obedient, and quick on his feet, and not a fool."

Zed's forehead wrinkled. "You sound as if you've made up your mind."

"Don't you think it's a good idea?" Rhani asked.

He frowned thoughtfully. "I agree with you, Dana's not a fool, and he's had formal training in several fighting arts. He's got good reflexes; he can fight." Zed grinned. "If he's not fighting Skellians."

"What's that supposed to mean?"

Zed flapped a hand. "Nothing, Rhani-ka. Have you spoken to Dana about this yet?"

"Not yet."

"Let me do it."

"As you wish," Rhani said. In the garden, Timithos was standing beneath a sprinkler's rain, trimming a vine. He looked utterly content. "This means, of course, that I shall have to take Amri with me."

"Why?" said Zed.

Rhani looked at him, exasperated. "Zed-ka, you don't listen. She's in love! And even if it's only spun-cotton love, she'll be miserable if she's left here while Dana's in Abanat."

Zed shook his head, smiling. "I keep telling you, Rhani; you shouldn't coddle slaves."

Rhani returned the smile. "I know, Zed-ka. But though in Amri's eyes I'm probably old and gray and doddering, I don't want her thinking that I don't know how it feels to be in love."

Chapter Six

The Abanat Sea, blue-green and flat as a plate, lay sparkling and glittering in the early morning sun. In the water the great peaks of the icebergs sat; Dana glimpsed them for an instant before the trajectory of the bubblecraft cut them from his sight.

"There," said Zed, "there's the landingport." Dana squinted down. He saw wide stone walkways, the green of trees, the silver ribbons of the movalong system, houses with black solar panels on their roofs. He was glad to see the city. Zed's precise directions and the bubble's display maps had brought him across the Chabadese waste over endless, featureless hills. Glaring light reduced visibility; landmarks were few, and subtle, and they shifted with shadow. He could see why it was dangerous to fly over Chabad at noon. You would end up flying in circles over the same humped hillocks unable to see past them, trapped like a fly in a bottle.

The landing field was clear below him; there was no other traffic. He touched the controls, slowing them to descent speed, and put the bubble into its spiral. This small field, Zed had explained, was maintained by the city for the private use of the Four Families. Before the dust from their descent had settled, the landingport manager was on the field bowing, smiling, and shouting orders to the porters. Rhani spoke with the manager. She looked crisp and cool in blue pants and a blue shirt. Zed leaned against a pylon, bored. The little port smelled of grease and hot metal. At one end of it stood a tall shuttle transport, an IS-class ship of the type that ferried passengers from the moon. Dana wondered what it was doing here—and then he realized that he knew it, had ridden in it: it was Zed's shuttle from the Net. Squinting, he could just make out on its side the design of the Yago "Y." He stared at it, aching for the feel of weightless flight and a starship, even a fusion-drive ship, lifting under his palms.

"Dana!"

Zed's voice sliced through Dana's longing cleanly as a knife. Hurriedly, he joined Rhani as she strode to the gate of the port. The gate had no Cage-field, not even a retinal scanner, but a metal bar and a smiling man sitting in a booth pushing a button to lift it. Dana wondered why he looked so happy at his task. The bar lifted. They were outside.

Heat slapped at them, bouncing off the streets and slideways. "This is a market district," said Rhani. The street was bordered on both sides by painted booths and shops sporting striped awnings. A musician played a flute; two naked acrobats balanced on their hands.

"What happens to the luggage we brought with us?" Dana asked. He glanced around. There were people all about them.

"The porters deliver it. Binkie—" Rhani turned. "You and Amri go on ahead."

"Yes, Rhani-ko," said Binkie. The pallid secretary and the excited girl pushed into the crowd.

Zed said, "Rhani, I have one quick errand to run. Shall I meet you at the house?"

"Yes." They embraced. Zed looked hard at Dana before he strode off. *Remember,* said the look. Dana's nerves shivered like a plucked wire. He was not likely to forget. Three nights before they were due to leave for Abanat, Zed had come to his room. He had informed Dana that he was to be Rhani's bodyguard. *"In Abanat, Rhani's going to need a bodyguard. Someone with quick reflexes and a fighter's skills, to escort her down the Boulevard, or to the park, or shopping."*

"Yes, Zed-ka."

"Binkie will tell you everything we know about her attackers. There isn't much. They call themselves the Free Folk of Chabad."

"Yes, Zed-ka."

"On the Net, you told me you've had training in the fighting arts. And every Hyper I know has been in a few brawls. You'll manage." He had stepped to the bedside. *"You'll more than manage."*

He had reinforced this command brutally and clearly with his hands.

Rhani thrust her arm through his: he jumped. "Come on."

"Where are we going?" He had to shout to be heard. All about them were laughing, calling people wearing red and orange and yellow and white, and just as many more wearing nothing. They all had black eyes. Rhani dragged him to a booth. She lifted something to her face. Now she had blackened eyes.

"Everyone wears sunshades in Abanat." She took a pair. "You'll need some too."

Wondering if it would not be simpler just to buy contacts, Dana picked up a pair of the primitive shades. They were bright yellow, huge and hideous. Tossing them back, he picked out a plain design that wrapped around his ears and covered his eyes. He stared at himself in a mirror. He, too, had grotesquely blackened eyes. "Ugh," he said. *"Where* are we going?"

Rhani said, "I want to visit a friend of mine."

The woman at the booth would not take Rhani's credit disc. "A gift, Domna. Only come back, and bring your friends." Rhani thanked her. The proprietor giggled with delight.

As they walked away, Rhani said, "That happens all the time."

"People know you?"

"Yes. I don't know why. I come to Abanat twice a year. Yet they all know my face in the markets." A group of musicians sauntered by. Dana grimaced at the clash of sounds. "Hungry?" She beckoned to a vendor and bought some food; meat wrapped in greens stuck on a wooden skewer. She offered Dana a bite. It was strange and tasty; spicy, and cold.

"That's good. What is it?"

"I don't know what the meat is. The shell is seaweed."

"Do all these people live here?" Dana asked.

"No." Rhani explained. She did not seem to mind his questions. "Most of these—" she gestured into the

street—"are tourists. Some are residents; they live in
Abanat two or three years till the taxes drive them out.
Some, a few, are Chabadese citizens."

"What do they do?"

"Cater to the tourists, work in the markets, make
things, entertain. Many of them are ex-slaves." They
arrived at another shop-strewn square. Rhani marched
toward a shop. It glittered with a display of miniature
birds, horses, trees, fish, animals of all kinds, colorful and
lovely, all of glass. Rhani went inside. Dana followed her.
He took off his sunshades. The store was carpeted, cool,
silent.

A tall, slim woman with gray hair came around the
counter. She and Rhani kissed. "Welcome back to
Abanat, Rhani-ka." Her skin was Cara's shade, milk-
chocolate brown. "You look well."

"I am well. How are you? How is the shop?" Rhani
turned in a circle. "It's bigger than the other. Who's
managing it for you?"

"I do the ordering and keep the accounts for both.
Erlin does the day-to-day managing when I'm not here."
While the two women talked, Dana drifted around the
shop, looking at the miniatures. A calligraphed sign
proclaimed them to be all handblown out of the finest
Chabadese sand. He found one of a dragoncat and
stooped to admire it.

A voice said, "May I assist?"

Dana straightened up. On the other side of the glass
counter, a young man with a red tattoo on his arm stood
smiling. "No, thank you," Dana said.

The young man continued to smile, mechanical as a
floodlamp. "Our prices are quite competitive with the
other market shops," he said. "All our miniatures are
handblown—"

More loudly than he'd intended, Dana said, "I don't
want anything!"

The woman speaking with Rhani looked up. "It's all
right, Jaime, he isn't a client." Jaime smiled and nodded.
His pupils were wide and fixed. He blinked, and blinked,
and smiled, as the gatekeeper at the landingport had
smiled.

Dana swallowed, feeling cold and a little sick. Rhani
was buying something, he could not see what. She

embraced the woman again, and beckoned for him to precede her from the shop. Outside, a woman was reading a newsheet. He could just make out the headline: "FOUR FAMILIES GATHER IN ABANAT," it said. He had to swallow again before he could speak. "Who is that woman?" he asked.

"That's Tuli. She was cook at the estate. When her contract expired, she took her money and bought a shop. This is actually her second store. She's doing well."

None of this was what Dana wanted to know. "Who's Jaime?"

"Jaime?" Rhani frowned, brow wrinkling. "Oh, you mean the slave. I think she bought him last year at the Auction."

Dana said carefully, "Is he retarded?"

Rhani was surprised. "No, of course not. By definition, only a person of full intelligence can commit a criminal act. The Net wouldn't even consider taking him. Ah—" she rubbed her chin—"you don't know. He was on dorazine, Dana. How odd. You're a drug smuggler, and yet you've never met anyone on dorazine."

Dana said, "I know what it does. It's a euphoric/tranquilizer."

"That's only a name," Rhani said. "It doesn't tell you what it feels like to be addicted."

"Do *you* know?"

She looked thoughtful. "I've tried it." She glanced at him. "I've never told anybody that. It makes you feel wonderful. Whatever you're told to do seems absolutely fascinating, the most interesting task in the world. You don't ever feel tired. Oh, and it helps you forget the past. I suppose, if you take it regularly, you even forget that you're a slave. It makes you smile a lot."

"You don't use it on your own slaves."

"We use it on the slaves at Sovka. Never on house slaves."

That's me, Dana thought. She was watching him, and he realized belatedly that she was carrying a boxed, wrapped package, and that he was supposed to be carrying it for her. That's what slaves are for, he thought, to carry bags, and open doors, and push buttons. It did not matter how mind-deadening the work got; after all, that was what dorazine was for. He held his hand out for the package. He could not meet her eyes. He tried to imagine living five years, ten years, in a soft, euphoric, drugged haze. He gazed at the shops; the goods in them seemed garish, the people buying them seemed equally garish, tasteless, *ugly,* tourists and slaves alike smiling the same wide, meaningless smiles. . . . Disgust cloaked guilt; irony burned a bitter taste on his tongue. For the first time, he felt justice in the turn of the wheel that had made him a slave.

He collected himself. He had stopped in the middle of the street, forcing people to eddy around him, keeping Rhani waiting. "I'm sorry," he managed to say. Rhani did not comment, and he wondered how much his face had given away.

They went swiftly now through a maze of streets till they arrived at what looked like a park: a lawn, fountains, green trees. It was barred from the street by an iron fence which was broken by a booth, a gate. "This," said Rhani, "is Founders' Green. This is the first park the Families made when the ice was towed from the poles." The smiling woman in the booth let them through the gate. The trees here were old and huge, older than the trees on the Yago estate. But the land was flat, the grass trimmed, not wild, and the bushes silent: there were no birds. Dana remembered Pellin's sky, her rocky cliffs thick with birds.

In one section of the park, a small fountain poured water from ledge to ledge in controlled cataracts. People sat on benches, or strolled on the lawn. "Domna Rhani!" A woman sitting on a bench leaped up. Dana tensed as she scurried toward them, blocking the way. She wore a flimsy, tentlike, sheer garment; she had a sharp face like a weasel's, and bright blue, bulbous eyes.

"How lovely to see you! I said to my household only this morning that it was certainly time for Cousin Yago to come to the city, but I didn't expect to see you walking in the park *today*. Is your brother with you? We are all looking forward to the Auction, oh, my yes. Abanat is filled with tourists: they are ruder than usual, my dear, be careful where you go. I was jostled on the street just the other day. But I am sure they do not treat a *Yago* that way. Shall you come to the parties? There is a party at Family Kyneth's in two days—or is it three days—and one at Family Dur's in three—or is it four days?—but why am

I telling *you* this when all the invitations are waiting for you in your house, oh, my, yes. I'm detaining you, look at me; you must be tired, flying all that way from your beautiful estate. Do commend me to Cousin Zed."

"Thank you, Charity," said Rhani. The woman beamed. As they passed her, she stared at Dana, a look of such desperate, clinical interest that he blushed. After a while, Rhani laughed.

"Who the hell is she?" Dana demanded.

"Charity Diamos. She is a cousin of Family Yago, and a horrible old bitch. She waylays people in the park and at parties so she can talk to them. Her household consists of five old women just like herself. In a few hours the news will be all over Abanat that Rhani Yago has bought herself a handsome young slave, 'Oh, my, yes!'" She imitated Charity Diamos' breathy gabble. "I suppose it's better for you to look like a whore than a bodyguard." She pointed ahead of them through the trees. "There's the house." Dana looked, expecting to see a house like the others that lined the Abanat streets, white or yellow or pale blue or rose, with upturned corners and ornate gates, but bigger. Instead, he saw a house like a block of stone, gray and huge. They had to negotiate a second gate to get to it.

A man stood on the front steps, in front of the open doorway. He had a white, full-moon face topping a fleshy frame. He had no hair. He wore sunshades. He bowed to Rhani. "Corrios." Rhani stretched to her toes, and, to Dana's surprise, kissed the man's white cheek. "This is Dana. Zed bought him from the Net to be my pilot. Dana, this is Corrios Rull, steward of the Yago house in Abanat. He doesn't talk much but he knows everything. Is all in order?"

The huge albino nodded.

"Is Zed here? Not yet? But Amri and Binkie have arrived. Dana, Corrios will show you where you can sleep."

The house was cool. It smelled musty. The ceiling arches seemed set very high. Lamps hung from iron hooks screwed into dark, wooden beams. A faded tapestry lined one wall of the entranceway. Corrios' hand fell on Dana's shoulder. "Come." The way was familiar: through a kitchen to a corridor lined with doors. Dana realized that this house and the house on the estate had been planned the same, or rather, that this house was the original from which the house in the hills had been duplicated. "Yours," said the albino, motioning to a door. Dana looked in. The room had a tapestried wall and a kerit skin rug on the floor. He shrugged. He had nothing with him to mark it with. His clothing and the auditor with the box of tapes were packed amid the rest of the Yago belongings.

The upstairs, too, was cool. The stone walls of the old house kept individual rooms private and isolated. Rhani went to her bedroom. There was a pile of mail on her desk; Binkie sat at the computer console. She glanced through the papers. Most of them were social. She opened the one from Family Dur. It was an invitation to a gathering to be held—untraditionally enough—in the morning, lasting through noon, at Dur house one day prior to the Auction. She would have to go to that, and to the party given by Family Kyneth, but she could, if she wanted, skip any others. After the Auction, Family Yago would host a gathering. "Binkie."

The secretary looked up.

"Accept the usual party invitations for us. You'll have to remind me of them. And you might as well begin to make arrangements for the Yago party. We'll hold it six days after the Auction. Hire a calligrapher to do the invitations."

Binkie nodded, unflurried. "Yes, Rhani-ka."

Rhani hid the package from Tuli's in the headboard of her bed. She had ordered it months ago on her last visit to the city. It was for Zed: a sculpture in glass, a special gift. She would give it to him next Founders' Day.

Amri brought in an immense tray, filled with cakes, candies, cheese, ice balls, treats to tempt the most tired palate. "Rhani-ka," she puffed, "the bags are here. Corrios is bringing them upstairs now."

"Good." Rhani went into the bathroom. She was hot from the flight and dirty from the street; she wanted a shower. Amri brought her a robe. Unbraiding her hair, she stepped under the spray. She ran it hot, and then turned it to cold. The washroom mirrors were steamy. She turned on the fan. Pulling the robe around her, she went into the bedroom, letting her wet hair hang loose.

Zed was there. Binkie was not. Rhani sat on the bed to towel her hair. She smiled at her brother. "Did you get your errands done?"

He did not immediately answer. He lifted a hand to touch her damp cheek. "You should wear your hair down more often."

"It's too much trouble."

He held out a wrapped and ribboned box on the palm of one hand. "For you."

"Zed-ka, you shouldn't!" She took it from him. She debated giving him the sculpture now, and decided to wait. She shook it. Nothing rattled. Pulling apart the wrapping, she lifted up the lid. Nestled in cotton lay a small golden cylinder decorated with thin jade stripes. She picked it out of the box.

"Careful," said Zed. He took it from her. "It's not what you think it is."

"What is it?"

"I had a hell of a time finding it. See this button on one end?" He turned it to show her a small gold button. "Press it firmly and a stun dart shoots out the other end, into whomever you point it at. Normal finger pressure won't trigger it. There's a matching chain in the box, so you can hang it around your neck." He lifted a gold chain from the box. Clipping the chain to the cylinder, he fastened it around her neck. It hung coldly between her breasts. Somewhat repulsed, she went to the wall mirror and stared at it.

"It looks like a pendant." She touched it with cautious fingertips. "Is it legal?"

"No," Zed said calmly. "But if you have to use it, I doubt that'll make a difference."

"Where can you buy such things?"

"In the Hyper quarter." He glanced around the room. "Where's Dana?" Rhani shrugged. She rolled the cylinder between her fingers. The chain stretched. She pretended to take aim. "He's supposed to stay with you!"

"Not in the house, Zed-ka."

"Even in the house." Zed swerved to the wall speaker and said Dana's name into it. Dana answered. "Come upstairs." Zed swung around. "Have you had a chance to talk to Corrios yet? He needs to know about the bombing. I want this house locked tight."

Rhani felt herself getting annoyed. "I haven't had time to talk to Corrios. I went to Tuli's shop, I bought some sunshades, and I met Charity Diamos crossing the park. I pissed, and showered. That's all I've done."

Zed looked contrite. "I'm sorry. I don't mean to rush you, Rhani. But I'm not going to stop worrying about your safety, especially when you don't seem to want to worry about yourself." Dana appeared at the door. "I want *you* where Rhani can reach you, even in the house. If that means sleeping on the floor outside her door, you do that. Understand?"

"Yes, Zed-ka," said Dana. He shrank back as Zed walked toward him.

Zed said, "I'll talk to Corrios. Then I'm going to the landingport. Those damn moronic porters lost the bag with my ice climbing equipment in it. They did the same thing last year, and it took a week to find it."

He clattered down the stairs. Rhani looked at Dana; his face was white. Her irritation with her brother spurted up again. What did he think he was doing, turning her slaves into zombies? Dana had proved his loyalty by saving her life. "Look at this." She touched the cylinder hanging over her heart. "Do you know what it is? If I press this button, the other end shoots stun darts. Zed was hunting for it in the Hyper quarter while you and I were listening to Charity Diamos." She stepped back, aimed, and pretended to press the button. "Pfft. No more Charity."

Dana's look lightened. "That would be no loss." He lifted the cylinder by the chain. "I've seen such things before." His fingers brushed her throat. She liked the touch. "I've never seen one of gold."

"Zed probably found the only gold one in Abanat."

When he heard Zed's name, his shoulders hunched.

Rhani chose her next sentence carefully. "I enjoyed walking through Abanat with you today."

That brought no reaction. Damn it, she *hated* it when he looked like that. One of the things she valued in him was his free spirit. With him, she had broken her careful rule, never to ask a slave about the past. Even with Tuli she had kept that rule. But it didn't seem to bother Dana to talk about Pellin, or his family. Maybe the ease with which he talked about his past meant he had reconciled himself to his future.

"Are you tired?" she said. "Does your head hurt?"

"No, Rhani-ka."

Rhani abandoned subtlety. "What's the matter?" she asked.

Dana said, "Does Zed really want me to sleep outside your door?"

"Oh, Zed." Rhani made a throw-away sweep of her hands. "He's getting on my nerves. Probably he does. But I don't want you to sleep outside my door. That would be uncomfortable."

Dana bowed his head. His hands knotted together. He said softly, "I will, though."

Rhani's temper flared. "Not if I tell you not to."

"If your brother tells me to, yes, Rhani-ka, I must."

"You forget," Rhani said icily. *"I own you."*

His yellow-ivory face grew automatonlike. Distantly, he answered, "Yes, Rhani-ka."

Oh no, Rhani thought, suddenly ashamed, I didn't want this. Her ill temper vanished. She laid a hand on Dana's forearm. "I'm sorry. That was ill-mannered of me. I know what an intolerable position you are in. You will not have to sleep outside my door. Don't worry about it. I'll speak to Zed."

The rigidity of his muscles lessened. She was inordinately pleased that he did not flinch from her touch. He needed to be distracted. She beckoned him to the tall bedroom windows, holding the curtain aside. "Look."

The windows looked west, at the turquoise ocean and at the shining bulk of the Abanat icebergs. They gleamed like crystal mountains in the sun.

Rhani felt Dana's tension leave him, as perceptibly as if the room temperature suddenly dropped. His hands lifted; his lips parted. He swayed toward the window in a graceful, unconscious gesture of flight.

He was not looking at the city, or at the sea, or at the ice.

He stared up, into the untrammeled depths of Chabad's sky.

Dana Ikoro slept badly that night.

He dreamed of Pellin, and then, a nightmare from which he woke crying, he dreamed about the Net. He had been on Chabad long enough to attune himself to its cycles, and his sense of temporal orientation told him that it was just after midnight. He turned the light on to drive the shadows from his mind. He felt restless, and also desperately tired. His body, less easy to discipline, was rebelling against the stern control he had put on his conscious mind: to wait, to watch, and above all not to fight. The luck would turn his way. A chance would come.

A hundred desperate schemes ran through his mind: to steal a bubble, to hide away on a shuttleship, to somehow get to *Zipper*. He told himself that every slave on Chabad had such thoughts. He turned off the light.

At breakfast, Amri, happily chattering, mentioned that Zed was not in the house. "He went back to the landingport to find that bag the porters lost."

Good, Dana thought. I hope it takes them hours to find it. It seemed to him that the whole household breathed more easily when Zed was out of the house. He did. He could deal with Rhani; saving her life had earned him her trust. But Zed—he shivered inwardly. He knew damn well that Zed did not trust him.

He knew that Zed was right.

Amri stared at him, troubled by his sudden silence. He grinned and crossed his eyes. Amri laughed. He took another piece of fruit from the bowl. Suddenly, he had an appetite. Corrios came into the kitchen from the hall, his big hands filled with paper. "Mail," he said. He gestured upwards with a jerk of his thumb.

"I'll take it," Dana said.

Approaching her room, he heard Rhani talking to Binkie. She sounded out of sorts. He knocked and stepped into the bedroom. Rhani was pacing the length of the space. She turned to glare at him. "Mail, Rhani-ka."

She rifled through it. "More party invitations," she said with contempt. "All they do in Abanat is go to parties. Do something with this junk."

Binkie took the pile out of her hands. In a noncommittal voice, he said, "There's a letter here from Dur House."

"Let me see it." She read it swiftly. "Ferris Dur requests permission to call upon me this afternoon. Thank you very much. I suppose I must say yes. Am I supposed to do something else this afternoon?"

"The manager of the Yago Bank respectfully asks to see you at your convenience."

"So he can waste time telling me he's making a profit? That's what I employ him for, to make a profit." Binkie said nothing. Rhani sighed. "Ah, well. I will send him a personal note fixing a time." She went to her desk. "And I should write to Ferris. There is paper here but no pen. Binkie, give me something with which I can write!"

Binkie handed her a pen. She scribbled two letters, and sealed them with a blue stamp bearing the Yago "Y." Suddenly she glanced at Dana, and smiled a rueful, deprecating smile. "I have the disposition of a kerit today. Binkie has been listening to me all morning. It's Abanat. I hate Abanat. I miss my garden." The printer whirred: the same soft sound as in her bedroom at the estate: a soothing noise. "I hope you slept better than I did. Have you been outside the house?"

"Not since yesterday, Rhani-ka."

"How are you going to escort me around a city you don't know anything about?"

This seemed to have no answer.

"What have you been doing this morning?"

"I ate breakfast, Rhani-ka."

She gazed at him, her head cocked a fraction to one side. "And now what will you do? Make beds?" She rubbed her chin. In a softer voice she said, "Binkie, let me have copies of the last four bank reports."

"Yes, Rhani-ka."

"And when you have done that, go outside. Take Dana with you. Show him how to use the city maps, and then you may separate to deliver these notes. Take your time. You work very hard, and you don't get holidays, or time to be alone, very much."

Binkie said, "Thank you, Rhani-ka." His tone was even, but his face blazed with joy. As he leaned over the computer keyboard, his hands shook.

Dana pictured Zed returning to find Rhani alone, her bodyguard out. "Rhani-ka, perhaps I should—"

"Perhaps you should both do as you are told," she said. Binkie handed her a stack of records. "Thank you, Bink. I have work to do, if you don't mind." It was clearly a dismissal. Dana shrugged, and walked out. He waited for Binkie to join him in the hall.

Downstairs, he remembered to pluck his sunshades from their hook. Corrios let them out. Heat rose from the pavement as he followed Binkie around the fenced-in park. The air was clean, dry, motionless, and very hot. Abanat streets were closed to all but foot traffic and the occasional emergency truck; travelers in a hurry rode the movalongs, which glided at the standard pace of ten kilometers per hour. The movalongs were jammed with gossamer-robed tourists. Morning was market time in Abanat.

A block away from Founders' Green, Binkie stopped. The black sunshades against his pale skin made him appear to be wearing a mask. He handed Dana one of the letters. "That one's for the bank," he said. "It's about six blocks from here, the other side of the Boulevard." He pointed to what looked like a bas-relief sculpture set into a piece of wall. A stylus swung beside it from a chain. "I'll show you how to get there." He picked up the stylus. Dana recognized a pressure-sensitive map. "We're here. That's the Yago house on the other side of the park. The city is divided into quadrants by its two main streets: the north-south street, the Promenade, and this east-west street, the Boulevard. The ocean's west. Auction Place is in the center of the city, where the avenues cross."

"The bank is—"

"There."

"What's that square in the northwest quadrant?" Dana asked.

"Main LandingPort."

"I've got it. Thanks." Binkie disappeared without a backward look into a gaggle of tourists. Dana looked in the other direction. Where Binkie went was his own business. He was not going to pry into anyone else's privacy, even in thought.

He went to the bank. The building was cool and filled with machines. People shuffled through it; it echoed, like a vault. The pressure-sensitive maps were all over the city; there seemed to be one on every wall. It would be hard for a child to get lost in Abanat. He delivered the note. Taskless, he went out into the crowded street.

Perhaps the luck had turned; fickle fortune smiling at him, radiant and deadly as Chabad's sun, mocking him with this sudden and revocable gift of freedom. He glanced around the street. No one was looking at him. *"Take your time,"* Rhani had said. He straightened his spine and lifted his head. He was a slave on an errand.

Mindful of the heat, he walked slowly north, toward Main LandingPort.

Rhani listened as Dana and Binkie left the house. Like a cat waking, she shook herself. She was ashamed of her ill temper. She made herself pick up the topmost bank report. She worked through the first page. The second page blurred. She could not seem to keep her attention on it.

Amri knocked. "Shall I straighten the room for you, Rhani-ka?"

"Yes, go ahead." She lifted the report. But the rustle of the sheets annoyed her. "Leave it. Go away," she snapped. Frightened, the girl scuttled off. Exasperated with herself, Rhani almost threw the paper to the floor. She laid it gently on the desk. She had not slept; she could not concentrate; none of this was Amri's fault.

It's Abanat, she thought. It distracts. She stood up. She could not be comfortable inside the grim old house. The park was close, a step. She would take a walk. Founders' Green was private and safe: the iron fence and the gates kept it cut off from idle traffic. Leaving her room, she went downstairs.

Corrios was in the hall. He grunted at her: it meant, *"All right?"*

"I'm fine," she said. Her sunshades hung from the hook. "I'm going for a walk."

Corrios stood in her path as she turned toward the door.

She had snapped at Amri; she would not snap at him. Gently, she said, "What is it?"

His face was distressed. "Don't."

"Don't what?" she said with heavy patience.

He jerked a thumb at the door.

Her pulse thudded. She said, "Did Zed tell you to lock me in?"

He shook his head.

"Then this is your own idea. It's a bad one."

He folded his arms. In the dim hallway, he was immeasurably bigger than she, a mountain. Rhani glared at him. Her fists clenched. "Corrios Rull, this is stupid. You are not going to keep me in if I want to leave." Her raised voice echoed down the hall.

He said nothing.

Tense with fury, Rhani said, "Very well. You've worked for Family Yago for fifty years. You'll lose that place in three seconds if you don't move from that door. One. Two." She opened her mouth to say, "Three." Corrios stepped aside. Rhani slid the door open and slammed it behind her.

She ran down the steps to the street, ears ringing with rage. She couldn't remember the last time she'd slammed a door. Sunlight fell like a hand upon her shoulders. She slowed. She unclenched her fingers, knuckle by knuckle. Anger was a waste of time. She dusted her palms together. There. She was no longer angry. She crossed the street to the Green and walked along it, tapping the fence. Shaded by thick tree trunks, the iron spikes were cool. She heard the voices of children quarreling in the park. She changed her mind. She walked south, to the broad, crowded Boulevard.

The entertainers were out: jugglers, dancers, musicians all competing vigorously for the attention of the tourists. At one street corner, an ebony-skinned acrobat performed a graceful backbend, muscles rippling. Rhani stood and watched her for a while. At last she went on. Her head began to feel hot. She touched her hair; it was dry as Chabadese grass. She had forgotten how the light in Abanat ricocheted off walkways and walls and clothing, and she thought: Stupid, you should have brought a parasol.

Oh, well. If she wanted one, she could buy one. She sauntered down the Boulevard.

Suddenly, across the street, she saw Dana. She lifted a hand to wave him to her. But the person—who, she realized, was in fact *not* him—did not see the gesture, and walked quickly by. The apparition was disquieting. She walked another block, and seeing where her feet had carried her, started to smile. She faced a gray house, much like her own. But someone had carved an axe, posed to strike, on the façade, in place of her own Yago "Y."

She went to it, knocked, and was admitted.

The Dur house smelled of wax, the wax of beeswax candles, imported from Belle. Domna Sam had burned them profligately, preferring them even to sunlight. Over the years the smell had soaked into the walls and curtains and rugs of the house and even into the stone shell itself. A slave ran within to announce her; a second slave ushered her through the front hall to the parlor. Ferris Dur rose to greet her. He was taller than she, and bulky—loose-fleshed, she thought. He had the pale complexion of someone who has spent little time in the sun.

In that, Rhani thought, if in nothing else, he resembles his mother. He had brown eyes, too, like Domna Sam. She had not thought very much of him, Rhani knew. "He plays with toys!" she had said once. "Toys, from a Dur!" Rhani had no idea what she had meant. Ferris was reaching to grasp her hand. She pressed his briefly, and drew her fingers back. He seemed to want to hold on to them.

"Rhani Yago," he said. "I just received your message. This is a pleasant surprise. Please be seated."

"Thank you," Rhani said. She glanced around the parlor. It was not a room she knew; Domna Sam had always invited visitors upstairs to her bedroom. Ferris had turned the room into his office, with desk and com-unit. It was filled with dark, heavy furniture and portraits of long-dead Durs. It had to be the only room in the house that didn't smell of candles. She sat in a chair. A slave came in with a platter of food and a decanter of chilled wine.

Rhani said, "I hope I haven't upset the workings of your household." The slave poured the wine. She wore a broad dorazine smile.

"My household would be in poor straits if it could not accommodate itself to a visit from Rhani Yago." Ferris snapped his fingers; the slave withdrew. "Are you comfortable?"

"Yes, thank you," Rhani said. She sipped the wine. "This is delicious."

Ferris flushed with pleasure. He was wearing a red robe, trimmed with kerit fur. He stroked the fur lightly. "I hope all is well with Family Yago."

Sweet mother, Rhani thought, is he always this stilted and formal? No wonder his mother couldn't bear to have him around! Let's see: I'm facing a dorazine shortage, the kerits are dying at Sovka, and people are trying to kill me. Matching Ferris' formal tone, she said, "Quite well, thank you. I hope all is well with Family Dur."

"Nothing's wrong that I can't handle," he said sharply. He smoothed the robe again. The unconscious gesture seemed to calm him.

Rhani said, "I admire your self-confidence."

He peered at her, and she realized that he thought, or feared, that she was making fun of him. What a silly, awkward man! She said, "Ferris, were you coming to see me this afternoon on a social visit?"

He shook his head. "No. I rarely make social calls."

Inwardly, Rhani sighed. "You know," she said, "I received your letters. I'm afraid I found them a little peremptory."

He looked abashed. "I beg your pardon," he said. "I'm afraid I pay less attention to the niceties than my mother did."

Domna Sam never bothered to be delicate either, Rhani reflected, but she at least knew how. She leaned back in the chair. The images of dead and forgotten Durs looked down their painted noses at her from the walls.

"Well," she said, "shall we talk business? As I recall, your letters said you had something very important to discuss with me. 'Business of import to Chabad . . .'?"

"Yes" said Ferris. "It is important. I would like to propose an alliance between Family Dur and Family Yago. A permanent alliance."

Rhani frowned. Clearly he was not talking about a kerit farm.

She said, "What sort of permanent alliance?"

He licked his lips nervously. "A marital alliance," he said, and went on before she could talk; "I know what you're thinking; Yagos don't marry. Neither do Durs. I am thinking of it primarily as a business arrangement."

Marriage? Rhani thought. He's crazy, that's all. He wants to marry me? She wondered if this could be one of Domna Sam's schemes. For Domna Sam's sake, she would listen. "Perhaps you could be more specific," she said.

He leaned forward. "I propose," he said, "that you and I marry, and have a child—at least one child, but that would be up to you—upon whom we could settle a joint inheritance. This agreement would enable our two Families to unite finances as well as lines. The investment advantages of such a merger would be tremendous. It could be profitable for both Families, and for Chabad."

Rhani rubbed her chin. "The other Families will be quite disturbed," she pointed out.

He shrugged. "So what?"

"It runs counter to all our customs."

"Yes," he said, "but then, it could create others." He reached, and took a piece of cheese off the mother-of-pearl inlaid tray. Rhani's glass was empty; she put it down. The slave shuffled forward to refill it. "No, that's enough," Rhani said, and the glassy-eyed woman stepped back. The vacant smile was distressing; Rhani looked away.

She rarely thought about it, but she had always taken for granted that someday, not soon, she would bear a child. Part of her responsibility as a Yago was to produce an heir. Until then, pills controlled her fertility. She had suppressed as soon as she reached adulthood what it felt like to *be* a child. When Aliza Kyneth's youngest was born, she visited the house, and Aliza had let her hold the baby. "I feel silly—clumsy," she had said, cupping the dark fuzzy head to her breast.

Imre took his son from her and cradled him with casual competence. He teased, "There's more where he came from if you drop him."

Would it, she wondered, have felt different, would she have felt less clumsy, if she'd been holding her own child?

With a slight shock, she realized that she was taking Ferris' proposal seriously.

He was watching her anxiously; so, she thought, must he often have watched his mother. "If what you really want is for the Yago and Dur finances to merge," she said, "why not propose a corporate merger?" She wondered what he would answer.

He shook his head. "We can't," he said. "The Founders' Agreement prohibits it. The only way to change something in the Founders' Agreement is to have a planetary referendum and add a section to the Constitution."

"And marriage between us does not constitute a violation of the Agreement?" she said.

"It would, if we did not put fifty percent of our joint capital in trust for the child, or children."

"What control would we retain of this capital?" she said. "Who would execute the trust?"

"On Chabad?" he said, surprised. "Anyone we like."

It was true. Rhani smiled, wondering if she could name as executor the Investment Committee of the Yago Bank. Arranging to place fifty percent of Yago Corporation capital in a trust might be difficult, but she thought it could be managed. Or did the statute mean fifty percent of her personal capital? She would have to read the Agreement—something she had not done in fifteen years—or, better still, discuss the entire scheme with her legal staff.

She would have to do that anyway, of course. She wondered what the other Families would say about it, and why none of them had ever thought of such a thing. They were so accustomed to inter-Family rivalry, to competition, to spying and bargaining and making secret deals. . . . Such a merger, she thought, would change utterly the balance of power on Chabad.

That was not an unattractive thought.

Hesitantly she said, "This could not be our private agreement, Ferris. Our legal departments would have to work out a contract."

"Of course." His voice was eager. "So you think it's a good idea?"

She scowled. "I'm not accepting the offer. I want to think about it."

"Yes, I understand," he said. He pushed the tray with foodstuffs at her. "Won't you have something to eat?"

Because she was his guest, Rhani took an applestick from the tray, and bit slowly through the red rind to the soft white heart. She wondered if Ferris thought they could be lovers. "You know," she said, "I have always preferred to arrange my own liaisons. . . ."

He flushed, deeply embarrassed. "I'm sure we can arrange not to interfere with each others' private lives."

She watched his fingers stroke the fur of his robe, wondering what he was like in bed. The prospects did not excite her. He probably liked to bed slaves. Slaves. . . . She thought of her brother. What would he think of this? "Is that all you have to discuss with me?" she said.

With the first sign of humor she had seen from him, he said diffidently, "Isn't that enough?"

Rhani felt suddenly very sorry for him, alone in this great house with only ghosts and slaves on dorazine for company. But pity, she thought, was a bad base on which to do business. It was too bad he was so unattractive. . . . She stood. Ferris rose. "Thank you very much for your hospitality, Ferris. I shall go home now."

"You will—"

"I will consider your offer," she said firmly.

He snapped his fingers. "My slaves will escort you," he said, and led her to the front door himself.

The street was hot. The two slaves kept Rhani between them as she walked down the Boulevard. One of them held a white parasol over her head. The tourists were all indoors, hiding from the heat, and the wide road was deserted; mutable as water, the stones seemed to dance in the brilliant, shimmering light.

Abanat *is* beautiful, Rhani thought with swift, possessive pride. Perhaps one day she would bring her daughter to this street, and tell her the history of the city. *"The fountain was built by Orrin Yago,"* she would say. *"Lisa Yago planted this tree."*

She hunched her shoulders. Marriage, and with Ferris Dur? It was strange even to think about. She pictured a daughter, a solemn, slender girl with hair the color of wheat, and almond-shaped, amber eyes. I will name her Jade, or Cecilia, or Samantha, Rhani thought. She squinted into the sun, trying to see the child's face, and realized that she was remembering herself.

Then she thought: People are trying to kill me! The image shattered. She looked up; there was her house. "You may go," she told the slaves. They bowed and shuffled away. Leaping up the broad steps, she hammered on the door. It opened. The hall was dark, and there seemed to be a lot of people in it. . . . She heard Binkie say her name, with a sound like a sob.

Chapter Seven

With some judicious bullying, Zed found his ice climbing equipment at the little landingport. It lay in a corner, under a pile of greasy rags where some porter had dropped it. He checked the seals; they were unbroken. The manager apologized a dozen times.

Zed watched the porters move around the port, frowning. He wondered when they had last had blood tests. They were not slaves—the only slave near the landingport was in the exit booth—but dorazine addiction was a constant problem among laborers, ex-slave or not.

"I want your people tested," he said to the manager. "I'm on my way to the Clinic; I'll have the clerk call you to set up a time."

"Whatever you say, Commander."

Main Clinic was in the city's southeast corner, six blocks from the Promenade. It looked, off-worlders said, like a Terran starfish; five long one-story buildings radiated from the center hub. The hub was CTD, Clinical Tests Department. Its spokes were Outpatient, Contagious, Surgery, Recovery, and Special Services. Outpatient's principal work was to coordinate and staff the mobile units that did the monthly dorazine tests. By Chabadese law, every slave on dorazine maintenance had to have a blood test every three months. The technicians who rotated to the mobile units called it "Going to Needle Row."

Zed stopped at the Outpatient desk. The clerk said, "I'll put it in the computer, Senior, but they probably won't get to it until after the Auction."

"Do what you can," Zed said. The clerk shrugged.

The wheel-like architecture of Main Clinic reminded Zed with pleasure of the Net. He followed the traffic flow through Outpatient to CTD. From there he walked around the rim of the core until he came to the entrance to Surgery. He walked to the interior of the building and leaned on the chief clerk's desk.

Her name was Yukiko Chun; she was a dark woman, withered as a dry stick, all snap and bark. "Senior Yago," she said, "welcome back."

"Thank you, Yuki. It's good to be home."

"Too bad you didn't get here earlier," she said. "We could have used you last week."

"Oh?"

"There was an accident at the Gemit mines." Zed's interest sharpened. Rhani will want to know that, he thought. "A surgical team flew out there. They had to do

some very tricky limb replacements." Her mouth folded
down severely; she was scolding him. As far as Yukiko
was concerned, surgeons had no private lives. She moved
them ruthlessly about to fit her schedules, knew their
every foible, and treated them all alike. "You want
morning or evening shift?"

"Wherever you're short," Zed said.

"I'll put you on Emergency call," she said. "Where are
you staying?"

"The Abanat house."

There was no exit to the street from Surgery; Zed
retraced his steps to CTD, and from there to Outpatient.
A woman came through the doorway; saw him; stopped.
Shyly she said, "Hello, Zed."

Her name was Sai Thomas. Like Zed, she was a senior
medic. They were old friends, and a little more. Some five
years back she had approached him with an offer. . .
"I've heard rumors about you," she had said. Oh, no, he
had thought, prepared to evade or to lie. "The rumors say
you like pain." She was forthright. "I'm high on the
Réage test, you know." The Réage test, Zed knew,
examined an individual's emotional and physiological
reactions to a situation of mutual, consensual, sado-
masochistic sex.

"I'm not," he said. It was the truth: he had no interest
in mutual pain. The thought of being vulnerable in the
ways he made his victims vulnerable terrified him.

"Tests have been known to be wrong," Sai said. "I
thought—" She laid a hand firmly on his forearm. "Zed, I
think you're very attractive."

Despite his better judgment, Zed had been moved.
"Sai, I'm not—I don't usually choose women for partners," he said awkwardly. Hell, I don't have partners, he
had thought.

They had gone to bed together. The trappings of
fantasy—silk and chains—excited him not at all. Sai was
gentle, patient, determined. Zed was hopeful, but even
the force of his practiced will had not made his body
perform: he could, at her request, bind her, but when it
came to inflicting pain he could not move. He was afraid
of what might happen if he did. Finally she had understood that it was not going to work. Sadly she said good
night to him. He had gone home and gotten drunk. He

spent the next night in Lamartine's, the one brothel in Abanat willing to cater to his tastes. That evening five years back had been the last time Zed had tried to break out of his psychosexual patterns.

She was sturdy, fair-haired, quiet—not at all like Rhani. Yet that night in her room he had seen only Rhani.

"How are you?" he said.

"Fine," she answered, "you?"

He respected her, and would not lie to her. "Things could be better. I'll tell you about it sometime. Family concerns."

"Anytime. Are you on the schedule?"

"Emergency, on call. And you?" They talked Clinic business for a while. She had been the anesthesiologist on the team that flew to Gemit. Zed questioned her about the accident, but she knew few of the details. She described the surgical work with pride.

"You should stop in Recovery and look at it."

"I'll do that."

He rode the movalongs back to the house. It was getting close to noon, and hot. He slid the front door back. The house seemed very dark. Binkie, Dana, and Corrios stood in a huddle in the hall. At the sound of the door, they looked up. Binkie's face grayed. Zed stepped in. The door slid closed. Something was wrong. He touched the hall intercom. "Rhani?"

Not even an echo answered him.

He said to them all, "Where is she?"

Dana answered, "We don't know. She went out alone. We were making a list of places to call."

Zed's mind filled with pictures of Rhani hurt, kidnapped, dead, somewhere in Abanat. Binkie babbled; he barely noticed the exculpatory whine. Dana's shoulders were hunched. Zed moved toward him. "I told you to stay with her." With grim satisfaction, he saw the color drain from Dana's face, and fear tighten the muscles around his eyes.

"Zed, I—"

"Shut up. I told you to guard her." He let his hand rest on Dana's shoulder, fingers caressing the pressure point. "Didn't I?"

Dana swallowed. In a half-whisper, he said, "Yes, Zed-ka."

Knocking interrupted the moment. Corrios hurried to open the front door. Rhani stood, framed in the light. Binkie gasped her name. She came inside, glancing swiftly from Zed to Dana. "Zed-ka," she said, "you promised. He's mine."

It was true, and she was unhurt. Nevertheless, Zed permitted himself a hard look at Dana before he took his fingers from Dana's arm. "Where were you?" he said to his sister. "Why were you alone?"

She said, with a look at the slaves, "It's a long story. Corrios, make us something cool to drink, please. Dana, Binkie—you may go." Dana bowed. The color was back in his face. He strode off toward the slaves' hall. Binkie nearly knocked a chair down in his haste to follow.

Rhani pointed to the dining alcove off the downstairs salon. "Let's sit there."

Subduing his impatience, Zed followed her to the alcove. She had not been hurt; probably she had not even been endangered.

But she could have been. He worked his shoulders to loosen the tension in his frame. She could have been.

They sat. Corrios brought a pitcher of iced fruit punch and a plate of pressed dried seaweed, an Abanat delicacy that Rhani loved. She curled her legs into the chair and looked at Zed over her drink. "Dana was not remiss in his job, Zed-ka. I sent him on an errand, and then decided, while he was gone, to go out. I don't want him punished for something that wasn't his fault."

Zed had to acknowledge the justice of that. "All right, Rhani-ka," he said. "But if you send him on errands and then go out, he won't be much use to you as a bodyguard."

"You're right. I should have waited. But the house was driving me crazy!"

He grinned at her, knowing what her mood must have been like. It always took her a few days to get used to Abanat. He sipped his drink; it was mixed to Rhani's taste rather than his, and was sweeter than he liked. "Where did you go?"

"I visited Ferris Dur. He was going to come this afternoon to see me, here. I ended up in front of his house, and decided to go in." She tilted her head, smiling. "It's odd, that he should be there, and not Domna Sam.

He's changed the house all around."

"What did you talk about?"

"Business," she said. She flicked a look at him. "Very important business. He wants to marry me."

Zed grinned, wondering what Ferris had really wanted. "That's probably the first proposal a Yago ever had. What did you say?"

She smiled. "I said I'd think about it."

"I'm sorry I asked. Truly, Rhani-ka, what did he want? I gather he didn't want to buy the kerit farm."

She chuckled. "Zed-ka, you don't believe me? I'm serious! Ferris Dur asked to marry me, and I said I'd think about it."

Zed shook his head. "The poor man has gone quite insane. But why torment him, Rhani? Tell him no, and let him breathe."

"I'm not tormenting him," she said quietly. "He wants to marry me, and father my child, who can then inherit the fortunes of our two Families. He called it a business agreement. It might not be a bad idea."

She meant it. She really was thinking about it. Zed's mouth went dry as the Chabad earth. The hairs on the back of his hands lifted. For a moment he felt utterly detached, observing his own physical reaction. Then panic set in. If Rhani married—it could not happen, he thought, it *can't*—she might leave the estate, or, worse, ask him to leave it, to make room for someone else.

He took a deep breath, trying to steady his thoughts. She *could not* ask him to leave her. He still desired Rhani; she was, in fact, the central human passion of his life. Knowing her, he had wanted nothing else, and, taken from her, he had denied himself all lesser sexual delight, and need, so denied, had changed and twisted inside him. There was nothing in him any more of the ardent, gentle boy she had desired as a lover. But she was still his loving sister, his friend, and touchstone to his innocence. . . .

He had learned to ignore his lust to strangle her occasional bedmates: they were not his rivals. His rival was Chabad, the Yago fortune, her work in which he now shared as her principal confidant and advisor.

She said, smiling, "Of course, it's early yet for me to think about having a child."

He said tensely, "I fail to see the use for the arrangement."

"Zed-ka, you're not thinking! Remember the Council meeting a year ago, when we argued for hours about using our capital for further exploration of Chabad? We couldn't decide which project to undertake, because none of us is willing to spend credits on a venture another Family will profit by. Imre wants to make a polar settlement. Domna Sam wanted to fund the undersea mining. Theo Levos supports seaweed farming. A concentration of capital would swing the balance of risk—" she turned a fist into a swinging pendulum—"to the other side. I can see value in all three projects. That's an example. It would be tricky. There would be problems."

"You sound like you've made up your mind."

"In an hour of talk? Of course I haven't. Zed-ka, what in the world is wrong?" She put her glass down and reached for his hands. Her fingers were clammy. "Oh, I know what you're thinking," she said. "Zed, this would be a business arrangement. We wouldn't have to live together, Ferris and I. I like my life the way it is. If I should marry Ferris Dur, I stay Rhani Yago. And you are still Zed, my friend, my brother."

They were both older now, and her hair had darkened over the years. But he still wanted her, and it terrified him, because he could not always dominate the responses of his traitorous nerves. She watched him, worried.

"What does he look like?" he asked.

"You really don't remember?" she said. "He's tall— broad, but not big-shouldered like you. He's bigger boned, but I'd bet he's not an ice climber. He looks sedentary, and he's so pale that he must spend most of his time indoors. He snaps his fingers to call his slaves."

How ostentatious, Zed thought. "Do you like him?"

She shrugged. "It wouldn't matter."

"It matters," Zed said.

"Do I like him? No, Zed-ka, I don't think I like him." She frowned. "Though—he's odd, Zed-ka. He's a puzzle. He's pitiful and yet he's very arrogant. It's as if he knows the meaning of words he says but not the implications?"

"Don't you think these feelings are important, Rhani?"

"Not especially," she said. "This is business."

Zed felt as if a ghost had walked into the room. Go away, old bitch, he said to it. You're dead. "Marriage by its nature is more than a business relationship," he said.

Rhani rubbed her chin. "Not if I don't wish it to be. Marriage is a legal relationship. It would be convenient if I liked him."

Zed said, "If you want a child, Rhani, take a lover and let him father one. You don't need to marry Ferris Dur because he challenged your Family pride."

"That's not fair, Zed-ka!"

"Isn't it?"

Rhani stood, rocking the chair, clumsy in her haste as Binkie. "You say that because you are afraid he will come between us. I tell you, the only people who can keep us from each other are ourselves. You're jealous. It's warping your judgment, Zed."

"You flatter Ferris Dur. He sounds much too pretentious to be jealous of."

"I said he was arrogant."

"I think you are being kind to the man. He's not arrogant; he's stupid."

Softly she said, "And am I stupid, too, for listening to his proposal, and for taking it seriously?" Anger lit her face, vivid as the Abanat lightning.

He bit his lip, preparing to apologize, when she said, "I do what is best for Chabad, Zed. You forget. Your perspective is narrower. I haven't said I'm going to marry Ferris Dur. But if I decide to do so, I expect your support. Not because you are my brother, but because you are the Net commander, and my heir, until I bear a child. Do I have it?"

The sun leaked through a crack between the drapes to stroke her hair, turning one lock of it to gold. He remembered her standing under the bitter pear tree at the estate, naked, her hair loose, long enough to sweep her thighs.

She was waiting for an answer. Despairingly, he said, "Rhani, I can't!"

"Very well," she said calmly, and her voice reminded him, terribly, of Isobel, their mother. Turning, she left the alcove, and with a firm, decisive tread, went swiftly up the stairs.

Dana woke convulsively; he shot up in bed, reaching for the light switch, before he realized that he had been awakened by a friendly voice, a hesitant touch. He blinked at Amri while he got his breath back. Sleepily, she explained that Rhani had decided she wanted to go to Sovka, three hundred and fifty kilometers north, and had instructed Amri to wake her pilot up. Dana looked out the window. It was night. "Do I have time for breakfast?" he asked.

"Corrios is making it."

By the time he finished a hasty meal of fish cakes and fruit, the sun was rising. Corrios came in with mail, an armload. Amri took it upstairs. Knowing that Rhani would want to skim it before she left the house, Dana dawdled in the kitchen. He cleaned the dishes and counters. Memories of the previous day crowded into his mind. He tried to shut them out. He did not know which of them was worse: Zed's anger, and his own moment of panic; or the pain when he realized that, Starcaptain or no, he could not get through the Gate to Main Landingport. . . .

"Dana! Where are you?" asked the intercom.

"In the kitchen, Rhani-ka."

"Go to the front hall. I'll be right down."

She came briskly into the hallway. She was wearing a light cream-colored jumpsuit; it glinted as if it had specks of mica in the cloth. Her hair was not in its accustomed braid; she had pinned it up with an ivory comb, and she seemed thoughtful, and a little sad. He knew—Amri had told him—that she and Zed had fought.

She was carrying a piece of paper. "Dana," she said, "have you ever heard the name 'Loras U-Ellen'?"

Her gaze was intent and formidable. Dana turned the name over in his mind. It was not familiar.

"No," he said. "I'm sorry, Rhani-ka."

"He's connected with the drug trade."

"No."

She frowned. "All right." She glanced at him. "Did you sleep well?" she said. "It's a long flight to Sovka."

"I'm fine, Rhani-ka," he said.

"Good. Then let's go." They went to the front door. She paused to tell Corrios that she expected to be back in the late afternoon to speak with the manager of the Yago Bank, and that, if necessary, she could be reached at Sovka. Outside the shadows were long in the streets. They cut across the park to the private landingport. A light breeze lifted the dust from the walkways, bringing a touch of salt and the scent of moisture to the air, and Dana wondered if the wet western breeze meant that the Chabadese winter was coming. Rhani would know. . . . But she walked silently, preoccupied, a little ahead of him, and did not speak until they reached the landingport mall.

The manager hastened to them. "Domna Rhani! How may we serve you today?" He sounded a little apprehensive.

"Good morning," Rhani said. "I should like the use of the Yago bubble."

He definitely looked unhappy. "Domna, in view of your previous custom—that is to say, in prior years—"

"Yes?" Rhani said.

"It's being cleaned," he finished.

"Fine," Rhani said, with exaggerated patience. "I commend your efficiency. Is there another bubble we can use?"

"Oh, of course, of course." He ushered them to a hangar. In it was an old model, two-person bubble, less roomy than the newer styles.

"I'm afraid this is not the most modern model we have," the manager said. "That one is being repaired."

Rhani shrugged. "This will be fine." They crowded into it. Touching the controls, Dana smiled. The first self-powered flyer he'd ever flown had been a model like this one. Till then, his only experience with flight had been hang-gliding off Pellin's seaside cliffs. The hangar roof slid back. He took the bubble into the air over the city. Rhani sat with her legs folded beneath her in the other chair. To please her, he sent the bubble scooting over the sea. The icebergs glistened out of the blue-green water. Rhani pointed. "See the seals?" she said. Dana gazed through the glass. Gray animals crawled over the lower slopes of the icebergs, sliding from there to the water, where they became infinitely graceful and mobile.

"I thought there were no large animals on Chabad," he said. He touched the computer keyboard, keying for maps of Chabad. The third projection showed him Abanat, the coast, and a route leading north-northeast to a dot labeled *Sovka*.

"Imports," said Rhani. "From the Enchanter labs.

They can stand temperatures that would dehydrate Terran seals in a few hours." The bubble completed its circle. They skated above the Abanat rooftops, a checkerboard black-and-white, and headed north. "But who told you there are no animals on Chabad? That's not true. There are kerits."

Dana said, "I meant, except for the kerits."

Severely she said, "You can't discount the kerits; not on Chabad. Kerits are mammals, omnivorous, and without known predators. A full-grown kerit can weigh as much as thirty-five kilos. During the day they stay within burrows; at night they run. They get water from plants. They never drink, or piss. Kerit kits are born fighting; the first thing littermates do is gang up on the weakest member. They eat grass and insects and grassmice and snakes and each other. They are absolutely untamable. They run in packs led by the females, and two hundred years of breeding have not affected them at all. Put a kerit born in the breedery into the wild, and in two days you won't be able to tell it from its cousins. Oh, and they stink, too."

Dana said, "Thank you very much."

"You're welcome," she said. "The kerit farm is an important source of income for Family Yago." She stretched her arms in the air. Her extended fingers touched the ceiling of the bubble. "I wonder how many of the people who knew me are still there. Fourteen years ago—not many, I guess."

"I don't understand," said Dana.

"No—why should you? I worked and lived at Sovka for five years. I was not Rhani Yago; I used the name Irene Sokol. I started when I was seventeen, cleaning cages with the slaves, and by the time I was twenty-two, I was assistant manager. I would have been made manager the next month. But my mother called me home." Again she stretched. "Look," she said, "there's the Levos estate." Dana looked downward. He saw a green circle surrounding a house. Someone was semaphoring with both arms. He dipped the bubble to say *Hello.*

Rhani clutched the arms of the chair. "Don't *do* that!"

"I'm sorry, Rhani-ka," he said. As she relaxed, he added, "I can stand this thing on its head. . . ."

"Well, *don't.*" But she stopped gripping the seat. "I

suppose you're an expert at this."

The words just came out. "I *am* a Starcaptain."

Rhani did not challenge the bitter assertion. "And my brother?" she said softly.

Stiffly, he answered, "Zed is a good pilot." She was gazing out the slitted window, shoulders hunched, fingers bunched in her lap, lips tight. He wondered what they'd fought about. It might be safer not to know.

With a disconcerting, telepathic flash, she said, "You know we had a fight."

"Yes, Rhani-ka."

"He's good at many things. . . . He's a senior medic and a surgeon, and a pilot; he runs the Net superbly; he is an expert ice climber. I don't know what I would do without him. . . . He is not entirely sane, you know." She said it matter-of-factly. Dana's hands jerked on the controls and the bubble craft sideslipped. He corrected quickly.

Rhani seemed not to have noticed. Her voice was soft, but her clasped hands whitened in her lap. "We were very happy, the summer before I went to Sovka. We weren't lovers. I was three years adult, but still virgin, and Zed was fifteen, half-boy, half-man, my playmate. . . ." She glanced at him. "Is there an incest taboo on Pellin?"

"Not within a generation, no," he said.

"Nor is there on Chabad, though closer than cousins may not marry. The gene pool here is small. But we were only playmates. My mother—" She paused. "My mother was a cold woman. She saw in me a reflection of herself. I think it made her furious, that I had formed an intimacy with someone—anyone—before she had me trained. When she discovered how intense our feelings had grown, she separated us. I went to Sovka. Zed left for Nexus the next year. We didn't see each other for six years. In Sovka, I was Irene Sokol. I could hardly send communigrams to Nexus to Zed Yago."

The landscape below was soporific; russet hills, as far as the eye could see. Dana filled a water cup. Sipping from it, he offered it to Rhani. She took it in both hands, drank, gave it back to him.

"I know what Zed did then. I don't know why he did it. He made himself a eunuch; he shut off all sexual feelings, rather than share them with a stranger, with someone who wasn't me. . . . But you can't do that, shut off your sex as if it were water in a pipe. So he learned to find release in other ways."

Dana's chest ached. He stretched, and realized he had forgotten to breathe. He took a deep breath.

"A telepath might be able to help him. But I don't think he wants to be changed. To be commander of the Net must be a careful sadist's dream. I use him: his skills, his needs, his devotion. Just as he uses me."

She knows, Dana thought, shaken. She *knows* what he is. For a moment, all the hatred born of his humiliation and pain at Zed's hands trembled in his blood, muscles, and nerves. He felt dizzy. He hated her, he wanted to kill her. There was nothing to stop him: she knew nothing about self-defense; he outweighed her by fifteen kilograms. It would be easy.

And then he saw her, a slender, amber-eyed, dark-haired woman, sitting at his side. She was not Zed; she had not hurt him. It was not her fault that he was her slave. He had known the risks running drugs to Sector Sardonyx and had chosen to do it anyway; for his present situation he had only the luck and himself to blame. Not Rhani Yago.

She was only a human being, like himself, equally imprisoned by her own choices, and equally lonely. "Rhani," he said. She turned to look at him. She was crying. Gently, he reached his hand to touch her cheek.

As the bubble descended through the opened roof of the Sovka hangar, Rhani stretched. "Sore?" said Dana. He punched a button. The roof closed. The hangar grew dark and silent. "So am I." They sat with shoulders touching.

She smiled through the darkness at him. She did not want to move. The last part of the ride they had talked together about Nexus, about Pellin, places she had not seen. . . . They had not mentioned Zed. It had been remarkably easy to forget that, in another place, at other times, they were owner and slave. She found Dana's nearness in the bubble comforting. "We have to go." She had told Binkie to call ahead to tell them she was coming. "They're out there now, waiting."

Dana strode beside her as she stepped, blinking, out of the hangar. The heat was blistering, and she was glad she had remembered her sunshades. As far as she could see, there was not a speck of green.

"Welcome to Sovka, Domna," the new manager said. Erith Allogonga was dark-skinned, dark-eyed, and extraordinarily compact; she weighed eighty kilos, carrying it easily on a short, muscular frame. From wrists to shoulders, her black arms were welted with scars left by the teeth of kerit kits whose lives she'd saved in birthing. She brought the others forward, introducing them and naming their responsibilities in case Rhani had forgotten since her last visit to Sovka, three years back.

They were the five section heads, the assistant manager, and Erith's secretary, a thin quiet woman with a scar on her forearm. Rhani remembered her. "It's good to see you, Marisa," she said warmly.

The woman inclined her head. "I'm honored, Domna."

Erith Allogonga said, "Domna, let's get out of the heat, and you can tell us what you want to see first. I should tell you, I think we've discovered what has been killing the kerit kits. On a hunch of Seponen's, we sent every bit of data we had, including the kits, to the Enchanter labs, thinking maybe we were dealing, not with a virus or bacterium, but with some weird genetic pathology. Their report arrived yesterday; I told Marisa to put a copy through the com-unit. The kits died of hemophilia."

Rhani had never heard of it. "What is it?" she asked.

"Incomplete clotting of the blood. Our analysis told us that much, but we'd never heard of hemophilia. Apparently it used to exist in human populations. Enchanter did a gene analysis. There's a mutation, a blood-factor deficiency, that's recessive in about half our breeders in Prime Strain."

"What can be done about it?"

"Stop interbreeding. Increase the gene pool. We've sent the hunters out once already. It means a temporary dilution of Prime Strain."

"Can't be helped," murmured Kay Seponen.

They walked to the entrance of the breedery, where a large sign said: OFFICE. Rhani glanced at the long, low buildings. Nothing had changed; the heat, the dust, the smells were the same. The buildings had a new coat of paint. The farm consisted of the runs, huge fenced-in spaces where the kerit packs lived, dug caves and tunnels, foraged, fought, and mated; the breedery itself, where the kits were born and the weak and deformed kits culled; the food and chemical units, and the skinning unit where the male kerits and some of the females ended up. Maintenance took care of the runs, mended the fences, fed the kerits, blocked off the tunnels when they got too long, and kept the kerits from savaging each other when they got feisty or bored. Rhani had started work in Maintenance, paired with a smiling slave from Ley.

She frowned, trying to remember the girl's name.

"Something wrong?" said Erith Allogonga.

"No—I was just trying to recall a name." Joann, that was it. Joann had pitied "Irene" because she, not a slave, had to mend fences and clean cages without benefit of dorazine. She had offered—a sacrifice, this—to share a tablet. The next day, they had carefully cut Joann's tablet in two. Rhani remembered the serene, soft look of the fields, and how intricate and interesting the wiring of the fence had seemed. . . . But Joann grew irritable. By nightfall she had not wanted to share any more dorazine.

At the office door, she turned to the section heads. "I'll ask Erith to bring me to the sections after I hear her report. That way you have time to alert your staffs, so that when I come in they can all be looking busy." Kay Seponen chuckled. Bevis Arno, head of Maintenance, looked relieved.

In the office, the reports were waiting for her on Erith's desk, unsmudged printouts, crisp and clean. "How far back do you keep records?" Rhani asked.

"The computer automatically eliminates them, Domna, after ten years."

Rhani sighed. Irene Sokol no longer existed, except in memory. She wondered what had happened to Joann. She sat in a chair. The reports were easy to read. Expenses had gone up; profits down, but the farm was still making money by a comfortable margin. "Any staff problems?"

"No," said Erith. "There's always a little friction between Maintenance and the breedery. Maintenance is always overworked, and the breedery staff wants repairs made last week. It's been like that for ten years, as long as I've been here."

Rhani nodded. Nothing had changed. An item on a sheet caught her eye: TOURS. "What's this?"

"You remember—we opened the breedery about two years ago to interested tourists. We get four and five a week during Auction season. Fewer the rest of the year." Erith Allogonga grinned. "They won't go in the skinning unit, they think the kerit kits are 'cute,' and don't understand why we won't give out souvenir skins."

Rhani laughed. She ran a hand along the soft fabric of the chair; it was scraped kerit skin. She rose. "Your reports look good," she said. "I'm very pleased."

"Thank you, Domna."

"I'd like to visit Food and Chemical: short visits, then the skinning plant, the runs, and the breedery. Are you expecting a tour today?"

Erith called, "Marisa, are we expecting any tours today?"

Marisa said, "Yes, in about an hour."

"Call me when they come," said Rhani. "I'd like to see people who think kerit kits are cute."

Chemical had three main tasks, as well as a host of smaller things to do: to mix and store the chemicals used for curing kerit skins, to identify and treat diseases, and to distribute dorazine to the slaves working on the farm. Its personnel were trained technicians, not slaves. Rhani, Dana, Erith Allogonga, and Dov I-Kotomi, the assistant manager, were greeted at the entrance by Kay Seponen. She escorted them through the labs, identifying the different divisions, and praising her subordinates by name. Technicians, bent over their slides, barely looked up. The machinery gleamed. "A properly dedicated staff," Rhani murmured to Kay Seponen.

Food, next to Chemical, had two divisions: one which fed the staff, and one which fed the kerits. The cafeteria looked as if it had been redone; it was larger and cleaner. Rhani sampled some fish. It was good. She shared it with Dana. "How's your stomach?" she asked.

"It depends," he said. "For what?"

"Seeing things without their skins."

"As long as they're dead."

"They're dead." Erith Allogonga led the way. Rhani smelled the familiar mixed odors of the skinning area: acid and blood. The conveyor belt was still, and the stools empty, where the skinners usually sat holding their sharp little knives, smiling.

The manager said, "We're not processing today, Domna."

Rhani went to the vat in which the skins were dipped. Climbing the ladder, she peered in. The liquid swirled sluggishly. It was a sophisticated compound, fixing the skins without dulling the color, shine, or reflective properties of the fur. Fixed and dried, the furs were packaged. From the skinning unit, they went to a plant at the edge of Abanat, where they were made into rugs, coats, gloves, muffs, and sold to the Abanat wholesale market. The rest were shipped offworld.

Erith Allogonga said, "Domna, shall we go to the runs?"

It meant going outside again, into the blistering heat. Rhani redonned her sunshades.

As they neared the runs, the smells grew familiar again. Rhani's pulse beat faster. She walked a bit ahead of Erith Allogonga. For five years she had eaten and slept with this stench in her nostrils. It steamed in the air: rank, heavy. Sweat prickled on her skin and dried almost instantly in the heat: it was midmorning, and Rhani guessed the temperature to be 40° C.

Nothing moved in the runs. Even this early in the day, the kerits might be in their burrows. Erith Allogonga caught up with her. She was light on her feet for so bulky a woman. "Try run six," she said. "They've been active there."

The runs were separated from each other by wire-protected lanes, and guarded by watchful slaves. These were the elite of the Sovka slaves; never given dorazine, they were even trusted with weapons. (Though the weapons could not attain lethal charge—all they could do was stun.) Rhani strolled down the lane beside run six. Dana stayed at her side. Suddenly, a white head poked from a burrow. Rhani caught Dana's arm. "See it?" she whispered.

"I see it," he said. He watched the kerit waddle toward them, and thought: Hell, it's ugly. He had expected it to be small and sleek, like fur-bearing animals on Pellin. It was fat, for starters; it had light gray eyes, and a small, snouty head on a squat body. It had no tail. It sat on its ass, front paws dangling, peering at them from about a meter away. Dana looked at the paws, noting the huge claws on them. Makes it easy for them to do all that digging, he thought. The fur was white, but not merely white: it was a sparkling, breathtaking white, almost a blue-white, remarkable as diamond. Incongruously, it reminded him of the color of the snow on Pellin's Kamerash Peaks. He crouched by the fence to see it better, spreading his fingers on the wire mesh.

The kerit sprang at him.

Lashing its front claws to the mesh, it clung to the metal, glaring viciously at him from the level of his waist. Balancing on huge, muscular back legs, it was suddenly twice its height. Its mouth opened soundlessly, showing two rows of small, sharp, even teeth. Seizing his shoulder, Rhani dragged Dana back from the fence. A man in a white hooded jumpsuit came racing down the lane toward them, brandishing a stun gun. Rhani said, "Stay still. If they care to, kerits have been known to climb the fence."

But this kerit was smart, or else it had been stunned before. It dropped to all fours, and sped, with a curious rocking waddle, back to the mouth of its tunnel. It popped in. Rhani, Erith Allogonga, and the slave relaxed. Rhani said, "Now the breedery."

On the way to the other building, she touched Dana's arm. "I did the same thing," she said, "the first time I saw one."

At the entrance to the breedery, Erith Allogonga dismissed both the assistant manager and the section manager. "I'm running *this* tour." She smiled as she walked in. She said to Rhani, "I have to be very careful; I'm always reminding myself I'm not the manager of only this section any more."

They walked through a pair of automatic sliding doors. Floor-to-ceiling, wire-mesh cages lined the walls of a big room. It was hot. All the other buildings had been cool. Erith Allogonga remarked, "The breedery is kept to approximately the temperature of the inside of the kerit burrows." The room smelled like the kerit runs. In a corner of the nearest cage lay a huge, white-furred kerit, sleeping. On top of, around, and possibly under her lay small, furry bundles, gray and white, teeth and claws glinting through their fur. Dana counted thirteen of them. Erith Allogonga said, "After birth, we have to drug them. During birth, they're undrugged; drugged females birth dead kits. But if we leave them undrugged, they turn on the handlers. They do anyway." She held her arms out. Dana stared at the crossed weals patterning her arms. Involuntarily, he glanced again at the peacefully sleeping kits.

"What happens to them all?" he asked.

"The non-breeding males are put in separate runs until they reach puberty. Their skins are perfect then. They're killed and skinned. Males kept for breeding go in with the packs. The imperfect females are culled out right away and killed. They can't be kept anywhere that they can smell the packs, or they tunnel to reach them. The males' claws are small; they rarely tunnel. As the females come into heat, they grow aggressive. Eventually they kill the males. We bring the pregnant females here a week before their time. These kits were born eight days ago. In another five, the mother and the female kits can rejoin the pack. Other females don't attack nursing females or the kits. We control the breeding cycle; the kerits' hormone balance is dependent upon diet. Fertility and aggression are controlled by the amount of meat they eat. When breeding, they fight for space, or food, or just for temper. They're born fighting."

Rhani said, "They're vicious little beasts."

"Horrible," said Erith Allogonga.

They entered the office through a back door. In a small room, Erith Allogonga produced a pitcher from a cooler, and two glasses. She poured wine for Rhani and for herself. Rhani gestured to Dana. He found a third glass, and filled it from the pitcher. The manager would serve Rhani Yago but not her slave; it was a perfect and impersonal example of the automatic Chabadese hierarchy.

Voices mingled in the outer office, where the secretary sat. Erith Allogonga said, "Domna, that's the tour."

Rhani cocked her head to listen. "They sound angry."

"They probably are. Since the litter deaths we've been keeping the tours out of the breedery, fearing some kind of contamination. The report from Enchanter came yesterday. I forgot to change the rule." She opened the inner office door.

"We were told we could see everything!" said an irate male voice. "What kind of a cheap place is this?"

The secretary answered in measured tones. "This isn't a tourist attraction. This is a factory. We produce a product. We reserve the right to limit access to parts of the plant when we feel that outsiders might interfere with the manufacturing process."

Dana saw Rhani nod in admiration. "Perfect," she said.

There was a moment's confused babble. The man muttered about a runaround. "That's right," a woman shrilled aggressively, "When my sister was here last year, she saw the babies. They were all in cages. She said they looked darling. I want to see them."

A rising clamor of voices supported her. "Tourists," said the manager. She rolled her eyes upwards. "I'd better go out there." She slid open the door. Rhani beckoned to Dana. They followed her. The outer office was crowded with people dressed in bright, flimsy gowns, holding sunshades, and parasols. They looked hot and tired; a few looked green from the bubble flight, or perhaps from the smell. Calmly, Erith Allogonga said, "I'm sorry. The breedery section of the farm is not open to visitors at the moment."

A thin, sallow woman with a taut mouth said, "Who are you?" She glared with suspicion at the manager. It was she who had spoken before.

"My name is Erith Allogonga. I am the manager of the Yago Kerit Farm."

"And who are they?" The woman transferred her gaze to Rhani and Dana. *"Important people,* that's for sure. If *you're* the manager, how come you aren't out here, greeting your guests, instead of leaving us to talk—to some ex-criminal!"

Someone gasped. The room fell silent as Marisa started to rise, her face bloodless with fury. Erith Allogonga put a hand on her arm.

The woman looked at Rhani. "I bet *you* saw the babies!" she said.

Rhani said, "That's right."

"How come you can go where we can't?"

Rhani said, unsmiling, "Abanat Production Quality Control Inspection Bureau. We can go anywhere."

The sallow woman opened her mouth and shut it again. She said, "But my sister—"

"One time has nothing to do with another," said Rhani. "The manager is perfectly correct in refusing you entrance."

"But why?"

"I'm afraid she doesn't have to tell you that. Neither do I. However, you may rest assured, the original reports of contamination are definitely false."

The tourists all took one step backward toward the door. "Contamination?" quavered one. "What reports?"

The original speaker said, "I can live without seeing the babies."

"I can live without seeing anything."

"I want to leave. This is my holiday, I didn't come here to get sick."

The sallow woman said, furiously, to Rhani, "We should have been warned! I'm going to report this! What's your name?"

Rhani said, "Irene Sokol."

The office emptied. As they streamed toward the hangar, Dana could hear the shrill voice in the midst of the other tourists, talking about her sister.

Marisa broke the awed silence. "Thank you, Domna." She was smiling, her face its normal color. Erith Allogonga began to laugh resoundingly. Dana remembered the woman's incredulous expression. He grinned. The grin became a chuckle. Rhani smiled. Finally they all broke up, leaning on the desk and shelves and on the computer, sweating, howling.

They stayed at the kerit farm for lunch.

Erith Allogonga pointed out: "Domna, it's near noon, and the flight back to Abanat is a two-hour flight. Wait till the heat has passed." Rhani agreed. They ate in the cafeteria, at a round table with Erith Allogonga and the section heads. As the staff filed in for lunch, Dana saw the heads turn to look, and heard the whispers go around. Occasionally, someone started laughing. They finished the meal—which was not bad, though not up to the standards of either Immeld or Corrios—with tall glasses of the ubiquitous Chabadese fruit punch. Rhani added sweetener to hers. Slowly, the lesser members of the staff went out.

Kay Seponen said, "Domna, I think you've halted the tours for a while, till the rumors die down."

Dov I-Kotomi said, "Not such a bad thing."

Rhani said, "Do they get in the way of your work? I'll have them stopped."

The section heads looked at one another. Kay Seponen said, "They don't really take up any time. The slaves like them. It's just that—you know. Tourists."

Erith Allogonga said, "I'd love to see the look on that woman's face when she discovers that there is no 'Abanat Production Quality Control Inspection Bureau'!"

Rhani sipped the punch. She was looking tired; her eyes had lost that animated gleam. Softly, Dana said to her, "Rhani-ka, if we're going to be staying much later, perhaps we should call Abanat. You don't want Zed to worry."

She pushed the glass away from her. "We won't be staying later. I've seen all that I came to see."

Erith Allogonga and the section heads accompanied them along the dusty path to the hangar. They crammed into the narrow seats. The bubble hummed under Dana's fingers; the hangar roof pulled back; the sky blazed in. They lifted toward it.

Rhani sighed. She wriggled against the hard padding of the seat. "I'm tired," she said.

Below them, the bubble shadow dipped and lifted over the contoured ground. Dana took them higher. Rhani had a smudge of dust on her left cheek. Curled into the seat, her pinned-up hair falling down, she looked like a dirty-faced child, done with exploring some wild and private wonderland. Dana smiled at her. "We'll be home soon."

"Not home," she corrected. "We'll be in Abanat. *Home* is the estate. May I have some water, please?"

Filling a cup, he gave it to her. She lifted her face to drink. The small agelines around her eyes stood out, clearly defined. She no longer looked like a child.

Dana felt a rush of tenderness for her. He reached out his hand to brush her cheek clean. She smiled. "My Starcaptain," she said. She turned her face toward his palm. In the hollow of his hand, he felt the lingering moist warmth of her lips and tongue.

Chapter Eight

On the way up the steps to the house, Rhani turned to look at Dana. Coming from the landingport, he had remained silently and watchfully beside her, a perfect image of a bodyguard. She touched his wrist, afraid of putting too much weight on their unexpected rapport. "Be careful," she said. "You will have to be careful."

"I know," he said. The door opened, and they went in. They separated at once: Rhani went to the stairway, Dana to the slaves' hall. She glanced at him before ascending the stairs. He was watching her from the hallway, his face impassive except for his eyes, which brimmed with warmth.

As she went upstairs, Rhani remembered that she had asked Tak Rafael, manager of the Yago Bank, to attend her that afternoon. She sighed, scrubbing her face. She felt dusty, begrimed, and hot. Perhaps she would have time to shower. She went into the bedroom.

Zed was there.

He looked weary and tense. Rhani's head stabbed with sudden pain; she could not bear the thought of a second fight with him, she would not. . . . She touched the intercom. "Amri," she said, "bring me something cool to drink." As she started to pluck the ivory pins from her hair, Amri entered with glasses and a pitcher of chilled wine.

"I'll do that," Zed said, as the slave began to pour. Amri left. Zed cleared his throat. "Rhani-ka," he said, "I was stupid, and jealous yesterday, just as you said. I will support whatever you choose to do, even if you choose to marry Ferris Dur. Can we be friends?"

She turned to him, deeply grateful. She reached a hand to him. He lifted it to his cheek. His face was grainy with exhaustion. "Thank you, Zed-ka," she said.

He let her hand fall and presented her with the glass of wine. "You look tired," he said.

"It's a long flight from Sovka. So do you."

"Yukiko called me in. I spent the morning repairing a badly shattered elbow."

She nodded, knowing that he had battled his way to his capitulation under the surgery lights. "They found out what was killing the kerit kits at Sovka," she said. "It's called hemophilia."

Zed frowned. "The name's familiar." He shook his head. "Tell me about it."

Rhani repeated Erith Allogonga's explanation.

"Of course." He leaned on the back of the chair. "It must have been a spontaneous mutation. As I recall, it was sex-linked in humans; females carried it, but it was expressed in males. . . . How many breeders were affected?"

"About half the Prime Strain breeders, Erith said."

Zed winced. "They'll have to be killed, and their kits as well, even the healthy-seeming ones. You can't continue to breed them."

"I know," Rhani said. "They've already sent the hunters out."

"It'll dilute the strain." Prime Strain kerits were so designated because of the color, texture, and superior reflectivity of their coats. "But I suppose it can't be helped. Something like this was bound to show up eventually."

Rhani drank and set the glass down. Recalling Jo's letter, she pulled it from her pocked. "Zed-ka," she said, "look at this." She held it out.

He read swiftly. "Loras U-Ellen has taken Sherrix Esbah's place. Who the hell is that?" He read further, and scowled. "Is not, as far as anyone can tell, dealing in dorazine? He'll go out of business in a week! How did he persuade Sherrix to—oh, I see. Probably a bribe. U-Ellen, U-Ellen. It's an Enchantean name, but I don't think I've ever heard it. Better tell Binkie to get the word out."

Rhani nodded. "I shall. I wonder what's going on, Zed-ka." She frowned, and her temple twinged with pain. She hated dealing with shadows, names, never faces. In five years, she had never met or even spoken with Sherrix Esbah. That, too, was a consequence of the Federation ban.

A step drew her attention. Binkie stood in the doorway. He spoke, not looking at Zed: "Excuse me, Rhani-ka. Tak Rafael has arrived, and waits downstairs. And you asked me to remind you; Family Kyneth's party is tonight."

"Oh, hell!" Rhani said. Her shoulders hunched. Parties, she thought with disgust. She did not want to go; her back hurt from the flight, she was hot, and tired, and her head ached. . . . She looked at Zed. "Zed-ka," she said, "would you go in my place? One of us has to."

Zed groaned. Rhani knew he hated parties, and never went to them unless she was there. But it was hard for him, as she knew it would be, to deny the direct request. "I wouldn't have to stay long," he said hopefully.

She smiled at him. "An hour or two," she said. "No more. You can tell them that I'm not feeling well, and you have to return to take care of me."

He sighed. "I'll go." He glanced at the clock display on the com-unit. "I'd better eat and dress."

"Come and see me before you leave," she said. She looked longingly toward the washroom. She had wanted to shower. It would have to wait.

"I will," Zed promised. He walked to the door. Binkie had vanished. "Don't waste your strength on that bank manager, Rhani-ka."

She grinned at him, amused despite her fatigue. "But, Zed-ka," she said, "he's *my* bank manager."

Zed left. Rhani rose from the chair and went to the washroom. Her eyes ached, and she patted them with a cold towel before scrubbing her face with hot water. She combed her hair out, braided it, and then, over the intercom, told Amri to bring Tak Rafael to her room. He entered quietly: a slim, brown man with gray-green eyes.

"Domna Rhani," he said, bowing slightly. "It's good to have you back in Abanat."

"Thank you," she said. She gestured to the com-unit, knowing he preferred to sit at it. "Please be seated." He sat. He was wearing Yago blue, and the only bright touch about him was the red frame of his sunshades. "I must confess that I have not had the time to read over all this year's earnings reports with the care they deserve." She brought the stool to sit beside him at the com-unit.

"I know you're a busy woman," he said. "That's why you employ me."

She smiled. "Yes. However, if you will bring the last

quarter's report on the screen—" he tapped out brisk instructions, and the display winked to life—"yes, thank you. I have a few questions. . . ."

His response to her questions, and the ensuing discussion, took two hours. The bank was making money, certainly; however, in certain divisions investments had drastically lost money, and Rhani wanted to know why. At the conversation's close, she requested Rafael to have the Bank's Investment Committee send her a policy statement, with examples of its application from the four prior reports. And—wondering a little at herself—she asked Rafael almost diffidently what he could tell her about Family Dur's current investments.

Cautiously, he said, "You probably have access to more of that information than I, Domna."

"Tell me what you know."

"They invest mostly through the First Bank of Chabad, of course. Aside from what they have tied up in mining and refining equipment, they've invested heavily in underwater mining gear, in the diamond market on Belle, in some of the newer Abanat housing projects and hotels, and in pharmaceutical supplies."

"These are stable investments? Nothing chancy?"

"I doubt that the Investment Committee at the First Bank of Chabad would authorize anything less."

She grinned at him. "I hope not." She rose from her stool. "Thank you for taking this trouble and time."

He rose and bowed. "As always, it is a pleasure to see you, Domna."

She called Amri to escort him downstairs. In leaving, he said, rather shyly, "You know, Domna, I recently learned that I'm not the only person in my family to have worked for yours."

"Oh?"

"I can trace my line back five generations on Chabad, and in each generation one member of my family was employed by yours. My great-great-grandmother was an accountant for Lisa Yago."

Alone at last, Rhani kicked off her sandals and sank onto her bed. The house was hot; the aircooling system was old, and needed to be repaired, or replaced. She let herself fall backward to the bed's cool, silky surface. Closing her eyes, she relaxed her tense muscles: images paraded through her head, Sovka then, Sovka now, the kerit cages, Erith Allogonga's scars, white on her dark arms, Dana Ikoro, her Starcaptain. . . .

It had been a long day. Uncharitably, she blamed Ferris Dur for that. If he had not made his offer, she would not have fought with Zed, nor found herself flying to Sovka in the middle of Abanat's heat. She touched the flat surface of her belly and tried to imagine herself pregnant. It would be simple enough to arrange; all she would have to do would be to stop taking the pills she had taken since she was thirteen, one each Standard week. She wrinkled her nose, wondering if she would like being pregnant. Some women did. The aircooling system clunked, interrupting her thought, and she made a mental note to ask Binkie to call someone to fix it.

Binkie . . . slaves . . . dorazine. Scowling, she opened her eyes. Damn Michel A-Rae! He was her foremost problem. If he had his way there would be no merger of two fortunes, for neither she nor Ferris Dur would have one. She remembered a book that Isobel had made her read, Nakamura's *History of Chabad*. Nakamura, a vigorous anti-slaver, had predicted that moral indignation and rising costs would force Chabad to end the slave system and replace it by hired labor. Michel A-Rae seemed to be providing the moral indignation, she thought. Maybe this was the beginning of the decline, and Nakamura had been right.

Slavery was not the most efficient system, she well knew. But the Chabadese adaptation of it worked, and Family Yago needed it. Yago money maintained the Net, ran the Auction, and profited from both. If slavery ended, Sovka would survive. But the Net would not. And what, Rhani thought, would Zed Yago do if the Net did not survive?

She sat up abruptly on the bed. She did not want to think about her brother, not now. Padding barefoot to the bedroom door, she slid it shut. Then, stepping from her jumpsuit, she curled naked on the bed and poured herself a glass of wine. A drop of sweat formed between her breasts and glided to her navel, making her shudder. On Chabad, even sweating was a luxury. She gazed at her own body, wondering where Dana was now: in his room, perhaps, talking to Amri, or listening to the music of—

what was that name?—Vittorio Stratta. Her nerves jittered with sexual tension.

The rapport between them had sprung out of nowhere. It was always that way for her. She remembered back two months, to the brief affair she had had with the young acrobat, and before that, to the love-time she had spent with Clare Brion. That had been lighthearted loving, swift, tender and fun.

She had never loved a slave. Wine glass in hand, she paced. She didn't even know if he wanted her. She traced, with her own hand, the path of his hand on her face. Surely, he did. She could call him, make him sit and talk with her; she could command him into bed, even. Her mouth twitched with laughter. Much good that would do. She wondered how she looked to him. Too short, too tall, too skinny?

She wondered if he was good in bed.

She heard his voice in her mind. "Yes, Rhani-ka. No, Rhani-ka." Slave manners, incongruous coming from a Starcaptain. It surprised her how swiftly he had learned them, until she recalled who had taught him. Zed had hated Clare; hated the nights when she had not come home, hated it even more when she brought Clare to share her bed. He hadn't met the acrobat. If she took Dana as bedmate, Zed would say nothing to her; he would take his anger out on Dana. That would be insufferable. Rhani scowled. This was insufferable, or soon would be. She could free him. Then Zed would not touch him.

But if she freed him, he would be gone off Chabad as fast as he could go, out of Sector Sardonyx, out of her life.

She didn't want that either.

She shrugged into a robe, yanking the sash tight, as if by constricting her breathing she could shut off her thoughts. She palmed the door open. "Binkie!" He entered. "I want this letter to go out to all Family Yago associates immediately."

"To Whomever, from Domna Yago: Family Yago would appreciate knowing whatever can be known about an Enchantean family surnamed U-Ellen. Thank you, very sincerely, Domna Rhani Yago." He tapped it out. She watched the message flit across the screen. "Thank you, Bink. Send that out, and when that is done, please set up

a file for me with all the material we have received to date
on Michel A-Rae."

Zed ate dinner in the kitchen.

Dana wandered in, saw him there, and left at once,
with a swift, "Excuse me." Zed watched him walk. His
body was beginning to regain some of its confidence; it
had resumed that Hyper glide. Zed smiled to himself. It
might be amusing, he thought, to spend some time taking
it away.

"Is there more wine?" he asked. Corrios poured it for
him. No, he would not do that. He had promised Rhani to
leave Dana alone, and anyway he had other things to do,
and not a lot of time. He pushed back from the chair.
Climbing to his room, he showered and dressed. He tied
his hair back with a silver clip, and reached into his closet
for his cloak. It was dark blue apton on the outside and
kerit fur on the inside, and it was trimmed in silver braid.

He went to say good night to Rhani. She was in bed,
tray of food beside her. She had not put her hair back in
its braid. It rippled over the pillows, shining like water.
Bending over her, he brushed the soft strands with his
lips. Rhani tugged at the ruffles on his shirt to straighten
them. "Zed-ka, you look fine," she said.

"Thank you. Why did I let you talk me into this? I'll be
back early."

She said, "Don't leave so early that Imre will think you
rude."

"I won't."

"Give him and the others my regards and regrets."

He gazed at her levelly. "No special message for
Ferris?"

"No," she said. "Anything I have to say to him, I can
say myself."

At the front door, Zed reminded Corrios to keep the
door double-locked and the alarms on. He crossed the
street to the park. Looking back, he saw the house
looming like a castle through the trees, light shining
through the slits in the curtains. There was no one in the
park tonight; no lovers coupling in the wet stems, no
children playing in the early darkness. It seemed ominous.

He zigged and zagged, taking a diagonal path through
the small streets, till he reached the Kyneth mansion on

the Promenade. It was a bigger house than the Yago
house: the Kyneths liked large families. The door fronting
on the Promenade was wide open. Two slaves flanked it.
They bowed as Zed walked between them into the foyer
of the house. Another slave took his cloak. Through the
doors into the main hall he saw the massed backs of the
guests. Voices shrieked. Just like the tourists, he thought.
Zed squared his shoulders.

The crowd splintered. Imre Kyneth walked out of the
crush, hands outstretched in welcome. "Zed, good evening! So pleased you could be here."

"Thank you," Zed said. He touched the man's hands
briefly. He had a great deal of respect for Imre Kyneth.
He was the oldest of the Family heads now that Domna
Sam had died; seventy-seven, very active, small and
spare, head of the Chabad Council, a brisk, effective
man. He had a brood of sons and daughters: no lack of
heirs. Family Kyneth controlled Chabad's most precious
resource: water. The long pipelines that kept Abanat
green were theirs, manufactured in their plants from steel
made by Family Dur. They owned and ran the water
purification plant. The ships that moved icebergs from the
poles to the city were theirs. They were a close-knit but
outgoing crew; the antithesis, Zed thought, of the individ-
ualistic, solitary Yagos.

Imre craned his neck to look behind Zed's broad
shoulders. "Where's Rhani?"

"She sends regards and regrets. She isn't feeling well
tonight. She knew you'd understand."

"Of course. Is it serious?"

"No," said Zed, "a mild indisposition, nothing to worry
about."

Aliza Kyneth sailed up to them. She was a massive
woman, tall and nearly as broad as a Skellian. She had a
strong-featured face; huge, black eyes; and hair that
snapped, it was so red. She dwarfed her older husband.
The white tent that fell over her in soft folds only
emphasized her size. "Zed, welcome back from the Net.
Imre, why do you keep him standing in the foyer? Zed,
Rhani isn't with you?"

"She's indisposed."

"That's too bad. We'll hope to see her at the Dur party.
Ferris will be disappointed. He had hoped she'd be
coming."

"He's here, then."

"Of course. See him there?" Aliza pointed at one of the backs. "Give Rhani our best and tell her we want to see her. Come in, mingle. Imre, someone else has come through the doors." She looked pointedly at her husband, who chuckled and went to greet the woman standing in the doorway. "Quick, Zed, if you don't want to be cornered. That's Charity Diamos."

"Aliza, I love you," said Zed.

"Drinks to the right."

Zed walked right.

The drinks table stood against a mirror-covered wall, so that people moving along it were reflected back to themselves. It made the large room look even larger. The Kyneth children were studded in strategic places. Slaves circulated, carrying huge trays brimming with food: fish in batter, sweets, cakes, pressed seaweed, Ley cheese, fruits. Zed picked an egg tart off a passing tray. The slave handed him a blue glass plate. Zed smiled, prepared to be social. It was what he'd come for. Theo Levos, head of the Fourth Family of Chabad, was holding court in the center of the room. He was a big, boisterous man, accustomed to space. Zed waited patiently for him to take a breath.

"Good evening, Theo."

"Zed Yago, you silent man! How long have you been standing there, saying nothing? Why didn't you say something?"

"I didn't want to interrupt your speech."

"Interrupt me. You Yagos are always silent."

"Rhani asked me to send you her regards."

"She isn't here?" Theo put his hands on his hips. Zed explained. "Sick? How can she get sick with a medic for a brother? I'm sorry she's sick, tell her that."

"I'll tell her."

"Say hello to Jen, she's somewhere about." He pointed to a small alcove lined with booktapes. Jen T'ao, his companion, mother of two of his three children, was standing talking with Clare Brion. Zed nodded stiffly towards the two women. Jen nodded back. There was a beautiful gold-and-black cavorting dragon embroidered on her red jacket.

"Zed Yago!" said a voice. Zed turned, inwardly cursing. "How lovely to see you! I said to myself as soon as I walked in behind you, how elegant he looks, oh, my, yes. But Imre tells me that Rhani is not well! Of *course* it can't be anything serious or you would not have left her side, all Abanat knows how devoted you two are to one another, oh, my, yes. We are all looking forward to the Auction. I'm looking for a new cook; my old cook's contract just expired, so inconvenient. I don't imagine I'll find anybody half as good. And then, there are so many tourists in residence this season that I'm worried one of them will outbid me. Of course, the Yagos *never* have to worry about that. Such a handsome young slave dear Rhani had with her the other day, crossing the park. A secretary?" She looked up at him, eyes brilliant with curiosity and malice.

"Her new pilot," said Zed.

"Oh, yes," said Charity Diamos.

"Excuse me," said Zed.

Escaping as swiftly as he could, Zed worked his way to the isolated, relative safety of the stairs. A well-dressed child sat on the lowest step. As Zed approached, he scrambled to his feet. "C-C-Commander," he stammered.

"Hello," said Zed. Like most of the Kyneth children, he had Imre's build, but Aliza's features and her thick red hair. "Which one are you?"

"Davi, Commander."

"You don't have to call me that," said Zed, amused by the look of worship in the boy's green eyes. He probably talked back to his father without a qualm. "My name is Zed. How old are you?"

"Ten. I'm the youngest."

"You Kyneths are hard to keep track of. Ten. When I was ten, I never got to stay awake for the parties."

"Did you want to?"

Zed grinned. "No." He tried to recall just how many Kyneth children there were. He didn't know all their names. Most of them worked with and for their father, on Chabad, but one, he knew, was studying engineering, and another was working toward being a medic. It was mostly the older ones and the very young ones, now, who could be found at home.

"I don't either." Davi tugged at the white ruffled collar of his shirt. "I hate parties."

"Why are you here, then?"

"All our slaves are busy. Mother told *me* to guard the stairs. I have to stay here until she sends me to bed. And *talk* to people."

"Zed," said a woman's voice, not Charity Diamos. It was Margarite Kyneth, Imre's heir. She was a tall woman; she overtopped him by half a head. "What are you doing, hiding in the shadows talking to the Brat?"

Davi scowled at his older sister. Zed said, truthfully, "Getting away from Charity Diamos."

"Oh. Poor man. Davi-ka, Mother wants you by the wine table." She reached a hand to pluck at Davi's lopsided collar as he slid by. He was still scowling. "What did you talk about?"

"Charity and I?"

"No, of course not. Who can talk to her? You and the Brat."

"He seems a smart child."

"He's more intelligent than I am," said Margarite. "Did he tell you he wants to be a Hyper?"

"No. But so did I, when I was ten."

"Me, too," said Margarite. "But I got over it. So will Davi."

"You sound certain of that."

"I am. The Family needs him. And, dreams aside—he's a Kyneth. That's what matters on Chabad. Excuse me." She walked toward the booktape alcove. Zed watched her regal pacing. She was practicing, he thought, for when Imre died, and she was the Family's head. Conversations faded in and out around him. *Auction, money, slaves, money, parties, tourists, heat, money, oh, my, yes.* Margarite was right. For the Families' children, there was no escaping Chabad. A woman pranced by, wearing a red brocade tent embroidered with blue feathers. Zed wondered if Rhani were sleeping, or if she were still awake, reading or working or perhaps standing by the window, looking at the stars. It was not as easy to see the stars in Abanat as it was to see them at the estate. The city lights paled them.

In the next room over music started up. Feet thudded. People danced. There were too many people in the place, too much noise, it was stuffy, and hot, and very bright, and he longed suddenly for the cool silences and white curving walls of the Net.

In a sudden lull he heard a voice like a fingernail scraping glass. ". . . Such a *handsome* young slave, oh, my, yes."

Davi wriggled by, holding a brimming glass of wine. He brought it to his father. Seeing Zed watching him, he flashed a sunny smile, and ducked around the circumference of the crowd to arrive at Zed's elbow. "Do you want some wine?" he asked. The heat had wilted the crisp, red curls on the back of his neck.

For an instant, Zed's mind rocked with fantasy: Davi drugged, helpless, bound to a bed under his hands. He caught his breath. Passing his plate to a nearby slave, he ruffled the boy's curls, a careful gesture, like a magician casting a counterspell. "No, thank you. See you later." Davi gazed at him worshipfully. Zed strode toward the knot of laughing, talking strangers like a man plunging headfirst into an icy pool.

He was listening to two men discuss three-dimensional chess—a game in which he had no interest—when Imre Kyneth appeared at his side. "Zed Yago," said the older man. "Have you a minute?"

"Certainly," said Zed. "Here?"

"No. Come with me." Imre led him out the back of the room through a high, arching doorway, to a small round door set in a paneled wall. "In here." He opened the door. The lintel was only a few centimeters taller than Imre. Zed had to duck. Inside the room, he could stand upright. Imre touched a switch. Lights came on. Zed turned. The room's walls were shelves from floor to ceiling, and the shelves were filled with old-style, bound-paper books.

"This is my den," Imre said. He smiled. "Every adult should have one."

"I'm impressed," Zed said. There was a desk to his left. Something about it was odd. He frowned. What—ah. It was out of proportion—at least, for him. He glanced back at the books. "Have you read them all?"

"Most of them. But not these, not literally. These I don't handle very much. They're originals. Most of them were manufactured on Old Terra. Some are actually of animal skin: vellum, it was called. I've got a few that are six hundred years old, made of cloth and leather and glue, and they still hold together. The temperature in this room is controlled, of course." He touched the light switch again, and a lamp nearby came on. Underfoot, its color matching the wood of the shelves, a carpet gleamed copper. "I'm glad you like it, Zed."

"It's very handsome." Zed touched the satiny finish of the desk chair. It was just a little smaller than the other chairs in the house. "What may I do for you, Domni?"

Imre scowled at him. "Imre to you, if you please. Are we strangers that we need to use titles to each other, or enemies?"

Zed grinned at the smaller man. "Imre, never that."

Imre sat. "I asked you in here to talk to you about Michel A-Rae. I had thought to speak with Rhani—"

"I will tell her what you say," Zed said.

"I am grateful. I invited him to this party, you know."

Zed was surprised. "A policeman? Why?" He did not think such an invitation had ever been made to A-Rae's predecessors.

"I wanted to see what he would say," Imre said. He steepled his hands against his chin. "I didn't expect him to accept, and he did not. He did, however, reply. We spoke over the com-unit screen. He called."

Zed nodded. "Yes. He did the same with me, when I was on the Net."

Imre looked relieved. "You've spoken with him? Then you know what he's like."

"As much as one can tell from a five-minute conversation," Zed said, "yes."

"He's dangerous," Imre said flatly. "A fanatic. His name's Enchantean, and I wonder if there might be something accessible and explanatory in his past. . . . He hates you, you know."

"I got that impression," Zed said. "It doesn't trouble me, Imre."

"It should. He hates your sister, too."

Zed's shoulders tensed. "How do you know this?"

"From what he said." Imre looked at his hands. "He called her several indelicate names, and made comments about—about the two of you—"

Zed said harshly, "You needn't elaborate. I've heard

them." Needing suddenly to move, he walked a slow circle around the desk. "Is there more to this, Imre?"

Imre nodded crisply. "Yes. I want to know what Rhani plans to do about the dorazine shortage."

Zed stopped pacing. "Has it begun to affect you?" he said.

"Yes," said Imre. "Our stores are particularly short over at the purification plant. Without dorazine, we cannot trust slaves to do the work there, which means that if there is no dorazine, we shall have to hire outside labor instead of purchasing slaves. And we are not the only ones. If we rely on an outside labor force instead of slaves, then the Auction will not go well, which means there will be an excess of slaves in holding cells—"

"You needn't continue," Zed said again, gently this time. "I know what will happen next." With no dorazine, the slaves could not be kept in the holding cells without security precautions, guards, even weapons. . . . This year might see the beginning of a reaction which could blow Sector Sardonyx apart. Metaphorically speaking, Zed thought. "I'm rather sorry Michel A-Rae did not attend this party," he said. And again he thought, I know him. Or knew him. He scowled, hunting through memory for the source of that elusive sense of familiarity.

He did not find it.

Imre Kyneth laughed shortly. "I'm not."

The two men looked at each other. Finally Zed said, "Imre, I must go. Rhani will be concerned; I said I would not linger."

"You wouldn't anyway," Imre said.

"I will tell Rhani what you have told me. How short of dorazine are you?"

"We have enough to last another three months."

"Stars!" Zed said. "That's short."

"Family Yago's stores are better, I gather," Imre said.

"I believe so," Zed said cautiously.

Imre stood. "You'll need it," he said. "Tell Rhani I look forward to hearing from her soon."

"I will," Zed said. "I'll find my own way out, Imre, don't move." He walked to the entrance. At the door, he glanced back. Imre stood beside a tall pole lamp, holding between his palms an old, skinbound book.

Part way to the front door, a voice said Zed's name and

a hand groped his shoulder. Muscles bunching, Zed turned. A pasty-faced stranger held his upper arm. He wore gold and red, the Dur colors, and Zed realized that he was looking at Ferris Dur.

He said, "Domni Ferris, kindly take your hand off my arm."

Ferris Dur let him go.

Zed smoothed his shirt. "My thanks."

Ferris Dur said, "Isn't Rhani here? Why is she not with you?"

Zed said, "She's at home, she isn't feeling well. I imagine she'll be well enough to attend your party."

"Has someone from the Clinic seen her?"

Zed said, "I am a senior medic."

Ferris stared at him. "That's right," he said. "I forgot." His shirt was grease-stained. Kerit bait, Zed thought, despising him. "She isn't seriously ill?"

Zed set his teeth. His fingers curled at his sides. "No," he said. "Now, if you'll excuse me. . . ." If you don't get out of my path in five seconds, Ferris Dur, he thought, I'm going to walk over you. Ferris stepped back: Zed took a deep breath and slid past him. Davi Kyneth was watching him with that damnable look of hero-worship, not two meters away.

"Bring my cloak," he snapped to a slave near the door. The slave brought it. "Please give my regards to your mistress."

The slave bowed, clear-eyed. "Commander."

The night, like most Chabadese nights, was cold and crisp. Overhead, the stars glittered like points of ice. Zed pulled the cloak closer to him. He walked north along the deserted Promenade. He thought, steadily, holding his mind to it; I shall have to tell Rhani about my conversation with Imre—and then pain welled up inside him; he swayed, body bunching as if he walked into a wind. A tormentor of children, is that what he was destined to become? I'll kill myself first, he thought. For a moment he wished that there could be an easier way out of what he had made of himself. He could go to Nexus, or better yet, to Psi Center, and put himself into the care of the telepaths. He could try again to find a lover. He could leave Chabad, be a pilot for a corporation, perhaps return to Nexus and train to be a Starcaptain. . . . But his attachment to Rhani had spoiled him for anyone and anything else, and he knew none of those would work.

He stopped suddenly in the middle of the street. He was hurrying to get home, and it was not his sister he was thinking of, but Dana, even Binkie. He breathed slowly and deeply until his tension subsided and his muscles slackened. He knew how to keep himself under control; choice as well as chance had gone to make him what he was.

The house was blissfully dark and quiet. On his way upstairs he heard Corrios walking around to the windows, resetting the alarms. We should have alarms on the estate, he thought. I wonder why we never thought of it. Because, he answered himself, we never thought that there we'd be accessible to harm. He glanced into Rhani's bedroom. She had fallen asleep with the light on. He walked through the scented dimness to the bedside.

"Zed-ka?" Her voice was thick. Eyes closed, she yawned.

He suppressed a moment of fury. What if it were *not* him? Dana should be here, should have been lying across the threshold. . . . He relaxed his fingers effortlessly. "Yes, it's me."

"Is it late?"

"Not very."

She opened her eyes. "Was Ferris Dur there?"

"Yes. He asked for you. I had an interesting conversation with Imre Kyneth. Remind me to tell it to you tomorrow."

"All right." Her lips curled in a sleepy smile.

Zed drew a fingertip across the smooth line of her cheek. "Good night, Rhani-ka," he said. He left her door ajar and went to his room. He leaned in the doorway, while desire shuddered through him, corrosive as poison, swift as a surgeon's knife. Walking to the window in his room, he flung it open and leaned on the sill, arms crossed, while the sweat poured off him.

The city lights glittered below him; the stars glinted austerely above. He looked up.

After a while, the compulsion died.

He stood quietly, frightened. His control was slipping. He had been roused close to action twice in one night, and he was only two weeks back from the Net. He had learned not to be greedy, learned to starve his system. . . . He rested his head in his hands. Fear and reproach were pointless. He could go to Lamartine's: they would not be pleased to see him, but for two hundred credits they would let him pick out a slave to do whatever he wanted to. Need would rest, satisfied.

A breeze touched his cheek. There was a sliver of moon in the west. He squinted at the evening sky. The glow of the city's lamps gleamed on the icebergs' slopes.

He bowed his head. Walking to his medic's case, he thumbed it open and picked from it a clear capsule: chloral hydrate, purveyor of dreamless sleep. He swallowed it dry and shut the case. Shedding his clothes, he unclipped his hair, closed the open window, and struggled into his bed.

He would take his needs to the exorcism of the Abanat ice.

Chapter Nine

The next day, carrying his ice climbing equipment over his shoulder, Zed Yago stepped from the movalong that terminated at Abanat's westernmost street. At his back, the dawn sky was clear and brilliant. A hill of orange grass separated the city from the beach. He walked across it, feeling the tough grass bow but not crush beneath his weight. The beach sand was fine as talc. Even this early there were tourists on the dunes, wearing sunshades and skinscreen and not much else. In two hours, hundreds of them would be lying in the Chabadese sun, slathered with skinscreen. The beach, with its breezes, was about the only place you could stay outdoors on Abanat and not collapse from the heat.

Zed walked north until he came to a paved walkway and a metal gate. The sign on the gate said, PRIVATE. On the other side of the gate sat a dock with boats. Zed pushed the unlocked gate aside; a squatting man with a hammer looked up, nodded, and returned to his repair work. Over his bowed head the Abanat icebergs loomed, deceptively lovely, terribly bright.

Icebergs are bits and pieces of glaciers. Even on

Chabad there were glaciers, left from a period some twelve thousand Standard years ago, when most of Chabad except the equator had been covered with ice. Chabad's current climate was the result of a massive dust cloud through which the entire solar system had been passing since that time: the interstellar dust, remnant of some long-vanished star, lowered the albedo and raised the surface temperature of the planet.

Every year, portions of the polar ice sheets wormed equatorward, broke from the mother ice sheet, and tumbled into the sea. The first Abanat iceberg, Primo, had been transported from the southern pole in the sixty-seventh year of the then mining colony. Before its arrival the colonists' water had come from desalinated seawater, carefully rationed and recycled. In colony year sixty-one, a dilettante Leyvian chemist working in the free lab at Kroeber University on Nexus had discovered and refined a non-toxic substance which retarded melting. Painted on a surface, it insulated just about anything solid from the inevitable absorption of heat. The chemist patented his find, licensed it to Family Kyneth, and then retired to grow rhododendrons on Ley.

Family Kyneth hired a platoon of chemical engineers and explained what they needed to be able to do with the substance, named Antimelt. In preparation for the event, they built four immense ships, known collectively as the Floating Islands. During the next five years, bubblecraft flew out every polar spring, looking for bergs. A properly massive berg was located in the sixth year.

It was five hundred meters thick, six hundred and forty meters wide, and two-point-four kilometers long.

It had calved from the south pole's Komarkova Glacier, and was moving north with the current. The Floating Islands went to meet it. They aligned themselves along its southern width, laid their tremendous prows against its icy wall, and shoved. The berg moved. Once out of the flow of the current, they maneuvered it to a halt and brought out hoses and nozzles and wet suits and airtanks and twenty-two tanks of Antimelt. Crews painted the berg from above and sprayed it from below with the retardant. The process took four months. Coaxing it at last to Abanat, they headed the monster berg toward shore, where its underpart ran aground in the Abanat mud. Around it they constructed an artificial bay, a giant bowl, and festooned the berg with pipes and sluices to direct and capture the freshwater runoff. The friction of the water wore away the paint; the berg melted slowly at the littoral line. As its volume decreased, the berg lightened, lifting from the sea. Every five years or so—at public expense—Family Kyneth manufactured more Antimelt, and sent out a crew to reapply it.

Without Antimelt, Primo would have lasted perhaps five years before diminishing beyond use. It lasted forty-five. In the one hundred twelfth year of the colony's founding, Family Kyneth sent The Floating Islands south and culled two more bergs, one a little larger, the other a little smaller than the first. They were called Primo II and Secundo.

Dumping his equipment bag into the nearest boat, Zed clambered in and pointed the craft into the bay. Ahead of him the visible portion of Primo II glittered like milk glass. Secundo, south of it, had an aqua tinge. From beneath the boat's bow, water lifted upward in a fine spray. A seal, curious and fearless, popped up three meters away to look at him. Zed increased the boat's speed, and the light shell lifted until it skated the surface of the sea. Primo II, sleeping giant, muttered to itself as he approached. All icebergs did that; they boomed and hissed as their ice melted and reformed. Abanat's icebergs, melting slowly, were more silent than most.

He felt peaceful, loose, and light. He took the boat around to the southwest face of Primo II. There were no seals here; they preferred the gentle slopes of the east face. A dock, a path, and a long, low building disturbed the iceberg's surface. Zed tied the boat at the dock and walked, carrying his bag, into the building. "Loren," he called.

She came from one of the supply rooms, one leg dragging slightly from the spinal injury she had received the day, four years back, that, claw climbing, she had fallen from the ice. She could not climb, but she could walk. "Wondering when you'd get here," she said. "I heard the Net was back."

She was like Yuki, obsessive. For Loren Basami, life happened only on or around the ice.

"Anyone else up?" Zed asked.

"Two." She named them. They were both claw climbers. Zed wondered how many of them there were now. Thirty? He flexed his fingers. He had brought traditional ice climbing equipment: crampons, ice axe and hammer, screws and pitons, boots. But he had also brought his ice suit and claws. "How do you want to go?"

"Clawed," he said.

"You can leave the bag in cubicle nine," she said.

Following her to cubicle nine, Zed shook out the soft, furry folds of the ice suit and laid it on the single chair. He stripped, and, unsealing the suit, stepped into it. It molded around him from ankles to neck. He worked his hands into the suit's arms and into the flexible framework of the fingers. Except for the deceptively mild stiffness of the struts that held the claws in place, they felt very much like surgical gloves.

"You want a bandolier?" Loren said. Zed shook his head. "Rope?"

"No." He laced on his boots. She bent to check the lacings.

"Belt holsters," she suggested.

Zed frowned. Finally he decided to take axe and hammer with him. He might tire of the claws and need the tools. He took axe, hammer, crampons, and his iceshades from the bag, and nested the axe and hammer into the holsters. "All right," he said.

He followed Loren to the sound room. The heavy door, closing, sealed out extraneous sounds; the seals' barking, the clatter of passing boats, the *lip-lip* of water. The rhythms of their breathing seemed unnaturally loud. With total impersonality, Loren ran her fingers over the crotch of Zed's suit until she found the thumbnail size disk that led to the suit's power pack. She pulled a lead from the machine at her side and attached it to the suit. She nodded, and Zed said his name. Most ice climbers chose their own names to signal their claws; your own name was the one thing you would not shout by accident on the ice.

"Zed. Zed." His voice sounded strange, but that was because, in the sound room, it was unmingled with all other sounds. "Zed." He repeated it, whispering, shouting, speaking normally, until Loren signaled him to stop. She changed the wire's position. "Yago," Zed said. "Yago."

"Enough," Loren said. Detaching the lead, she
snapped the protective patch on the disc.

Zed extended his hands. "Zed." The claws slid out.
They were five centimeters long, light, rigid, very strong,
made of a steel-and-ceramic laminate. Zed's fingers
crooked to follow the curve. "Yago," he said. They
retracted. He repeated the ritual, changing his voice, and
the claws responded each time. "Good."

Loren said his name. The claws did not move. "All
right," she said. She opened the sound room door. They
walked out of the building. "Take trail four," she
directed.

"Right," Zed said. He had done it once, some years
ago, but by now it would have changed, as, beneath the
coating of Antimelt, compressed by the climbers, ice
shifted and reformed.

"If you don't come down by nightfall, we'll come get
you," she said. She always said that. Occasionally a
bubble did have to come and pick some exhausted climber
from the ice. But for a clawed climber, unpartnered,
unbelayed, there were only two ways down. One was to
reach the east face trail, where steps had been chopped
into the ice. The other was to fall.

"See you," said Zed. He walked to the trail marker,
and stopped at the foot of a blue, near-vertical wall. He
fastened his iceshades around his head and strapped the
crampons on his boots. Now his feet had claws: ten
pointing down, two pointing out of the toes of each boot.
Primo II towered over him, pitiless and stark. Its snow
cover had long gone, melted in its journey toward the
equator; what gleamed above him now, rucked and
crevassed and thousands of years old, was Chabad's polar
ice.

Beneath the ice, showing only occasionally on the
surface of the berg, lay the water system's pipelines. They
were set off by red markers, and the climbers stayed out
of their way. The pipelines halted a few meters above the
waterline. Nothing disturbed the ice above that point; not
sunlight, not the friction of an occasional storm wind, or
the great wreaths of fog that gathered around the ice
peaks and blew inland in gray plumes. Zed examined
what he could see of the trail. About twenty meters up
was a ledge. He could not see farther than that because of

the glitter in his eyes. Foolish to wait any longer, he thought, and his heart began to beat with increased strength. "Zed," he said. The claws slid out. He reached, chopping as high as he could into the frozen blue surface with his left hand. Kicking the front points of his right foot into the ice a meter up the face, he pushed upward, swinging his right hand at the ice. The claws gripped. He was up. He set his left front points in, leaned his weight on them, and worked his left-hand claws free of the ice. He reached upward, struck. Stepped and kicked his right foot. Ice climbing was not like rock climbing, where there were projections to cling to, boulders to grab, the safety and strength of rock. He leaned out, keeping his heels low and his muscles loose, snaking slowly up the milky blue wall, dancing on the tips of his fingers and toes. Despite the cooling breeze, it was hot—32° Celsius—and sweat slicked his skin within the ice suit. It was the best material ever developed for climbing ice: made of apton and kerit fur, it was supple, nearly weightless, and it fended off cold at the same time as it reflected back light.

But it was not perfect. Pressed against the ice, Zed's palms began to ache. More than once he hung by claws alone, kicking to get his front points more solidly into the ice. His forearms hurt. He should have started with axe and hammer. He should at least have taken rope and set up a belay. He told the thinking, doubting brain to shut up. Left hand. Right foot. Right hand. Left foot. Do it over again. Sweat stung his eyes till they burned. The interior of the ice suit was at body temperature; it would stay that way. His hands were numbing. He worked his way around a bulge so big he could not see around it. He knew what was on its other side: more ice. It rippled mercilessly overhead, as high as infinity. His foot slipped. He kicked it in again, went up another twenty centimeters, and found himself at the ledge.

It was a wide ledge, roomy enough to sit on and still have room to stand and turn around when it was time to start again. Zed waited for his hands to warm up. He wiped the sweat from his eyes, and before his head could tell him why he should stay on the ledge a little longer, just a little longer, he began climbing. He used the claws. He had gone from looseness to tension and now he was loose again. He felt as if his skin were soaking in a warm oil bath. The physical, the sensory, the real took hold of him like a great inexorable hand. It thrust him up the mountainside. He cursed the heat, the glare, the numbing cold that sealed his flesh to his bones. He couldn't feel his fingers. He looked down once.

The sea glittered like blue-green crystal below him.

The second ledge turned out to be sixty meters up. This ledge, too, was wide. Zed muscled onto it. "Yago," he said, and his claws slid back. He worked his cold, tired, and cramped hands forward and back, till the blood began to return to tingle and burn them. It was a welcome pain. His mouth quirked, and he leaned back against the adamantine ice face. Pain cleared the senses; it made the world seem bright and sharp. Zed wondered what Dana Ikoro would think of that.

For a price, there was a further refinement of ice climbing technology available on Chabad. The operation was tricky, but surgeon Ja Narayan had been known to do it. Zed knew two climbers who had had it done. The bones of the hands and forearms were removed, the flesh laid back, and artificial bone was joined to real bone. At the tips of the fingers, the artificial bones ended with retractable claws. The operation destroyed the feeling in the hands, and, when the claws were extended, the hands could not be closed.

At a party, Zed had heard some learned guest of Theo Levos discourse on "the ultimate egotism" of ice climbing. The speaker claimed that it was an unconscious confirmation and symbol of this egotism that a claw climber shouted her or his name over and over again at the ice. This, the philosopher remarked, revealed the fundamentally decadent nature of Chabadese society. The listening guests nodded, and refrained from pointing out that the speaker was the guest of a Levos, and was standing in the heart of that decadent society, being served by slaves, drinking decadently imported wine.

Zed had refrained from strangling the idiot. He asked the man if he had ever done any ice climbing. The answer had been, "No, certainly not!"

Zed grinned, remembering. He'd rarely heard anyone make less sense. After a very little time on the ice, the shouted name became meaningless, a noise without objective referent. It ceased to have an owner; it was just a word, unconnected.

He stood on the ledge. Glancing at his left wrist, he checked the small suit chronometer which told him how long he had been climbing. It did not surprise him to learn that he had been climbing for nearly three hours. His shoulders and forearms ached; he ignored them. A cool wind fanned his cheeks. He smelled the sharp, tangy scent of the ice. He said his name; the claws came out. He chopped his aching arm into the ice wall and stepped upward, setting the front points of his right foot.

He climbed.

At breakfast that morning, Rhani, remembering Zed's comment from the night before, waited for him to join her. Finally, when Amri came into the bedroom to remove the plates, she realized that he was not coming. "Amri, is my brother still asleep?" She said.

Amri shook her head. "No, Rhani-ka; his door is open. He isn't in the house."

"Do you know where he went?"

"No. But I think he left early this morning."

Corrios, padding up the stairs with the mail, said, "Yes."

"Do you know where he went, Corrios?"

"Ice," the big man said succinctly.

"Ah," Rhani said. She took the mail from the tray. She wondered what had happened at the party to send Zed to the ice. She doubted very much that it had been his conversation with Imre.

Could it have been meeting Ferris? She considered that, then shrugged. As she did so, her fingers encountered a letter with a crest on it.

It was from Ferris Dur. She opened it. It asked after her health and sent regrets that she had not come to the party. There was also a letter from the Abanat police. She tore it open quickly. Officer Tsurada wrote: *"We are having some difficulty in tracing the Free Folk of Chabad. They are either smaller than we thought, or more tightly organized. Only a few of our informers have even heard of them, and their information is sketchy and has proved largely useless."*

"Wonderful," Rhani said aloud.

"I beg your pardon, Rhani-ka?" said Binkie.

She looked up. "Good morning," she said. "I didn't

hear you walk in." She held the letter out to him. He perused it.

"I'm sorry, Rhani-ka," he said.

"So am I." She stretched. "Is there anything else in that pile that I should look at?"

He fanned through the rest of the letters. "They seem to be mostly invitations, Rhani-ka."

"Feh." She stretched again. Her body felt tense and light. Perhaps she had slept in an odd position. Rising, she paced around the room once. "Zed isn't here," she said to Binkie. "He's ice climbing."

He bowed his head. She wondered where Dana was. She had a swift, unexpected memory of his hand against her cheek, and shivered.

Turning to the intercom, she called him. "Dana!"

"Yes, Rhani-ka?"

"Come to my room, please." She stepped away from the intercom and smiled at Binkie. "Bink, I shall not need you this morning."

He bowed. "As you wish, Rhani-ka. I—" he hesitated, then said, "I have some errands to run in the city. May I—"

"Of course," she said. "Go ahead."

"Thank you," he said, and left. She heard Dana's step outside the room, and his voice, as he paused to give Binkie greeting. Did he want her? she thought. She thought so, yes. He came into the room. He was wearing a light gray jumpsuit, and the pale sheen of the fabric made his hair look even darker.

"You wanted to see me, Rhani-ka?" he said.

She smiled at him. "I wanted your company. Zed is ice climbing—" she watched him for a response, and was disappointed—"and I have a lot of work to do. I hoped you would sit with me."

He sat on the stool. "As you wish, Rhani-ka."

His obedience both pleased and annoyed her. Damn it, she thought, that's something Binkie would say. But then she remembered that Dana and Binkie had something important in common. She went to the com-unit, sat, and tapped in the information code for what she wanted. The screen blinked numbers and then said, IDENTIFY. She pressed her left thumb against the cool plastic.

Dana had come silently to stand at her side. "What are you doing?" he asked.

"I've requested a breakdown of our present storage and usage figures on dorazine. We have to allocate the limited supplies to serve the strongest need. At present the need is greatest in the Barracks: after the Auction the demand on our stores will drop, but if the situation does not change, we may have to start using one of the legal dorazine substitutes, although they are not as effective. Zed says the best of them is pentathine."

"I see," he said.

She was aware of everything about him: his arms, scant centimeters from her own, the set of his head, his eyes, dark as jet, his smell—it reminded her, somehow, of rainwater. Impulsively she asked, "Dana, where did you go the other day? The day I was so irritable."

She could see at once that it was not a good question, and almost wished she could call it back. He looked at the screen, and swallowed. "I went to the Landingport, Rhani-ka."

"Main Landingport?" she said. He nodded. "What happened?"

He bit his lower lip. "The alarms went off, and I was Caged."

She felt a rush of sympathy for him. "You didn't know that slaves are not permitted within Main Landingport."

"I should have known." His face worked. "I didn't think. Seeing the ships—I forgot I wasn't a Starcaptain."

"What happened when the Cage came down?" she asked, curious. Normally, she was only half-aware of the electronic net that sat shimmering above every gate. She had never seen anyone Caged.

"The guards drew their stuns. They questioned me. I—" he caught his breath—"played stupid. They logged my name through the computer and told me to get out."

"What do you mean, they logged your name?"

"They recorded that Dana Ikoro, a Yago slave, had been Caged at Abanat Landingport." His voice was even, but Rhani could hear the tension under it and understood what it was he would not say.

"Hmmph." She frowned, and then, slanting a look at him, ordered the com-unit to show her the Cage records logged at Abanat Landingport over the last two days. In a moment, a line of names winked on the screen. She ran through them: they were mostly tourists who had tried to get into Communications or Compsection with inadequate I.D., a belligerent crew member from one of the shuttleships, a drunk off the street—there. DANA IKORO, SLAVE, FAMILY YAGO SYSTEM #56488B. With care—she had never done this before—she directed the computer to expunge the record.

As she pressed her thumb to the screen, verifying her right to order this operation, Dana said, "What are you doing?"

"Clearing the record," she said. She leaned back in the chair. "Now if anyone—my brother, say—should look this information up, your name is no longer on it. You are Yago property; I can do that."

She had thought he would be pleased. But his face only grew more strained. "If your brother asks me," he said, "I have to tell him, just as I told you. How will I explain to him that the incident is not on the record, if he looks and does not find it there?"

"You will say I took it off for reasons of my own," Rhani said sharply.

He nodded. After a moment, he said, "Thank you." He sat on the stool. Rhani turned to the board and directed it to show her the dorazine figures again.

She could not but admire his self-control. She had not asked him why he had gone to Abanat Landingport: it might have been to watch the ships—and it might have been to look for a way offplanet. If that was what it was, she didn't want or need to know.

She concentrated on the figures on the screen. Right now, her concern was the Auction. There had to be enough dorazine for the Auction. After the Auction—she cued the screen to detail and asked the computer to break down the figures. How much of the dorazine allocated to the Auction was used there, and how much of it was actually used once the Auction was over, to quiet the slaves still in the holding cells?

Some. Not much. Nevertheless, pentathine could safely be substituted in those cases, and that would save—the computer added it up—almost five thousand unit doses. Good. She smiled, pleased, and turned to tell Dana what she had just discovered.

He was no longer on the stool. Instead, he was standing to one side of the window, gazing at the street. "What is it?" she asked.

He beckoned. Curious, she crossed to look out. "Don't stand in front of the window," he said. Puzzled, Rhani went to his side, and he moved back so that she could take his place. "There's a man in the park," he said. "I think he's watching the house."

Rhani tensed. "What man?"

"Look at the gate," he said, "then look left, about ten meters this side of the big tree. He's wearing brown." She gazed at the green jumble. All she could see was the children in their bright-colored clothes, no man. "I don't—" she began, and then did see him. He was staring fixedly at the house.

Despite herself Rhani stepped back. Angry, she said, "Who the hell is he?"

"I don't know," Dana said. "A wacko, perhaps." He tapped his temple. "Someone a bit crazy."

"In Founders' Green?" Rhani said. "How did he get through the gate?" She strode to the com-unit and, clearing the screen, told the computer to connect her with the Abanat Police Station.

"Officer Tsurada, please," she said when the communications clerk answered. "This is Rhani Yago; I have priority."

"Yes, Domna," said the clerk. The screen blanked.

"Is he still there?"

"Yes."

Fuming, Rhani waited for the screen to show her Sachiko Tsurada's face. Instead, the screen flashed VISUAL TRANS UNAV. PLEASE STANDBY. "I'm standing by," she muttered.

Sachiko Tsurada's voice sounded through the com-phone. "Domna, I'm patched through to you. How may I assist you?"

"Still there," said Dana at her back.

"There's a stranger in Founders' Green," Rhani said. "He appears to be watching the house, this house."

"Can you give me a physical description?"

Rhani scowled. "I can," Dana said.

"Do it," she said.

He crossed to the com-unit. "He's about 1.8 meters tall, pale skin, dark hair close-cropped to his skull, his clothes are brown with I think greenish trim—"

"Eyes?" said the com-phone.

"I can't see them, he's too far away." He glanced at the window. "Rhani-ka, maybe you'd better see if—"

"I will." She stood to one side of the window and gazed obliquely down. He was still there. Dana spoke with Tsurada for a moment and then joined her.

"Officer Tsurada says that there will be police along in five minutes to check his I.D."

"Good."

Five minutes seemed to take a long time. Finally, she saw four people wearing the cream-colored jumpsuits of the Abanat police force approach the gate. The watcher seemed unconcerned as they traversed the flagstone paths. Two of them converged on him. She saw him reach into a pocket and produce I.D.

"They must have a miniscanner," Dana said, with interest. "Or else—" He did not finish. Or else what? Rhani thought. After some conversation, the man walked quietly out between the two police officers. It all looked very calm and cordial. Unconcerned, the children played around the fountain.

The com-unit beeped. She crossed to it and punched the phone line. "This is Rhani Yago," she said.

"Domna, this is Leander Morel, Abanat police. You requested we examine the identification of a stranger who appeared to be watching your house."

"Yes, I did. Who is he?"

The man on the other end of the line cleared his throat. "Domna, he is a member of the Federation Police Force, Drug Division. We verified his identification and requested his name, but he refused to divulge it, something he has a legal right to do. We questioned him, but he informed us that he would answer no questions and that all inquiries as to his assignment should be directed to his chief, Michel A-Rae. We asked him to leave the park, which he did."

"A Hype cop!" Dana said.

Rhani gazed at the blank screen for a moment. "Thank you, Officer Morel," she said at last.

"Our pleasure, Domna. Anything else?"

She rubbed her chin. "Founders' Green is a private park. I don't like strangers there. Can we—" She let the sentence hang.

Morel cleared his throat again. "I'm sorry, Domna," he

said. "You can ask your lawyers, of course, but I don't think there's any way you can keep the bastards out."

Dana chuckled. Rhani grinned. "Thanks, then. No further business." She cleared the line. "The drug police," she said. "What the hell are the drug police doing, watching *my* house?"

Dana could not answer her.

Rhani asked the same question of Zed, that evening.

He had come from the iceberg just after noon, and had gone to his room saying only, "If anyone wakes me, it had better be for an emergency." His face was darkened on forehead and cheekbones, and he looked unbelievably weary. But in four hours he had awakened, ravenous, and strode into the kitchen to ravage Corrios' stores. He then showered, and joined Rhani in her room. As he entered the room, Dana—who was lying on the rug—scrambled up, tense. He had been sitting on the floor, absorbed in a booktape Rhani had given him.

But Zed simply nodded to him. Crossing to Rhani at the com-unit, he bent and lightly kissed the back of her neck. She turned in the chair. "Zed-ka." She smiled at him, face a softer mirror of his own, and he let his fingers trail along her cheek. Dana looked away.

"How was the climbing, Zed-ka?" Rhani said.

"Good," said Zed. He sat in the chair. "Very good." Dana looked at him curiously. He was tuned to Zed's mood; he could not help it. The Net commander sat with head thrown back, arms loose along the sides of the chair, throat exposed—Dana had never seen him so relaxed. He seemed sated, not with the intense sensual pleasure of another person's pain but with something deeper and less terrible. Suddenly his head moved: he looked at Dana, and grinned.

"Ever been ice climbing?" he said.

"No," Dana said. "Mountain climbing, on Pellin."

"Ah," said Zed. "Ice is different. You should try it sometime."

Rhani turned her chair to face him. "Zed-ka, the drug police were watching this house today."

Zed straightened. "What? Tell me." Rhani did so. Their faces gleamed in the soft lamplight, profiles matching. Dana listened and watched, marveling at how alike they were, and how unalike.

Zed tapped his fingers on the chair arm. "I wonder why they bothered," he said. "They can't think you invite your suppliers to your home."

"I don't know," Rhani said. "If I could find someone willing to sell me dorazine, I might." She bent over the com-unit. "Zed-ka, let me show you what I did today."

Rising, Zed went to peer over her shoulder. Figures flashed in green across the screen. "If we substitute pentathine for dorazine here, here, and here," Rhani said, "we can save sixteen thousand unit doses over the next three months." She cited figures. Dana's attention wandered.

He glanced at the viewer in his hand. The booktape Rhani had given him was a Nexus historian's *History of Chabad.* He was surprised she even owned it, since the historian made no pretense at objectivity: he was venomously anti-slavery. A sentence from it ran through Dana's mind. *"The wealth and febrile pleasures of the tourist-minded aside,"* Nakamura had written, *"Chabad is and remains a prison. None of its citizens are free: some are slaves, the rest, jailers. This latter category includes the members of the so-called Four Families."*

He had glanced through the index for references to the Yagos, but found none about Rhani, Zed, or the Net. He grinned, thinking of what wonderfully nasty things Nakamura would have said about the Net.

"Dana," said Zed's voice above him, "what are you doing?"

Dana snapped the viewer off. "Reading, Zed-ka," he said. Zed reached toward him, and the pulse began to hammer in his throat.

"Let me see."

Dana relinquished the viewer. Zed turned it on, advanced the pages, and chuckled. "Nakamura! Where did you find this?"

"I gave it to him," said Rhani.

"Having institutionalized a pernicious, retrograde system and made of it an economically stable one, Chabad and her sister worlds in Sardonyx Sector defended that system to the Federation diplomats through a series of legal rationalizations," Zed read. "Nakamura is so pompous when he thinks he's right," he said, dropped the viewer

on Dana's lap. "I'd bet Michel A-Rae loves him. Rhani, don't you have a file on Michel A-Rae?"

"Certainly." Rhani instructed the com-unit. "Here it is."

He read it over her shoulder. "He's young for his position; he's only twenty-eight. An Enchantean, trained in police work on Santiago in Carnelian Sector and on Old Terra. That's interesting. Trained in the drug unit on Nexus. Hmm. Also trained as a Hype navigator but never finished—Dana!"

"Yes, Zed-ka."

"Could you have known him?"

Dana frowned, turning the name in his mind. "I don't think so. Is there a picture of him?"

"Come and look," said Zed. Dana rose, leaving the viewer on the rug, and went to stand behind the com-unit chair.

He gazed at the photo on the screen. Dark hair, dark eyes, his skin the chocolate-brown typical of many Enchanteans. . . . Dana shook his head. "He looks like a lot of people," he said.

"Yes," Zed agreed.

Rhani read from the file. "Family connections unknown; personal history unavailable due to I.D. ex. What is I.D. ex?"

"I.D. exchange," Zed said. "Where does it say that? When did he do it?" He bent forward eagerly, scanning the file.

"What does it mean?" Rhani demanded.

Dana said, "It means he changed his name."

"Oh."

Zed said, "He was how old—eighteen? Stars. His family must have *loved* that. He took his majority money and told them to fuck off. Where did he go? Ah, Nexus. Then Santiago and Old Terra, and back to Nexus again." Zed grinned. "I knew some folks on Nexus who'd made three or four name changes."

Dana nodded; so had he.

"Can you do that?" Rhani said.

"Sure. You apply for it at Compcenter. They verify you have no intent to defraud, take all your money, give you ten percent of it or the amount of your majority money, whichever is less, and change your name, removing all trace from their records of the person you were and of the change."

"Why do people do it?" Rhani asked.

Dana and Zed looked at each other. "To escape the past," Zed said. "To obliterate all traces of a person you no longer desire to be. . . ." He stepped away from the com-unit.

"I want to know who Michel A-Rae was," Rhani said.

Zed picked up the viewer from the rug. He turned it on and off again. "I don't see how you can, Rhani-ka. The legal record no longer exists."

Dana said, "Maybe his name will tell you something."

Rhani said, "Of course! All Enchantean names are formal. Now, what does 'A-Rae' signify?" She punched instructions to the com-unit. Zed crossed to her. The three of them stared at the screen.

"A-Rae. Unclassified name, believed invented. Pun on Enchantean local dialect. Means 'no one.'" Rhani snorted and blanked the display. "Well." She rested her hands on her lap. "How remarkably useless." She swiveled the chair. "I'm hungry. Dana, will you tell Corrios we'd like to eat, please?"

"Yes, Rhani-ka."

Dana found himself wondering who Michel A-Rae had been. If A-Rae had not been there in Sardonyx Sector, driving away the dorazine trade, then he, Dana Ikoro, would have slipped unremarked onto Chabad's moon. It was A-Rae's doing that he had been brought to the attention of Zed Yago. Bastard, he thought, sanctimonious, fanatic—he heard himself fuming, and laughed.

"Glad you've got something to laugh about," said Binkie sourly. He was sitting in the kitchen, gnawing at some bread and cheese.

Dana ignored him. "They want to eat," he said to Corrios. The big man nodded, eyes unreadable behind his sunshades.

"Has Rhani asked for me?" Binkie said.

"No," Dana said. And then, because though he did not like the pallid secretary, they had something in common, he said, "Zed's back from the ice."

"I figured," said Binkie.

Dana went to the dining alcove. Amri sat there, playing with a three-dimensional game. She turned it this way and that, trying to make the counters fall through holes. "Can you do this?" she asked as he approached, holding the layered cube out to him.

"Nope," he said. "Rhani wants to eat, kitten."

"Oh," She laid the game aside. "I'd better make this room ready. Why do you call me that?"

He shrugged. "A nickname. Don't you like it?"

She smiled at him. "I like it." Hair like a blown cloud around her head, she went into the kitchen.

While Zed and Rhani ate, Dana, Corrios, and Amri stayed in the kitchen: Corrios to watch and Amri to serve the meal, Dana because he liked keeping Amri company. After dinner, he went to his room. He had just put Stratta's "Fugue for Three Flutes" in the auditor when the door of the room opened suddenly and Zed walked in.

Dana froze, sweat prickling the back of his neck. Memories of the last time Zed had come to his room were unpleasantly fresh in his mind. Zed gestured to the auditor. Dana shut it off. The Net commander grinned at him. "Relax." He tossed something underhand onto the bed. It was the viewer, with the booktape still inside it. "Rhani mentioned at dinner that you were the one who noticed the watcher in the park," Zed said.

"Yes, Zed-ka."

"That was good. It occurred to me that the Hype cops may not be satisfied with hanging around in the parks. How good are you at noticing a shadow?"

Dana licked his lips. "I don't know," he said.

Zed snorted. "You were a smuggler, Dana. You know enough to look behind you."

"Yes," Dana said. "But it's easier to spot a shadow in the Hyper district—"

"I know," said Zed. "But when Rhani goes out, I want you to watch. A-Rae might be having her followed."

"Or you," Dana said.

Zed nodded. "Or me. Thank you for reminding me. We don't know what he wants, after all. Maybe he thinks I'll lead him to the Yago drug dealer." He grimaced. "One thing I'll say for A-Rae, he isn't subtle." He stepped back. "Good night."

"Good night," Dana said, astonished. Zed's footsteps echoed down the hall. Night, Dana thought, night was the safe time. . . . Memories of the Net engulfed him, and he shivered.

He closed the door firmly, and turned on the auditor again. "Fugue for Three Flutes" filled the room. Dimming the lights, he undressed. The sheets were fragrant and cool; as he slid between them, Dana thought of Rhani, Rhani and Zed. She had said specifically that they had not been lovers. She's beautiful now—she must have been lovely at seventeen, he thought.

He closed his hands to fists, remembering the warm, liquid touch of her tongue on his palm. She wanted him; he knew it, and it terrified him, knowing that if Zed found out about it, it could cost him his sanity, if not his life. He assumed she usually took lovers when Zed was on the Net. What must that be like for him? Ridiculous to feel sympathy for Zed Yago—but he recalled the moment in the bedroom that afternoon, when Rhani asked why people changed their names, and Zed had answered, "To obliterate all traces of a person you no longer desire to be."

He turned out the lights. Now the only illumination was the city light seeping through the window. The house was still. Stratta's flutes wove fluid serene patterns. Dana wondered where Tori Lamonica was now. He let breath hiss through his teeth, thinking of the Hype, the vast, vertiginous darkness wreathed in hieroglyphs of ruby dust, and him with his ship vibrating beneath his feet. . . .

He shifted to lie on his side. Now he could not see the window. Rhani Yago. If she wanted him—well, she could have him. He was her slave. And maybe, if he pleased her enough, maybe she would free him.

Maybe.

Chapter Ten

The morning of the day before the Auction, Abanat children flew kites.

Rhani could see the kites out her washroom window. As she dried her face, she watched them dance in motley array and imagined them to be a flock of birds. There were all different colors and styles of kites to be seen: box kites, parafoils, lozenge kites, parawings, dragons, skates, Musha kites: many were silver with the blue "Y" imprinted on them. The Yago Bank had been giving those away all week. The children were gathered on the brown-red lump of a hill known as the Barrens; Rhani could just make them out, dark figures against the northeast sky, dressed in bright reflective colors as if they were mimicking the kites.

She had not flown kites on the Barrens the day before the Auction. Other children did that; Yagos did not. She walked out of the washroom to her bedroom. Amri was waiting for her, holding in her small arms a length of silver cloth. Taking it from her, Rhani twisted it about herself in stylized folds.

Amri watched, rapt. "That's beautiful, Rhani-ka," she murmured.

"Thank you," Rhani said. "It's called a *sari*. The style of it comes from Old Earth." She had learned to wear it from her mother, who had learned to wear it from her mother, Orrin, and Orrin from Irene, and Irene from Lisa Yago. Originally, it was worn over a tight-fitting, short-sleeved blouse. But the blouse was binding, and Rhani chose to do without it. The fabric was apton; sleek and light. She tucked the final folds of it around her waist, and swirled the long trailing end of it up about her head. "Where's the pin I set out this morning?" she asked. Amri picked it from the table. Rhani let the end of the cloth drape over her shoulder, and stood still to let Amri secure it with the simple silver pin.

Around her neck she hung Zed's gift, the pendant with the miniature stun charge. Her hair was tightly braided into a cap on her scalp. As she turned toward the dressing alcove, a knock on the door told her that Dana had arrived. "Tell Dana he may come in."

He was wearing the clothes she had instructed Binkie to have made for him: dark blue trousers, a dark blue tunic, sandals, all very plain. He was wearing sunshades pushed to the top of his head. "Good day," she said to him.

"Good morning, Rhani-ka," he said. His voice was stiff. She frowned, wondering—ah. He was not wearring the earrings.

"Did Binkie not give you the earrings?" she said.

He held out his right hand. The sapphire clusters lay on his palm. "I don't want to wear them."

She rubbed her chin. "Why not?"

He said, "Hypers wear earrings. On Nexus it's an insult for anyone not a Hyper to walk the streets wearing earrings, or any other kind of jewelry."

Rhani said, "This isn't Nexus, and anyway, you are a Starcaptain."

"I am a slave," he said.

Exasperated, Rhani scowled at him. This was the man who, on the way to Sovka, had said defiantly, "I am a Starcaptain." Had Zed been tormenting him? She was sure not. Gently she said, "We do not keep such custom in Abanat. It would please me if you would put the earrings on."

He bowed. "As you wish, Rhani-ka."

She turned in a circle, wanting him to notice her. "What do you think?" she said.

"The cloth is beautiful!"

Nettled, she glared at him. He pretended not to see it. Damn it, why would he not look at her? "Close your eyes," she ordered. He obeyed, eyelids trembling slightly. She gestured to Amri. The girl trotted into the dressing alcove and emerged, carrying the black wig. Rhani sat on the stool and Amri fitted it over her scalp. It was light as a hat; the hair was artificial, but so fine that it felt natural. It hung just past her waist. She swung her head from side to side, and hair swept across her neck, shoulders, and back. Dana's eyes were still closed. She said to him, "You may open your eyes."

He did, and focused on her. She grinned and spun in a circle; the hair made a sweeping arc. "Well?" she said.

He said, "Are wigs Abanat custom, or a Yago adaptation?"

"I had it made years ago," she said. "It was just a whim."

Dana wondered what lover she had last beguiled with the toy. The black hair deepened the tint of her skin to bronze. The pendant gleamed against her throat, and the silver cloth wrap she wore hugged her like a second skin. He said honestly, "*You* are beautiful, Rhani-ka."

She smiled. "I thank you." She slipped her feet into a pair of waiting silver sandals. "I'm ready. Let's go."

Amri went ahead of them down the stairs. She went to the slaves' hall, and Dana heard her open one of the storage bins. She returned with two parasols; Dana took them both, assuming he was expected to hold Rhani's for her, but she took it from his hand. Binkie and Corrios were standing near the door. "I'll be back after noon," she said to them. "Zed is at the Clinic, and I expect he will be there till late in the evening."

"Yes, Rhani-ka," said Binkie. Corrios nodded.

"I'm at Dur House, of course. If you must reach me there, send a live messenger. Don't use the com-unit."

Binkie said, "Yes, Rhani-ka."

Corrios opened the door. Rhani snapped her parasol open and up as she stepped into the light. It made a circle of shadow at her feet. She squinted, and half-turned back to the house. "My sunshades."

Dana got them. Corrios closed the door. They went down the steps and across the street into Founders' Green. Dana glanced around but if anyone was watching them he could not see it. There were few people in the fenced-in park. They traversed it, exited through the gate, and turned west to walk along the Boulevard. Rhani's wig made Dana nervous; it was as though he walked with a stranger, who might vanish at any time.

As if she had read his thought, she slipped her arm through his. "Don't get lost," she said.

The sunlight battered the parasols. Strolling slowly in the heat, they passed a row of ornate, curlicued gates. People rode the movalongs, passing those who chose to walk. Silver-sided bubblecraft, rotors whirring, hovered like giant birds over the city. They crossed a market square: a naked man balanced on a tightrope wire above their heads. A woman with a blue bottle in her hand was sitting beneath a tree, singing. A peddler waved sticks of self-igniting incense: the smoke made Rhani sneeze. In the center of the square stood a fountain: water spurted out of a shallow pool through and over the frame of a geodesic dome.

"That looks like fun," Dana said.

Rhani nodded. "Once in a while, when Isobel wasn't home, Corrios used to take us, Zed and me, to play in the fountain. It was fun."

He wondered what kind of childhood she had had, if fun was something she could only have in her mother's absence. He could not ask that—not yet. But he could ask, perhaps, about another thing. "May I ask you something?"

Her arm tightened on his. "Go ahead."

"Corrios has no tattoo scar."

"Corrios was never a slave."

"Then why is he on Chabad? There are plenty of worlds he could live on which get less sunlight."

"He chose to stay," Rhani said. "He was born on Chabad. He has worked for Family Yago for fifty years, since he was fourteen."

"That makes no sense."

"Perhaps not," said Rhani. "Corrios was born sixty-odd years ago to one of my mother's slaves. Such things do happen. By Chabadese law, a child born to a slave becomes a ward of whatever person or Family owns the parent who claims it. His mother claimed him. Corrios was brought up by Family Yago. At the termination of her contract, his mother chose to stay on Chabad. Isobel offered to make a formal transfer of wardship, but the woman refused. She wanted no part of her son. Corrios stayed at the Yago estate. At fourteen he became an adult and asked Isobel if he could stay at the estate, to work. He did Cara's job, he was cook, he was steward. When I was ten, Isobel made him caretaker of the Abanat house. He is well paid; he can afford passage to anywhere in the Living Worlds. He doesn't want to go. I have asked him."

Dana said, "It sounds incredible."

Rhani said, "I don't see why. It's not a bad life, even for an albino on this planet, working for Family Yago." She smiled. "The manager of the Yago Bank told me he can trace his family's service to mine back through five generations."

She spoke as if such loyalty was to be expected. He realized that she was used to being deferred to, served, by other people. She had Cara, Immeld, Corrios, Timithos, Amri, himself, even Zed, as accessories. She seemed to have no friends, unless the people she saw at parties were friends. And Binkie. It was easy to forget about the silent secretary. He moved softly; he rarely spoke unless Rhani spoke to him. And Rhani thanked him, and used him as ruthlessly as she used one of the household machines.

He wanted to ask about Binkie, about Amri. But he did not think—how strange Chabadese etiquette was—that she would tell him about them; they, unlike Corrios Rull, were slaves. "Doesn't that wig make your head hot?" he asked. He was sweating beneath his clothes.

"A little." She shook her head, and the hair moved. "It's very finely woven."

They went by a musician bending over drums, and their steps quickened to the rhythm of the drumbeats. "In Abanat, do you often have daytime parties?"

"No." Rhani smiled. "Maybe Ferris Dur wants to start a fashion. Family Dur is the First Family of Chabad, and other Families follow its lead in social matters, sometimes."

"Does Family Yago give parties?" he asked.

"Of course. This year it's planned for six days after the Auction." She glanced sideways at him. "You know that the Auction is tomorrow."

"I know," he answered.

His tunic was sticking to him. He started to ask where they were going when he saw, beyond the pastel walls of smaller houses, a huge barrackslike house made of gray stone. "Dur House?" he said. Rhani nodded. A red-and-gold flag fluttered over its entrance. There was a design on the flag: an axe, single-edged, short-handled, poised to strike.

"The Dur crest," Rhani murmured. As if quoting, she added, "If you oppose the axe, it cuts."

The front door of the house was open. A slave stood like a statue in the entrance. From the other side of the Boulevard, a small crowd of people approached the steps to the house, all finely dressed, all carrying parasols. Dana counted nine of them. Leading the group was a small, spare man beside a statuesque woman with glorious, flame-colored hair. Rhani halted. "That," she said softly, "is Imre and Aliza Kyneth, and their children." Unobtrusively she slid her hand from his arm.

Dana expected her to wave or call to them. But, with a twist to her mouth that reminded him suddenly, vividly, of Zed, she stood politely aside, as if waiting for the procession to pass. The small man inclined his head toward her, acknowledging the deference. Then he stopped on the first step and turned around. "Is that—Rhani?"

She grinned. "Good day, Imre. I was hoping that you

wouldn't recognize me so that I could tease you later."

The red-haired woman laughed. "That's quite a disguise," she said, and bent to kiss Rhani's cheek. "How nice to see you, my dear. Are you well?"

"Yes, thank you, Aliza," Rhani said. "I am sorry that I missed your party." She nodded to the tall woman behind the man. "Margarite."

"Domna."

"Shall we go in?" Imre Kyneth said. He gestured Rhani to go ahead of him. She lifted the long skirt of her gown from the front and snapped closed the sheltering parasol.

Dana took it from her. He did not know what to do; should he follow at the tail of the Kyneth procession? She seemed to sense his confusion. "Stay near me," she murmured, in the middle of a sentence addressed to Aliza Kyneth. A lot of people were pressing up the steps. A pale man with black, short hair was greeting people in the doorway. He wore red-and-gold—Ferris Dur, Dana thought. He watched Ferris greet Rhani; he held out both hands, and seemed to want to talk with her. She said something light to him, pressed his hands, and moved on.

Dana stayed at her elbow. Once inside the house, his job changed somewhat; he became escort, and ceased to be bodyguard. Rhani put her hand on his arm as they stepped into a hallway. Music flowed from somewhere; he heard the tinkle of bells, and a stringed instrument playing in minor tones. About seven meters ahead of them a voice said loudly, "Look at that, will you?" The hall grew suddenly, inexplicably cold. The crowd moved forward to a narrow room in which the walls were pearly-white. . . . "It's ice!" said the same voice. Dana looked around, and then up. All four walls and the ceiling of the room had been coated with ice.

Here and there, curtains were drawn back to allow bright bands of sunlight to wink through to the room. The sunlight seemed to have no effect on the ice. Slaves circulated through the room carrying trays with different kinds of wine. Dana said, "Rhani-ka, do you want me to stay with you all the time?"

Under the black wig the angles of her face looked different. "No. But be where I can find you if I need you." A woman with feathers in her hair greeted Rhani, stepping between them. Dana stood by uneasily. He felt embarrassingly conspicuous. He couldn't see how to obey her without turning into an obstacle for every person in the room to walk around.

The babble of voices grew loud, as more people poured in from the hall. There were adults here, no children, except for a slender white-gowned girl, and the curly-haired Kyneth boy, who appeared to be about ten years old. A woman with blue eyes stopped to stare him up and down. He recognized Charity Diamos. He followed Rhani to another room with wood-paneled walls. He realized he was not alone. There were slaves all over the house, serving food, carrying drinks, standing like statues at their owners' elbows; the Chabadese paid no more attention to them than they did to the sunlight. Rhani beckoned. He went to her. She told him to get a drink for the woman she was talking to. He relaxed. He was invisible, to everyone but Rhani. He delivered the glass. His only worry was that he would lose sight of her and be unable to find her again because of her disguise.

He was not totally invisible. Leaning against a pillar, he felt a long-fingered hand grope slowly, intimately down his thigh; in the crush of people he could not even tell whose it was. The pungent odor of marijuana swam through the jumbled scents of wine. Within the two rooms he estimated there were close to two hundred people. The rooms were getting hot. Dana wondered what would happen when the ice walls started to melt. It was hard to stay detached among this many people. . . . He gazed at one of the windows; through it he could see the brave flutter of kites riding the currents of the sky.

The longing for escape, for freedom, for the Hype rose in him, and he clamped hard on it. He turned to face the party, looking for Rhani. He did not see her. Squinting, he turned in a circle, looking for black hair topping silver cloth. He found Imre Kyneth, Aliza Kyneth, Margarite Kyneth, even Charity Diamos—no Rhani. His throat began to dry. She might have tired of the wig, and removed it. Prowling through the two rooms, he looked for russet hair and silver cloth. He found three people in silver, but none of them was Rhani. He grabbed the arm of a nearby slave. "Have you seen Domna Rhani Yago?" The slave shook his head, smiling an unnerving dorazine smile.

She had to be in the house. He circled both rooms again. He felt trapped between the ice walls. He could not find her. His bladder ached. Surely she could not be in danger, not in this house. . . . Maybe she had gone to another floor. He watched the slaves with food trays until he located the door to the kitchens. Toiling cooks ignored him as he walked through it. He found a stairway leading up, and took it. Glancing upward at the curving hallways, he wondered if he would find his way back, and then laughed at himself. He was a Starcaptain, a navigator in the Hype. There was no chance, on this world or off it, that he was going to get badly lost!

Rhani sat on the edge of a chair in Ferris Dur's bedroom.

She wanted, very much, to be somewhere else. This was the room that had been Domna Sam's. It reeked of candlewax. She gazed at it. Ferris had changed it: the bed, with its red-and-gold drapes, was the only piece of furniture in the room that had been there while Domna Sam was alive. She had died in it. Everything else was new: chairs, com-unit, and desk, and all was made of metal, foam, and plastic. Ferris perched on a chair of extruded black foam, wearing red-and-gold. It looked incongruous. He had even retiled the floor, in black tiles. Rhani wished that he had left the place alone.

She wondered what he had done with the black kerit fur rug. It had been a gift from Orrin Yago to Samantha Dur, at Ferris' birth. A black kerit was the equivalent of an albino on Chabad. They did not survive in the wild, but the Sovka breedery nurtured a special strain. They were the fur market's greatest prize.

Ferris said, "Rhani, have you had time to consider my proposal?"

Reluctantly Rhani turned her attention to him. It was hard to keep out the memories of the last time she had been here. Domna Sam had been lying in the great canopied bed, face a mottled blue, surrounded by support systems and oxygen tanks, an old woman who would not admit that she was dying. . . .

"Have you?" he said.

She said, "I am still considering it, Ferris."

"But you have not rejected it," he said.

"Not yet."

"Good." He leaned back in the foam chair. Even in this room he looked awkward, Rhani reflected, but less so. Maybe he would grow into it.

"How are things at Gemit?" she asked.

He blinked. "How are things at Sovka?" he countered.

"Quite well," she said. "I was there on an inspection tour a few days ago. What problems there were appear to have been solved."

"I am glad for you," he said. "Gemit is presently in turmoil. But it will resolve itself. I don't know if you heard—we had a serious accident, several people injured."

Rhani stared at him. Why was he telling her this?

He smiled—it made his pouty face seem rather attractive. "It seems strange to be talking honestly, doesn't it?" he said. "I am trying to get us both accustomed to thinking of each other as allies."

Of course. Rhani rubbed her chin. She contemplated telling him—it could not hurt, now that the problem was solved—about the kerit kits. But he had spies in Sovka and would know it. . . . "How are your dorazine stores?" she said casually.

He pleated the silk over his knee. "Somewhat depleted. My agents tell me they have been having difficulty buying."

"It's planet-wide," Rhani said. "The new head of the drug division of the Federation Police is a fanatic antislaver. He's been concentrating all his forces in this sector."

"I see," he said.

It was almost like sex, like foreplay, this cautious testing. Sex—Rhani frowned, and then smoothed her face quickly. She did not want to have sex with Ferris Dur, even to have a child.

"Rhani," he said. She glanced at him. He was standing, leaning over her. She had not heard him move. "I hope you will not find it necessary to consider too much longer." His voice was almost pleading. She wished he would sit down, she disliked having to look up to people. Why, she wondered, was this so important to him? It could not be because of the business arrangement; he was not financially minded. . . .

Was it, she wondered, that he wanted her to tell him what to do? He was used to that, after all; he'd lived most of his life with Domna Sam standing at his elbow. She rose. He did not step back. Instead, he put his hands on her shoulders.

The black metal chair trapped her; she could not move back. "Ferris!" she said sharply. His fingers slid wetly over her bare skin. Angry, she tried to pull away from him, and he poked his face at hers, jerked her toward him, and, with graceless haste, pressed his lips on hers and stuck his tongue into her mouth.

She tore away from him, furious. "Damn it, Ferris, let me go!" she said. But he had already let go, and stood now irresolute and pale, hands opening and closing.

"I thought—" he began.

"You didn't think!" she said. She rubbed her lips.

He glared at her, petulant again. "You don't have to shout."

Sweet mother, she thought, he's like a child. Suddenly, behind her, she heard the sound of a door opening, and a familiar, welcome voice said, "Rhani-ka?"

Ferris, pale face reddening, glared over her head. "You were not summoned," he said. "Get out!"

Rhani said, "No. Stay." She turned around, smoothing the cloth over her breasts. The black wig had slipped, straggling fake hair over her right eye, and she adjusted it.

Dana said, "Domna, I'm sorry to disturb you. Binkie sent a messenger. You're needed at the house."

His face was shuttered, the perfect mask, but Rhani thought she detected amusement there. Did it please him to see her embarrassed? Ferris had regained his poise, what there was of it. "My regrets, Domna, that you have to leave."

"I am sorry," she said, glacial. "I will be in touch with you soon, Domni."

They went down a kitchen stairway. Dana stayed a pace behind her. At the foot of the steps, she waited until he was level with her. "Was there really a message?"

Behind the decorous look, she was sure that he was smiling. "No, Rhani-ka. That was a lie."

She nodded. "We'll leave anyway," she said. He bowed, and slid the kitchen door aside for her. They walked through the ice-walled parlor. It was largely empty; the guests had gathered in the wood-paneled room for the entertainment. Finger bells tinkled and a dancer came in, body slick with oil, naked except for a sequined loincloth snaking around muscular thighs.

The Boulevard was bare and hot. Rhani remembered their sunshades and parasols. She did not want to go back for them. It was close to noon; after the entertainment the slaves would serve a lunch: salads and cold fish and pickled greens and ices. She glanced at Dana, strolling quietly by her side, and wondered what he had seen or heard or guessed. She had no idea how long he had been outside the door. She slid her arm through his. "He wants to marry me," she said.

He sniffed. "That man?"

"His *name* is Ferris Dur," she said, "and he is head of the First Family of Chabad. You'd do well to remember it."

He said, "I beg your pardon, Rhani-ka. I meant no disrespect."

The sun blazed on the white pavements. "What are you thinking?" she asked. He did not answer, and she stopped. He faced her. "Tell me."

He smiled. "I was thinking that in bed he looks as if he would be—unimaginative."

His eyes looked very dark in the brilliant noon light. Coldly, Rhani said, "It would be a business arrangement."

"I see," he said. He coughed. "Are you going to tell your brother about his unbusinesslike conduct?"

Rhani frowned, and turned to walk again. "You mean, am I going to tell Zed that Ferris kissed me and that I didn't like it?" She watched their shadows moving almost directly underneath them. "No. Zed would flay him, or want to."

"Or me," Dana pointed out quietly, "for letting it happen. I'm your bodyguard."

"Even Zed could not expect you to throw yourself between us," Rhani said tartly. Sweat slithered from beneath the wig and dried on her neck. "I hadn't planned to tell him."

The air tasted coppery with the intense heat. The house banners hung limply, looking sodden. Three people, arms about each other, stumbled slowly down the Boulevard.

One of them, a woman with a blue bottle in her hand, was singing. The tune wavered, off key. "Drunks," Rhani muttered, disgusted. She watched them fold up onto the pavement, giggling. The singer peered at her as she and Dana came abreast of them; she was moaning the words of a popular song.

"Rhani-ka," Dana said, his voice clipped, "let's walk this way—" Gently, he tugged her to the center of the street. The drunks were still staring at her. Suddenly the woman raised her arm and brought the bottle smashing down on the stone. The sound was shocking. Dana shouted as the woman leaped to her feet. She no longer looked drunk. The jagged glass gleamed in her right hand.

Rhani screamed. Hands gripped her shoulders; Dana half-lifted her and threw her to one side. The woman was coming toward her. She caught her balance in time to see Dana kick the bottle into the air. It glittered in the sun and shattered to bits on the ground.

Dana dived at the woman and brought her to her knees. He hit her on the side of the head, hard. The other two drunks were on their feet and running toward him. One of them swerved and came at Rhani. Gasping, she dodged his outstretched hands. The man's features seemed huge and monstrous in the distorting light. She heard Dana swear, and the sound of someone falling. The man grinned and came at her again, and she turned and ran, frightened and furious that she had to run, that she had never learned to fight.

A weight hit her back. She slammed down on the stone. Pain skewered her right shoulder, and she screamed. Her attacker cursed her and pinned her wrists behind her, and she screamed again at the agony lancing through her right shoulder and arm.

"Yago bitch!" the man growled. She heard footsteps near her ear. The man yelped and released her wrists. She heard heavy breathing and the scrabble of feet on stone. She sobbed, not daring to move. Something clinked beneath her: it was the pendant with the stunner that Zed had given her. I could have—I should have—her thoughts moved slowly. A shadow stooped over her, and she stiffened.

"It's me," Dana said. He was breathing hard.

"Where—?" she asked.

"They ran," he said. "They're gone. Are you hurt?"

Rhani tried to turn. She couldn't use her right arm. It seemed strengthless, sickened with pain. She sat up. There was a bleeding scrape on Dana's cheekbone. "My shoulder hurts," she said, and gagged as Dana's fingers probed lightly along her neck and down her collarbone.

"Dislocated," he said. Without warning, he grabbed the shoulder with one hand and with the other pulled and twisted the dangling useless arm. She screamed again; tears sprang into her eyes. The shoulder throbbed. Dana put his arm around her. "All right, that's done."

"What did you do?"

"Put it back in place." She wriggled her fingers. They moved. Tentatively she swung the arm. "Can you stand?" he said. He helped her to her feet. The brooch on her shoulder had opened, but miraculously it had stayed in the cloth instead of driving itself into her flesh. The careful folds of the sari had unraveled. Fingers trembling, she wound them back about her. Dana said again, "Come on."

"Your face—" She reached to touch the blood.

"It's nothing, it'll keep. Damn it, Rhani, stop shaking and walk! We've got to get you home."

She had lost her sandals. Barefoot, she staggered. Dana kept his arm around her. She couldn't stop shaking; it was noon on Chabad and she was shivering with cold. It's shock, she told herself. The blood made a starry pattern on Dana's cheek. She would have to call the police. Her stomach churned. Anger overwhelmed fear. She had been attacked in Abanat, her city, on a street whose contours she knew as well as she knew her own hand. Her breathing steadied. She wondered if, by some luck, Zed would have finished at the Clinic early. He might even be home.

They rode the movalong to Founders' Green. At the edge of the park, looking into that soft green wildness, Rhani's fear returned. "I can't go in there," she said. "I won't go in there."

Dana nodded. Tersely he said, "Better not." They climbed the steps. Rhani's feet were sore. She was shaking with fatigue. The door opened before they reached it, and Corrios came out to the step. Before she could speak, he bent and swept Rhani up in his arms. She put her head on his shoulder. His bulk was comforting. Swinging around, he carried her into the front hall.

The feel of the house restored Rhani's strength. Corrios seemed ready to carry her to her room. "Put me down," she said. She ignored the dull throbbing pain spreading in her right side. Amri and Binkie hovered near her. "I'm all right. Dana has a cut on his face. Amri, bring us something to drink, and run a bath for me. Binkie, leave a message at the Clinic for Zed. No specifics, just say that I want him to call. And then get me a line to Officer Tsurada of the Abanat police." She walked upstairs without help. Binkie babbled fatuously beside her: *Was she hurt, had she been alone, did she want a medic?* "Of course I wasn't alone," she said. "Dana was there." She stripped off the torn, dirty sari and put on her robe.

The pendant bounced on her neck. Stupid, she told herself. You could have used it, at least. Irritated, she took it off. Amri brought a tray with a pitcher and glass, and went to run her bath. She was snuffling. Binkie leaned over the com-unit, struggling for self-control.

"Rhani-ka," he said huskily, "I have Officer Tsurada on display." Rhani went to the screen. Sachiko Tsurada looked grimly back at her.

"Domna," she said. "My deep sympathy and regrets. I hope you are not badly injured."

"No," Rhani said. "I was simply shaken up."

"Can you tell me what your attackers looked like?"

"I'll try," Rhani said, sitting in the chair. "There were three of them, two men, one woman." She tried to picture their faces, but the features she had seen so intimately in the strong sunlight came back to her now impossibly blurred. "Wait," she said, and told Binkie to find Dana. After a few moments he came to the bedroom. There was a white gel patch on his cheek. "The police need to know what those people looked like," she said.

He nodded. "I'll try." She let him have the chair. She was aching now, as if every muscle had been strained. She half-listened to Dana's description; "Fair skin, dark hair, nose broken to the left. She was right handed. There might be some fingerprints on the shards of broken glass."

Amri said, "Rhani-ka, your bath is ready."

Rhani tottered to the washroom. The mirrors were

steamy. She slid her robe from her shoulders and handed it to Amri. The slave gasped. "Rhani-ka, your side!" Rhani looked at herself in the clouded mirror. Her right side was blue from shoulder to hip. She lowered herself into the hot water, and had to clench her jaw tightly to keep from crying.

The heat eased the soreness. She leaned forward to let Amri soap her back. Her legs stung; they were scraped from her fall on the pavement. She lifted her hands to free her hair from its coils and remembered the wig. It was not there. She did not remember when, during the struggle, it had gone.

"Rhani-ka," said Amri, "your beautiful dress is all torn."

"It doesn't matter," Rhani said. She leaned against the wall of the tub. She stayed in the bath until the water cooled. At last, moving slowly, she eased herself from the washroom. Her skin was reddened where it was not black and blue.

She drank a glass of fruit punch, savoring the sweetness of the cold drink. Probably, she thought, it would be good to eat. But she had no appetite for food. Amri opened the bed for her, and she climbed between the sheets.

The face of the woman with the bottle slid waveringly into her mind.

"Yago bitch," they had called her. She pictured the police hunting them through the streets. Tears sprang traitorously to life beneath her eyelids; she lay weeping, furious at her body's weakness. She was Rhani Yago, *Domna* Rhani Yago, what was she doing, lying in her own bed crying like a child?

Amri crept in. "Rhani-ka, are you in pain? Can I get you something?"

"No," Rhani said. She rubbed her face. "Has Zed called yet?"

"Not yet, Rhani-ka."

"Is Dana there?"

"I think he went downstairs again," Amri said.

"I want him," Rhani said.

"I'll go find him."

"Thank you, Amri," Rhani said. She struggled up. She wanted to be sitting up when he came in, sitting, and not crying.

The door slid aside. He came into the bedroom. "You sent for me, Rhani-ka."

"Yes," Rhani said. The traitor tears began to run down her nose again. She didn't know what she wanted from him. Reassurance . . . the knowledge that he did not think less of her because she was helpless in a fight? "Damn it, I—" She had to stop, and blow her nose. He turned, and vanished into the washroom, to emerge carrying a wet cloth and a dry towel. Sitting on the bed, he wiped her face with the cloth and patted it dry, just as if she were four years old.

"Better?" he said.

There was neither reproach nor scorn in his voice. Rhani put her head back in the pillows, and her heart, which had been knocking against her rib cage like a demented pendulum, regained its equilibrium. Measuringly, she gazed at him. She knew what she wanted. "Close the door," she said. He left the bed and shut the door. She pulled the blanket to one side. Walking back to the bedside, he stood gazing at her. She moved in the big bed, making a place for him there. "Come inside."

He stripped. In the soft arrested daylight behind the curtains, his body looked hard and cold. But against hers it was warm. He touched her gently, cautious of her bruises. He wasn't clumsy. His weight on her was uncomfortable; she gestured, and he rolled, pulling her on top of him and easing himself into her in one motion. His hips lifted to meet her. Lowering her head, she began to stroke his chest with her hair. He teased her nipples with eager fingers, and she saw his lips soften and sigh with pleasure as she began to ride.

Chapter Eleven

After the loving, Dana rose and opened the curtains.

Light filled the dark room, spilling down the paneled walls. The afternoon bustle of tourists through the streets came faintly upward, noise without words, like the distant rushing of a river. The house was quiet, except for the labor of the aircooling machine. But, Rhani thought, why do I think of rivers? The rivers run underground on Chabad.

Dana came back to the bed. He leaned over it to kiss her, and she stroked his hairless yellow chest, feeling for the heartbeat beneath the skin. The room smelled of sex and semen.

"I must go," he said.

"Yes." He bent to her, kissing her eyelids, nose, ears. She captured his mouth and brought it to hers, enjoying the taste of him.

When she let him go, he dressed. Noiselessly he slid the door ajar. He closed it behind him. Rhani stretched and rolled onto her belly. She could still smell him in the creases of the sheets.

Her bruises ached. She watched the sunlight move on the dark wooden walls. Finally she rose, went to the washroom, and stepped into the shower. The water felt good except on her scrapes. She returned to the bed and pulled it into some sort of order, straightening the covers and plumping the pillows. Then she got into it, knowing that she should be up and working, and not caring. The stillness of the big house was soporific.

Zed's step on the stair woke her from sleep. He was coming two at a time. The room was cool. The sky outside the windows was a brilliant shimmering purple.

Zed slid her bedroom door aside without bothering to knock. He crossed to the bed. She lifted her hand to him. "Zed-ka."

He sat on the edge of the bed. He was wearing a green gown, tied at the throat. "Did you come through the streets like that?" she asked.

"Yes. Clinic garb. Are you all right? I came as soon as I could. All the juniors are on Needle Row, or at the Barracks. I was working Emergency." His face was drawn.

"I told Binkie not to tell you!" she said. "He was only to tell you to call. . . ."

"I have been calling," he said. "And calling. There's been no answer for six hours."

"Oh." Rhani glanced at the com-unit. The message light on its side flashed steadily. "I—I was asleep."

"City Computer said the line was not malfunctioning. I was worried. I came home. Binkie told me there was a second attack. Three people, one of them with a bottle?"

"Yes, that's right. I wasn't hurt, just shaken up. My side aches."

"Tell me about it." She described the attack as best she could. "Let me see your side." She drew back the coverlet to show him the bruises. They were purple-green, very big, and ugly. In places, the flesh was puffy. Clinically, carefully, he touched her ribs. It hadn't occurred to her that they might be broken.

"You see," she said, "I'm fine." She smiled at him to prove it.

He did not return the smile. "Rhani, do you want to go back to the estate?" he said.

"Run away, you mean?" He nodded. "Absolutely not. What would you have me do on the estate, build a Cage-field? Live behind bars? No. I am going to the Auction tomorrow, and in six days we will have the Yago party. We will leave after that, as we always do. Family Yago built this city; I will not be chased out of it!"

Mildly, he said, "I had to ask."

"I suppose you did."

"Did you notify the Abanat police of the attack?"

"Of course." Rhani got out of bed and reached for her robe, wincing a little at the ache in her right arm.

"What is it?" said Zed quickly.

"My arm . . . I fell on it. It got wrenched out of the socket. Dana put it back." His name resonated in her mind, like a bell ringing. She turned her face away in unaccustomed dissembling from her sharp-eyed brother. She turned the lights up. The purple had faded into a soft, shadowless blue, herald of darkness. She wondered how long it would take him to learn that she and Dana had bedded. Amri might let it slip. Corrios would not. Binkie would not say two words to Zed by choice.

She called the kitchen on the intercom. "Amri, tell Corrios that Zed and I will want dinner in the dining alcove." To Zed she said, "Are you hungry? You must be. I am. When I left the Dur party they had just begun to serve lunch."

"You left early," he said. "Was it so tiresome?"

"Yes," she said, half-smiling as she recalled Ferris Dur's mouth against her own. So clumsy. Not like Dana.

"Very tiresome. Zed-ka, don't you want to put on other clothes?"

He glanced at his Clinic greens. "Oh. Yes." He rose, and then came to her, and very gently, as if she were made of glass, put his arms about her and buried his head in her hair. "Rhani," he whispered.

She held him lightly. "Zed, I'm all right. I'm all right, twin."

"Yes," he whispered, and let his arms fall.

Dana watched Zed and Rhani walk side by side down the curving marble stair.

As he had been the first time, at the estate, he was struck by their likeness. But now he could see beyond it, beyond the fact that their eyes were amber, their hair red-brown—Rhani's dark, Zed's lighter—their height the same, their voices similar. They were different as light and dark, different as pleasure from pain. He remembered the springy weight of Rhani's hair on his throat, and shivered. And what am *I* now? he thought. Slave, Starcaptain, pilot, friend, lover, bodyguard. . . .

Amri pushed past him, carrying a tray. He retreated from her path, into the kitchen. Zed and Rhani went into the dining alcove. Corrios was bending over his pots, muttering. Binkie sat on a stool, eating. His look was unfriendly.

Corrios jabbed Dana in the ribs with an elbow. "Eat," he said.

"All right." Dana filled his plate and sat on another stool.

He tried to think of something lighthearted to say to Binkie, and couldn't. They sat in silence, and ate. Suddenly Amri came from the dining alcove. "Dana, Zed wants you."

"Wants me—now?" Dana said, half rising. Amri nodded. Dana swallowed. Binkie looked at him, expressionless. Dana's hurts began to ache as he walked from the kitchen. His left arm had been scraped on the stones of the Boulevard, and there was a dark, painful knot where he had been kicked, on his left thigh.

He walked to the dining alcove. Rhani was there. He was careful not to look too long at her. Be careful, warned the blood hammering through his chest, be very careful. He called upon the discipline he had learned on Nexus, and shut Rhani's presence from his consciousness. Then he turned, to face the one person who could, if he chose, obliterate that self-control with a touch.

"You sent for me, Zed-ka."

"Yes," said Zed. He leaned back in his chair. "Tell me about this attack today."

"There were three of them," Dana said. "They were waiting for us, approximately halfway between Founders' Green and Dur House, on the Boulevard. They pretended to be drunk. It was noon, a perfect time; there was no one on the street for blocks. Rhani's black wig didn't fool them: they must have known she had it on."

Zed frowned. "Black wig?" he said to Rhani.

"I wore that black wig, the one I bought four years ago," she said. "And the silver sari."

He nodded. "Go on."

Dana thought back. "The woman with the bottle went for Rhani first, I think. Yes. I got between them. I kicked the bottle from her hand." He grimaced. "It was a stupid move, but it worked. I brought her down and hit her. The second one tackled me and we rolled around for awhile. The third one went after Rhani. He was twisting her arms when I got to him. I pulled him off her and they all got skittish and ran. There wasn't a soul in the street to see it."

"Was it difficult, chasing them off?" Zed asked.

Dana's thigh throbbed. "It wasn't fun."

Zed said, "What did they want, do you think? To kidnap Rhani? Hurt her? Frighten her?"

Dana considered that. "I—I don't know, Zed-ka," he said. "They couldn't have wanted to kill her or they would have done it from a distance, and I never would have seen their faces."

Zed locked gazes with Rhani. "It makes a pattern," he said.

Rhani was nodding. "Yes. The day after tomorrow I should get a letter from the Free Folk of Chabad."

Zed's gaze shot to Dana's face. "You did well," he said.

"Thank you, Zed-ka," Dana said.

"Tell me"—Zed sipped his wine, still looking at

Dana—"was there no way to put one of them out? A knock on the head would have done it, and the police would have had someone to question."

Dana swallowed. He had been expecting this question, and dreading it. Truthfully he answered, "When I pulled the third one off Rhani, I was afraid for her; I thought she'd broken an arm. I let him go without thinking."

Eyes like bits of crystal bored into his. Then Zed said, "All right, Dana. Go back to the kitchen."

Safe in the kitchen, Dana leaned against a wall. Amri touched his arm, her round face anxious. He smiled to reassure her. "It's all right, kitten," he said. "I'm not even bent." But his heart was still pounding. He had told the truth, but not all of it. If Zed had pushed, he would have learned that Dana had chosen not to try to capture one of the attackers. He could not face bringing someone back to the house so that Zed could break the poor fool slowly and painfully apart.

He sat, and finished his cooling meal. Corrios cleaned the kitchen. Rhani and Zed left the dining alcove; Dana heard them laughing on their way up the stairs. Amri straightened the alcove. Finally she came into the kitchen. "I'm done," she said to Corrios. The albino checked the food storage bins and coolers, nodded to them all, and stalked out.

Amri flicked off the kitchen lights. "Are you going to stay here?" she said to Dana.

He nodded toward his empty plates. "I want to clean those up."

"I can do it," she offered shyly.

"No," he said, "that's all right, kitten. Go to bed."

She left. In the quiet dark, Dana put the plates through the cleaning unit and set them in their places. Alone like this, he could pretend that he was free on Pellin. Suddenly he realized that he was not alone. Binkie had been sitting on his stool, silent as a wall, watching him.

Dana stared at him. "Aren't you going to bed?" he said.

Binkie stirred, and slid from the stool. Almost pleasantly, he said, "What the hell business is that of yours?" He reached out and gripped Dana's arm. Dana froze—it was Zed's grip, thumb poised, ready to drive nerve against bone.

Angered, he thrust the secretary from him. "What do you think you're doing?" he said.

In the dim light Binkie's features were bleak, hard as stone. "You're lucky, you know that," he said.

Dana said, "I don't know what you mean."

Binkie smiled at him. "Rhani," he said, very softly. "Who do you think turned off the com-unit alarm?"

Dana felt himself blushing. He was glad the light was dim. "So?" he said belligerently. "I owe you for it."

"That's right," Binkie said. "You do."

"Let me know when you want to call the debt in," Dana said sarcastically. He walked to the entrance to the slaves' hall. Binkie did not follow him. As he went into his bedroom, Dana wondered why Binkie had turned off the com-unit alarm. Simply to get Dana in his debt? Or was there another reason? Did Binkie have a secret he wanted protected, a lover perhaps, some treasure hidden in Abanat that he visited on those rare occasions Rhani gave him a morning off?

Stars, Dana thought, we live in the same house, we are fellow-victims of the same man, and we know nothing about each other, nothing at all.

The next day was the day of the Auction.

From the maps, Dana knew that the Auction was held in a square at the center of the city: Auction Place. It was sunny. He wondered if it had ever rained the day of the Auction. Both Rhani and Zed would attend it, of course, and he would be at Rhani's side, as her bodyguard. He washed and exercised. He was dressing when Amri tapped on his door. She was wearing pale yellow, and Dana was reminded of his first meeting with her on the estate. More than ever she looked like a butterfly.

She held out a pair of blue boots. "These are for you, from Rhani," she said.

Dana took them from her. They were very light, and he wondered what animal's skin they were.

Amri's errand was not complete. "Rhani says she wants you to wear blue, and the sapphire earrings that you wore yesterday."

"All right," Dana said. Wondering why it mattered what he wore, he changed his clothes. His thigh felt almost normal, and the gel on his face had dried. Peeling it off, he felt the contours of the cut with his fingertips. He looked in the mirror: its edges had knit. It would not even leave a scar. He hurried into the kitchen. Now he could hear clearly the sound that had awakened him: the musical chiming of many bells.

Binkie sat on a stool, the same one he had occupied the night before. He too was wearing blue: the fresh clothes were the only sign that he had left it. "Better eat something," he said to Dana. "You'll need it."

They assembled in the front hall: Rhani, Zed, Dana, Binkie, Amri. Rhani was dressed in silver and blue; Zed in the silver Net commander's uniform with the Yago "Y" on its sleeve. The sight of it made Dana's stomach contract into a tight ball. Rhani's hair hung loose. A topaz at her throat accentuated the amber of her eyes. She spoke to Zed; the conversation had evidently started in her room. "Zed-ka, I don't want to talk about my bruises, or about the attack. I want to go to the Auction and have a good time. We can be serious and worried tonight."

With punctilious courtesy, Zed said, "Whatever you wish, Rhani-ka."

The bells had stopped. Corrios held the door open for them. They went outside. In the night, the city had erected flagpoles all along the Boulevard from which a splendor of flags was flying: the flags of the Four Families and the flags of all five worlds in Sector Sardonyx. Below them, all of Abanat seemed to be moving in one direction: eastward, toward Auction Place. It was early. The lighter-eyed folk were wearing sunshades, but most of the people in the streets were carrying theirs. Dana pushed his to the top of his head. Rhani said, "The banks and businesses close today; everyone goes to the Auction. It's one of our holidays." She and Zed went down the steps together. Dana, walking beside Binkie, saw the secretary's face contort at the word *holidays* as if he smelled something rotten. They joined the throng. Dana moved to walk at Rhani's right shoulder. She chuckled. "No one will attack me today, Zed-ka. I have two bodyguards."

She rested her fingers for an instant on Dana's bare left arm. Dana screened his reaction by pretending to stumble and regain balance. Zed glanced at him curiously. Dana said, "I'm not used to walking in these boots."

Zed said, "You're growing worldbound." The word

described the inevitable dissolution of agility and grace that happened to Hypers who lived too long away from the starships.

"I hope not," said Dana.

Zed looked at him with a momentary rare sympathy. "It will happen," he said.

Dana looked away, into the blue sky, past the city and the dry, contoured hills. It happens to others, he thought. It isn't going to happen to me.

Binkie said, in his ear, "You want to know about the Auction?"

Dana was grateful for the change of subject. "Please." Listening to Binkie, he was careful to keep his eyes on the crowded, kaleidoscopic street.

"The long buildings flanking Auction Place are called the Barracks. The slaves are kept there, clothed, fed, drugged with dorazine, from the time they leave the Net."

"How many?" Dana asked.

He thought he had lost Zed's attention. But the Net commander answered the question: "The capacity of the Net is four thousand slaves. This year it transported three thousand, six hundred and seventy-nine."

"Thank you, Zed-ka," Dana said.

"They bring the slaves in lots from the Barracks," Binkie said. "The lots are divided according to skills. Laborers come first. They're picked up by the building contractors, the landingport, the city maintenance department, and the Gemit mines. Later come the skilled laborers, technicians, craftspeople, professionals, and specialty lots. There's a break at noon when everyone hides. We've missed the first lot, and maybe the second."

The Boulevard broadened. "My dear," said a voice to Dana's right, "it's all automated. You slip your credit disc in the slot and punch the bid you want. The screen shows the last bid recorded. You'll see. It's fun to get there early, when they've just opened the bidding on a new lot. You can bid knowing your bid will be topped. Like gambling!"

Like bees in a swarm, the crowds of people streamed into Auction Place. White-walled buildings reflected sunlight into the glittering crowd. Bodies trapped the heat. Dana wiped the sweat from his face. The open space simmered like a pot on a fire. Whispers rose: *"Rhani*

Yago, Yago, Yago." Tourists turned around to stare. Serene in her silver tunic, Zed beside her, Rhani strolled forward. People backed to make way for her.

Binkie jostled Dana from behind. "There."

Doors like black mouths opened in the buildings' white sides. Dana saw that there were platforms lining the square, parallel to the buildings, about a meter off the ground. People marched out the doors. "Those are the slaves," said Rhani. Men and women in blue uniforms walked at their sides. The slaves wore white. Directed by their keepers, they positioned themselves on the platforms at regular intervals. A whisper informed Dana that this was the last of the skilled laborers' lots.

Rhani walked to a platform. Dana looked up. A woman slave stood above him. A screen told him who she was. AMALIE O-THORIS, it read. AGE: FORTY-NINE, GENERAL MACHINIST. CONTRACT: FIVE YEARS. DORAZINE DOSAGE: 1.75. She seemed oblivious to his scrutiny. She stared into the sky, over the bobbing heads of the people in the square, toward the distant horizon.

Binkie said in Dana's ear, "The city'll buy her to keep the movalongs running. Or else she'll go to Gemit. They need machinists in the mines." Dana wondered what Amalie O-Thoris' crime had been, and what her final price would be.

"Excuse me," said a voice. Dana backed away. A dark woman read the information on the screen. She bit her thumb, and then inserted a disc in a slot and punched buttons. Numbers shuddered into orange life. She wore a white jumpsuit with a dark insignia on it: the Dur crest, the axe lifted to strike.

Dana said, "If you buy her, where will she go?"

"The mines," said the woman in white.

"See?" hissed Binkie.

The air steamed with the smell of thousands of sweating, perfumed bodies.

Dana stared at the motionless figures, tucked into invisible niches on the platforms. "Isn't there any shade?" he said.

Binkie said, "For slaves? No."

Rhani turned around. "The lots stand for an hour. In that hour they get three breaks in which they may sit down. They drink as much water as they need. And most of them are on dorazine, which can make even an uncomfortable situation pleasant."

Binkie murmured syllables which might have been, "Yes, Rhani-ka." Worming through the crowd, peddlers hawked tarts and seaweed and jelly cakes and ices. A woman sold balloons with the Yago "Y" imprinted on them, and tiny silver flags. Dana heard a drum, and the tinny clash of finger cymbals. On the platforms the slaves shifted and sighed, trapped in dorazine dreams.

Staying close to the platforms, Rhani and Zed strolled around the square. Dana noticed a woman with the Yago "Y" on her tunic make a bid on a short, thick-shouldered man. Numbers changed on the screens. Beneath one screen two buyers stood, glaring at each other, jaws outthrust, punching alternate bids. Zed bought Rhani a seaweed cake. The peddler would not let him pay for it.

"Zed! Rhani!" A woman sailed toward them. Dana recognized the majestic redhead Rhani had greeted on the Dur steps. She was wearing a white gown; in the bright sun, she moved with the grace and strength of a square-sailed ship. "My compliments to the Yago Net. Imre's managers report that they have filled their labor reserve, and I have a new gardener, so we are all pleased."

"Thank you, Aliza," said Zed.

"Have you heard about the Gemit accident?"

"I did hear something," Rhani murmured vaguely.

"Oh, hell," said Zed. "I heard about it from Sai, at the Clinic. I meant to tell you. They'll be buying today. A week ago, wasn't it, Aliza? Sai didn't know the figures; all she wanted to talk about was the limb replacements."

"Two full work teams put out of action," said Aliza.

"That's too bad," said Rhani pleasantly. They smiled at one another.

A bell rang. Blue-clad attendants walked onto the platforms to guide the slaves back to the Barracks. The platforms stayed empty for about five minutes, and then another lot of slaves came out through the doors. "Which lot is this?" said Aliza Kyneth.

Zed answered, "The technicians' lot."

Dana asked Binkie a question which had been puzzling him for some time. "What happens to the slaves who are not bought?"

"Dealers buy them," Binkie explained. "They're taken

from the Barracks and housed and fed at the dealers' expense. Then when a slave's contract runs out in midyear, or if the slave is manumitted, or dies, immediate replacements are available. Of course, the dealers' prices are higher than the prices usually paid at Auction."

Aliza Kyneth had been listening. "That is correct," she said, with approval. "Rhani, your secretary is very concise."

Rhani smiled. Binkie bowed, his pale face flushed.

The bidding on this lot was brisk. The Yago household and Aliza Kyneth made a conspicuous knot in the traffic flow. A clever peddler released a sackful of artificial butterflies into the air. Wings powered by the sunlight, they fluttered and soared in graceful imitation. The crowd shifted toward the east side of the Place as people rushed to buy them.

A voice at their backs said, "Good morning, Domna, Commander."

They turned around. A man in black stood facing them, flanked by other people in black. On the front of his shirt was a silver insignia. A Hyper, Dana's mind registered, and then he recognized the silver symbol; and a cop. Rhani did not know him, Dana could tell from her face, but Zed did.

"Rhani-ka," he said, smiling only with his lips, "let me introduce you to Michel A-Rae, Sardonyx Sector's very own nemesis."

Without fuss, Aliza Kyneth turned her bulk broadside to them, making a shield of herself to block the gaze of any interested tourists. Rhani nodded to the black-clad man. "Good morning," she said. "I trust you are enjoying the Auction."

Stars, she's cool, Dana thought, admiring her composure. A-Rae looked much more individual in person than he did in his photographs. In his left ear he was wearing a black pearl earring, and Dana guessed that it had a transmitter in it. He was weaponless, as far as Dana could tell, but the two people on either side of him were carrying stunners conspicuously clipped to their belts.

"I am not," A-Rae said. "But then, I didn't expect to. Some things we do out of duty. This is one of them."

Rhani smiled sweetly. "That is very noble of you, Captain A-Rae."

He pursed his lips. "I'm surprised you know my title."

Rhani said, "I know a little about you. I must confess, I would like to know more."

"Really?" He seemed amused. "Like what?"

"Well—" Rhani rubbed her chin—"I would like to know why you appear to have a vendetta abainst Chabad. Were you ever a slave?"

One of the flanking drug cops gasped. A-Rae shook his head. "No, Domna, I was never a slave. I am Enchantean. When I was a child I was taken to watch the loading of the Net shuttles. It horrified me. When I grew older I found that my own family was deeply engaged in supporting and profiting from the slave system, and I found that horrible, too. I repudiated my family and have since dedicated my life to the destruction of slavery."

"For no other reason than moral repugnance," Rhani said.

"Does one need another reason?"

"You don't," Rhani said. "I might."

A-Rae stuck his thumbs in his belt. "Since your mother built the Net and your brother is its commander, I would not expect you to share my feelings," he said. "But then, I have always assumed that people who profit from human pain have no morals." He looked directly at Zed. Dana saw Zed's shoulders go back.

Rhani laid a hand lightly on her brother's arm. "I think you are being rude, Michel A-Rae," she said.

He grinned mirthlessly at her. "Does my rudeness upset you, Domna? And yet, you can stomach *this!*" He swept his hand toward the immobile, sweating slaves.

Dana's stomach hurt with tension. Rhani seemed able to ignore it. "This repels you," she murmured. "Yet you are not distressed by prisons?"

"In prison, a person may retain some measure of dignity. There is no dignity in being *owned*." Despite himself, Dana nodded. Out of the corner of an eye he glimpsed Binkie's face: the secretary/slave was drinking in A-Rae's every word, lips parted, eyes wide.

"I see," Rhani said in a tone of polite disbelief. "You have, of course, been to prison, and know."

A-Rae scowled. "No, Domna, I have not been to prison. Is this all you want to know from me?"

"Well," Rhani said, "I admit I am curious to know why

your people are watching my house."

A-Rae raised his thick eyebrows. "My people—I presume by that phrase you mean my staff, Domna—are not watching your *house*."

"Me, then?"

He grew grave. "That is Federation business, I am afraid. You know I cannot answer questions about Federation business."

Dana thought: he is enjoying this, isn't he. He thinks he is humiliating Rhani Yago, and he likes it. The realization disturbed something deep within him. He waited to hear what Rhani would say.

She simply nodded. "You must have wounded your family deeply when you changed your name," she said. "Have you reconciled yourself to them at all, after so many years?"

A-Rae's dark eyes smoldered with anger. "My family is also none of your business, Domna!" he said, clipping the words out. He touched the shoulders of his two companions briefly. "This is my family!"

"Very touching," Rhani said.

Her lack of excitement seemed to infuriate the man. "You are so sure that you are untouchable, aren't you?" he said. "You are wrong. I hope to prove to you that you are wrong."

One of his companions murmured placatingly in his ear. His face worked, and then smoothed to a polite mask. "Domna, if you will excuse me," he said. The three cops stepped aside and bent their heads together.

The Barracks' bells chimed. Zed said softly. "He is so *damn* cocksure." Dana glanced at the Net commander. Zed was gazing at the little huddle the three cops made, his eyes grim.

Rhani tightened her fingers on her brother's arm. "He is an uncivil boor," she said. "But I would prefer that you did not create a scene with him in public, Zed-ka."

Zed scowled. "He said you have no morals."

"I don't care what he thinks of me, Zed-ka."

Dana said, "His companions have stunners."

Zed's shoulders stiffened. "You think they'd use them? On me?"

"The way they feel about you and the Net? Yes," Dana said.

Zed glared at him, and Dana thought for a moment that he would end up being the focus of Zed's evident rage. But the Net commander nodded. "You are probably right," he said. He was still watching the spot within the swirling mélange of color where the black-clad cops stood.

Aliza Kyneth, who had listened to the entire exchange, said, "Rhani, I admire your calm."

Rhani smiled. "Isobel always said I was too excitable."

Aliza Kyneth said, "Isobel would have been proud of you this morning." She turned her back on A-Rae. "That man is irritating, but an insect."

"An insect with a sting," Rhani said.

"Perhaps," Aliza said. She beckoned. "Walk with me, Rhani. I have something to ask you."

"Certainly, Aliza," Rhani said. She withdrew her arm from Zed's. "Excuse me, Zed-ka."

Dana hesitated, unsure if he should follow Rhani and Aliza, or not. He turned to ask Zed what to do. "Zed-ka, shall I—" But Zed was not listening. His eyes were fixed on a point some fifteen meters away.

Dana wondered if he were contemplating what he wanted do to Michel A-Rae. The Net commander seemed welded to the stone underfoot.

Suddenly he moved, slicing through the mass of tourists as if they weren't there. A murmur of resentment marked his passage. Dana went after him. "Excuse him," he said. "Excuse me. Excuse us." It took him a few moments to maneuver his way through the packed crowd. When he finally broke free, he realized he was a meter from the platforms. Ahead of him, Zed stared upward, deaf to a spatter of speculative comments.

Dana looked up.

A woman slave stood gazing quietly over the throng. Her hair was long, loose, and reddish, like gilded chestnut in the light. She was slender, and not very tall. Her eyes were brown. She looked, Dana saw with incredulity, very much like Rhani. Her spare, neat, triangular face was Rhani's, and the set of her eyes was Rhani's, and the sharp line of her cheekbones was Rhani's. She stood like Rhani, head a little to one side, feet parallel and apart. She appeared to be Rhani's height. Dana tore his eyes from her to look at the screen.

DARIEN RIIS. AGE: TWENTY-SIX. COMPUTER TECHNICIAN. CONTRACT: FOUR YEARS. DORAZINE DOSAGE: 1.25. She was ten years younger than Rhani.

Zed's fingers clamped like steel claws on Dana's upper arm. "Where's Binkie?"

"I don't know, Zed-ka."

Zed let him go; Dana caught his breath. "Find him," ordered the Net commander. "Go find him."

Dana looked around. Binkie had been at his elbow, as had Amri. Where the hell had they gone? Zed was staring at the woman again. Dana plowed away from him, looking from side to side, trying to remember where they had been standing before, trying to retrace his steps. He wondered where Rhani was, and how she would find them in the press. All the faces about him seemed equally vacant, equally unfamiliar. He felt panic fluttering in his nerves, and forced it away. He would find Binkie only by staying calm.

Hands clutched him. It was Amri, bright-eyed, beaming delight. Someone had given her a butterfly. She opened her cupped palms to let light touch it; the wings flapped slowly. "Do you know where Binkie is, kitten?" he said.

"Over there, by that platform. He told me to get lost." She giggled.

"That wasn't kind of him."

"He's talking to someone," said Amri, "and he doesn't want me to listen." She said with dignity, "I don't listen to people that I don't even *know*."

A high-pitched bell signaled a rest period. Chairs mushroomed up out of the platforms behind the slaves. Most sat. Some, too drugged to care, did not. "Wait here," said Dana. He pushed toward the platform till he saw Binkie. "Binkie!" he shouted. The secretary was talking earnestly to someone with short hair and what looked to be a pressure bandage on one arm. He maneuvered to them. As he reached them, the stranger—woman, he thought—looked at him and melted back into the crowd. Binkie whirled, snarling.

"What the hell!"

"Sorry," Dana said, "but I have no choice. Zed wants you yesterday."

Binkie cursed with unmistakable venom. "Where is he?" he asked, more quietly. Dana pointed. They slogged back, collecting Amri, who was patiently waiting for them. Binkie looked to see what Zed was gazing at. His head went back, and stayed there. He stood, openmouthed.

Zed said, "Buy her."

"But—"

"You carry the household credit disc. Buy her." Fumbling the disc in haste from his pocket, Binkie inserted it in the slot. Zed said, "Stay here. Overtop all bids for her. You understand, Binkie?" His fingers curled like claws at his sides.

"Yes, Zed-ka."

Some of the tension drained from Zed's face and hands. He turned on Dana. "Where's my sister?"

Dana stammered, and then caught himself. "Walking— there." Through the crush he caught a glimpse of Aliza Kyneth's dress and flying red hair.

Zed squinted into the sunlight. "Ah. I see. With Aliza. Go to her."

Dana went to Rhani's side. She had a quizzical look on her face, as if she had just tasted something new and wasn't sure she liked it. "Aliza, I'll help if I can," she was saying.

"Thank you," Aliza said affectionately. "That's all I ask." She lifted her chin. "Now I must find Imre. He will be looking for me." She strode regally away, a whale among minnows.

"Take my arm," Rhani said. Dana linked his arm through hers. She was quivering with laughter. She pressed her hip to his; the little joining made him shudder. "Imagine—Aliza wants me to help her arrange a surprise party!"

"Why is that funny?" Dana said, puzzled.

"Because I hate parties. Aliza says she wants this one to be a party even I will enjoy. It's for Imre's birthday. Where's my brother got to?"

For a moment Dana had almost forgotten Zed. Bleakly he answered, "Buying a slave."

"Buying a slave! For the household?" Rhani frowned. "Why?"

"Come." He brought her to the platform on which Darien Riis stood.

"Zed-ka, why are you. . . ?" The question trailed into

silence as Rhani looked up.

Zed said, without turning, "Her name is Darien."

A bell rang. The slaves stirred in reflex. The buyers in the square shifted, talking loudly. The bidding on this lot had ended. The slaves moved into line like the figures on an ancient clock. Darien Riis, age twenty-six, property of Family Yago, disappeared through a door. Zed said, "Let's go." He took Rhani's hand and drew it through his arm, as had Aliza Kyneth.

Dana said softly to Binkie, "What happens now?"

The secretary said, "She'll be tattooed and delivered to the house tomorrow morning."

Like a package, Dana thought.

Zed said, "Binkie. Call the Barracks when we reach the house. Tell them to keep her until we have left Abanat. I don't want to see her until we're back at the estate."

"Yes, Zed-ka," said Binkie.

At the edge of Auction Place, the crowd thinned out. Dana moved up to walk at Rhani's right shoulder. Her arm brushed his, by accident, it seemed. She began, "Zed-ka, why. . . ."

Zed's left hand sprang upward in an abrupt gesture of denial. It silenced her. The Net commander drew a deep breath. "Don't ask," he said.

Rhani bit her lip. The Boulevard was clear before them: they were out of the square. In the distance a bell rang. Dana looked back, but could not see. He held his hands up to shield out the light.

A new lot of slaves was being shepherded through the vaultlike doors.

Chapter Twelve

They were almost to the steps of the house when Dana saw someone he knew. At first he could not put name to face. She was half-turned away from him. . . . Then she turned around, and he saw her clearly.

It was Tori Lamonica.

Her brown-gold hair was short; the last time he'd seen her it had been long. Hands in her pockets, moving with graceful strides, she was traveling away from him, walking north. She wore lavender and black, and her Starcaptain's medallion gleamed through the lace of her shirt front. Gold hoops dangled from her ears. She was frowning, not looking his way, and for one wild moment, Dana drew breath to shout at her. . . . But they had reached the steps, and Rhani was looking at him.

The street was very quiet; most people were still at the Auction. Above, Corrios drew back the doors. Amri, carrying her solar-winged butterfly, seemed the only one of them who was not subdued. Binkie went immediately toward the slaves' hall. Rhani went upstairs. Dana went to his room. His head hurt from the glare of the sun—he could not believe he had actually seen Tori Lamonica out there. What the hell was she doing on Chabad? he wondered. She had to have sold his dorazine weeks ago. Had the proximity of A-Rae's cops kept her from getting offplanet? Could she have stayed for other reasons? He tried to remember what he knew about her, her amusements and habits—but Hypers did not talk about each other much. About the only thing he could remember Russell saying of her was that she jacked cargoes, was a superb pilot, and played an ancient Terran game called "Go."

Rhani's voice saying his name brought him out of reverie abruptly. "Dana, come to my room, please."

"Yes, Rhani-ka." He went upstairs. She was sitting at the com-unit. Dana glanced at the door to make sure that it was tightly shut, and bending, touched his lips to the crisp, clean silk of her hair.

She said, so softly that he barely heard it, "Have you ever heard of Cherillys' Law?"

He scowled. The name was familiar. . . . "I think so, but I don't remember what it is," he said.

"It's also called Bradley's Hypothesis." She recited, *"For every bit of organized matter, organic and inorganic, within a given macroscopic universe, there is one exact molecular duplicate within that universe."*

"Yes," Dana said. "Now I remember. It depended on some very theoretical mathematical models, and it was never proved."

Still softly she said, "In ancient times on Old Earth they believed it was bad luck to meet your double. It meant you were going to die soon."

Dana scowled. "Rhani, you know that's nonsense." He grabbed the back of the chair and leaned on it until it turned. "Where did you encounter Bradley's Hypothesis?"

She shrugged. Her cheeks were flushed. "I don't know. I must have read it somewhere." She stood up suddenly. "Don't hang over me," she said sharply, and he gave her room to pace. After a while she said, "When I came back from Sovka, I was lonely. Zed was on Nexus; I was trapped with Isobel, learning to be Domna Rhani Yago. I read a lot in those months." She thrust her hands in her pockets and hunched her shoulders. "Zed and I—we used to pretend we were twins. When Isobel separated us, I felt as if I were being pulled apart, as if there were two of me, one in here—" she tapped her chest—"one somewhere else, free. I never thought I'd meet her."

Her melancholy irritated him. "That woman's not your twin," he said. "Her name's Darien Riis, not Rhani; she's not from Chabad; she's a computer technician; and her eyes aren't gold, they're brown." He paused. "And anyway, she's not free."

Sudden mischief lit Rhani's eyes. "My dear, the resemblance is striking, oh my yes!" She laughed. "You're right. I'm being stupid."

Dana wondered if he dared tell her about Tori Lamonica. "Her hair's redder than yours, too."

"I know," Rhani said. "She doesn't look like me. But—you couldn't know this—she looks like what I used to look like. My hair was redder when I was younger." She rubbed her chin. "Zed's fascination with her— disturbs me." With evident pain, she said, "He wouldn't talk to me the whole way home."

"At all?"

She nodded. Suddenly she came back to the com-unit keyboard. She punched a set of symbols, and the screen printed out: RECORDS OF THE YAGO NET: CURRENT YEAR: HOLDING. She sat on the chair and keyed in further instructions. The screen said: CARGO ROSTER: HUMAN. There was a pause, and then the screen flashed, in bright green letters, IDENTIFY.

She pressed her thumb to the screen.

Dana said, "Are those the Net records?"

She nodded. "They're only accessible to authorized

persons. Me, Zed, the Net staff, the Barracks staff, the Clinic—"

Dana said, "That's a lot of people." He remembered what his first computer instructor had said: *"Anything that anyone can put into a computer, someone else can find. All you need is the time to look."* "I suppose I'm there, too."

"Yes," she said, "you are." The screen began to fill with words. Dana read them over Rhani's shoulder. DARIEN RIIS: SEX: F; AGE: 26; PROFESSION: COMTECH; LENGTH OF CONTRACT: 4 YRS; PLANET OF ORIGIN: ENCHANTER; DORAZINE DOSAGE: 1.25 TID: CRM STATUS REGIS: 79R. Rhani frowned and touched a key. The green letters did not change.

"Are you looking for something more?" Dana asked. He was fascinated.

"There should be information about her offense," Rhani said. "I forget what 'Status 79' means, but 'R' denotes restricted information. I wonder what's going on."

"Can you override it?"

"My thumb print should have keyed in an automatic override. Whoever fed the computer the original data made an error. Or else there's a defect in the override circuit." She tapped the keyboard. "I've asked it to define 'Status 79.'"

The screen printed: STATUS 79: PERSONAL VIOLENCE AGAINST INDIVIDUAL ADULT.

"Oh," said Rhani softly.

Dana found himself wondering what circumstances or combination of them had driven a redheaded twenty-six-year-old Enchantean computer tech to an act of personal violence. Rhani touched a fingertip to the slick plastic screen, as if trying to feel the pinpoints of light. Then she erased the words. "You're right," she said. She swung the chair around.

"Right about what?"

"She's not my twin. My twin would never commit a crime of violence against an individual."

"How do you know that?" Dana said.

Rhani rubbed her chin. "Because I wouldn't." She rose. "Thank you for your comfort," she said.

She looked very solitary, standing in this room which smelled of her, her voice husky, even, and formal: Dana wanted to go to her, to hold her, to feel her upright body curve and soften against his. . . . He couldn't do it now. Now she was not his lover Rhani, but Domna Rhani Yago. She doesn't need a twin, he thought; she herself is twins, as Zed is, as I am, surgeon/sadist, slave/Starcaptain.

Someone knocked sharply on the door, and then slid it back. Zed leaned in. "Rhani-ka, I'll be at the Clinic if you want me," he said. He closed the door before she could answer. Startled, Dana glanced at Rhani. It was not like Zed to be so brusque with her. She had not moved, but her shoulders were hunched as if against a blow, and her face was thinned and drawn.

Dana went to her and put both arms around her. She laid her head against his chest. He could feel her breathing deeply—finally she sighed and stepped away. "I'm all right," she said, with something of a child's defiance in her tone.

"I know you are," he said.

She brushed her hair back from her face with both hands and lifted her face to his.

The kiss was lingering. As they disengaged, Rhani sighed—with pleasure, with melancholy? Dana didn't know. Her glance at him seemed oddly calculating. Was she working out the next time she could take him to bed? He felt as if she had made some kind of decision about him, a decision she did not intend to tell him about.

She thumbed the intercom. "Binkie? What is your file number on Loras U-Ellen?"

Binkie's voice said, "Number 1216, Rhani-ka."

"Thank you." She walked to the com-unit and sat before it. A little apologetically, she said to Dana. "I still have work to do."

She tapped the com-unit keys. "You remember I asked you about Loras U-Ellen? Well, the reason I asked you if you knew the name is that he appears to be a drug dealer."

Joltingly, Dana remembered Tori. "I told you when I first met you, Rhani-ka," he said, "I don't really know the drug dealers."

"Yes. That's right." She continued to touch keys. "I'd like something cool to drink," she said. "Would you ask Corrios to make me up some fruit punch?"

She was Domna Rhani Yago again. "Yes, Rhani-ka," Dana murmured.

The kitchen was cool and empty. Dana wondered where everybody was. "Corrios?" he called. No one answered, but a noise from the dining alcove drew his attention there. He walked toward it. Halfway there, he met Amri. Her blue eyes were reddened, and she was sniffling.

"Kitten, what is it?" he said. He curled an arm around her, as he would have embraced a weeping brother or sister. "What's wrong?"

She said, "Binkie yelled at me."

"What? Why?"

"Because I asked him who he was talking to, on the steps."

"What?"

"Someone came to the back and they talked. I just wanted to know who it was. I didn't mean to snoop." She knuckled one eye.

"Is that what he said?" She nodded. Dana contemplated finding the secretary/slave and telling him as nastily as possible what he thought of this. Amri snuffled again. "Never mind, kitten," he said, wondering for the hundredth time how old she was, and what she could possibly have done to make her a slave on Chabad. "He's a *kamsharrah*."

"What's that mean?"

"It means he's the sort of man who would sell his mother's body to be eaten by goats."

"Ugh!" Amri made a face. "That's horrible. Is it a Pellish word?"

"Uh-huh."

"I don't think he is," she said. She looked suddenly thoughtful. "I think he cares a lot about his family. He's from Enchanter. When he first came here—to the estate, it was—he showed me a picture of his little girl that he carried with him all the time. But then he tried to run away, and Zed—" She paused. "You know. After that, he stopped talking about his family, about anything." She blinked. "I need to wash my face."

He hugged her, and let go. "Rhani wants some fruit punch," he said. "Is Corrios out?"

"He's asleep," Amri said. "He likes to nap around

noon. I'll fix it." She grinned suddenly, and gave him a little push. "Go back to her. I can bring it up."

Dana returned the grin. "All right," he said. As he ascended the stairs, he decided that he would have to stop thinking of Amri as a child. That little shove had not been a child's reaction. Maybe, he thought, maybe Amri's artless look is just an act. Or no—not an act—a persona, a mood put on to hide what she was really thinking and feeling. We all wear one, he thought grimly. We must, or the contradictions between what we were and what we are—between free being and slave—would rip us apart.

Suddenly, three steps from Rhani's door, he was shaken with such rage that he had to lean against the wall. Damn this place, damn Sardonyx Sector, and damn and double damn the people of this planet, who had stabilized and made functional a social system based on degradation and drugs. The realization that he had helped to make it work contributed to his horror. He found himself thinking of Michel A-Rae with sympathy. Let him bring it down! he thought. I don't care what they put in its place: a room with bars is more merciful than this. At least, inside a room with bars, you would not constantly have to see what you had lost.

"Dana?" called Rhani.

"Coming," Dana said. He straightened, breathing evenly, consciously relaxing the tension that shuddered through his flesh. Finally, he slid the door aside, hoping that none of his feelings—his true feelings—were showing on his face.

Rhani sat on the bed, surrounded by printouts. "Amri's making punch," Dana said.

"Thank you." She looked up, pushing her hair away from her face with her wrist. "Come look at this."

He sat on the bed beside her. She laid the printout in his lap. "What am I looking at?" he asked.

"A summary of the information on Loras U-Ellen. Personal data, family data, economic interests."

"Uh." He scanned it. "How can he be forty-seven and ninety-three?"

"The old one is his father. This is him." She pointed to the paragraph. "Unmarried, three times liaisoned, father of seven children, three of whom live with him . . ."

"I see it." Dana read the paragraph quickly. "What the

hell is a *pinoth?"* he asked.

"It's an Enchantean flute," Rhani said. "He plays in an amateur orchestra."

"Really?" Dana wondered what music they'd played, and if they had ever heard of Vittorio Stratta. "He's independently wealthy?"

"He's officer of a corporation," Rhani said. She leaned over the page; a strand of her hair tickled his throat. "Please note what corporation it is." She pointed to the relevant line. "Pharmaceuticals, Inc. They manufacture pentathine, a legal dorazine substitute."

Amri leaned through the doorway. "Rhani-ka, I have your punch," she said.

Rhani glanced up. "Thank you, Amri. Put it down."

Amri laid the tray on the footstool, poured some punch into a glass, and brought it to Rhani.

"Thank you," Rhani said. "That's all." Amri left. "What the hell is a corporate officer doing, sneaking around the back alleys of Abanat, pretending to be a drug dealer?"

Dana shrugged. "I don't know. I don't know anything about corporations, Rhani-ka."

She gazed at him, startled.

"We don't have them on Pellin," he said. "All the industries and products belong to everybody. It's been that way from the time the colony was founded."

"Oh," she said. She rubbed her chin. "Well, it's most uncharacteristic behavior, take it from me." She was frowning as she studied the printout. "Sweet mother, they're a huge family! I wonder how they keep it all straight."

Dana half smiled. For a moment, his mind leaped back to his own big family. On Pellin, every family had an official recorder, some member of the clan with a capacity for retention and a real historical sense. His Aunt Kobé could recite the lineage of everyone in the clan for three generations. There were so many of them that when they traveled to the northern mountains for *shamshama,* the yearly traditional reunion, it took three huge wagons to carry them all . . . . Soon there would be one more. His sister, Anwako, was pregnant for the second time; that had been four, no, six months ago. She had probably already had the baby. The baby's father had blue eyes, her last letter had said, and the rest were taking bets as to whether the baby's eyes would be black, like those of most of the Ikoro clan, or blue . . . .

"Well?" Rhani said.

She had asked him something. "I'm sorry," Dana said. "I was thinking about something else. Would you say that again, Rhani-ka?"

She gazed at him impatiently. "I asked you what you thought was the best way for me to contact Loras U-Ellen."

"Send him a letter," Dana said.

He meant it flippantly. But Rhani's hard gaze told him that he had made a mistake. "I beg your pardon," she said. "This must be very boring to you. You may go."

Dana swallowed, and rose. He had not meant to offend her. Sweet mother, he thought, I don't understand this woman sometimes. . . . "Rhani-ka, I'm sorry," he said. "I was trying to be funny. It was out of place. I'd like to help." And as he said it, an idea lurched out of the back of his mind and roared at him. "You said—" his throat was abruptly tight, and he coughed to clear it—"you said he is on Chabad, pretending to be a drug dealer?"

"Yes," she said. "More exactly, he appears to have bribed my regular dealer, Sherrix Esbah, to leave the planet, and has taken her place. But he is *not* dealing dorazine."

"How did you find *that* out?" he asked.

"Jo Leiakanawa, the Net navigator. Remember when Zed left the estate for Abanat, a few days after you came? I had written several times to Sherrix, and still not heard from her. Jo had spoken to the dealers about Family Yago business before. Zed asked her to investigate Sherrix' silence for me."

"You could do that again," he said.

Her shoulders hunched. "Zed would have to do it," she said. "Talk to Jo, I mean. And he—" She took a deep breath. "I don't know what is happening to him."

Nothing good, I hope, Dana thought. Trying to sound casual, he said, "You know, I could do it, Rhani."

She did not misunderstand him. "Find Loras U-Ellen for me." She leaned back on the bed, studying him.

He sweated beneath that amber gaze. There were moments when she was very like her brother. "He must be in the Hyper district," he said. "I could go down there, talk to people."

"They would talk to you?"

"I think so." He touched his left arm with his right. "I would have to hide this, of course. And I'd need some money, a credit disc—"

"Your medallion?" she said.

Do you have it? he wanted to shout. But, warned by her tone, he shook his head. "No. That's not necessary."

Leaning back on the bed as she was, the outline of Rhani's body showed clearly through her pants and shirt. He could not help looking at her and finding her lovely. For a moment, he became aware of the gulf between them, not of age or even, so much, of wealth, but of experience. Each had knowledge the other could not even dream of. And, under her penetrating, meticulous gaze, he saw himself mirrored—and felt himself wanting.

Quietly she said, "Dana, you do know, don't you, what my brother did when Binkie tried to escape from the estate."

His mouth drying as if scoured by wind, he nodded.

"Good. I—I would not want it to happen to you."

He caught his breath. "Wouldn't you stop it?" he asked.

She sat upright, shoulders hunching. "I would try. I'm not sure I could." She gazed at him, and said, not flinching, "I cannot always control him, you know."

"Why do you let . . ." he started, and stopped, afraid that he would indeed overstep bounds.

But to his astonishment, she said, "Why do I let him what? Be what he is? How can I prevent it? He is a medic, he knows what he is. If he wanted, he would go to Psi Center and put himself under the care of the telepaths. Why do I let him work for me, command the Net? Because it is safer than any other choice I can think of."

"Safer for Zed," Dana said. "Not for his victims."

She rose and faced him. "Do you think I don't know what he does? I do—more or less. I have seen the effects from close up. On another world, he would have to find willing victims. Do you think he couldn't? There are worlds where they would not even blink at what he does."

"Not many," Dana said. It irked him that she should

presume to tell *him* about other worlds. *He* was the Starcaptain.

"We will not fight," she said simply. "But don't try to escape when you are in the Hyper section of the city."

"I won't," he said, standing in his turn. Now their eyes were on a level again.

"When shall you go?" she asked.

He wanted to say to her: Now. Free me. I will do this for you anyway, I will help you find Loras U-Ellen, and then I will leave. Free me. But something held the words back. He could not bear to think that she would refuse him, and he knew she would.

He gave the question some thought. The Auction would disrupt everybody's normal patterns. He could not be sure of finding Tori Lamonica tonight; it was pure luck that he had seen her today. "Tomorrow—perhaps the day after tomorrow," he said.

"Fine. I will have Binkie make you a four-day credit disc. Your limit will be one hundred credits." She paused and then said, "I assume that will be sufficient?"

"To buy a few drinks at some Hyper bar?" he said. "Oh, yes."

"Good. I don't know how you plan to do this—but I needn't. What I would really hope is that you can convey a message to Loras U-Ellen for me. I want to meet him."

"That's the message?"

"Yes." Walking to the footstool, she poured herself more punch and returned with the glass to the bed. She sat down and pulled the printout to her lap. She looked up. "Thank you, Dana," she said. "You've helped me a great deal."

The aircooling system, overloaded, thumped in irritation. Dana started to sit down and then realized that she did not want him there. "You're welcome," he said, with irony, and knew as he reached the door that she had not heard it.

"FEDERATION OFFICIAL CALLS FOR SECTOR REFERENDUM!" the PIN headlines screamed in the morning. "A-RAE CALLS SLAVERY IMMORAL, ASKS FOR FIVE WORLDS TO VOTE." The picture with the newscan was of Michel A-Rae and Rhani Yago at Auction Place.

Rhani, grimly reading the article below the headline,

thought that it was clever of A-Rae to make his call for a referendum the day after the Auction. She wondered when she had first started thinking of him as an adversary.

Binkie was going through the rest of the mail. The pile was extra-thick because of the one-day lull. Most of the letters were formal replies to the Yago party invitations. "Is there anything in that stuff I should see?" Rhani said.

"Not yet, Rhani-ka," Binkie answered.

Rhani returned her attention to the PINsheet. "FEDERATION OFFICIAL CALLS FOR SECTOR REFERENDUM."

Well, he could do that, of course. Any Federation oficial above a certain rank could suggest a vote on any question involving Federation law. "A-Rae signs the first petition." There was another picture, of Michel A-Rae signing a piece of paper. For there actually to be a sector-wide vote, a petition would have to be made to the government of each world, signed by one-tenth of its citizens.

Of course, A-Rae was an Enchantean. Rhani tried to recall the last Chabadese census figures, and could not. "Binkie, what was the total from the last planetary census?" she asked. "To the nearest million."

Leaving the pile of mail, he bent over the com-unit. "Five million, Rhani-ka."

"Citizens or total head count?"

"Total head count."

"How many voters?" Tourists and slaves, of course, could neither petition nor vote.

"A little under two million," he said.

Rhani rubbed her chin. All A-Rae would need was two hundred thousand valid signatures on the petition.

Were there two hundred thousand voters on Chabad who did not support the slave systems? She didn't know. She wondered what the voting population figures on the other four worlds were, and decided that she didn't want to know. She went on reading. "A-RAE RESIGNS AS DRUG CAPTAIN." He had to do that, of course. His job demanded political neutrality, and he had just abrogated that. "HENRIETTA MELONES BECOMES ACTING CAPTAIN." She was probably his second-in-command. Eventually the Federation bureaucracy would name someone else to the post, but that could take months.

Rhani wondered how long A-Rae had been planning to

make this suggestion. There was no guarantee at all, of course, that any of what he wanted would come to pass. He had six weeks to obtain sufficient signatures on the petitions—not merely the petitions on Chabad, but those on Ley, Sabado, Enchanter, and Belle. Even if the question was actually put to a vote, how could A-Rae count on the outcome of a referendum? *Maybe he knows something I don't,* Rhani thought. For the first time in a long time, she was beginning to feel outmaneuvered. She simply had no idea what A-Rae might do or say next.

I have to find out who he is—was, she thought.

Amri's excited voice sounded on the intercom. "Rhani-ka, look outside! There are people all over the steps!"

"What?" Rising, Rhani went to the window. The morning sun blazed over the streets. Below her the steps of the house seemed covered with people, strangers. "What are they doing?" she said aloud.

"Rhani-ka, you might want to look at this," Binkie said. He was holding a dirty sheet of paper in one hand.

She scowled. "I know what it is," she said. "What does it say?"

"You will never be free of us until you have freed the slaves," read Binkie.

Rhani felt like shouting. *What in six hells is that supposed to mean?* "Fools," she said. "Put it in a safe place, Binkie. Officer Tsurada will want it."

She gazed out the window again. "Who are all those people, do you think?" she said.

Binkie shrugged. "Sightseers," he said. "Curiosity seekers."

"Tourists?"

"Some of them are probably tourists." He hesitated, and then said, "Like the people on the sector worlds who come to see the Net load. They make a holiday of it."

Rhani scowled. She found that picture mildly repugnant. "Well, I don't have to have them on my steps," she said. "Call the Abanat police for me, please, and ask for Officer Tsurada." She walked back to her chair, stabbing the intercom on the way. "Corrios, I would like breakfast now, please."

Before Amri had even brought the breakfast tray, Sachiko Tsurada came on the com-line. "Good morning, Domna," she said. "I understand you have a small crowd around your house. We have dispatched two units to move the people away."

"Thank you," Rhani said. "I appreciate that. But that was not the principal reason I called you. I received another communication from the Free Folk of Chabad. It says, 'You will never be free of us until the slaves are free.' Something like that."

Tsurada said calmly, "We would like to have it. I will send a messenger to collect it. I trust you are recovered from your experience?"

"I barely noticed the bruises this morning," Rhani said truthfully.

"I am glad." The policewoman cleared her throat. "I assume you have seen the PINsheet this morning, Domna."

"I have," Rhani said.

"You might be interested to know that Michel A-Rae, now resigned from his post, has dropped out of sight since his interview with the PINsheeters. We are doing our best to find out where he is; we assume that he is somewhere in the city."

Rhani said, "I'm sure he'll emerge as soon as PIN stops printing his name. He seems to like publicity." But as she said it, she wondered if it was true. The more she thought about him, the more enigmatic he became. "Officer Tsurada, do the Abanat police have any information about A-Rae's past?"

Tsurada said, "We know he had an I.D. exchange."

"Yes," Rhani said, "I know that too. Have you any information which predates that change?"

Tsurada shook her head. "No, Domna. I am sorry."

"So am I," Rhani said. "Thank you, Officer." The door slid back. She turned, expecting Amri. But it was Dana. He brought the breakfast tray into the room and set it on the footstool. It warmed her to see him.

"Good morning, Rhani-ka," he said. As he straightened, his hair fell across his forehead. He pushed it back. It had gotten long, she thought, seeing the way it framed his face. She wanted to touch him, to feel his hands on her skin. . . . She felt drunk. She swallowed.

"Are those people still on the steps?" she said, and was surprised to hear her voice come out as it always did, calm and clear.

Dana went to the window. "Almost gone," he reported. "There are two or three still there, arguing with the police. I think they must be PINsheeters; they have cameras."

Rhani scowled. She glanced at Binkie. "Thank you, Bink. That's all." He went to the door. Rhani licked her lips. "Dana," she said. He turned toward her.

A step sounded in the doorway. Zed walked in.

He was dressed in blue-and-silver. His hair was pulled back in a silver clip. He crossed to Rhani. She held her hand out to him, and he took it. His fingers were warm. "Good morning, Rhani-ka," he said softly. She wanted to ask him . . . but she would not.

"Good morning, Zed-ka," she said. She glanced toward Dana; he was standing near the window, face and eyes studiously blank.

"Have you seen the PINsheets this morning?" she said to her brother.

"No. Should I?"

She gestured toward the bed. "Take a look."

Dana said, "Rhani-ka, you have a call on the com-line."

Rhani turned toward the com-unit. The light was blinking. "Answer it," she said.

Dana stepped to the unit. His hands moved over the board: the light ceased flashing. Imre Kyneth's image appeared on the screen. Rhani went quickly to Dana's side. "Good morning, Imre," she said. Dana's hip brushed hers. Behind her, from the bed, she heard Zed exclaim.

"Good morning, Rhani," said Imre Kyneth. Aliza stood behind him, vast as a pavilion in her immense white robe. "Have you seen the PINsheets?"

"Yes, Imre, I've seen them."

"What do you think?" said Aliza.

"I haven't decided," Rhani said. "I haven't had my breakfast yet, for one thing." The words came out with more force than she had meant them to have, but the smells rising from the tray behind her were making her stomach ache for food.

Imre said, "I am sorry, Rhani. But I have already had my breakfast interrupted by seven people, including Theo and Ferris. I think the Council needs to meet."

The Chabad Council was made up of two houses: the Lower House, in which sat representatives from the Abanat districts, Gemit, and Sovka, and the Upper House, which consisted of the heads of the Four Families. A place in the Upper House was hereditary. To be a member of the Lower House, you had to be elected by a majority vote of your district: all Chabadese citizens could vote, but to run for the Council, you had to meet certain requirements, including those of residency, previous service to the community—a vague one, that—and one having to do with money. Poor people did not attain office on Chabad. But then, there were very few poor people on Chabad, and most of those were transients, not citizens. The Lower House held most of the official power; the Upper one, in theory, simply gave advice and consent. In practice—since consent could be withheld in more tangible ways than in Council—few decisions were taken by the Lower House that had not first been approved by the Four Families.

Rhani wondered what the Council would do in this situation. Referendum procedures were fairly fixed. "Why, Imre?" she said.

"Because," Imre said, "I think it likely that A-Rae will find sufficient signatures to ratify his petitions."

"Oh." Rhani rubbed her chin. If that were so. . . . "Do you also think he will win the referendum?" she said. Odd, she reflected, how we speak as if A-Rae were alone in his opposition to slavery. Talk about wishful thinking. . . .

Imre looked grim. "It's possible. It must be made plain what will happen to Chabad if he does."

"Not only to Chabad," said Aliza. "To the sector. The Council has a responsibility to meet. What do you think?"

Rhani's stomach rumbled. "I think I need my breakfast, Aliza," she said. "I shall eat, and talk to Zed, and call you. Will that be satisfactory?"

Imre smiled. "Of course, my dear," he said. "Meanwhile, you should expect a call from Ferris. He is agitated."

"Thank you, Imre." She did not want to talk with Ferris Dur, not now. She waited until the line had cleared, and then instructed the com-unit to hold all calls. Then she turned, to find Dana by the window and her brother seated on the bed.

Zed said softly, "I would very much like to have one uninterrupted hour alone with Michel A-Rae. Just one hour." His fingers curled. Dana flinched, and Rhani saw it.

"Zed-ka. that would not help matters at all," she said.

"It would relieve my feelings," said Zed. He scowled. "You know, ever since he first spoke to me while I was still on the Net, I've had the feeling that we've met somewhere, not here." He shook his head. "I must be wrong."

Rhani wondered if he could be right. "Do we have any associates among the Hype police, Zed-ka?"

He laughed. "I doubt it, Rhani-ka. They have a reputation for being incorruptible and unapproachable." He slapped the PINsheet. "Can A-Rae do this? I know a Federation official has to be of specific rank to make such a call."

Rhani said, "I'll ask the lawyers. But I'm sure he can." She watched the com-line light blink on, to tell her that someone had called and left a message. She wondered if it was Ferris. "Imre thinks the petitions will have enough signatures to ratify a referendum."

"I heard," Zed said. "I hope he's just being cautious." Shoulders slumping, he rubbed his eyes with the heels of his hands.

"Zed-ka, when did you leave the Clinic last night?" Rhani asked, alarmed.

"After midnight."

"Zed-ka—" Rhani put her fists on her hips, prepared to scold, and remembered Dana's presence. She could not be angry at Zed in front of Dana. "Dana," she said, "you may go."

He bowed, and left the room. Rhani advanced on her brother. He rose. "Rhani," he said gently, cupping her cheek with his palm, "I know what you want to say. Don't."

It stopped her. His fingers curved around her cheek. She wanted to shout, to tell him that he could tell her anything, that if something was wrong she needed to know, that she trusted him and always would. . . . Dark patches stained the skin beneath his eyes.

Unable to scold, she hugged him lightly and stepped back. "Let's eat."

"I'm not especially hungry," he said. Picking up a muffin, he broke it and handed her the larger piece. "I wish Corrios would make egg tarts."

"I'll ask him to," Rhani promised. She bit into a blueberry. The sweet juice spurted onto her tongue. Blueberries, like all fruits and vegetables, were imported to Chabad. Forty years back an agricultural commune from Sabado had brought in citrus tree stock and had erected massive greenhouses. With careful temperature control, the commune insisted, they could produce three crops a year, and the Levos Family, against advice, had invested money in the plan. It had all sounded workable, but within two years the greenhouses had had to be abandoned. Those advising the investors had not bargained for the unrelenting alkalinity of Chabad's soil.

Zed tore apart a second muffin. "These are pretty good," he said.

Rhani ate another piece slowly, watching the sunlight pattern on the walls. She sat on the bed, leaning back on one palm. "Zed-ka," she said, "have you ever wondered how historians will write about us in their books?"

His eyebrows went up. "What put that in your mind?"

She pointed to the PINsheet. "That. If Michel A-Rae has his way, they will say that under its fifth generation of inhabitants, Chabad's economy collapsed."

"Do you think that he will?" Zed asked.

"I don't know," Rhani said. "I hope not. Lisa Yago helped to found this colony. Irene was a member of the first Council. Orrin went to Nexus. Our mother built the Net. What will they say about me?"

"What would you like them to say?"

Rhani said, "I would love to have them tell how Rhani Yago established Chabad's independence from outside influence by purchasing the dorazine formula from The Pharmacy."

"Oh ho," Zed said. He smiled at her. "I should like that, very much."

"Or," she said, "they might also say that Rhani Yago changed the political and economic structure of Chabad by uniting the influence and fortune of two great Families in the person of her daughter."

He froze for a moment, eyes shuttering, gaze turning

inward, smile gone. Then he said, "You have decided to do it."

She nodded. "Yes."

His mouth quirked suddenly with amusement. "Have you told Ferris Dur?"

"Not yet."

"I see," he said. "Thank you for telling me first. Are you doing this to placate history, Rhani-ka, or to appease our mother's shade. . . ?"

I am doing it because I want to, Rhani thought, and because I have found a way to do it that will afford me pleasure. . . . But this, above all, she could not say to Zed.

"It seems right," she said, determined not to grow angry. "Domna Sam used to tell me to trust my intuition."

"Pilots are taught that, too," Zed said. He gazed around the room. "Our mother never had any to trust."

Rhani was astonished. Zed rarely mentioned Isobel, and he had deliberately mentioned her twice in the last minute. He's upset, she thought; about Michel A-Rae, about me, about Darien Riis. . . . She did not want to think about *that*. On impulse, she leaned across the bed to the compartment in the headboard, and brought out the wrapped sculpture that she had bought at Tuli's.

"Zed-ka," she said, "I was saving this to give you on Founders' Day, but I think I want you to have it now." She passed it to him. "Be gentle with it, it's glass."

He unwrapped it, methodically folding the paper and laying it aside. As the sculpture came free, it caught the light and glittered, and Rhani heard her brother's sharp intake of breath. It was a statue of a man standing on an ice slab; the man was blue, the ice black. The man held an ice hammer, and wore an ice suit with the hood folded back. Tuli had promised that the etched details would be exquisite, and they were: in the curves and hollows of the climber's tiny profile, the maker had managed to render Zed Yago's portrait.

"Do you like it?" she said.

"Rhani-ka, it's stupendous," he said. He rotated it gently, face momentarily unguarded in his appreciation of beauty. "I love it. Thank you." He kissed her forehead.

Rising, he crossed to the door, carrying the radiant blue figure in both hands. "I'll put it in my room. I'll have to warn Amri not to touch it."

As he reached the door, he turned back. "I'm going to the Clinic again today," he said.

"Now?" Rhani exclaimed. He nodded. Wait, she wanted to cry, wait, we have to talk, I need your advice. . . . But he had gone. She heard his footsteps in the hall, the sound of a door sliding back, and silence.

The laboring aircooler wheezed. She sat rigid, fists locked on her knees. Finally she stood and went to the com-unit. She checked the message—it was indeed from Ferris Dur—and instructed the unit to connect her with Imre Kyneth.

A woman's image formed on the screen. "Good day," she said, "this is a recording of Nialle Hamish, Domni Imre's secretary. Would you kindly leave your message?"

"This is Rhani Yago," Rhani said. "Imre, I think we should wait a week to assess public reaction, and then call a Council meeting. Let me know if this seems good to you." She switched off, waited a second, and called Ferris.

He came onto the screen immediately; himself, not a recording.

"Domna!" he said. "I hoped you would call."

He was agitated; she could see that from the state of the fur trim on his robe. She braced herself to deal with it.

"You've heard, of course," he said.

"I've heard," Rhani said. "I've suggested to Imre that the Upper House request a Council meeting in a week."

"Why wait?" Ferris said. "This petition is a threat!"

"A threat is not an attack," Rhani said. "Besides, it seems more in keeping with our dignity if we do not appear to be frightened of it. If we meet now—" She let the sentence finish itself in his mind, and then said, "But the referendum is not why I called, Ferris. I called to give you my response to your proposal—the proposal of import to all Chabad. . . ."

"Yes," he said, leaning forward. "Yes?"

"Yes," she said. "I will marry you, Domni Ferris." She held up a hand before he could speak. "I will have my legal staff draw up the contracts for merger and settlement of our mutual properties upon a child."

"Our child," he said.

She said, *"My* child." His jaw slackened as he understood. "That must be part of our agreement, Ferris, or else we do not have one."

His brown eyes grew indignant. He twisted the robe's fur with both hands. "All right," he muttered. "I can accept that."

"I am pleased," Rhani said, and switched off. She had not bothered to sit: now, leaning on the back of the chair, she breathed slowly, calming her senses, calming her mind.

She went to the bathroom, covered her hair, and took a shower. As the water streamed down her body, she looked at herself as if she were a stranger even to herself. She tried to imagine what it would feel like to be pregnant, and could not. I could ask Tuli, she thought. Tuli has a child. Tuli has a son. What if I should have a son? She imagined herself holding a boy child like the youngest Kyneth, with black hair, not reddish hair. . . . It would not matter, she thought. She stepped from the shower and toweled herself dry. Then, facing her mirror, she reached for the little vial of pills beside it.

One pill every seven days kept her infertile; she had been taking them for twenty-three years.

She watched in the mirror as a woman in a bathroom just like her own put a vial of pills into a disposal.

Then she went to the intercom. "Dana?" she said.

He answered, "Yes, Rhani-ka?" In the background she heard the lilt of music, and Amri asking a question.

"I want to talk to you," she said. "Please come now to my room."

Chapter Thirteen

The room was dark. Rhani had drawn the heavy curtains over the windows; Dana did not know why. She was sleeping now, curled on her side, head on the pillow. Her unbraided hair fell across her face and veiled her breasts: lips parted, in the shadowy bedroom she looked like a sleeping child. Dana bent closer. Her eyelids flickered but did not open; she was dreaming. He wondered what about. He stretched, feeling sad despite the lingering remembrance of pleasure. For three days now she had called him to her bed. The loving had been good, splendid and passionate, and yet—he sensed behind her gaze as she smiled at him and called his name the presence of another person, another face. He did not know whose.

Some previous lover's? he thought. Zed's? That frightened him. For the fiftieth time in three days he pictured Zed walking in and finding them in bed. *"I cannot always control him,"* Rhani had warned. The image made his scrotum contract. He lifted on an elbow. Rhani opened her eyes. She smiled, and stretched like a cat. "Hmm?"

He stroked her flat belly. Her skin was soft as silk. "Rhani-ka, I should go."

"Why?" she said. Lunging, she wound her arms about his neck and pulled him to her. "Bored?"

He breathed her smell. "No," he said into the side of her neck. "Oh, no."

She released him. "What is it, then?" She teased him with one groping hand. He trapped it in his own.

"Rhani-ka, stop."

"What for?"

"Because I should leave."

She sat up. Her hair fell over her shoulders. "What do you have to do that is so important?"

He said, "It's been two days since the Auction. Don't you want me to find Loras U-Ellen?"

"No," she said, and in the same breath, "Yes. Yes, I suppose so." Once again she seemed to look through him to that other face. He felt sullen, sulky as a child whose promised treat has been withheld. He wanted to shake her, and to say: You don't love me, and my body's nothing special. So what's this all about?

But then, his own motives were none too pure.

"What are you thinking?" she demanded.

He gazed at her, finding her beautiful. "I was thinking how strange this is," he temporized.

She laughed, and sat up suddenly. Her breasts swung. Her nipples were small and pinkish-brown; the nipples of a woman who had never had children. Leaning forward, she kissed him quickly. "Better go if you're going."

He left the bed and dressed before she changed her mind.

"You'll need a credit disc," she said as he started toward the door. Feeling somewhat sheepish, he turned back. She opened the compartment in the headboard of the bed and handed it to him. He took it, pulse quickening.

"You look so happy," she said thoughtfully as he once more began to leave the room. The hairs on the back of his neck stood up. Her tone was wistful . . . . Relax, he ordered himself, relax. She isn't Zed, who would sense the presence of the joy and question until he knew what source it sprang from. This is Rhani.

"Loras U-Ellen," he said. "I'll return as soon as I can."

"Don't forget the curfew," she said. Oh, *hell,* Dana thought. He had forgotten that unaccompanied slaves had to be off Abanat's streets one hour after sunset.

It doesn't matter, he thought. I can go back tomorrow, and the next day, and the next, until I find her. "Thank you, Rhani-ka," he said. He left the room. The hall was bright, and he squinted as he went downstairs. Amri saw him and shot him a knowing look from the dining alcove.

It was just past noon, and he guessed that Corrios was asleep. He walked back to Amri. "Kitten, I may be back late," he said. "I'm on an errand."

She nodded. "Binkie's out, too," she said. Jumping up, she came to him and put a hand on his forearm. Her clear blue eyes were guileless. "Dana, Binkie doesn't like you, you know."

"How do you know?" he said.

She shrugged. "I just do."

He accepted it. "Thanks, kitten. I'll remember." He went to the front door, remembering at the last minute to lift his sunshades from the rack. He stepped outside. The air shimmered with heat. He went slowly down the steps, feeling the sunlight fold like a cape around his shoulders and back.

In Founders' Green, the fountains were playing. He watched them for a while. Suddenly he saw Binkie crossing the street, coming toward the house. Dana gazed along his trajectory. . . . At the corner of the street was a figure in black striding swiftly west. He thought: Even tourists should know better than to wear black in Abanat—and then remembered who might wear black anyplace, anytime. Binkie came abreast of him and started to pass him; Dana reached out and clamped a hand in the front of Binkie's blue shirt.

"Who was that?" he said.

The secretary said, "What the hell business is that of yours?" He tried to pull away; Dana tightened his grip.

"That was a Hype cop," he said. "Why are you talking with the Hype cops?"

The secretary glared at him. "You have no right to question me," he said. "Let go."

Dana held on. "I want to know," he said.

"You're a fool," Binkie said. Contempt edged his tone. "I think you like it—being a slave."

Dana wanted to hit him. "What the fuck makes you think that?" he said.

Binkie snorted. "The way you spend your days."

Dana flushed. "I can't exactly refuse," he said defensively.

"Why not?" Binkie said. "She won't rape you. She's not Zed."

"Keep your voice down!" Dana said. It was not like Binkie to be so reckless with his words. He dropped his hand from Binkie's shirt. "You've been acting odd lately," he said. "Amri's noticed it—I don't know why Rhani hasn't."

"Because all she thinks about is hopping into bed with you," the secretary said. "I'd sooner bed a kerit." He started to brush past Dana.

"Hold it." Dana caught his arm. "I still want to know what you have to say to the Hype cops."

Binkie looked him up and down. "It seems to have escaped your attention," he said, "that I don't want to tell you. What do you think I'm doing? I'm buying my way out of here. Like you."

Dana was silent. It was true, of course. His fingers loosened. "I don't like being a slave," he said quietly.

"Then you ought to have noticed," Binkie said, "that the only person fighting the slave system in this sector is an ex-Hype cop, Michel A-Rae."

Dana scowled. "I'm not used to thinking of the Hype cops as allies," he said.

Binkie stared at him. "Sweet mother," he said. "You're a child. You—but I forget. How long have you been a slave? Under a month, right? Try it for a year,

Dana. Try it for four years. Wait a little while, until Rhani gets bored with your body, or Zed finds out you've been her lover. You've pushed what he did to you to the back of your mind, because you have to, I know, but it can happen again. And your lover Rhani won't save you from him because she needs him a hell of a lot more than she needs you. How long is your slave contract for?"

Dana swallowed. "Ten years."

Binkie said, "How old will you be in ten years?"

"Thirty-four."

"Think about that. And then tell me *I'm* odd." He went up the stairs. Dana heard the door close.

Slowly he went down the steps. Stars, he thought, Binkie's right. . . . He scowled, and kicked a pebble. He felt shamed. He had been defending the very system of which he was a victim. But it was a legal system, he thought, and besides, was it wrong of him to have saved Rhani Yago's life? He tugged at his left sleeve. The shirt was one of Rhani's, and the sleeves went to his wrists, hiding his slave brand. She had offered him one of Zed's shirts, but he had refused it. If slavery is abolished, they will have to put something in its place, he thought, and that won't feel any better to the people in jails. . . . He wondered what it would be like to live in a cell, or whatever they let prisoners live in. What if they voted in something worse than slavery: forced labor, or brain-wipe?

But slavery was already a kind of forced labor, and dorazine addiction produced a temporary brain-wipe. The arguments went around and around in his head. Suddenly, a face popped in front of him. "Excuse me, citizen, can you tell me what you think of the referendum?" It was a PINsheet pollster. The man crowded him expertly, camera poised, one hand thrusting out a hand mike. "Your name, citizen?" he pressed.

"Fuck off," Dana said. The man sighed and turned away. PINsheets littered the walkways. Dana passed one newsstand; a woman with mirrorshades and sandals on— and nothing else—was listening to the news through headphones. Dana's foot crunched on a sheet. The headline said: "PETITIONERS CLAIM 40,000 SIGNATURES IN 3 DAYS."

The PINsheeter had found someone who would talk to

him. She wore a light yellow apton robe that billowed about her like a cloud: not a citizen, Dana thought, but a tourist. He dawdled, listening to her comments. She hoped the referendum would fail, though, of course, since she was from Sector Cardinal, it was none of her business, but after all, Chabad's methods with criminals were not *so* awful; on her world, China II, rehabilitation sometimes took *years,* and anyway the slave system made Chabad so intriguing, so different to come to!

"Would you own slaves?" the PINsheeter asked.

The tourist looked uneasy. "I don't know."

"Do you know anything about dorazine addiction?"

She backed away, suddenly shy. "Oh, no. No."

Dana grinned mirthlessly, because if he did not laugh he would weep. The woman's rationalizations were painfully familiar. Halting at a map, he located the nearest movalong going north. Exultation coursed through him. Careful, he told himself. He had a credit disc in his pocket and the freedom of the streets, but he was not free.

As he neared the Hyper district, sound captured his attention first. In the narrowed streets, behind a closed door, someone was drumming. The insistent patter, like hail on the hard ground, thrust his imagination back in time to Liathera's, on Nexus.

Careful. Be careful.

A man came yawning from a doorway. His face was streaked with glitterstick and he walked, like all Hypers, with the recognition in his bones that gravity is just a local condition.

As unobtrusively as he knew how, Dana followed him.

He had no idea who the yawning man was: a pilot off a shuttleship, perhaps? A crewman from one of the passenger liners? The man turned two corners and, with another gaping yawn, sauntered into a doorway. The door opened to his palm. Hard night, Dana thought, breathing in the heavy odors of marijuana and wine. An acrid smell caught his attention as he moved further down the nameless street. . . . Coffee, he realized. He walked quickly to the corner. Sure enough, the smell grew stronger. He had located at least part of what he was looking for: only a Hyper bar would serve coffee.

As he strolled through The Green Dancer's swinging

door, he remembered coming in to Chabad's moon with the chatter of the shuttleship pilots welcoming him. He tried to recall names, *Seminole*—he remembered *Seminole*. With Juno on the stick. He wondered if Juno came here often. Just within the doorway he halted to look. It looked like every other bar he knew. Small tables and rugged chairs. Booths in the back. A curving bar that ran the width of the front room. Over the bar was hanging an awkwardly painted picture of a figure in green veils: supposedly, Dana guessed, a Verdian dancing a *K'm'ta*. Dana wondered if Chabad had any Verdians on it. If it did, they would come here. Bars for the Hyper community were not simply places to meet friends, drink, listen to music, and fight.

A mean-looking woman with frizzy, white hair was standing behind the bar. Dana went to her. "Red wine." He slid his credit disc across the dark-brown neowood surface. She poured a glass of syrupy red wine for him and flicked the disc back.

"First one's free," she said.

"Oh." He was not certain what that meant. He decided that it could only mean that the bar bought everybody's first drink of the day. A pleasant custom. He took the glass of wine to a table. Food smells wafted from an unseen place; broiled fish and seaweed cakes, cheap Chabadese food. He would have lunch, he thought. It was wonderful to know that he could order food if he wanted it, that he could buy clothes—shirts with long sleeves—and jewelry—earrings that were not blue—musictapes, booktapes . . . but he could not buy a weapon, the disc would not pay for that. Nor could he rent a bubble.

He sipped the wine. It was awful, dreadfully sweet. People drifted in, spoke to the bartender, whose name, it seemed, was Amber, picked up drinks, and ambled to seats. He wondered if the Net crew came in here. Of course, they must. A woman stalked in wearing a scarlet feather in her hair, and he wondered what it was: a signal, an identification, or just decoration?

The coffee smell grew stronger. Dana glanced toward the bar: Amber had poured herself a mug of it, which told Dana a small fact about her. People who drank coffee had once lived on New Terra, Old Terra, or New Terrain, or had shipped with someone who had. Russell drank coffee.

It was Russell who'd told him that. And there was a lot more he said that I should have listened to, Dana thought.

Zed Yago's voice whispered in his mind, *"Didn't your mother ever tell you not to skop Skellians?"*

Fuck off, Dana replied. He sipped the wine and discovered he had nearly emptied the glass. He returned to the bar. "More wine, please," he said to Amber. This time she took his money.

As she slapped his credit disc down, she said, "We don't often see strangers in here."

It was, of course, a question, and it delighted him because it meant that, whatever else he was, he was still a Hyper. Amber would never trouble to question a tourist. He leaned an elbow on the bar. "I'm looking for a friend," he answered.

She stepped to the other end of the bar to pour a drink for a chunky man wearing a loader's harness. Dana let his gaze wander to the tables. They were crowded now; the noon heat had driven the stragglers off the streets. A girl in blue glitterstick was talking to the woman with the feather. Amber came back. As she set up fresh glasses on the counter, she said, "This is a friendly bar."

"Seems to be," he agreed. "I'm looking for a particular friend." He rested his hip on the bar stool. "I'll bet you know everyone here."

She looked straight at him. "I don't know you."

"My name is Dana Ikoro," he said.

Turning away, Amber pressed a button. Ice clattered into a cooler behind the bar. "I've heard the name," she said.

The hairs on the back of Dana's neck stirred. "Where?"

"In here," she said. She cracked her thumb knuckles. "From the Net crew."

"What did they say?" Dana asked, trying to keep his voice casual.

She gazed at him from beneath the bird's nest tangle of hair. "They said that some Hyper named Ikoro had been picked up by the Narc Control and funneled to the Net. And that he ended up as meat for Zed Yago."

Meat. Yes. That he had been, and was. Dana's throat soured. "Did they say anything else?"

"They said they thought he was a Starcaptain."

Dana said, "That's true."

Her eyes, which were green as Pellin's grass, searched his face. "And the rest."

Old woman, he thought, if you pity me. . . . "The rest is true, too."

Her face did not change. "Welcome to The Green Dancer, Starcaptain."

"Thank you," Dana said. "I'm looking for Tori Lamonica."

Amber ran a hand through her hair, not improving it. "I know her," she said. "She comes in here."

At their table, the woman with the red feather in her hair and the girl in blue glitterstick were glaring at each other. Suddenly the girl said loudly, "Well, you can just shinny, if you feel *that* way about it!"

"Excuse me," Amber said. She ducked from behind the bar and went to the table. The girl in glitterstick-blue was standing.

There was a whispered argument, finished when Amber jerked a thumb toward the door. The woman in red stalked out. Amber returned to the bar. "Want some lunch?" she said.

"Sure," said Dana, fumbling out his credit disc.

Amber thumped the flat of her hand on the bar. "Lunch time!" she said. People at the tables stretched and rose and came to the bar. The girl in glitterstick yawned and came around the end of the bar. She went in the back; in a few moments she emerged with three plates of food on each arm.

Amber put a plate in front of him. The seaweed looked overcrisp, but the fish smelled—and tasted—fresh. Dana put his empty glass where the bartender could see it. After a while she refilled it.

"Buy you something?" he said.

She snorted. "Think I'd drink my own liquor?" Closing her hand suddenly around his glass, she took it away and dumped out the wine. Before he could protest, she filled it with a darker liquid. "Try that."

He drank. The wine was smooth and dry, not cheap. "Thank you," he said.

"Lamonica comes in evenings," she said. "If she comes in tonight, I'll tell her you're looking for her."

Dana wondered if Tori Lamonica knew he had been

taken by the Net. He decided she must. "I'd appreciate that," he said. "Tell her that I'll come back tomorrow night."

She said sharply, "I want no trouble in the bar."

"There'll be no trouble," Dana promised.

The girl in glitterstick sauntered to the bar and took the stool beside Dana. "Amber, may I have a drink?" She smiled at Dana, and her voice went up half an octave. "Hello?"

Dana grinned at her. "Sorry," he said, "I'm shinnying." He drained the glass of good wine before heading toward the door.

Outside in the street he stood, breathing deeply, while sweat rolled down his arms. Dust blew down the narrow roadway. He wondered who the girl was; she looked too young to be a Hyper. Amber's daughter? Some star-crazed kid? Maybe she had taken antiagathics and was really two hundred years old. He rubbed his eyes with both hands. Somehow he had not realized before that, even if—no, *when*—he managed to escape, the information about what had happened to him on the Sardonyx Net would never leave him. . . . From star to star, sector to sector, it would follow him around; in every place he drank, he would hear his own name, and then Zed Yago's, and people would stare.

Fuck, he thought. Damned infertile son of a syphilitic goat—he thought in Pellish. He walked from the building, wishing that he could stay, sit on the barstool, drink Amber's wine (even the cheap stuff) and tell glamorous lies. But he had to go back. He made himself stop swearing. If he let himself grow too angry, one day it would come out at the wrong time.

The moment he entered the Yago mansion he knew that something was wrong. As he returned his sunshades to the hall rack he saw that Rhani's were not there. He went to the kitchen. Amri was sitting on a stool, eating chobi seeds. "Is Rhani home?" he said.

She jumped like a startled cat. "Oh. No. She went out."

"Alone?"

Amri nodded, and her bland face grew troubled. "Yes. Corrios said she should wait for you but she said she didn't want to."

Dana groaned. "Did she say where she was going?"

Corrios entered. "Tuli's," he said.

Tuli's. That was the glass shop in the market square. He remembered the package. "When did she leave?"

Corrios glanced at the wall clock. "Half an hour ago."

"Maybe I can catch her," Dana said. "Why the hell didn't you stop her?" he said to Corrios, but the big man only shrugged.

"How?"

Don't open the door, Dana thought savagely. Hide all the sunshades. Lock her up.

Seizing his sunshades, he loped to the front door. At least, he thought grimly, if Zed comes home, he'll find us both gone. He cast his mind back to that first confusing day, trying to recall their movements through the streets. . . . They had gone from the little landingport to the market square. He hurried down the steps. Twice on his way he thought he saw her and crossed the street to find he had been chasing a stranger. Once, for five minutes, he got lost. At last, he found the square. It was easy to pick out Tuli's shop window: it shimmered.

As he started across the square, he saw her. She was moving quite slowly through the throng of shoppers. Her hair was loose; sunshades hid her eyes, and she was wearing the gold pendant that Zed had given her.

He went to meet her. As he neared her, she stopped, waiting for him. Her face looked tense; the lines around her mouth suddenly prominent. "Rhani-ka," he said, "why didn't you wait for me?"

She did not answer.

"What's wrong?" he asked, alarmed.

She sighed, and put her arm through his. "I wanted to talk to Tuli," she said. "So I went to the shop. When I got there—" She paused. "I've known Tuli for eight years. I thought we were friends. I went in. She was behind the counter, waiting on a customer. I said her name. She called me Domna Rhani. She wouldn't smile at me. I saw a sheet of paper on the wall and went to read it. It said that anyone wishing to sign the petition calling for a referendum on the maintenance of slavery in Sardonyx Sector should see the proprietor of the store."

Dana did not know what to say. As noncommittally as possible, he said, "You were surprised?"

Rhani's normally husky voice was rough with pain. "I just wanted to talk."

"Did you expect an ex-slave to be in favor of slavery?"

Her fingers bit into his arm. "I'm not that much of a fool! But she need not have called me Domna Rhani. And I did think she might have the grace to remain publicly neutral."

Dana said, "I'm sorry you're upset."

"I'm not upset, I'm angry! At myself." With a choppy gesture, she thrust her sunshades to the crown of her head. "I have feared what this referendum's outcome might do to the economy of this planet, if A-Rae's position won it. Now I fear that, whichever side wins or loses, the feelings released by the issue will break Chabad apart. I should have foreseen it."

She was, Dana realized, quite serious. "Rhani," he said, "you aren't responsible for the destiny of an entire planet."

The cacophony and color of the market square swirled around them like storm winds around the eye. Rhani gazed at him. She was only a little shorter than he. . . . She was wearing blue pants and a blue shirt. The shirt had a red dragon embroidered on its back. The gold pendant glinted in the soft hollow of her throat. She said, "You are wrong. I am."

They began to walk then, threading slowly through the clumps of tourists. That's crazy, Dana thought. No one runs a planet; that's fantasy.

But it was not fantasy, he thought. This woman strolling at his side had the power to make decisions which affected the politics and the economy of this and four other worlds.

A series of shouts from behind them made them both turn. Rhani started to walk toward the noise. Dana caught her arm, remembering his responsibility as bodyguard. "Don't," he said, "it isn't safe."

"Move aside please!" came an amplified shout. Three Abanat police officers sliced briskly through the crowd. Two of them were carrying Federation-issue stunners.

Like members of a herd, the tourists began to bunch toward the shouting. "Come on, let's get out of here," Dana said. He held Rhani's arm. Shopkeepers came from their doorways to gaze into the square, and a few of them looked curiously at the two people moving steadily away from the confrontation. Dana watched, but he could not see anyone who stared for very long.

"This way," Rhani said, changing directions. Dana followed automatically. Soon they had reached the Boulevard, and, crossing it, were heading toward Founders' Green.

The woman at the gate smiled and bowed and passed them in beneath the cool, green trees. "Why do you always walk around the city?" Dana asked.

Rhani chuckled. "It's the only exercise I get," she said. She grinned. "Besides, the movalongs are for tourists."

They stopped beside the fountain to watch the water cascade from rock to artistically placed rock. "I love waterfalls," Rhani said.

Dana said, "There are worlds with more waterfalls than Chabad has rocks."

She shook her head. "I doubt that," she said. Then the left corner of her mouth turned up in amusement. "I told a lie," she murmured, putting her hand on Dana's arm.

"What?" he said.

Her amusement broadened. "Walking is not my only exercise."

The spray from the fall had left a veil of drops against her hair; they looked like sequins in the trees' concealing shade. Dana glanced toward the Yago house. . . . "No one can see us," Rhani said. She reached for him.

But Dana held her off. "Rhani-ka, it's not safe," he said. "We may be being watched. The Hype cops—"

Rhani scowled. "Damn," she said softly. "I was trying to forget about them."

As they walked from beneath the trees, Rhani said, "How did your errand go?"

Dana tensed. "I've made a step toward contact," he said.

"What's your next step?"

"I must go back tomorrow night."

"You are being very vague," she said. They walked into sunlight, and the sweat jumped on Dana's arms and neck. "I presume you mean to be."

He said, "I would prefer to be, yes."

She turned to face him. Pushing back her cloud of hair with both hands, she said, "I dislike being ignorant,

Dana." Behind her, the tines of the iron fence gleamed darkly in the stark Chabadese light.

Dana said, "Rhani, if I tell you what I do and who I see, I break a confidence. Even more than that—I break Hyper tradition. I promised you Loras U-Ellen. Will you trust me to keep that promise?"

She did not like being cornered; he could see it in her face. She cocked her head to one side. "How long till I have him?"

"I don't know," he said. Sweet mother, he thought, she had better trust me. If she doesn't, I shall have to tell her a pack of lies.

He did not want to lie to a Yago.

She nodded. "All right. I will trust you."

"Thank you," he said.

She said, "Don't be a fool, Starcaptain. What should I do, give you to Zed? Let him discover that we have been lovers?"

He said grimly, "Zed would never hurt you."

"I know that," she said. Her shoes rapped crisply on the path. Ahead of them sat the second gate, and, looming over it, the façade with the Yago crest. "Leave it, Dana. Let's not go over it again." They walked through the gate. "Oh, no!" Her voice rose in dismay. Dana looked past her. PINsheeters with cameras and recording equipment swarmed over the steps of the house.

There was no way to go around, under, or over them, Dana judged. He glanced at Rhani. "Well, Domna?" he said.

The muscles of her face tightened. Then, to his surprise and admiration, she smiled, and walked forward.

The PINsheeters saw her. Courtesy, and their knowledge of her status, restrained them for brief moments. Then they scrambled toward her. Dana stepped in front of her, putting himself between her and the rush—"No!" she said. He stepped back, jolted.

She pointed. "You, you, you, you, and you," she said. "Get me to the house with as little time lost as you can manage and you may have an interview with me indoors."

They did not hesitate. "You got it, lady," said the one in front, a tall black woman in a bright yellow tunic and pants. She was carrying a camera. "Form wedge—hup!"

As if they had practiced the maneuver, the five turned, and Dana realized that the other four wore yellow badges, that Rhani had not, in fact, selected at random. . . . "Let's go!" They moved out. The other PINsheeters, seeing what had happened, swore at them. But the woman in yellow simply grinned and put her shoulders down, thrusting ahead, ignoring the angry noises. Dana hung back, as did a man with a yellow badge, in case the disappointed PINsheeters decided to crowd them from behind, but nothing happened. Corrios opened the door. The lucky PIN team began to point cameras in all directions. "What the hell update is this?" said the black woman.

"Six," said a short man with a vidscreen in his hands.

"No," said someone else, "seven."

"Can we go into the kitchen?"

"How about upstairs?"

The tall woman pointed at Dana. "Who's he?"

Smoothly, Binkie appeared and took charge. "Citizens, Domna Rhani suggests that you set up your equipment in this room." He slid back the door to the large parlor. "She'll be with you in a moment; she asks you to remain here until she arrives. The interview will last twenty minutes."

"Hell," protested the tall woman, "we deserve more time than that! We got her through, didn't we?"

"Shut up, Teddy," said the short man, "or she'll throw us out."

"Twenty minutes," Binkie said inexorably. He gestured to the door. Grumbling, the PINsheeters entered the parlor. Corrios came from the kitchen balancing a laden tray on one palm.

After the interview was over and the PINsheeters had left the house, Rhani lingered in the parlor. It was not a room she liked; the furniture and the decorations were heavy, dark wood. It reminded her of her mother. She rubbed a hand across the nappy velvet of her chair. The PINsheeters had left exceedingly pleased. She had answered about two-thirds of their questions and had given them a headline for their update: "RHANI YAGO SUPPORTS REFERENDUM!"

What she had said was, "If the petitions support a

referendum on Chabad, then I support it, too."

"What do you think of Michel A-Rae?" Teddy Corinna, the tall woman, asked her.

"I think he is inexperienced," Rhani had answered in her most patronizing tone. "But well-meaning."

She had meant to patronize: she hoped that A-Rae's pride would pique him to a response. Perhaps he could be teased into a few stupidities. Most people could. The sillier he sounded, the more his support would drop, and his supporters, embarrassed, would grow silent.

The PINsheeters had drained two carafes of wine and eaten a pile of spice cakes. Rhani took a handful of the only food left on the table, chobi seeds. As she stood, someone tapped on the parlor door. "Rhani-ka," said Binkie's voice, "Officer Tsurada is on line."

"Thank you, Bink." She turned. "Is there still a mob on the steps?"

"No, they've gone." He looked with distaste at the litter left by the PINsheeters. "I'll call Amri to sort this out."

"Thank you. Do you know what the call's about?"

He smiled and shook his head. "No, Rhani-ka. Officer Tsurada would never tell *me*."

"No, of course not," Rhani said. "I forget, sometimes—" She smiled an apology. "Is my brother still at the Clinic?"

"As far as I know, Rhani-ka."

I wonder, she thought, if he is staying away because he cannot bear to be with me, now that I have decided to marry Ferris Dur?

She did not want to think about Darien Riis.

Cracking a chobi seed between her teeth, she wondered what Binkie would make of the wedding news. She would let him know, of course; in fact, she thought, I should discuss it with him now, before all the legal negotiations start. As she climbed the stairs to her bedroom, she found herself longing to be home at the estate. Soon, she promised herself. Soon. After the party.

Which would happen in three more days. She made a face as she crossed the room to the com-unit. The screen was on standby mode. She thumbed the com-line open. "Rhani Yago here."

A face flickered elusively, then resolved into Sachiko

Tsurada's features. "Domna. We have uncovered some rather interesting information."

Rhani tensed. "About what?"

"The Free Folk of Chabad. The next to last message you sent us retained a fingerprint on it. We 'grammed the Nexus files; they sent us back an 'R' classification."

"I'm sorry," Rhani said, "but I don't know what you're talking about."

Tsurada giggled, embarrassed. "I'm sorry. When we checked with Nexus Compcenter, which has all human records stored and available to it, we were told that though they had an identification for the print we sent, they could not release it."

"What does that mean?" Rhani said.

"It means," said the policewoman, "that the Free Folk of Chabad have been getting some very high-level assistance."

"Assistance—" Rhani scowled. Who would help a dissident organization to plan—rather ineptly—an assassination?

She knew. Officer Tsurada was watching her, eyes grim. Her wrists began to ache, and she realized that she had been gripping the back of the com-unit chair. She released it, and sat. She hesitated, and then said, "Officer Tsurada, is there any chance that either you or Nexus Compcenter made a mistake?"

Tsurada shook her head. "No, Domna. Unfortunately."

Rhani nodded. "I see," she said. Beneath the calm she hoped she was expressing, she could feel rage rising. "Perhaps we should say no more." This was an open line; anyone with the right equipment could be listening to the call. "Tell me, Officer Tsurada—the last time I spoke with you, you were working on a missing person case. Did you locate the object of your search?"

For a moment, Tsurada's gaze reflected only bemusement. Then her puzzled eyes grew clear, and her mouth straightened. "No, not yet, Domna. But we will." Both women smiled. The Abanat police had not let located the present whereabouts of Michel A-Rae.

"That's good to know. Please keep me informed. Thank you for apprising me of this information." Rhani watched the image flicker out. The background noise of the police station thrummed in her ears. With a stab of her thumb, she broke the connection, and, suddenly enraged, slammed her fists on her thighs. Fury fought briefly with pain. So the Free Folk of Chabad were getting high-level, *Federation*-level assistance, were they? Damn Michel A-Rae!

She rose and walked to the window. Holding the curtain aside with one cautious hand, she gazed into Founders' Green, looking for a watcher wearing tell-tale black. No one was there but children, and watchful slaves. She wondered if A-Rae could have subverted one of the slaves. She let the curtain fall. Crossing her arms over her chest, she walked to the com-unit. Zed needed to know of this. But as her hand moved, she hesitated, and then drew it slowly back. She would tell him, yes, but not now, not while it seemed to hurt him to be in the same room with her. She wondered if she could be wrong in assuming A-Rae's part. No. Who else would exert such power on behalf of a group whose only object appeared to be to kill Rhani Yago? Or, if not to kill her, to frighten her, demoralize her. . . . She stopped, her arms tensing in a grotesque hug. Could A-Rae have actually planned this—this process, created the Free Folk of Chabad, to frighten her into some complex error of judgment? Or—her chest hurt—was there someone else behind A-Rae? Or even someone else behind the Free Folk of Chabad?

Dropping her hands to her sides, she forced herself to stop pacing, to breathe, to slow down. Simple is best, she thought, remember Occam's Razor. Don't complicate the situation; it isn't necessary. She rubbed her neck, which ached, and discovered that her palms and sides were wet. She felt as if there was no one she could trust, except Zed, no one who might not be an enemy.

You're being silly again, she told herself. Amri wouldn't betray you, she hasn't the capacity. Corrios would kill for you. Tuli—she dismissed that thought. Clare, Imre, Aliza—what's the matter with you, Rhani Yago? Do you really think you've lost all your friends?

There was nothing she could do about Tsurada's information: she had no influence on Nexus. She would simply have to be cautious, leave the house as little as possible—never alone—and wait until the Abanat police located Michel A-Rae. After the party she could return to the estate, and she could bear Abanat for four more days; it was not as if she had no work to do. She walked to the intercom. "Binkie?"

"Yes, Rhani-ka."

"Please come to my room."

In a moment he was at the door. She gazed at him, wondering; could he betray her? Beneath her silent scrutiny, he grew progressively more pale. Finally, he said, "Is something wrong, Rhani-ka?"

"I don't think so," she said. She gestured at the com-unit. "I should like you, please, to call Christina Wu's office. Ask her to come and see me, soon. Within a week, if that's possible." Christina Wu was chief of Family Yago's legal staff.

"Yes, Rhani-ka." He sat in the com-unit chair. Rhani watched his fingers tap the keys. She wondered what it was like for him, knowing all her business, privy to information which no other single person, except Zed, had. He was always obedient, meticulous, even detached.

He consulted her schedule before speaking with Christina Wu's appointments' clerk. They spoke for a few moments, and then Binkie swung the chair around. "Rhani-ka, will an appointment the morning of the party be convenient?"

"Yes," she said. He made the appointment, thumbed the line silent, and rose again.

"Thank you, Binkie," she said gravely. Sitting on the bed, she motioned him to the footstool. "Tell me now about the party preparations." As he recounted the details—two hundred invitations had been sent out (hand-delivered by hired messenger), one hundred seventy of them had been accepted, the food, drink, and service would be catered, a theater troupe had been hired to perform a popular Chabadese comedy—which one piece of her mind heard and absorbed, she thought, when I marry Ferris Dur I should make some gesture, some symbolic reference to a change of state. What? Buy something, sell something, endow something?

She suddenly knew, and grinned. Of course, that was it. She would free her house slaves.

Chapter Fourteen

Dana Ikoro sat at a table in The Green Dancer, waiting for Tori Lamonica.

His right shoulder brushed a window. He breathed on it, and rubbed the moist patch with his sleeve. He could see, through the glass, the lights of Abanat, and beyond them, the reflection of that light off the icebergs in the bay. The bergs, remote, frosted with fog, seemed like bits of another world. Between him and the bay the noise and hubbub of the landingport stirred. Under his left elbow, someone had scratched in the neowood tabletop, "KILROY WAS A NARC."

He had been waiting for an hour. He could wait three hours more. Across the room, Amber saw his expression and grinned at him. The bar was crowded. At the largest table, which was round and two meters in diameter, ten people were playing a game with seven counters, all different colors, and strange six-sided dice.

Four of the ten were pilots; the loudest of them was a woman in a diaphanous robe. That was Juno Kouris, *Seminole*'s pilot. The slender, quiet woman next to her was navigator Lyn Cowan, also off *Seminole*. They wore matching torques on their necks. The name of the game was "Triple"; Dana had heard of it but never seen it. He wondered if Lamonica played it, too, and if it was anything like "Go."

Rose, the girl in glitterstick—today it was red—slung her tray in his direction. "How you doing?" she shouted.

"Fine," Dana said, holding his hand over the mouth of his glass.

"Good." In a softer tone, she said, "Amber says, watch the door." Dana's stomach muscles cramped. He shifted in his seat, stretching his legs into the aisle and then pulling them back as a man in a ragged thermal suit stumbled toward him.

The door opened; a wave of cold air swept in. So did four people, two human, two Verdian. One of the humans was Tori Lamonica. She was wearing green, a deep green that looked almost black. Her medallion hung around her neck. She walked to the bar and leaned on it to talk with Amber. She accepted a drink, and strolled in his direction, halting at the tableful of gamesters. "Hey, Tori, man, how's tricks?" said Juno, rising to kiss her on the mouth. "Want to play?"

Dana could not hear Lamonica's reply. She shook her head, punched Juno's shoulder with the hand that did not hold the drink, and continued down the aisle. She sat opposite him. "Good evening," she said. Her clothing was undecorated, which was uncharacteristic for a Hyper, but she was wearing gold hoops in her ears, and she had dyed her left eyebrow green, and her right one white.

Her drink was green, with a froth of cream on top. Dana lifted his wine glass. "To the luck," he said. His voice was not quite steady.

She lifted her own glass and let it clink against his. "I'll always drink to the luck."

Dana waited until she set the glass down again. Cream dappled her upper lip, and she wiped her mouth with one hand. "How've you been?" he said.

"Well enough," she answered. "You?"

"It's been better."

From the round table came a shout. "Hey, you can't make that move; it's illegal!" A glass shattered.

Juno rose. "Who said I can't?"

"Shut up," said Lyn Cowan. "Roll it again."

"But I like what I just rolled." Protesting, Juno sat. Lyn kicked the glass under the table. The overhead lights flickered, then came back on.

Lamonica said, "I was surprised when I heard you'd followed me. I figured you would turn around, maybe go back to Nexus."

I should have, Dana thought. But I didn't know. How could I know? "So you heard," he said.

She nodded. "I'm sorry." She rubbed her thumb along the side of her glass.

"Leave it," Dana said. He didn't need apologies. At the table to his left, someone lit a dopestick. He took a deep breath. The man saw him and, grinning, passed him the stick. He took the smoke into his lungs.

Careful, he told himself. Remember, you can't stay out all night. He offered the stick to Lamonica; she shook her head. "It makes me cough," she explained. "So does tobacco. How did you find out that I was still on Chabad?"

"I saw you," Dana said. "The day of the Auction you walked by the Yago house."

She looked startled. "So I did. I was just walking. I like Abanat; it's a beautiful city." She lifted her glass, and he sensed her embarrassment. "Maybe you don't think so."

"It'll do," he said. "I was surprised to see you. I thought *you'd* gone."

She said, "I wanted to. But I had some trouble selling my cargo."

Dana said lightly, "Your dealer left town?"

Her left eyebrow, the green one, twitched. "Now, how the hell did you hear that?"

He grinned. It was all falling into place. Truly luck had turned for him. . . . The man at the next table held the dopestick under his nose. He breathed in.

"Thanks." Dana smiled. "Let's talk business, Starcaptain."

Both Lamonica's eyebrows went up. But she turned in her chair and signaled to Rose. The girl waved a hand. Lamonica turned back to him. "Talk," she said.

Dana sipped his wine. It went like water down his throat. "You know," he began, "that I work for Family Yago." She nodded. "Family Yago buys dorazine." He watched her face. "The name of Family Yago's dealer in Abanat is—" he paused—"Sherrix Esbah."

Lamonica leaned forward in her chair. "Go on," she said.

"Sherrix Esbah has left Chabad. The name of the person who has taken her place is Loras U-Ellen."

If anything, Lamonica's bland face grew more impassive. But her left eyebrow twitched again. "So?" she said.

"Here," said Rose, leaning over the table, drink in hand.

Lamonica dug out a credit disc and slapped it on the table. "You want another?" she said to Dana. He shook his head. Rose made a face at him. Glitterstick lines striped her breasts, hips, and back. Her nipples were lightly touched with rouge. "Sure?" Lamonica pressed.

"I'm sure," Dana said. Rose shrugged and stalked off. "So," he said, "Family Yago has an interest in this man."

He was pleased with the choice of words. An interest.

That was something Rhani might choose to say. "In fact," he said, "Rhani Yago would like to meet him."

"So?" Lamonica said.

"Have you met him?"

"I might have."

"Could you reach him again?"

"I might."

"Family Yago would be grateful if you could pass that message on to him."

Lamonica smiled. "How grateful?" she asked dryly.

"Fifty credits," Dana said.

"One hundred."

"Seventy-five." He did not have one hundred credits left on the credit disc.

"Ninety."

"Eighty-five," he said.

"Done." She grinned. "A good night's work." She raised her glass, drank. "How do I tell U-Ellen to respond?"

Dana scowled. Rhani had not told him that. . . . She would not want U-Ellen to use the com-lines, that was certain. He remembered the responses to the party invitations lying strewn about the room, piles and piles of them. "Tell him to write her a letter," he said.

Lamonica nodded. "They do that a lot in Sardonyx Sector." She stretched; the gold hoops glinted in her ears. "Pay me, man."

Dana fished his credit disc from his pocket. The transaction unit, he guessed, was at the bar. He started to stand— "No need," Lamonica said. She put two fingers in her mouth and gave a piercing whistle. Amber and Rose looked around. No one else moved. Lamonica made a signal, two-handed this time, and Rose picked up her tray. She halted at the gaming table to take drink orders, and then moved on to them. On the tray was a squat gray metal box: a PCTU, a portable credit transaction unit.

He was surprised to see it; most bars did not trouble to provide them, unless in addition to selling liquor and drugs they sold other things—stronger drugs, or sex. But then he remembered the gamesters. Rose set the box on the table. "I didn't know you were playing," she said.

"We weren't," said Lamonica. "I won a bet." Her green brow lifted. "And you've got my disc."

"Oh! Sorry." The girl brought it from the pouch around her waist. She laid the black plastic token in Lamonica's palm. Their fingers touched just a little longer than necessary. Lamonica smiled. She pressed a button on the unit and thumbed her disc into the alpha slot. Dana found the beta slot and inserted his.

Swiftly, Lamonica instructed the PCTU to transfer eight-five credits from the disc in the beta to the disc in the alpha slot. The machine burped. TRANSACTION COMPLETE, it printed on its display line. The green letters burned in the shadows and then winked out. The discs fell from the slots. "Is that really all?" said Rose.

Lamonica picked up the unit and laid it on the girl's tray. "For now," she said. The back of her hand stroked Rose's glitter-streaked thigh. "For now."

Rose made a musical noise in the back of her throat, held the tray up, and glided softly away.

Dana began to sweat. His throat felt tight. He told himself it was the effect of the dope, no more. Lamonica was watching the girl at the bar. He coughed. She flicked a glance at him. He lowered his voice. "I have a second deal to propose to you."

"Hmm." The Starcaptain sipped her drink. "That's the fourth proposition I've had tonight." She gazed at him across the rim of the glass. "Go on."

"It's private, it has nothing to do with the Yagos, and you can name your own price, within limits."

"I like it already," she said, and yawned.

Someone tapped Dana's left shoulder. His muscles spasmed, and his throat soured. For an instant, he was sure, *sure* that the person who tapped him—who had moved so silently up to him that he had not even heard the footsteps—was a cop, or worse, was someone wearing a Net uniform. . . . "Hey," said the man at the table to his left, "want more?" He leaned forward, brandishing a smoking dopestick. He wore a shirt with a landingport insignia on it, and his narrow head had been shaved bald. "You know, you're cute. How come I haven't seen you before in here?"

Dana sighed. "Not now, friend. I'm busy," he said.

"Oh." The man jerked his hand back. "Oh, sorry." He sounded wistful.

Lamonica chuckled. "You were saying?"

Dana wiped his hands on his knees. "You'd have to pick up a cargo on Chabad and deliver it out of sector undetected."

From her nod, he knew that she had caught the minute stress he had put on the final word. "A legitimate cargo?" she murmured.

"No."

"We're talking smuggling. What size and type of cargo—drugs, furs, gold, jewelry?"

Dana swallowed. "Me," he said. Locking his fingers around each other, he watched them shake.

He had practically memorized the relevant passages in Nakamura's *History*. Softly he explained to Lamonica, "By Federation law, a slave's credit is frozen until his time of servitude is up. He can't touch it, but neither can anyone else. That means I can't pay you until we get out of Sardonyx Sector. But I can pay you."

"Don't you still own *Zipper*?"

He shook his head. "'*The offended state has the right to confiscate any real property,*'" he quoted.

"What does that mean?"

"It means that Chabad—in fact, Family Yago—owns *Zipper*." He sipped his drink. He was still shaking. He remembered another sentence from the *History*: "*In the last two hundred years, there have been eight hundred forty-two known attempts at escape; of these, twenty-three succeeded.*"

"How could it be done?" she said.

"I can't get into Main Landingport," he said. "You'd have to come and get me."

"Where?"

"The Yago estate. It's about one hundred kilometers east of here."

"How?"

"I'll walk out the gate, around noon," Dana said. "It's been done before. With reflective clothing—" which I can steal, he thought— "I can live a few hours in the heat. You'd have to pick me up quickly; timing's crucial."

Lamonica scowled. "And if the Abanat police come after me?"

"I don't see how they can. But it would help if, sometime between now and then, *Lamia* was hidden near the Yago estate."

"I won't hazard *Lamia*," she rapped out.

"I won't ask you to," Dana said evenly. "If they overtake us, you can put me out and take off." She nodded, obviously relieved. He forced his imagination not to dwell on that, on what would happen to him then. . . . Binkie was right, he knew. Rhani had as good as told him that if he attempted escape, she would not be able to protect him.

Sweat rolled from his hair and down his neck. He gulped his drink. Lamonica said, "How would I know when to come for you?"

"I'll tell you."

"How?"

"Over the com-line. I'll use the bar as a drop point. I'll leave a message addressed to Russell O'Neill in navigator's coding. The message will contain a Chabadese date. Disregard the month; look at the day, and add five to it. If it says twenty-two, it means twenty-seven; if it says forty-three, it means day three, next month."

She tilted her head to one side, her bland face thoughtful. "It sounds good. Can you get to a com-line?"

"I can."

She rubbed her nose. "I have to be offplanet in ten weeks."

Dana smiled. "I don't intend to wait that long."

"What if—" She hesitated. "What if you're caught?"

"That's your risk," he said simply. His stomach hurt.

"You couldn't not tell them."

He shook his head. "Will you do it?" he said. He would not beg. He leaned back in the chair, trying to still his shaking hands.

She laid her right hand, palm down, on the scarred table. "I'll do it," she said, and her eyebrows jumped. "Hell, I jacked your cargo."

For a moment he did not believe her, and then relief shuddered through him. He breathed a great gulp of air. He let his left hand rest atop hers. "Thanks."

She rose. "It's been good talking to you," she said. She strolled unceremoniously off. He watched her stop at the gaming table, speak to Juno, lay a hand on Cowan's shoulder, and angle toward the bar. When he glanced at her again, she was leaning on the bar, centimeters away from Rose. All right, Starcaptain, you can leave now, he thought, but he could not leave, not yet. All his muscles seemed to have turned to water.

Finally he could stand. The man at the next table watched him with saddened eyes as he went toward the door. Amber grinned tightly at him as he passed the bar. He opened the door; the bar lights flickered, and cold air eddied through it. "Close that!" someone yelled. He stepped outside, filling his lungs, and shoved his hands in his pockets. The noise from the bar seemed louder now that he was not in it.

The air shivered. His skin contracted. He looked up as a deep roar began to hurt his ears. Over the tops of the old, grimy houses, a shuttleship was rising from the Landingport's field. He leaned against the wall and watched it go, wondering where it was going—the moon? The Net? Not the Net, the Net was empty. His eyes pricked with tears. The city lights made it hard to see the stars, but they were there, he knew, and beyond them was the Hype. Soon, he promised himself, soon—the wind slapped coldly at him, and he shivered, chilled—soon you will be gone from here, offplanet, you need never come back again: . . . He closed his eyelids, seeing in the patterns behind his eyes the slow curling red dust of the Hype.

As he came around the corner of the street leading to the Yago house, someone called his name. "Dana, wait!" He turned. It was Binkie. He looked very pale. "Get out of the light!" he whispered, and his hand closed on Dana's arm.

Dana let the secretary/slave steer him into shadow. "What is it?" he said.

Binkie's voice was grim. "Brother, you'd better not go near the house."

Dana's stomach began to hurt again. "Just tell me," he said.

"Zed," said Binkie succinctly. "He and Rhani had a fight. I heard your name. Rhani sent me out to wait for you, to tell you to stay the hell away."

"The curfew—" Dana said.

"Fuck the curfew," Binkie said roughly. "You idiot, Zed *knows*."

Sweet mother—Dana looked at the house. The lights were lit in Rhani's bedroom. Against the curtain, Dana thought he saw a familiar shape. "How did he—who told him?" he said.

"I haven't the faintest idea," Binkie said. "Pull yourself together, man. Take this." He thrust something soft at Dana, who took it automatically. It was a cloak. "You'll need it."

Yes, Dana thought, and with clumsy hands he wrapped it around his shoulders. "How long should I stay away?" he asked.

"*I* don't know," said Binkie. "Six hours? I've got to get back inside. Keep moving. Good luck." He hurried away. Dana watched him go up the steps. Corrios opened the door, his big frame plain against the light. Keep moving, Binkie had said. Dana started to walk silently east. If he kept moving, he could probably evade the police patrols.

An hour before curfew, Dana had not yet returned. Alone in her bedroom, feeling like a kerit in a cage, Rhani paced back and forth, back and forth.

She was worried about him. And, she admitted to herself, she was feeling guilty, because she had sent Dana to the Hyper district to find Loras U-Ellen without consulting Zed. Outside her windows, the city gleamed like a jewel, all the street lights blazing on the wide white streets. She strode to the window and, leaning close to the glass, looked out. People strolled past the house, arm in arm, laughing, talking. . . . None of them was Dana. She scowled at the street and resumed walking. How many years would it take her to tramp a ring into the glossy wooden floor?

"Rhani-ka, would you like some dinner?" That was Amri, standing timidly in the doorway.

"No. Unless—ask my brother if he wants to eat." Zed had come back from the Clinic early, and had gone straight to his room.

The girl went away. Rhani heard her knock, heard her speak, heard Zed answer. Amri returned. "Rhani-ka, he says no."

"All right. Thank you, Amri." She glanced at Binkie, who was sitting at the com-unit logging names into the computer, names of the people who were coming to the party. "Bink, have you eaten?"

He looked up. "Yes, Rhani-ka, thank you. I ate about two hours ago."

Damn, Rhani thought, oh damn, damn. . . . Finally she squared her shoulders and went down the hall to Zed's bedroom. She tapped on the door. "Zed-ka, it's me." She heard his step, and the door drew back. She glimpsed the rumpled bedclothes, his booktapes, a light. He was holding a viewer in one hand. He looked tired. "Zed, I'm sorry to disturb you," she said. "But I'm worried about Dana. I sent him on an errand three hours ago, and he hasn't returned."

For a moment he gazed at her as if he had no idea what she was talking about. "What?" he said. Then his voice grew sharp. "Three hours? That's too long. It's almost curfew."

"I know," she said.

"Where did you send him?"

She sighed. "To the Hyper district."

"What?"

"Yes. I hoped he could take a message to Loras U-Ellen."

"What message?" Zed asked.

"That I want to see him. But that's irrelevant. Dana should have been back by now."

Turning, Zed tossed the viewer on the bed. "Yes. Did you ask if any of the slaves have seen him?"

She shook her head. "I thought perhaps he might have gotten hurt."

"Hurt!" Zed snorted. "He's a Starcaptain, he's been in and out of the Hype, he's not going to get hurt in some backwater city."

"It isn't!" she protested.

Zed smiled. He no longer looked preoccupied. Closing his door, he went ahead of her to her room. "No. But it's not very big, and he lived six years in Port City on Nexus. Do you want me to call the Clinic?" He glanced around the room. "Where's Binkie?"

"I don't know," Rhani said. "He was just here."

Zed leaned over the com-unit. He riffled the stack of party responses with a finger. "Dull work." Seating himself in the chair, he instructed the computer to hold all prior operations, and punched the direct line number for Main Clinic. "This is Senior Zed Yago," he said to the clerk.

"Please consult your records and the records of all the district clinics for any report of injury or accident to one Dana Ikoro, about 1.7 meters tall, black hair to the shoulderblades, ivory-yellow complexion, thumbsized scar on the inside of his left thigh, deformed knuckle on the left fourth finger—" Rhani listened, fascinated, to the clinical, dispassionate description— "a tattoo, the 'Y' in blue. He's a slave."

They saw the top of the clerk's head as he played with his machinery. He looked up. "Senior, we have no such record, nor do the district clinics."

"If he comes in to any of the clinics, send immediate direct-line notice to the Yago house."

"That is our usual procedure, Senior."

"Then I'm sure you'll follow it," said Zed. He blanked the screen. "So." His voice was measured and grim.

So, that syllable said, you trusted him and he has betrayed that trust. *He's mine, now.*

Binkie walked in, saw Zed, and stopped. "Do you want me, Rhani-ka?" he asked.

"No," she said. "Wait—" he turned to face her— "Bink, do you know where Dana is?"

"No, Rhani-ka." He was very pale. He waited for her to speak again, clenching and unclenching his thin hands unconsciously. Irritated despite her sympathy, Rhani waved him away.

He walked like a man escaping a prison cell. He was one step into the hall when Zed said, "Binkie, come back here." Binkie froze, and turned. His face was ice-white. Rhani glanced at her brother, frowning. She did not like him to give Binkie direct orders.

Zed said, "He's lying, Rhani-ka." He stood, and stepped away from the chair. "Can't you see he's lying?" He glided toward the terrified slave. Rhani put a hand out to stop him. He halted. Binkie was breathing like a runner. "Binkie, I want the truth."

Binkie licked his lips. "I—" He swallowed. "I did see him. He was here about two hours ago."

"Here?" said Rhani.

"He came to the back door of the house. I was putting paper into the disposal bin when he dropped out of nowhere and took a cloak. I asked him where he was going and he said, 'Out,' and then he laughed. He wished me luck and said he hoped he never saw me again."

"No," Rhani said.

Binkie was shivering. "Rhani-ka, I swear it's true!"

"But it's stupid!"

"I agree," said Zed, "it's stupid. But he was bound to try to escape. Even Binkie, who should have known better, trudged out the estate gate. He must have made some connection in the Hyper district, perhaps found someone he knew . . ."

"No," Rhani said again. Her heart thudded. "He wouldn't—"

Zed crossed to her and put his arm around her shoulders. "Rhani-ka," he said gently, "are you saying that because you're sure he wouldn't run away, or because you thought he wouldn't and you don't want him to?"

Rhani let her head rest against her brother's cheek for a moment. "Both, I think," she said. But it was my fault, she wanted to say; I let him go to the Hyper district, I even gave him one of my shirts to hide the "Y"—She remembered Binkie with pity. "Bink, you may leave."

Once again Zed sat at the com-unit. He called the Abanat police, and described Dana all over again for them. "Treat him gently," he added.

Why say that? Rhani thought, and did not say it. She knew why. Zed wanted Dana unhurt, because he wanted to do the hurting himself.

Going to the window, she slapped the curtain aside. There was no way he could get offplanet, of course. She imagined him hiding like an animal, somewhere in the cold, clear night, and wanted to weep. Hands on the sill, she leaned forward until her forehead touched the glass. If she were a telepath, she could call him. She turned. Zed was talking to the A.P., smiling, and her stomach muscles clenched. Dana, she thought—Dana—you stupid, stubborn, treacherous fool!

He called the house an hour after midnight.

Rhani, drowsing on the bed, woke to the soft insistent beep of the com-unit. She knuckled her eyes and then stumbled to the screen, expecting to hear the deferential voice of a police officer. "Yes?" she said. "Rhani Yago here."

"Rhani?" said a whisper.

"Yes," she said, "who is it?" And then she knew.

"Dana!" She glanced at the clock. Sweet mother, it was late. "Where are you?"

"A public line. I had to call. Are you all right?"

"What?"

"Are you all right?"

"I'm fine," she said, not understanding. "Dana, come back, *please.*"

"Is it safe?"

She fisted her hands on her lap. "Yes," she said, "I promise. It will be." Now, she thought, now I must make that true. . . .

"All right," he said. The connection terminated. Rhani yawned, and then grinned at the blank screen in moronic joy.

"Zed!" she called.

In a moment he came through the door. Like her, he was wearing the clothes he had worn all day. "What is it?" he said.

"Dana called."

Zed's eyebrows lifted. "Really? What did he say?"

"He's coming back."

"Is he." Zed's voice was noncommittal.

Exasperated, Rhani said, "Zed-ka, what is wrong with you?"

He said, "Rhani, it could be a feint. He must know the patrols have his description. Where did he say he was calling from, did you ask?"

"I asked," she said. "A public booth."

Zed ran his hands through his hair, smoothing it flat. "We can check that." He sat at the com-unit. "There'll be a memory of the call in the computer which should contain the location he called from. Let's see."

Rhani went to the intercom. "Amri," she said, "Dana's coming back. Please have some hot food ready for him."

"Yes, Rhani-ka," said Amri's tremulous voice.

"Well, that was true," Zed said. "He did call on a public line."

Rhani swallowed. "Zed-ka," she said, "this is important, please. I need to talk to you."

He cocked his head to one side. "About Dana?" he said.

She took a deep breath. "Yes. I don't—"

The alarm rang.

Rising and falling like the breathing of a giant, it wailed into the night. At first she did not know what it was. Then she remembered the alarms. Someone's trying to get in, she thought. Dana? No, why should he not simply knock? The Free Folk of Chabad?

"Rhani, wait here," said Zed, sprinting for the door. Rhani hesitated for an instant, and then thought: Why the hell should I? This is my house. And I won't be any safer here than there.

Sliding the door aside, she headed for the stairway. Zed was shouting below. Amri was standing in the slaves' hall, hair floating to her waist, rubbing her eyes. The clamor of the alarms went on and on—a shrill, panicking sound. "Binkie?" Zed called. "Corrios?"

Corrios came from his room. He was wearing a sleep robe and sunshades. But it's night, Rhani thought. She walked the rest of the way down the stair. "Where's Binkie?" she said.

Zed came from the slaves' hall, and she realized that he had been opening the door to every room. He turned in a circle, hands on his hips.

Corrios answered her. "Gone."

The shriek of the alarm was making Rhani's head ache. Why? she thought. A roar answered her. The entrance-way was suddenly filled with flame.

Amri shrieked. A window burst. Thick black smoke boiled toward her. Choking, Rhani shouted Zed's name into the fire.

"Rhani, get to the kitchen!" She could not see him through the smoke. Ripping her shirt over her head, she held it around her nose and mouth as a screen. Amri was still screaming—a terrible, tearing sound. Something big moved through the pulsating darkness, and the screaming stopped. Step by step, Rhani felt her way toward the kitchen. Zed intercepted her before she could reach the back door.

"It's blocked from outside," he said. "Let's go to the storeroom."

"We'll be smothered," Rhani said. Her eyes watered.

"It's vented, and it's big. There's a lot of air inside even if they've found the outer vents." He pushed her ahead of him. Corrios grunted as he opened the door.

The stairway was space-black. Rhani thought insanely:

Wait, I'll get a light. She giggled at the image of herself walking down the steps with one of Domna Sam's malodorous candles in her hand. Zed went down the first few steps and reached back to grip her fingers. "Come on," he said. "Keep coming."

"I can't see," she said.

"Step down, Rhani-ka. I won't let you fall." Smoke was blowing through the open doorway. The alarm stopped, at last. Coughing, she stepped into the tense, dry darkness. Corrios came after her. He closed the door.

"Level ground in a few steps," said Zed.

She remembered Amri. "Amri?"

Zed's fingers tightened on her own. "Amri's dead, Rhani."

She nodded, remembering the terrible screaming. "Damn them, damn them," she said. "What an ugly death. . . ."

"No," Corrios said. "Neck broke."

"Did you do it?" she said.

"Yes."

"Rhani," said Zed, "if you put your hands in front of you, you'll feel a wall."

Stretching her hands in front of her, she touched plaster. It was rough and coarse. Wearily she leaned on it, and it scraped her bare shoulder. She had dropped her shirt. Corrios spoke, his voice diminishing as he moved away from her, "Storage bin, storage bin, cooler, cooler, water pipe, heater, filter, air chimney."

"Where?" said Zed. "Rhani, come." She moved across the hot cellar. She touched something cool. The water pipe, she thought. She breathed hot air. It was Binkie, she thought, with pain. Binkie lied. Binkie set the fire.

Zed came back to her. "The air vents are open, Rhani-ka," he said.

"What does that mean?" she said.

"It means," Zed answered, "that we're going to live."

Overhead, something huge hit the ground. The ceiling quaked and throbbed. "Is the house falling?"

"Pieces of it," Zed said.

The cellar was stifling. She could not cry. She leaned against Zed, feeling his fingers stroke her hair, as the shuddering went on and on. . . .

Chapter Fifteen

As Dana came from the shadows on the north side of the Boulevard, he saw flames. For several minutes, he realized, he had been hearing the wail of a siren. Vaguely he wondered where the fire was, if it was a fire, and how big, and how close it was to the Yago house. . . . As the realization of just how close it was hit him, he started to run. Bubbles darted overhead; a white chemical, half-liquid, half-smoke, poured from their snouts. He raced past Founders' Green and came to a skidding stop, knocking a knot of spectators apart. They snarled at him. He stared. The Yago house was gone. The walls still stood, but the roof had vanished, as had doors, windows, the inner corridors, the whole second floor—fire had eaten it away like vitriol. The chemical quencher sprayed down by the Abanat Fire Department draped itself in long crystalline coils on the ragged frame, the stone steps, the street. Workers in protective suits and carrying canisters and hoses waded through the terrible wreckage, pouring white clouds on the sparks.

"I hear they found a body," a woman's voice said. She was one of the spectators. "I wonder whose."

Dana swallowed. No, he thought, staring at the debris, eyes smarting from the smoke, no, it isn't possible. . . .

"Move along, please," said an official voice. Dana stepped back as a light blazed in his face. "Move along—hold it!" Hands grabbed for him. Sweet mother, he thought, I ran all the way right into the arms of the Abanat police! He turned from a wristhold and braced himself to run when someone fell heavily on him from behind. It hurt. He bucked. Two people hauled him upright. "Name?"

He shook his head.

They yanked up his sleeve. The light played over his face again. "It must be," muttered someone. "There's the 'Y.' Name?"

"Who're you?" he said.

The answer was a backhand blow that knocked him off his feet. He sprawled on his stomach as they tied his hands behind him. "Name," the voice said venomously.

He swallowed back blood, and coughed. "Dana Ikoro."

They dragged him up again and shone the light in his eyes. He closed them, and was cuffed. A second voice said, "Handle him gently, remember?"

The first voice said, "Hell, he's fine." Dana opened his eyes. Four police officers were standing around him.

"His face is puffing," said one.

The man who had hit him scowled. "Who cares what his face looks like? Handle him gently. I'll handle him, all right. The man who gave that order is roasting somewhere in that fucking fire."

"They haven't found all the bodies yet," said one.

Dana said, "What happened?" His head hurt.

The man who had hit him turned on him. "That's what *we're* going to be asking *you*. There's no freedom for slaves when their owners die victims of a crime. There's been one body found already in that inferno." His face worked. "I think you ought to see it. You like well-done meat? We need someone to identify it." He sank his fingers into Dana's upper arm. "Come on."

Crystals crunched beneath their feet as they walked toward the remnants of the mansion. Suddenly a voice lifted in a shout; the word echoed. "Alive! Alive!" The man holding Dana stood still; the others started to run toward the cries. A bubble, dipping low, sent out a flare of white light. Dana squinted. Etched darkly in it, three people appeared out of nowhere, out of the ground, in the very core of the ruins. One of them was Corrios; he had an arm across his face. The other two stood close together and were exactly the same height.

The firefighters cheered. Dana leaned on a police bus. His jaw ached from the blow. Zed and Rhani walked toward him. They were surrounded by police. Amri died, he thought. The searchlight winked out, and the bubble soared upwards. Tears stung uselessly at Dana's eyes.

Voices gabbled near him. Suddenly, someone said, "Wait." A hand fell on his shoulder. "Dana." It was Zed. Dana's sight crept back. There was a dark, dirty smear across Zed's cheek, and his clothes were torn. "Dana, *why did you run?*"

Dana licked his lips. Zed's grip bit his shoulder.

"Binkie told me to," he said.

Zed nodded, and let go. "Get those cords off him," he ordered.

The man who had hit him said, "But, Commander, you said he was a runaway, and we thought—"

"I was wrong," said Zed. He sounded unutterably weary. "Damn it, untie him, he doesn't have that kind of mind."

Dana stood passively as someone cut his bonds. He rubbed his wrists. "Rhani—"

"She's all right," Zed said. "Come on." Dana followed him, wondering where they were going. Zed answered the unspoken words. "We're going to the Kyneth house; they're putting us up." To the police he said, "Have you found the other one, yet?"

"No, Commander, we haven't."

"Keep looking," said Zed.

The doors of the police bus slid back. They went inside. A man's voice said, "Let me help you, Domna." Rhani stepped into the bus. She clambered onto the seat. She looked at Dana, and then at Zed. Corrios came in hesitatingly, squinting at the ceiling light. Without his sunshades, his face looked small, and somehow rather naked. The door slid closed, and the bus took off.

Rhani said, "Are you all right?" Dana realized she was talking to him. He wondered what he should say.

"Not really," he said. He tried to smile, so that if she wanted to, she could pretend it was a joke. "Are you?"

"No," she said. She crossed her arms over her breasts. Sweat and dirt streaked her skin. He wondered where her shirt had gotten to. "Amri's dead."

Zed said quietly, "Don't think about it, Rhani-ka."

She said, "I have to think about it." Her mouth worked. "Damn him! Oh, damn and double damn him! I wish there was a hell, so that he could burn in it."

Who? thought Dana. He had never seen her like this. The level of rage was frightening. Her eyes were like hot copper in her dirt-stained face. "You don't know," she said. "You don't know what it feels like to hear someone scream as she burns."

She was talking to him, Dana realized. "No," he said. "I don't."

"That craven, lying, deceitful—" She took a breath.

"I'll see him dead, I swear it. I'll watch him die." Hands balled into fists, she shut her eyes. Zed put his arm around her, and, sighing, she leaned her face against his shoulder. Steadily, he stroked her head.

Binkie, Dana thought. It must be Binkie she means. Corrios was here, and Amri was dead. The bus went up and down, and deposited them on the Promenade in front of Kyneth House. The door was open, and Aliza Kyneth waited on the steps.

She glided forward, and folded Rhani in her arms. Margarite Kyneth was standing in the doorway, flanked by several slaves. "Bath," said Aliza, "food, and sleep. Rhani, Margarite will escort you upstairs." She kissed Rhani on the cheek and pushed her toward Margarite, who grasped her hand as one might grasp the hand of a child. "Zed, I rejoice to see you whole. There is a room prepared for you next to Rhani's, in the family wing."

"Aliza—" Zed began.

She lifted a hand, and stopped him. "Zed Yago, if you thank me I shall be very displeased. There are rooms ready in the slaves' quarters for your slave and for your employee, if this will not offend him." She looked at Corrios.

The big man muttered something incomprehensible, and shook his head.

Dana was very conscious that his clothes were torn and filthy. He wanted to thank the woman for letting him into the house. . . . Stars, he thought, I'm lightheaded. He leaned forward to catch his balance and found himself sitting on a step, stomach roiling. It's that damn spray, he thought. I must have ingested some chemical.

Zed's hand on his neck shocked him into urgent sense. Blood pounded in his head. His legs trembled. "I'll see you later," said the commander. "Don't go to sleep." He went up the steps. Dana shut his eyes. He was tired. *Don't go to sleep.* Oh, god, he thought, not *now.* He forced himself to stand. One of the slaves helped him climb the steps. Inside the warm, fragrant house he sagged against a wall, hoping that Zed would forget, would collapse, would leave him alone. He had a lot to hide—too much, he thought. The slave led him into a vaulted passageway and then into a room. It was papered in white and green.

"This is yours," he said. He showed Dana the washroom and then mercifully left. Dana sat on the bed. I think I should wash, he thought. But now that he was sitting it was hard to move. He felt his eyelids tugging downward. No, he thought, don't. You don't want to be unconscious when Zed shows up. *If* Zed shows up. Damn him. Looking with distaste at the grime which caked his arms and his clothing, he let the cloak fall and levered himself to his feet.

The room Margarite brought Rhani to was large and pink. Rhani thought, I hate pink. She heard water running for a bath. Slaves moved in and out of the chamber, bringing blankets, clothing, food. The food smell made her mouth water, but when she tried to eat, she couldn't. She took off her clothes, and a slave brought her a robe, pink, furry, too big.

Margarite stalked in. "Rhani, do you have the strength to speak to my father?" she said.

"Of course," Rhani said, rising from the chair she was sitting in. Imre entered the room. Even in the middle of the night he contrived to look dapper, though his cheeks were bristly. "Domni, thank you for receiving my household," she said.

Imre reached for her hands and held them. "Rhani, don't be ridiculous," he said. "Every house in Abanat is yours tonight." His worldliness deserted him. He said, "My dear, I am—we are—we are all so terribly sorry!"

She could appreciate the sentiment. But— "No," she said. "We are sad. The people who made this fire happen will be terribly sorry."

Imre's eyes grew startled for a moment; then he veiled the reaction with an expert's calm. Releasing her hands, he said, "Apropos of that, the Abanat police called. An Officer Tsurada. She asked me to tell you they are holding a runaway slave of yours, as well as some other people."

"Binkie." Rhani's whole frame tightened.

"That was the name," said Imre.

"Does Zed know?" Imre shook his head. "Good. Don't tell him. Instruct the Abanat Police to hold him until further notice from me." She heard herself, and flushed. "Imre, I'm sorry. It's unforgivable of me to give you orders as if you were my secretary."

He smiled at her. "It is eminently forgivable. I'll be glad to speak to the Abanat police for you, and I won't tell Zed anything. Is there anything else you need?"

"Thank you, no." A new house, she thought, a new world—oh, Amri!

"Then we will leave you. You need not fear for your safety in this house. The police have ringed it with a near-army, and there will be a member of my household guarding your door and Zed's door all night."

Rhani bit back a comment on the efficacy of police armies. "Does Zed know that? Better tell him, or that guard will be unpleasantly surprised if my brother decides to leave his room in the middle of the night."

Imre said gently, "My dear, it *is* the middle of the night. But I will tell him."

He left, with Margarite half a step behind him. Rhani went to bathe. The bathroom was huge, almost as large as the bedroom; it had stained-glass windows and gold-leaved fixtures. She scrubbed until her skin hurt. When she emerged from the giant sunken tub, a slave was waiting with towels, scents, powder. "Leave them," Rhani said. "I can do it."

"Yes, Domna."

Cleansed of the stench of fire and death, she climbed naked and unscented into the roseate bed. The pink sheets were cool, delicious. She recalled curtains crawling with flame. Don't think of it, she told herself. The door of the room slid open. "Rhani-ka?"

She lifted on an elbow. "Zed? Come in, I'm awake." Zed came in. He wore a dark green robe; his shoulders strained the seams. "Whose clothes are you wearing?" she asked him.

"Imre's. You?"

"I think these must be Margarite's. You're all clean." She lifted his hand to her cheek. He held it there. She could feel him trembling. He went to the washroom and she heard the water running.

"They like lavish washrooms in this house. My bathtub is big enough to dive in." He wandered back, carrying a glass half filled with water. "Here." He held both hands out to her. On his upturned left palm were two black-and-white capsules.

"What is it?" Rhani said.

"Sleep."

"I don't want it," she said, drawing back.

"Take it. You need it, we both do. Take one. The other one's for me."

She hesitated. Finally she took one, tossed it into her throat, and accepted the glass. Zed put the other capsule in his mouth. She swallowed, feeling the pill slide down her gullet: artificial oblivion, she thought. How easy. She handed Zed the glass and watched his throat work. He put the glass on the marble stand beside the bed. "Why don't you lie down?" he said.

She lay back against the pillow. "I'm not sleepy yet."

He smiled. "Don't worry. You will be."

A worry hit her. "I don't want to dream."

"You won't." He sat on the edge of the bed.

Reassured, she let her muscles unkink. After a while, she felt herself becoming remote. Good, she thought. But as the night closed around her, infinitely long, she managed to say, "Zed-ka. Dana—did he know?"

She felt him stir. "I think not," he said.

"I don't think so, either."

His fingers stroked her cheek. "Don't worry about it, Rhani-ka. Sleep now." The bed moved as he rose. "Good night, twin."

"Good night, Zed," she whispered.

In the hall, Zed nodded to the woman who stood, stun gun in hand, to the left of Rhani's door. She returned the greeting but her gaze did not move from watchful perusal of the hall and the shadowy treads of the stair. Zed tongued the unswallowed capsule from his mouth. He had one more thing to do before he could rest. He strode down the corridor and found a slave. "Show me where the people who came with us are."

He meant to move silently but his weariness betrayed him; his steps echoed down the slaves' hall. When he opened Dana's door, Dana was already awake. A lamp shone in one corner. The room was narrow, unadorned: it held a bed, a wardrobe, and little else. A shelf doubled as a desk. In a recess near the shelf stood a slat-backed chair. Zed pulled it close to the bed. Turning it around, he straddled it, and, crossing his arms, leaned his weight on the upright back.

Dana's hair was wet, and the room smelled soapy. One side of his face was puffed and bruised. Zed tapped his own cheek. "Does that hurt?"

Dana shook his head. "No, Zed-ka."

He sounded shaken, but not in shock. Good. "How did it happen?"

"A police officer hit me."

Both his hands were clenched on the sheet as if he feared its being taken. Zed leaned more obviously on the chair back. Dana's hands relaxed. Zed said, "This evening Rhani sent you on an errand."

Dana tensed again. "Yes," he said.

"To locate Loras U-Ellen."

The tension remained. "Yes."

"Did you?"

Dana swallowed. "I found someone who can, Zed-ka. I paid her eighty-five credits to deliver Rhani's message."

"And then?" Zed prompted.

"Then I left to return to the house. Binkie met me at the corner."

"In the street."

"Yes. He said—" his shoulders lifted, "he said that you and Rhani had had a fight, and that you were very angry. He said Rhani sent him to find me, to warn me not to come back. He brought me a cloak." He glanced toward the wardrobe. "It's there."

Zed wondered if it was one of his. "Was that all he said?"

Dana nodded, and then said, "No—he told me to stay away for six hours. That's all."

"Did he say what Rhani and I were fighting about?"

Dana's eyelids flickered. "No," he said.

Zed stretched. Dana watched him move. Zed let his hands drop to his thighs. "Binkie set the fire," he said softly. "He sent you away so that you'd be blamed for it, after everyone but you and he was dead. He told us—in such a way that we would believe him—that you were planning to escape." Dana's eyes went wide. "I told the police to look for you. Then you called. Binkie heard Rhani tell me that you called. He went out the door. The alarms went off, and in the confusion, he triggered the fire, I don't know how, yet, and got away. He may have had help. They'll catch him, of course. Rhani, Corrios, and I got safely to the cellar. I suppose he didn't think of that. Amri was standing too near the source of the explosion. Her clothes flamed."

There was genuine shock in Dana's face. "That bastard," he said.

"Yes," Zed agreed, and rose, kicking the chair away. "Did you know it was going to happen, Dana? Did Binkie tell you, did you help plan it? Is that why you stayed away?"

It took a moment for the accusations to register. Dana's mouth opened. "No," he said. "No!"

Zed walked to the bedside and leaned over him. Dana recoiled until his head touched the wall. Cupping his chin, Zed felt with careful fingers for the pulse beneath the jaw. It raced. He found the nerve and pressed inward, lightly, as Dana breathed in gasps. Then he waited until he felt the deep involuntary shaking begin to rack Dana's muscles. "If you lie to me," he said, very gently, forcing the frightened man to listen, "if you lie, I promise I'll rip you apart."

He let the words linger, and then dropped his hand. Dana did not move. Sweat beaded his face. Zed said, "Let me hear it again."

Dana whispered, "I didn't know."

Zed watched the trembling fade. Before it could vanish completely, he reached out and ran a fingertip over the ugly bruise on Dana's jaw. "I believe you." Lightly he tipped Dana's chin. "But I'm tired, I've watched an innocent child die tonight, and my temper's very short. And I know you, Dana. You are lying to me, about something."

The muscles around Dana's eyes contracted, released. He said, "Yes, I am. But it doesn't have anything to do with Binkie, or with the fire—none of that. It isn't my lie, it's someone else's."

Zed nodded. "So," he said, "you want me to let you go on telling it."

"Please," Dana said.

Zed wondered what he should do. With a hand at Dana's throat, he searched the young face, looking for pride, for the telltale conceit of the manipulator. He didn't find it. A strong part of him wanted to reject the plea, to force Dana to speak—it would take ten minutes, no more—but that, he knew, was anger talking. It had not been easy to sit in the hot, darkened cellar and wait for the fire to burn out, or to be put out, feeling Rhani's terror and knowing that he was frightened too, frightened, and impotent. . . .

He lifted his hand. It was one of his rules: he played fair with his victims. Walking to the door, he slid it open, and turned around. Dana was staring at him, his pale face a study in disbelief. Zed said, "I owe it to you, I think. I told the police to treat you gently, and they didn't. Another time, and I might not leave—but it's late, and we're both tired, and this isn't my house. I'll let you have one lie, Dana."

Rhani lifted her head from a pillow.

For a moment she couldn't remember where she was. The texture of the sheets was unfamiliar. Sunshine through pink (pink?) curtains suffused the room with rosy light. The light made her think of fire. . . . Her fingers curled in the sheets; she remembered flames, the curtains like a torch, and Amri screaming. Her sinuses ached with the tears she hadn't cried. This was the Kyneth house, yes, and she had arrived here the night before in a police bus, with Zed and Corrios and Dana. But not with Binkie—Binkie was in a cell, Binkie had killed Amri, Binkie had burned her house.

She scrambled from the bed. An embroidered bell-pull dangled down the wall; she pulled it. In a moment, someone knocked on her door. "Come in," she called. A slave entered with clothing in her arms.

"Domna," she said, trying to bow with the burden, "these are for you." She put them on a chair and trotted into the bathroom—to run a bath, Rhani thought. Rhani looked through the pile of clothes. Her own filthy pants were nowhere in sight; Aliza must have taken them to give the computer a pattern, and then discarded them. There were four shirts, four pants, two tunics and a dress, all in fabrics and colors she liked, silky silvers, and blues, amber, and red-browns.

"What time is it?" she asked the slave.

"Domna, it's three hours past dawn."

Rhani hated such circumlocutions. She hunted through the room until she found the wall chronometer. It was in the headboard of the bed. Throwing on the pink robe, she strode into the washroom and splashed her face with cold water. The bath was waiting for her. She bathed quickly. Kyneths evidently preferred baths to showers. When she emerged from the bath, her skin felt silky-smooth; the slave had poured some kind of scented depilatory oil into the water. When she returned to the bedroom, swathed in a towel bigger than she was, the bed was decorously rearranged and the slave had drawn back all but the inner curtains. Through their gauze, Rhani saw the mathematical sprawl of Main Clinic, and, farther north, the brown, bald pate of the Barrens. Her mind jumped. She had to talk to Imre, and to Zed; she had to find a new secretary, she had to talk to Dana. She wondered if he had managed to locate Loras U-Ellen.

She dressed in blue-and-silver. She missed her room; it was hard to think in this alien place, where the pastel colors made the air seem fuzzy. She wanted the hard bright dimensions of her house. She had never cared for it, before.

And Binkie had burned it. Anger shook her like a benediction. The door opened wide; Zed came through it. He, too, was dressed in blue-and-silver, the Yago colors: she hugged him fiercely for a moment. Once more their responses had run alike. Twin! she thought.

"Did you sleep?" he questioned.

She smiled at him. "Always the medic. Yes, Senior, I slept very well."

"What shall you do this morning?"

Binkie. But she was not going to tell Zed about Binkie. "Things," she said, vaguely. "I need a new secretary."

"I thought I would go and look at the house," he said.

"I doubt it can be rebuilt," she said gently. "Not as it was."

"I wouldn't want it as it was. Would you?" he inquired.

"I don't know," said she. "I hadn't thought about it."

"I thought you didn't like it," he said.

I didn't, she thought. But that house had been begun by Lisa Yago. It symbolized something; it contained more than just their personal history. Suddenly she grew suspicious. Imre might not have kept his promise. "Why are you up so early?" she said.

"Why are you?" he countered.

She grinned, and said lightly, knowing he would not believe it, "Zed-ka, I'm hiding something from you."

But to her dismay, he did not laugh. "Are you?" His gaze sharpened. "Rhani—" He was interrupted by a knock at the already opened door. Calling good morning, a slave came in with a tray piled high with papers. Amri carried the mail like that, Rhani thought, and her heart wrenched in her chest like a squeezed toy.

Aliza Kyneth followed. "Good morning, my dear," she said. She gave Rhani a kiss, and the smile which she might have given her eldest daughter, and turned to Zed. To Rhani's astonishment, her brother stood ummoving as Aliza kissed him. "Did you sleep?" she asked, looking at them both.

Zed said, "Yes, Aliza. Thank you."

Rhani said, "Very well, thanks." She pointed to the tray. "What's this?"

"Letters that came for you in the morning mail. Most of them were hand-delivered. They came from all over Abanat—expressions of sympathy, probably offers of refuge—" She smiled without malice—"Who would have guessed a Yago would ever need refuge, on Chabad?"

"None of us," Rhani said. She sorted through the letters. There were notes from Ferris Dur, from Theo Levos, from all the lesser Abanat families, from the Yago businesses, from the banks, from Charity Diamos—she held that up for Zed and Aliza to see. They laughed. There was an impressive communiqué from the Lower House of the Chabad Council, offering sympathies and unspecified support. There was a letter from Clare Brion. She read that; it said, in part, *"If there's anything I can do, please call me."* There was no letter from Tuli. In the midst of the mail was a printed communication from the Abanat police, telling her that Ramas I-Occad was in custody at Main Police Station, along with five self-confessed members of the Free Folk of Chabad. She slipped that into a pocket. At the bottom of the pile, a PIN headline said: "YAGO HOUSE OBLITERATED!" She made a face at it.

"Rhani, Aliza, if you'll excuse me—" said Zed. He started toward the door. A third slave walked in holding yet another tray, on which sat six or seven different kinds of breakfast dishes. Zed lifted an egg tart off the tray and strolled out.

Rhani said to Aliza, "I want to hire a secretary."

Aliza said, "Of course, my dear. In the meantime Imre has instructed one of his secretaries to assist you in whatever you need. Her name is Nialle Hamish; she is very capable."

"*One* of his secretaries?"

"He has three," Aliza said. "I'm sorry, my dear, will you need more than one? I know we can—"

"No, no," Rhani said hastily, "one will be fine. I've never needed more than one."

Aliza pursed her ample lips. "That one must have been superb."

"Yes," Rhani said, "he was. What happened to the slave who came with me last night, and to the house steward?"

"We lodged them both in the slave quarters."

"I want to see Dana. The slave."

Aliza gestured to one of the women and gave her a swiftly murmured order. "And ask Nialle to come here," she added. "Rhani, before you begin to plan, let me assure you that you may call this house home for as long as you like."

Rhani shook her head. "Aliza, you are the most generous person I know," she said. "But I can't believe that your staff will welcome having to care for two households. As soon as we can, Zed and I will go back to the estate. We can live there."

"But you will rebuild the house?" Aliza exclaimed.

"Certainly," Rhani said.

A step sounded in the hall. A pudgy woman bowed from the doorway. Rhani recognized her from the phone tape. "Domna," she said, "I am Nialle Hamish."

Rhani smiled at her. "Please come in," she said, liking the woman's voice and bearing. She seemed calmly competent. "My household calls me Rhani-ka. I'm grateful that Domni Imre can spare you from his work long enough to help me. I need first to deal with this." She indicated the tray of mail. "They all need answers and some of them will need handwritten responses. Can you find me a calligrapher?"

Nialle said, "I myself am a calligrapher, Domna. I beg your pardon—Rhani-ka."

"That's wonderful," Rhani said. The breakfast smells

in the chamber grew suddenly tempting. Stepping to the laden tray, she picked out a strip of broiled fish.

Aliza said, "Rhani darling, I will leave you now. If you need anything, you have only to tell Nialle." She swayed to the doorway. In a few moments, Dana walked through it. He too was wearing fresh clothes, and his face was swollen—why? Rhani thought.

He stopped meters from her, and bowed. "Good morning, Rhani-ka," he said.

She wanted to tell him: I believed that you had run. She wanted to ask him: Would you go? And she wanted to hold him, to touch him. . . . "If you don't mind," she said to Nialle. At once the secretary left the room, and the slaves followed her. Rhani waited until the door clicked shut before she closed the distance between them. She laid her hands on his arms. He smelled of the same bath scent she did. He gripped her, murmuring her name, and then let go suddenly.

"I forgot your side."

She laughed at him. "It's healed." She touched his cheek very gently. "How did you come by this?"

"A policeman," he said, "last night. When they thought *I* had burned the house."

"Binkie burned the house."

"I know," he said.

"How did you know?"

"I guessed. He wasn't there, you see. And then Zed told me, last night."

"Did my brother—?" She could not finish the question. But he understood, and shook his head, seeming bemused.

"No. He didn't." Rhani put her hand on his chest. Under the soft fine weave of his tunic, his heartbeat trembled, rapid as freely running water. "Binkie—he told me to run away. He said, *'Zed knows.'* You can guess what I thought."

"Oh, I can." She could, vividly. The shared vision pulled them out of each others' arms. He hesitated, then touched her hair.

"I was so worried for you, Rhani," he said.

"And I for you. I'm so glad you called me. If you hadn't—"

"I almost didn't," he said. "But something about

Binkie's manner troubled me. He was just—odd." He drew a breath. "Stars, I was stupid."

"We've all been stupid," she said. "Have you eaten? Come and eat."

She watched him eat. He did not appear to be tasting much. After his pace slowed down, she said, "Did you reach Loras U-Ellen?"

Hand halfway to his mouth, he halted. "I found someone who could. I paid her eighty-five credits. I told her to tell him to get in touch with you, by letter."

"You're sure the message will reach him?"

He looked surprised. "Yes," he said, "I'm sure. She—when she says she'll do a thing, she'll do it."

Who? Rhani wanted to ask. But she remembered that she had promised to trust him—and besides, she did not want to watch his eyes grow secret as he considered how best to lie. "Binkie's at Main Police Station," she said. "Zed doesn't know. I want to see him."

Dana looked thoughtful. "Can't they bring him here?"

"No," she said. "Zed would know. He's gone now to look at the—at the house, but he might come back. Besides, I want to see him *there,* behind locks and doors and bars."

"What about the Free Folk of Chabad?" he said.

"They're locked up, too." She felt in her pocket for the police communiqué. Pulling it out, she passed it to him.

As he read it, she ate another strip of fish.

"Ramas I-Occad—?" he said.

"That's Binkie's full name," she said.

"Sweet mother. Why did you call him *Binkie?*"

Rhani said, "It was the name of a toy I once had."

Dana stared at her. "A toy? A toy what?"

His tone annoyed her. "What difference does it make? A toy animal, as I recall. Stuffed. It was some ancient Terran creature—a giraffe." She stretched her hands apart. "It had a long neck. Dana, this is all irrelevant."

"Yes," he said. "It must seem so, to you."

She scowled at him. "Will you please make sense?"

He flushed. "I'm sorry, Rhani-ka. I—please forget it. If you want to go to the Abanat Police Station, then we'll go. Now?"

"Are you fit?" she said bluntly.

He nodded.

Rhani thought: I'd better warn them that I'm coming. She glanced around the pink room, looking for com-unit and screen.

If it was there, she could not see it. Walking to the door, she opened it and stuck her head into the hall. "Nialle?" The secretary popped from another room. "Thank you very much for your patience. Please come in now." Nialle, smiling, came into the room. "I was looking for the com-unit."

"Of course, D—Rhani-ka." The round-faced woman went to a section of the pink-papered wall and pressed what appeared to be a heat-sensitive plate. The wall revolved, presenting them with a compscreen, a com-line, and a computer keyboard.

"That's rather nice," Rhani said. "Would you connect me with the Abanat Police Station? Ask for Sachiko Tsurada, Officer Tsurada."

"Certainly, Rhani-ka." Nialle's small hands skipped delicately over the keys. Watching her, Rhani was painfully reminded of when Binkie had first come to be her secretary. She had bought him during Auction, struck by something about him—his reticence, perhaps? She was no longer sure; whatever it was it had shone through the dorazine haze. He was a reticent man, a private person. Once he had relaxed in her presence and grown used to the household customs, he was pleasant, even funny, to be with. They had joked together; they made each other laugh. She had spoken to him of her childhood, and he had shared with her—a little, very little—his wishes and his griefs.

She could date precisely the summer night when the laughter had ceased.

She had not wanted him to be so hurt. She had warned him, more than once. But he had not listened. . . .

"Rhani-ka?" said Nialle.

She brought herself to the present with an effort. "Yes?"

"I have Sachiko Tsurada onscreen."

She went to the com-unit. Tsurada's dark face looked out at her. The edges of the screen were blurry as people flowed in and out of focus at Tsurada's back. "Domna Rhani," said the policewoman. She sounded and looked exhausted. "I'm glad to see you safe." She coughed. "We have your slave here: Ramas I-Occad. He is formally charged with the attempted murder of his owner and the actual murder of Amri Utasdatter, also a slave. We also have five members of the Free Folk of Chabad in custody. Their names are—but you don't want to know their names, do you, Domna? They are all members of the drug detail of the Federation Police Force."

Rhani heard Dana gasp. "That's crazy," he said.

"We have signed confessions from them, Domna," said Tsurada. She smiled. "We also have their resignations waiting for the acting captain to accept."

"You have evidence besides the confessions?" Rhani said.

"The fingerprint belongs to one of them. And we have all their equipment. You may even recognize one or two of them, Domna. They swear the attacks were never meant to kill."

Rhani said, "I believe them. Do you have A-Rae yet?"

"No. We cannot find him." Tsurada sounded angry.

"Sweet mother," Dana said. "The Hype cops turned assassins?"

Rhani said, "Officer Tsurada, I'd like to come see Bi— my slave."

"We have his interrogation in the computer, Domna. Do you want to read it?"

"No. I want to talk to him. You said—" she hesitated, and then continued—"you said formal charges have been filed against him. I did not file them."

"The law files them, Domna. The process is automatic." Tsurada rubbed her eyes. "I'm sorry, I should have been more clear. I-Occad has not only been charged with attempting your death, Domna. He has been tried and convicted."

"That's quick," Dana muttered.

Rhani said, *"I want to see him,* Officer Tsurada. Sentence is *not* to be carried out until I do. If I leave this house now, the movalong will bring me to your doors in approximately thirty minutes. I'll be there. Wait for me."

"Yes, Domna." Tsurada broke the connection.

Nialle said softly, "Will that be all, Rhani-ka?"

Rhani's lungs felt tight, as if she had not breathed in a long time. "Yes," she said. "Dana?"

"Yes, Rhani-ka. We can go. But—"

She frowned at him. "What is it now?"

"I think you should not take the movalong across town," he said. "Your picture is on the front page of every PINsheet."

"Oh, damn." She had not considered that. "You are right."

Nialle said, "There is a bubble hangar on the roof, Rhani-ka. We can hire a pilot—"

"I have a pilot," Rhani said.

Chapter Sixteen

A regiment of chiefs stood waiting in the bubble hangar of the Abanat Police Station. Sachiko Tsurada stood among them. She looked startled when Rhani walked straight to her. "Domna Rhani, may I present to you—" She started putting names to faces. The bubble hangar was cool and dark. An elevator waited, run by a smiling slave. They went down, quite far down. One of the important people explained: "Domna, the cells are two stories below the ground floor."

Dana stayed as close to Rhani as he could. The coded lights on the walls, the noises, the smell of drugs, the bars all reminded him of the Net. Tsurada pointed out the various rooms they passed. The room with machines and a bed, she said, was the interrogation room.

Rhani said, "You use drugs."

"Of course, Domna." She named the drugs they used. Dana wondered if Rhani thought the police used her brother's methods of extracting truth. Drugs were faster. But the spiritual kinship between the police cells and the Net made him shake. He listened to Tsurada's voice without hearing the words. She was so tired that when she spoke, she sounded like a bad tape.

"The cells for sentenced prisoners are this way, Domna." Tsurada ushered them into a corridor. Dana had expected the strong lights, the sweet, druggy smells, and the silence. But he had also expected more bars. There were no bars in the wide hallway. Prisoners sat or lay in a honeycomb of tiny cells, visible through glass walls. The walls were textured with anti-noise insulation.

"Can they see us?" Rhani asked. There was a remote quality to her voice. Dana found it disturbing. She seemed unaffected by the sights and smells.

"No," Tsurada said. "That's one-way glass." Most of the prisoners lay on cots. They looked asleep. A few of them sat upright, staring at bare walls. They wore light gray, ugly clothing. Not one of them looked up as the three visitors went past. Tsurada halted in front of one cell. A man lay curled on the bunk, back toward the hallway.

"That's I-Occad," she said.

"I want to go in there," Rhani said.

Dana said, "Rhani-ka, there must be a panel through which you could speak." The thought of entering that small, bare room popped the sweat out on his palms.

Officer Tsurada said calmly, "You can if you like, Domna. There's a guard at the end of the hallway watching each cell through a monitor. That light"—she pointed to a small red light on the cell wall—"shows that the machines are on. He's drugged; you're in no danger."

"Please," said Rhani. Tsurada took a plastic disc from a pocket and slid it into a slot near the door. The door folded back. Rhani stepped inside the cell. Dana followed her.

The door closed. Outside it, Sachiko Tsurada stood, waiting, Dana realized, until they were through. Binkie lay unmoving on the narrow bed. "Binkie," said Rhani. Dana thought perhaps the man was asleep—and no wonder, after a night of interrogation, he thought—when suddenly Binkie moved his head. Slowly he pushed himself to a sitting position. He needed both hands. His feet were bare, and Dana wondered if the floor was cold. Bare feet—he remembered the Net. He was *not* going to think about that now.

Binkie was gaunt; he'd lost weight overnight. Head canted to one side, he stared at Rhani. His eyes were fixed, the pupils dilated. He ran his tongue around his lips. "Rhani Yago."

There was no deference in his voice, and no fear, either; simply exhaustion.

Rhani said to him, "Were you always one of the Free Folk of Chabad?"

As if she had not spoken, he said, "They told me you

were alive. I was glad of that, a little. I was sorry that the fire killed Amri. I wanted it to be your brother." He might have been remarking on the heat. "I don't have to talk to you," he said. "I talked to the police all night. Why don't you ask them questions?"

Rhani said, meditatively, "We were friends, once."

He coughed. "To you we were friends."

"Was it all an act, then?" she said evenly.

He gazed at her without speaking, and then, suddenly, rubbed his face with both hands. When he lifted his head, his skin was blotchy. "I suppose not," he said. "Is that why you came, to know that? Do me a favor, then. A friendly favor. Don't call me Binkie. My *name* is Ramas I-Occad." Dana shivered, remembering without wanting to how Zed had stripped him, methodically, of even his name. And then had given it back to him.

Rhani said, "All right. Ramas—will you tell me what happened?"

"What happened?" He laughed weakly. "Zed happened. Your brother." His face worked. "No, that's not entirely true. There's more. I don't expect you to understand it." His voice was a monotone. "I never denied my crimes. On the Net they gave me dorazine, and everything they did seemed just. I don't remember the Auction. Then you bought me, and brought me to the estate, showed me your work, taught me to use your machines. And you talked to me, like a human being. I began to believe I was a human being. But—" he coughed—"that isn't true, I know now. Unless you wanted me to do something for you, you never looked at me. I was invisible, a thing, a machine that turned itself off when you didn't need it."

"I never thought you were a thing," she said.

"There wasn't even dorazine," he said. "That's when I began to go mad, I think. You don't know how cruel it is, Rhani Yago, that you don't permit your house slaves to take dorazine. We work for you, we stay ourselves, we act, we think, we are sane, we are almost free—" He coughed again. "But you can't be free *and* a slave." He looked at Dana. *"You* know what I'm talking about, don't you? But you had your music. I'm sorry about your tapes."

Dana swallowed. "That's all right." Binkie was correct;

he did understand. He remembered a moment during that first week at the estate when he had almost walked out the gate.

"So I ran," said Ramas. "I knew I couldn't escape. I just had to get away from *you*. And your brother brought me back—and you let it happen! Two days and nights screaming my guts out—did you pretend not to hear it?"

Rhani's face darkened. "I tried," she said. "I tried to stop him."

"No," Ramas said. "I won't believe that, because I don't believe you can't. I think you *like* what he does."

Sweet mother, Dana thought. He watched Rhani's face whiten at the accusation.

"You're wrong," she said tonelessly.

"I'm right," said the slave. "He worships you. He would never do anything you didn't want him to do. You call him twin—he's your other half, Rhani Yago. You're kind, gentle, generous to your slaves—because he is there, to do what you will never have to do. I used to picture you standing outside the door of the room he put me in, listening. Did you do that? Did you watch?"

"Stop it," Rhani said, with fury.

He laughed at her. "Make me. Hurt me."

Dana said, "Rhani, you don't have to stay here. We can go."

Ramas laughed, and coughed in the middle of it. "That's right, protect her. Remember though, what I said. She won't protect you." He leaned against the wall.

"No," Rhani said, "I want to stay. I still want to know about the Free Folk of Chabad."

Ramas nodded. "I'll tell you," he said. "Why not? The police will if I don't. They were all Hype cops. I didn't know that when I offered to help them. No, that's not what really happened—they approached me. In the mail. Your mail, which I opened every day. They asked me to be their spy, no more than that, to tell them where you went, who you saw, what your schedule was—I did. I told them everything. I rather hoped they'd kill you. If your owner dies, you go free."

"Not if it's discovered that you had a hand in it," Rhani said.

"I know, but I thought they were smart. After the bombing, the police didn't know where to look. It took a while before I saw that they didn't want to kill you. You were smart, you guessed that." He coughed, and licked his lips. "I'd like some water," he said.

"Where is it?" Rhani asked. He pointed to a spout on the wall. There was a cup on a hook beside it. She filled the cup and handed it across the little cell to him.

He drank it thirstily. "The fire?" she said.

"The fire—the fire was my idea."

"The Hype cops didn't know?" Dana said.

"They knew. They gave me the equipment. But they thought I would time the fire for daylight, for some time when there was no one in the house."

"Did you send me away to save my life?"

"No. I hoped they'd blame you for the fire. Since they weren't going to find my body either, I figured they could blame me, or you." He grinned. "Michel A-Rae planned it, every bit of it, except the last part. He wants to bring you down, Rhani-ka." His tone was suddenly vicious. "I hope he does it. He's got something else prepared for you, something I know nothing about, so even the drugs can't make me talk about it. He despises you. But he hates your brother more—even more than I do."

Rhani's face lost color at his tone. But her voice was still calm as she said, "He's stupid, to think I would react to threat by panicking."

Ramas said, "Yes. He is stupid. I could have told him you don't frighten easily." He slumped against the wall. His hair fell across his eyes, and he made no move to brush it away. "Leave me alone," he said. "Go away. I've answered your questions, and I'm tired. I suppose they'll kill me tonight, and then you won't have to think about me anymore."

Dana said, "What do you mean, they'll kill you?"

Rhani and her slave looked at him with identical expressions on their faces. Ramas answered, his tone irritable. "I tried to kill her. It's in the contract—if a slave kills his owner, or tries to, he's executed."

"You knew that, and you still tried it?" Dana said.

"Sure." Ramas grinned like a death's head. "Are you telling me that, given an opportunity and a way to blame someone else, you wouldn't try to kill Zed?"

Dana swallowed. "I don't know." The thought of trying to kill Zed made him sick, because if it didn't work. . . .

"Zed's not my owner, though."

"There's no difference," Ramas said. "She's just as bad as he is."

Dana saw Rhani's hands twist together. "I don't believe that," he said.

"More fool you." He held out the cup. "Water, please." Silently Rhani refilled the cup and gave it to him. "Thank you, Rhani-ka." There was rage in the last syllable. Dana tensed. His gaze flicked to the steady red of the scanner light. It was on, and Sachiko Tsurada still stood patiently waiting in the hall.

Suddenly Rhani stepped forward. Kneeling, she put a hand on the slave's knee. "Ramas—Binkie. Aren't you afraid?"

He looked at her, shrinking a little toward the wall. A tremor shook him. "Of course I am." He swallowed. "I don't want to die. I—" He halted. "Oh, leave me, *please.*" His pale face was chalk-white.

Rhani said gently, "Are you sure you want me to?"

A communication passed between them, a silent, mysterious thread. Hope? Dana thought. Love? He did not understand what was happening. Rhani looked at the door, which from this side was gray and opaque. "Officer Tsurada," she said, "I want to speak to you."

The door folded back and Tsurada stepped to the doorway. "Yes, Domna?"

"What happens now?" Rhani asked. She was still kneeling.

The policewoman looked faintly embarrassed. "Well, he's confessed. The sentence is automatic. Normally, we would wait until evening, when we would drug his food and then—" She did not finish.

"What drug do you use for the sentence?" Rhani said.

"Morphidyne."

Dana had heard of it. It gave release from pain, but was said to be terribly addictive. Of course, in this case it wouldn't matter, he thought. The smell of the hallway was beginning to sicken him. He breathed deeply to push the nausea back.

Rhani said, "Binkie?"

The slave's hands trembled. "I—oh, this is hard."

"I'll stay," Rhani said. She sat beside him on the narrow bunk and looked at Officer Tsurada. "Do you have any objections to that?"

Tsurada looked bewildered. "No, Domna," she said. "But it isn't—usual."

"I don't care," Rhani said. "Go and get your drug, Officer."

Tsurada left the room. Dana wiped his palms on his pants; he was sweating badly now. When Tsurada returned, she held a cup with a small black pill in it in one hand and a loaded syringe in the other.

"Which do you want?" she said.

Ramas stared at her laden hands. He nodded at the syringe. "That's faster, isn't it?" he said hoarsely. Dana felt dizzy. He put a hand on the white wall to hold himself upright. I refuse, he thought, I absolutely refuse to be sick.

"Yes, it is," Tsurada said.

"That's what I want." He looked at Rhani. "You said you'll stay. To the end?"

"To the end," she agreed.

Officer Tsurada shut the folding door. She lifted the syringe to the light, checking the solution, Dana thought. "Your left wrist, please," she said. Ramas pushed his left wrist at her. It was trembling; he tried to stop the tremor with his other hand, and could not. Rhani reached to the man who tried to kill her and cradled his hand between her own. Tsurada inserted the needle under the skin. The vein stood up. She pushed the plunger, and then drew it back a centimeter: blood backed into the tube, turning the liquid pearly pink. Ramas sighed; under the impersonal lights his face seemed translucent. Tsurada pushed the plunger the rest of the way in.

When she drew the needle out, a drop of blood welled on Ramas' wrist. His mouth opened. He licked his dry lips, tried to speak, tried with muscles weaker than a baby's to contract his fingers. He couldn't. "I'm cold," he whispered. He went loose, like a sack with its stuffing out of it. "Tell my daughter—" he started to say, and then the lines on his taut face smoothed. He breathed shallow, soft gasps that did not fill his lungs, and died.

They went into the hall. Dana balled his hands until his knuckles ached and concentrated on seeing. Rhani was talking with the policewoman about the Hype cops.

"What will happen to them?"

"They're Federation officials," Tsurada said. "They'll be shipped to Nexus, tried, and I expect convicted."

"Did they tell you anything about A-Rae's current plans?" Her voice was cool, unfazed, unfathomable.

"Only that he had expected to have to hide."

"I was thinking about what Binkie—Ramas—just said."

Tsurada shook her head. "No."

"Has the rest of A-Rae's staff gone with him into hiding?"

"He seems to have taken a core, maybe ten people, with him. The rest are milling about on the moon, under the command of Henrietta Melones, the acting captain. Word is that a replacement has already been designated for the position, and that the person—whoever she is—is on her way here." They reached the elevator, entered it, went up to the ground floor. Dana felt his stomach muscles settle.

Rhani said, "I would like to see the reports of the interrogations made on the five police. Are they available?"

"They're in the computer, Domna. I'll make sure they are released to you."

"Thank you. You are very kind." The elevator wormed its way to the roof.

They stepped into the bubble hangar. Rhani said polite things to Sachiko Tsurada, pressed her hands, dismissed her. Dana waited. His guts had relaxed, but his nerves were so tense he felt as if his skin were on fire. Rhani climbed into the bubble after him. The roof pulled back, the sky blazed down, and they were free. He sent the little machine into the light. He said, "Where do you want to go?"

She glanced at him in surprise. "The Kyneth house."

He directed the bubble south. The Promenade unrolled beneath them. Rhani sighed. "Wait," she said. "Go west." He took the bubble winging out over the lambent icebergs. "Are you all right?" she said.

He nodded. "I didn't think you noticed."

She raised her eyebrows. "Of course I noticed." She leaned forward, filled a cup of water, drank it. "Dana, you've never watched anyone die, have you?"

He shook his head.

"I have. My mother died at home. So did Domna Sam. Death isn't strange to me." The blood had risen under her skin so that its honey color deepened to bronze. "But it wasn't easy, witnessing that death. I did it because it wasn't easy."

He said, "I don't understand you."

"I know that. I don't expect you to." She leaned her head back, leaving her throat exposed. Something in the posture—he could not remember what—reminded him vividly of Zed. "I have my secrets from you, as you have yours from me. Binkie—" she halted, and then continued—"Binkie was right, I was cruel beyond belief when I let Zed have him. I should have put him on dorazine."

Part of Dana's mind agreed with her, and wanted to say it. But he found himself thinking: you couldn't help it, you didn't know how he felt—excusing her ignorance, denying the self-admitted culpability. "Don't put me on dorazine," he said. "I'd be of no use as a pilot."

"And Binkie would have been no use as a secretary."

They sailed over the iceberg peaks. On one of them Dana spotted a small toiling figure. An ice climber? he wondered. "May I ask you. . . ?"

"Ask," she said.

"What was Binkie's—Ramas'—crime?"

"On Enchanter, you mean?" Rhani sighed. "He ran an arson ring for profit. He was the administrator, not the one who made the flames."

Dana recalled Binkie saying to him, his first evening at the estate, *"I could be an arsonist, or an axe murderer."* The bubble plunged on a downdraft, and he righted it automatically. He licked his lips and said, "What about Amri?"

"What about Amri?" Rhani asked.

"What was her crime? She was so young, so childish—"

To his horror, Rhani laughed. "Oh, Dana," she said, and her voice was weary. "You poor innocent. Have you never met a person who'd been brain-wiped before?"

"Brain-wiped?" he said, incredulous. "Amri?"

"Twice," Rhani said. "She was a thief, Dana; an imaginative, incorrigible thief. The first time she was sentenced—she was just fourteen—the court judged her capable of rehabilitation, and sent her for treatment. She returned to her profession the week they released her from the clinic. They did a minimal brain-wipe—they call it a therapeutic wipe. It didn't take. They did a slightly deeper one the next time. Finally, in desperation, they delivered her to the Net. The Clinic telepath suggested that slavery might set up some kind of pattern of restitution."

Dana said, "Was it—was it working?"

"How do I know? Amri never stole from me, if that's what you mean."

"It's hard to believe—she seemed so pure."

"Brain-wipe does that. Let's go back now." As Dana swung the craft to the southwest, making a spiral toward the sun, she said, "I blame Binkie for that, for that death, above all. Amri deserved a chance to be something other than what she had been."

There was an acid taste in Dana's mouth. He felt a fool: he had thought Amri innocent, and she was simply a felon who had been trapped too many times. Starcaptain/slave, child/thief: Chabad kept transforming what he thought he knew. It was unfair. He was reminded of toy holograms he'd played with; when you turned them, the figure seemed to move, and yet when you looked again, they hadn't, and when you tried to touch them the smooth plastic casing pushed your hand away.

He had done that as a child on Pellin. Stars, he was still a child, as much a child as Amri, anyway. . . .

"Dana!" Rhani gasped. Dana jumped in his seat.

Somehow they had gotten too close to another bubble. Dana saw the pilot's mouth opening and closing impotently. He veered left as the other craft spiralled down. They missed each other. Fighting the wash of air that bobbed them like two corks, Dana said, "Thanks!"

You idiot. It was not Rhani's voice, and it came from inside his head. *This is Tamerlane Orion, Abanat's chief pilot. Where did you train, you fool? Don't answer me, I can't hear you. But watch what you're doing over my city, if you please, or I'll let you explain to Zed Yago how you nearly killed his sister because you weren't paying attention to what else was sharing the spacelanes.*

"Dana, what is it?" Rhani demanded. "What's happening?"

Signing off, the voice said grimly.

"Dana?"

"A minute," Dana said. His head was ringing. His contact with telepaths had been mercifully limited. He had had one examination by the telepaths on Nexus to qualify for his medallion; it had left him sick for a day.

He swallowed. "The chief pilot just communicated with me," he said.

Rhani looked at him as if he were out of his mind. Cautiously, she said, "How? I didn't hear a thing."

"You don't—oh." He was surprised. "He's a telepath. Rhani-ka."

"Really?" She rubbed her chin with one hand. "That's odd; I didn't know that, and I've met him."

Being very, very careful, Dana brought the bubblecraft the rest of the way across Abanat, and headed down toward the Kyneth roof. The hangar top was already open for him. He felt as if he needed to sleep, or else to scream long and loud where no one could hear him. He wished devoutly that the destruction of the Yago house had not also included his musictapes.

They settled into the hangar. "Wait," Rhani said into the shadows. Dana turned off the machinery and sat, hands in his lap. She leaned against him. Her hair blew against his mouth. He glanced at her and saw age lines, strain lines, at the corners of her eyes and lips. "Dana, do you hate me?"

"Hate you?" He was shocked. "No."

"Despite what Binkie said about Zed and me?"

He let his hand touch her cheek. "No. I don't hate you."

"I'm glad. I should tell you—" She stopped.

"Tell me what?"

"No," she said. "Not yet. Let's go in."

He held her back. "Rhani, you have to—" Her mouth came up to his. Like pieces of a puzzle locking into place, they embraced. Her fingers stroked his back. He breathed her scent. Her breasts and hips moved against him, and he felt his body move to answer.

This *can't* go on, he thought, and groaned as she touched him.

"Rhani." He captured her hands and folded them between his own. "Rhani, tell me something."

"If I can."

"How long are we going to stay in this house? Three or four days? A week? Two?"

"Perhaps a week," she said.

"And then we'll fly to the estate. Will Zed stay in Abanat?"

"Of course not. The estate is his home. He may fly to the Clinic if they call him."

"How frequently might that happen?"

She shrugged. "Once a week."

"Your brother is perceptive," Dana said. "How long do you think it will take him to see that we have been lovers?"

"You're forgetting something," Rhani said.

"What?"

"Darien Riis."

It was true; he had forgotten her. What was that nonsense Rhani has quoted to him: Cherillys' Law, that was it. "I don't know what difference she'll make," he said, "and neither do you. Rhani, if Zed realizes that I've shared your bed, he'll kill me, or worse. He can do worse."

"What do you want me to do?" Rhani said.

I have to ask, Dana thought. "Free me."

Her amber eyes locked on his face. "What will you do if you are freed?"

"Leave," he said.

"But you said you'd find Loras U-Ellen for me."

"I will. I have. T—my friend will contact him; I'm sure of it."

"I'm sure of nothing," she said. Her eyes gleamed, luminous in the dusky space. "If I don't free you, Dana, will you try to escape?"

"I'd be a fool to do so," he said, thinking of Tori Lamonica, of his ship, of the Hype. . . .

"But will you?" she insisted, shaking herself free of him, gripping his shirt with both hands. "Will you?" She answered herself. "Probably."

"I could tell you a lie," he said.

"Don't," she said. "I don't want you to lie to me." She ran her fingertip over his mouth. "Dana—listen. I need you. I can't tell you why, not now, only that I do, that your presence here is vital to me in a way you cannot know. Please, please, be patient.''

He said, "Will you free me, Rhani?''

She said, "I will, Starcaptain. But not now.''

"You won't tell me when.''

"No." She gripped his shoulders, hard. "Dana, don't try to escape. Please trust me.''

"It's not you I don't trust,'' he said. He released the bubble door. "After you, Rhani-ka.'' She climbed from the bubble. He closed the bubble door and walked to join her on the stairway to the house, thinking as he did: Rhani Yago, I'll trust you—just as much as you seem willing to trust *me*.

The Kyneths ate communally, at a wooden table so huge that lifting it would tax the strength of a family of Skellians.

Zed sat next to Davi Kyneth. The boy's nearness had frightened him, but after a while he relaxed. Eleven people sat at the table, nine Kyneths, Zed, and Rhani. The wood literally groaned as the slaves heaped it with food. All the Kyneths, big ones and small ones, ate hugely. Looking over the ruins of the house had been depressing, and Zed was surprised to find that he was hungry. He had gone from the house to the Clinic, but they had nothing there for him to do, and after an hour of wandering around Outpatient, he had come back to the Kyneth house and fallen asleep.

Rhani was eating. He watched her narrowly; there was an intensity about her that disturbed him. She had told him, just before dinner, about Binkie's death. After the initial shock—no, he thought, not shock, *anger*, admit it, Zed Yago, you wanted him for yourself—he had stopped questioning her. She was eating with an appetite now; internally, he applauded. She had been running on her nerves for hours; she needed fuel.

Imre and Vera, a middle daughter, were having a ferocious argument. Imre blew out his cheeks and bristled his beard; Vera tossed her red hair and slammed a fist on the table. Nobody but Zed seemed to notice. Aliza called down the table to Rhani; something about the weather. Rhani raised her voice in answer. As she did so, she glanced across the table at Zed. Speech was impossible, but he read in her eyes what she was thinking: *How different this all is!*

"C-C-C-Commander?" said Davi. He held up a breadstick as if he thought it might talk to him.

"I told you not to call me that," said Zed. "Didn't I tell you my name?"

"Yes, but—" He squirmed in the cushions.

"What is it, then?"

"Z-Z-Zed."

"Good. Did you want to ask me something?"

"Yes, please. Is this the kind of food that people eat in space?"

"Real food, you mean." Zed took the breadstick and bit it. "Sometimes. It depends who you are, and if it matters to you what you're eating, and what kind of a ship you're in." The bread had a sesame taste.

"In the Net?"

"The Net carries real food, much like this, though not with this—variety. When you're the size of a space station, food, even for several thousand people, doesn't take up all that much space. It would if it were for more than three months, but it isn't. And also, most of those people sit all day, or sleep. They don't need very much to eat."

"What about on a little ship?"

"Tell me what kind."

The boy blushed. "An MPL?"

"Big enough for captain and crew: six at most. That one?" He grinned at the boy. "You've been studying. Most MPLs carry food bars. It isn't always easy to navigate in hyperspace; a trip can take longer than you thought. Rather than guess what you need, and stock up on real food, and maybe run out of it halfway, you load with food bars. They compress; you can take as many as you like, as long as you also take a water supply."

One of the younger girls said, "Doesn't that get boring?"

"Very. But in the Hype, either you're bored stiff anyway, or you're so busy concentrating on saving your skin that you can't taste what you're eating." A slave put a large platter of egg tarts in front of him. "Unlike the food this household eats, which, I attest, tastes stupendous."

Aliza smiled. "Rhani said you like egg tarts."

"And breadsticks," said Zed with his mouth full. Davi turned red.

A sister observed with clinical interest, "Look, the Brat's blushing."

Davi's ears turned scarlet with embarrassment; he started to get up from the table. Imre yelled at his daughter good-humoredly. Zed dared to put a hand on the boy's shoulder. "Stay."

Aliza rapped for silence. The children quieted; heads turned. "I don't know what Family Yago will make of Family Kyneth hospitality," she said, "with all of us behaving just the way we always behave. Yelling." Imre chuckled. *"You're* as bad as *them,"* said his wife, referring to their children.

"Worse, I hope," said Imre. "Think of the years I've had to practice in."

Aliza said, "I am well aware of them. Now, my loves, Rhani wishes to talk to Papa, so minors and middle kids, upstairs."

There was a general howl. Vera said, "What are we supposed to do upstairs?"

Aliza said, "Play."

Dead silence greeted this remark. Vera said, "Mother, even *Davi's* too old to *play."* Davi nodded vigorous agreement.

Imre said, "Get out of here! Shor, Yianni, Margarite, you stay."

Zed whispered to Davi as the boy stood up, "What are middle kids?"

"Over fourteen but under twenty. There's Vera and Caspar and Jory and Sandor and—"

"Wait a minute! How many of you are there?" demanded Zed.

The boy grinned. "All together? Counting Mother and Father, twelve. The others aren't here; they're learning things."

The slaves cleared the table. Rhani held onto a plate of seaweed. Zed kept the egg tarts. Wine was poured. One of the slaves was sent upstairs with a plate of candies: "To keep the peace," observed Aliza. "Or they'll be half-killing each other, and we'll have to send Zed up there to patch wounds."

"I told you she'd have us earning our keep," said Zed

to Rhani, gesturing with his spoon.

She smiled dutifully. She was too far from him; the other side of the table felt a continent's width away. Isolated from her, he felt trapped. He sipped the red wine—it was good wine, Enchantean wine—slowly, uneasy.

A slave dimmed the lights. Rhani struggled with the heavy cushioned chair, and Margarite shot up and wrestled it back for her. She rose, saying, "Do you mind if I pace? It makes it easier for me to think."

Imre said, "Go ahead, my dear."

She had let her hair loose. In the somber light, it looked dark, almost black, certainly not red compared to the brilliance of Aliza's tresses. Zed felt a worm of desire for her, deep in his bones. He tensed, forcing it deeper.

"I have a story to tell," said his sister, gazing at her hands. "I don't know where it starts, or ends." She thrust her hands in her pockets, hunching her shoulders. "I mostly know the middle. One piece of it began on the Yago estate, on a summer night, two years back. Or perhaps it began even earlier, when my secretary, Tamsin Alt, left Chabad, and I replaced her with a slave named Ramas I-Occad.

"But I won't start it that far back. Let me start with a letter I got just recently, before the Net came home. It was a threat. I'd been threatened before, but no one had ever carried one out, so I didn't take it seriously. I don't even recall what it said, anymore. But it was signed, 'The Free Folk of Chabad.'"

Zed was surprised—astonished, in fact. It was unlike Rhani to disclose Family business to anyone. But perhaps a threat to her, because it was personal—damnably personal, he thought—was not quite Family business. He sat quietly, containing his restlessness, while Rhani described the letters, the estate bombing, the police visit, and the attack in the street which Dana Ikoro had thwarted.

She spoke dispassionately enough, but when she talked about the woman with the broken bottle in her hand, Yianni got up and walked around the room, clearly upset past bearing. She halted it there to let them all catch their breaths.

Aliza said, "Rhani, that's an incredible story. We—the

Families—have always been exposed, but rarely have we been actually attacked."

"Ah," Rhani said, "but this was a very special group of dissidents, Aliza."

Why? Zed thought. He was suddenly annoyed at Rhani. Why was she making him sit through this?

"Now," she said, "I want to go back again, to another part of the story. This starts even farther back, on Enchanter, I believe. As far as I can tell, it begins when a fourteen-year-old boy is taken to observe the loading of the Net."

Imre said, "Yianni, sit down. You distract us. Rhani, please go on."

"He was a very sensitive child, or a very ethical child, or a very impressionable one. I'm not sure. At any rate, the sight—and information he received, which delineated some sort of basic family complicity in a practice he found repugnant—affected him a great deal. So much so, that at age eighteen he changed his name and went off to become a Federation official dedicated to the destruction of the slave system in Sardonyx Sector. I speak, of course, of Michel A-Rae."

Imre said politely, "I didn't know you knew so much about him, Rhani."

"He told me most of this himself," Rhani said. She stepped to the table and, lifting her glass, took a sip of wine. The Kyneths watched her every move, as if they were watching a masque, a mime, or a play. "Now, at the beginning of my story I mentioned a slave I bought, Ramas I-Occad. I called him Binkie, and he was my secretary—a tall, pale man. You might remember him, Aliza. You complimented him the morning of the Auction."

"I remember," Aliza said.

"I didn't know it at the time, of course, but he hated me." She squared her shoulders. "Part of it was my fault. Part of it was someone else's fault—" she looked, bleakly, at Zed—"and it may be that that part, too, was my fault. He thought so, anyway. So. Our dedicated policeman comes to Sardonyx Sector. He may once, indeed, have been a moral man. But times have changed him. He takes all the legal steps possible to destroy the slave system. But he also takes a number of illegal steps. He forms—out of

his own staff—a group of seeming rebels. He calls them
the Free Folk of Chabad. And, on the off-chance that it
might prove a fruitful approach, he suggests that they
write to Rhani Yago's secretary and ask him to turn
informer on her, for them. Perhaps they know what
happened on that estate, on that summer night, two years
back."

Imre said softly, "Rhani, you shock me. His ability to
turn his staff into assassins bespeaks a level of corruption
in Federation service which I did not suspect was there."

"None of us did, Imre. But I should emphasize, A-Rae
did not want assassins. The attacks were never designed
to kill me. They were designed to frighten, to keep me
off-balance and afraid."

Margarite said, "You mean, Michel A-Rae got members of his staff to attack you? To burn your house?"

Rhani nodded. "I was not supposed to be in it. That
addition was Binkie's idea. He hoped I would die in the
fire, and that with my death he'd be free."

"Where the hell is Michel A-Rae now?" Yianni said.

Rhani smiled. "No one knows. The Abanat police are
searching for him. He's still on Chabad. According to
Ramas I-Occad, he has one more scheme to set in motion,
something special he has prepared for me. I want you to
help me find him, Imre."

It was like watching a masque or a play, so that, even as
he caught his breath in fury, Zed saw himself listening and
reacting as if he were one of the players. He did not
move. He found himself contemplating Michel A-Rae's
motives with an almost intellectual passion. *I wonder
what it is that disturbed him,* he thought. *Could someone
he knew—a friend, teacher, lover—have been a slave?*

Then a slave opened the door. Stepping into the
reverberant silence unnerved her; she fumbled, and
dropped a plate. The clatter made them jump. Zed felt
something break in his mind. His dark self, released,
writhed. He wanted, simply, to kill Michel A-Rae.

The blood burned in his eyes, so that he saw the room,
Rhani, the Kyneths through a true red haze. His hands
clenched, every tendon and muscle curling. Then he felt
an unexpected pain in his left hand; it jolted him from his
murderous state. He opened his fist, grimacing. He had
been holding a spoon, a piece of fine silver, as all Kyneth

tableware was. He was still holding it, but it no longer looked like a spoon, and it was bloody. He had driven its edges into the flesh of his hand.

He picked the mess from his left hand with his right and deposited it upon the table. As he reached for a cloth napkin to staunch the bleeding, Aliza exclaimed. "Zed! What—Lela, get a cloth from the medical kit, and hot water."

"Just bring a clean cloth and a gel bandage," Zed said. "I'll attend to it later."

"It needs more than that," Yianni said. Slender, swift, a redhead like all the Kyneth children, he came forward, napkin in hand. Zed recalled—he was the Kyneth who was studying to be a medic. He pulled a candle close to Zed's chair and went down on one knee, reaching for the injury with unconscious grace.

Zed's system shrieked. "No!" he said shortly. He pulled the hand back. Yianni looked up, still kneeling, startled. Then, without comment, he laid his napkin in Zed's lap and returned to his chair.

The slave, Lela, brought a sterile cloth, hot water, and gel. Zed fixed a rough bandage.

Imre said, "Zed, do you need a tourniquet? Surgery? Perhaps a cast?"

Zed laughed. It eased the tension. "No, I'll live." He glanced at Yianni. "Thank you."

Aliza said, "Your sister has a fine sense of drama."

Zed smiled. As always, pain, whether his or another's, had sharpened his senses. He sipped the wine, admiring the play of light on Rhani's hair. Yianni Kyneth was studying him over the rim of his own goblet.

Imre said, "Rhani, I will of course do everything in my power to help the Abanat police locate Michel A-Rae. How much of this do you intend to make public?"

"As little as possible," Rhani said. "The confessions of the ex-police are, of course, already public. And I expect the Abanat police to make public their warrant for A-Rae's arrest."

"Imre," said Aliza, "what if the Chabad Council were to offer a reward to persons assisting the Abanat police in that endeavor?"

Imre cocked his head at Rhani. "What do you think, my dear? In this matter, you are the most injured party."

Rhani said, "The A.P. might find it somewhat demoralizing. But I suppose, if they haven't located him in a few weeks, we might."

"Who is Henrietta Melones?" Margarite said. Imre shot his daughter an approving glance, and then answered her.

"No one we need be concerned with," he said. "My sources on the moon tell me that this is the highest Federation rank she has ever held, and that there is no chance of her being named captain, as opposed to acting captain."

Silence descended. Aliza rose, a pillar of light in the dark room. "Yianni, get the light, please." Yianni rose and vanished into the darkness. The overhead chandelier came on. "Is there more, my children?"

Zed tensed. He watched his sister, suddenly afraid that she would tell the Kyneths about her alliance with Ferris Dur. But she simply shook her head.

"Good," said Aliza. "Then—since we have all received enough shocks to our nervous systems to make sleep imperative—I, at least, am going to bed!"

Imre rose from his chair. "I always go to bed with my wife," he explained.

Zed walked to Rhani. She held out her hand and, when he laid the bandaged one upon it, she drew it to her lips. "Can you forgive me for that?" she said.

Zed said, "It isn't incapacitating."

Behind them, Yianni Kyneth coughed. "Excuse me," he said, "but are you sure, Zed, that you won't need help in tying that?"

"I can manage," Zed said. He put his arm around Rhani as they walked from the room. As he escorted her up the stairs, he regretted that he could respond to such overtures only in his own devastating way.

He rummaged in the Kyneth's vast medikit: spray anesthetic allowed him to stitch the deepest cut. Recovering the hand with gel, he went to the room he'd been given. Through the window drape he saw lights in the sky: the city was giving the tourists a fireworks display. No wonder the children had been quiet, he thought. He watched as the night sky over the Barrens sported a white-hulled ship with indigo sails, a gold-and-purple dragon, and a green kerit. For a finale, a great silver wheel bloomed in the sky and burst in a shower of glittering sparks. In the adjoining bedroom, someone produced a series of muffled shrieks which turned into giggles. He wondered what it would have been like to grow up in a house filled with siblings, permitted to yell, to giggle, to argue with one's parent. He wondered how he might have turned out if he had grown up a Kyneth.

He walked down the hall, to say good night to Rhani. But the guard at her door said, "She's asleep, Commander. She turned the light out ten minutes ago."

"Thank you," said Zed. Feeling cheated, he returned to his room. He had just taken off his shirt when a tap sounded on his door. He opened it.

His visitor—I should have known, Zed thought—was Yianni Kyneth.

"I want to talk to you," he said. His eyes were hard and direct.

Zed said, "Come in." He gestured to a chair—the rooms in the Kyneth house always seemed to have lots of chairs in them. Yianni shook his head.

"I don't want to sit. I want to know what happened tonight," he said firmly.

"What happened?"

"Between us. There was something." His gaze was like a knife. "I won't let it sit and fester. I don't do things like that. If we talk, perhaps we can discover what it is."

Zed said, "I know what it is."

Yianni stared at him, perplexed. "Well, out with it!"

Zed drew a breath. Oh, hell, he thought. "Better sit down first," he said grimly. He told it clinically, as he had told very few people—not even Sai Thomas, who would have listened and tried to understand. Jo Leiakanawa knew. So, of course, did his victims. And there were two telepaths who knew, on Nexus. Yianni listened. He kept his eyes on Zed's face. At one or two points he grew a little white about the mouth. When Zed finished, Yianni cleared his throat.

Zed said, "You don't have to say anything."

Yianni said, "I do." There were tears in his eyes. "I— oh, mother, I'm sorry. I shouldn't have made you speak." He rose. "I'll go."

"Wait," Zed said. He stepped forward, not knowing himself why he made the request. Yianni waited. Zed reached out with his right hand, the good hand. Yianni straightened, a lift of the shoulders; he was steeling himself. Gently Zed touched his cheek. It was rough with a day's beard.

"Don't apologize," he said. "It was right. I needed it. Thank you—though I warn you, I may never be able to look at you again. But you're going to be a fine medic, I can see that. And if things had been different, you would have made a fine friend."

Chapter Seventeen

The next morning there were dark shadows beneath Zed's eyes.

Rhani noted them when he came to her room to give her his morning greeting. "Zed-ka," she said, holding out both hands. He mirrored her. She had forgotten about the bandage on his left hand and the sight of it gave her a small shock. He kissed her cheek.

"Good morning," he said.

Something was wrong with him. She watched him circumnavigate the room. He ended up by the window. He lifted the drape, frowned, let it drop. It's odd, she thought; I pace to order my thoughts, Zed paces when he doesn't want to think, or at least, to speak. "Now it's my turn to ask you," she said, gently teasing. "Did you sleep?"

"Not very well." He made another restless circuit of the room, again stopping at the window. "Rhani—" he paused. It was not like Zed to start something, even a sentence, and not finish it. "Rhani, I want to go to the estate."

For a moment, she thought nothing, nothing at all. Then she thought: It's come then. She had been braiding her hair at his entrance; now, remembering, she felt behind her head for the braid. It had loosened. She pulled the thick strands tight and wrapped a sequined elastic band around the end. Zed was a blocky shadow against the window drape. "What will you do there?" she asked.

He said, "Walk in the garden. Read. Sleep."

"How will you get there?"

"Rent one of the bubbles from the landingport."

She imagined him walking across the lush garden lawn. *I wish I could go too,* she thought. *I hate being here, in a house not my own. We could go back together, the four of us, Dana and Corrios too. Timithos would be glad to see us. . . .* She remembered that she had not spoken with Cara and Immeld, though she had told Nialle to call and reassure them.

"Rhani? May I go?"

Zed's voice recalled her. She gazed at him across the pink room. "Go," she said. "You need it. If I need to talk with you, I'll call you. And please, Zed-ka—" she remembered what Binkie—Ramas—had said, that Michel A-Rae hated him. "Please be alert."

"If I see any bubbles without markings coming toward me, I'll turn around and come back."

They hugged. His mouth tasted of sesame. Rhani thought. *He breakfasted already. Probably he is already packed, not that he has much to take with him.* She wondered what had occurred between last evening and this morning to disturb him.

She would *not* ask him about Darien Riis.

Nialle had sorted through her mail but had tactfully not opened anything: she was, after all, a borrowed secretary, her wage paid by Family Kyneth. Rhani went to the tray of mail. Most of the letters were sympathy notes, more variations on an inevitable theme. One was a communication from Christina Wu which said, tersely, *"Obviously our appointment must be postponed. I am sorry about your house. Call me."*

Rhani frowned. She had forgotten that she had an appointment with Christina for the morning of the party—which, she thought ironically, would have been today. That was what she needed a secretary for, to remind her of such things. Binkie would have remembered. . . . Her hands clenched, and the thick notepaper creased. She did not want to remember Binkie.

Nialle came in. "Good morning, Dom—Rhani-ka."

Rhani smiled at her. "Good morning. Thank you for sorting my mail."

"It's my job, Rhani-ka," the secretary said.

"I know. But I appreciate it. Would you be so kind as to connect me with Christina Wu's office. I'd like to speak with her, if she's free."

"Certainly, Rhani-ka." Nialle pulled the com-unit from the wall and sat in the plastic chair. "There is a call for you, Rhani-ka," she said.

"From whom?"

"From Domni Ferris Dur."

Ferris. . . . Rhani sighed. She knew what he would say. He would offer his sympathies upon her loss of her house, and whine because instead of coming to him she had chosen to shelter with the Kyneths. He would then ask her how the contract arrangements were proceeding. As if she did not have other things on her mind! Ah, well. She had said she would marry him, and she would, there were good reasons to do it. . . . At least, she thought, marriage no longer carries with it the certainty of a sexual relationship.

Nialle said, "Domna Rhani, I have Advocate Wu online."

Rhani went to the screen. "Christina," she said to the small woman with the heart-shaped face who gazed at her, "you could have called me back."

"Don't be ridiculous," the lawyer said briskly. "Are you all right?"

"I'm fine. Don't you read the PINsheets?"

Christina grimaced eloquently. "Never," she said, "when I can help it." She grinned rakishly out of the screen. "I assume you made an appointment because you wanted to see me about something important; if it had been trivial you would have dropped me a note. Would you like to make it tomorrow? I have time." Her eyepatch glittered. She had lost one eye in a freak accident some years back. The damage was reparable but the surgery had left scars, and she had chosen to cover the eye rather than display it. Today's patch was shaped like a blue butterfly.

Rhani was touched by the offer; she knew how much in demand Christina's abilities were. She also knew that little went on in Abanat that Christina Wu was unaware of. "Thank you, Christina," she said. "What time?"

Christina flapped a hand. "Let our secretaries arrange that." She blanked the display. Nialle looked at Rhani inquiringly.

"Rhani-ka, do you have a preference?"

"No," Rhani said. "Make it to Christina's convenience. And when you have finished that, please connect me with Domni Ferris Dur."

A slave answered the call to Dur House. Rhani heard him say, "One moment, please, while I transfer the call downstairs." There was a pause, and then Nialle was beckoning to her.

"Domna, Domni Ferris is online."

"Thank you, Nialle," Rhani said. Tactfully, Nialle went out the door. Ferris was glaring at her from the screen. Behind him, where she expected to see the ugly, heavy furnishings of the study, she saw boxes and coarse draperies. It looked like a warehouse."

"Why didn't you call before?" Ferris was saying petulantly. He plucked hard at a sleeve. "I was worried about you!"

It was on the tip of Rhani's tongue to tell him that they were not married yet, and that under no circumstances, married or not, was he ever to think he had the right to call her to account.

But she could see from his face and from the state of his clothes that he meant what he said—he *had* been worried for her. So she said only, "I'm sorry, Ferris. I've been doing very little."

"Of course, I understand," he said, mollified. "I just wish—that you had come here. There's as much room here as at the Kyneth house, and we are—I mean—this is—" He halted, confused. And with surprising dignity, said, "This is your house, Rhani. I want you to believe that."

"Thank you, Ferris," Rhani said, gently, although she had no intention of ever living in Dur House. The ghost of Domna Sam would haunt me, she thought.

"I was wondering, Rhani," he said diffidently, "do you plan to rebuild the house?"

"I do." She would—though it would be quite different from the house Lisa Yago had commissioned. For one thing, she thought, I'd like a house all on one floor, maybe even with sunken rooms.

"Good," he said. "Then I may be able to help you."

She gazed curiously at him. She had never heard Ferris speak with such confidence about anything. She said, "I hope you may, Ferris."

He grinned. "You'll see," he said, "I will. How are your lawyers doing with the contract drafts?"

She said, "Ferris, don't push me."

He retreated at once. "I beg your pardon."

Once again she was conscious of his unhappiness. Somewhere in the core of him was a wound, or a place that had never grown and still retained a child's defenselessness. . . . To ease him, she said, "Ferris, might I call upon you to do me a favor?"

He said, "Of course," and his fingers ceased twisting the silken tassels of his gown.

"The Dur Family has extensive contacts throughout Abanat, I'm sure," she said. Ferris nodded proudly. "Would you instruct them, through whatever channels you use, to be alert for the appearance of Michel A-Rae?"

"Surely. And if he is found, I suppose you would like to be notified *before* the Abanat police?"

"Precisely," she said, and thought: That's something Domna Sam might have done! "My thanks."

"I am glad to do it," Ferris said. "And—Rhani—" he fumbled into a sentence—"I am sorry for anything I might have done the last time you were at my house—"

"I have already forgotten it," Rhani said. "Good day, Ferris. I'll call you." Putting the unit on hold, she said loudly, "Thank you, Nialle." Nialle entered, with Dana at her back. He was wearing blue velvet, and she found herself thinking, in painful imitation of Charity Diamos: Oh, my dear, Rhani Yago certainly clothes that handsome young slave *well*. . . .

She nodded to him, conscious of Nialle's solid presence in the room. He bowed, said, "Good morning, Rhani-ka," and handed her a letter.

It was from Corrios. He was resigning.

"How did you get this?" she asked.

"He gave it to me," Dana said.

"Do you know what's in it?" Dana shook his head. She passed it to him. "Go ahead, read it." As he did, she heard the phrases of the note in her mind—"many years' service . . . appreciate your trust . . ." She felt as if a piece of her childhood had just crumbled to dust, leaving a gaping hole in what she had thought was a sturdy edifice.

"Will you accept it?" Dana asked.

"Of course." She took the letter back, wondering where Corrios would go. The letter said he wanted to leave Chabad. Perhaps he would find some gray planet, some world where it was always twilight, cloud, and mist, where the sun hid, not the people, where he could walk in the light without sunscreen and shades. Was there such a world? she thought. Dana might know.

She passed the letter to Nialle Hamish. "Please arrange for a bonus of three thousand credits to be paid to Corrios Rull, and tell him that Family Yago will pay his transportation costs to anyplace, in or out of sector."

"Yes, Rhani-ka," Nialle said. She took the letter. "About the party—"

"Yes?" Rhani said.

"I took the liberty of extracting the list of acceptees from the records of the computer. Do you want me to write to them and cancel the event?"

"Sweet mother," Rhani said, "they'll know by now, won't they?" Nialle's bland face looked mildly surprised. "Oh, I suppose that's a good idea. Yes, do that, but send the cancellations through the computer net, Nialle. There's no reason for those letters to be calligraphed."

"Certainly, Rhani-ka."

Dana was watching her. She wondered what he was thinking. She wondered if there was a room in this big house where they could hide, and make love, and not be disturbed. . . . "My brother is returning to the estate today," she said. His shoulders lifted at the first two words, and fell with relief after she said the rest.

"Will we be going anywhere today, Rhani-ka?" he said. He is pretending, she thought, amused, to be the utterly obedient slave.

"I don't know yet," she said. "Possibly. I will call you." He bowed and went to the door. She wondered what he would do until she called him. Read? The house had books enough. Listen to music? She recalled, suddenly, Binkie's hateful words: *"I was invisible, a thing, a machine that turned itself off when you didn't need it. . . ."* No! she thought. I don't do that. I won't do that.

She glanced at Nialle. The secretary was bent over the com-unit, instructing the computer to send the notice of the Yago party's cancellation to a list of addresses.

Quietly, Rhani walked into the bathroom. Light from the stained-glass windows patterned her flesh as she opened all the cabinets until she found the room's medikit. Trust Aliza Kyneth to put a medikit in every room, she thought. She looked through it for the meter she knew was there. Finally she found it, took it from its protective case, and stuck it under her tongue. Sense told her that even if she had conceived, it was too soon for the meter to register the changes in her mucus and saliva—but she needed to check. Impatiently she waited one minute and then pulled it from her mouth and gazed at the bulb. If she was pregnant, it would be orange.

It was pale pink, its usual color.

Washing the meter, she returned it to its case and closed the medikit. Odd—she was impatient now for it to happen. Yet she was young for pregnancy, for a Yago, and she ought—according to Family tradition—to be feeling intruded upon, resentful, apprehensive, or at least indifferent. Maybe it had something to do with age, she thought. Maybe her mother, and her grandmother, and her great-grandmother should have had children early, instead of doing what had become the Family custom and extending artificially the period of fertility. She gazed into the gold-framed mirror, seeing through her own image the smaller image of a girl's, a girl with red-gold hair and a solemn face. . . . Sweet mother, she thought, with a sharp, intense hurt that was purely of the heart, if my mother had borne me at thirty, even forty, she might have loved me, *wanted* me, instead of seeing me as the rival who would inevitably wrest her power from her. . . .

Over Chabad's landscape, Zed pushed the bubble to its top speed. The ground unrolled beneath him. For once there was no solace in the flight, the solitude, the instantaneous obedience of the machine. He wanted to be home. His sandals were dusty with the ashes of the Abanat house. Home was a green circle on an arid hillside; home was the estate.

He had called ahead from the little landingport to tell Cara that he was returning early and alone, and that Rhani would follow with Dana as soon as she could. "Yes, Zed-ka," she said, and then said, "Excuse me, Zed-ka, but you should—" but he had blanked the screen.

It was rude, but he had not wanted to wait.

As he came over the grounds to the hangar he saw Timithos waving a broad arm, and the red flash amid the bushes of one of the dragoncats. His heart rejoiced. He dropped the bubble into the hangar and hurried to the house. Cara was downstairs. She said primly, "Welcome back, Zed-ka."

He smiled at her. "Thank you, Cara."

Immeld strolled from the kitchen. "Zed-ka," she said, "I made egg tarts."

Zed grinned. He was almost surfeited with egg tarts. Not quite. "Thank you, Immeld," he said. He heard her saying something else but he was already past her, going up the stairs. It felt strange to be coming back without Rhani, without luggage, medikit, ice climbing equipment—his personal metaphors of permanence. He walked into his room. Everything was polished and tidy. The skeleton hung in its corner. Zed slid a hand along its scapula, and grinned at his shelf of booktapes. In the silence of the next few days, before Rhani came home, he might indeed have some time to rest, even to read.

He touched a bare space on a shelf. The glass sculpture Rhani had given him, now melted and unrecognizable in the wreckage of the house, would have fit right there. Too bad, he thought. Pushing apart the terrace drapes, he felt for the handle, found it, and slid the door aside.

A woman sat, cross-legged, on the terrace, a watering can at her feet.

She rose instantly. She was barefoot. Her gaze was steady, her eyes normal, not dilated or fixed—but the steady look was a shade too direct. She was frightened of him. The fear did not tantalize or excite him. She tilted her head to one side, evidently waiting for him to speak, to react, or tell her what to do. . . . He felt his chest tighten with tension. He couldn't breathe. He gasped, and the tension broke, shattered like ice breaking.

Cara had entered his bedroom at his back. With anger in her tone, she said, "I tried to tell you. You wouldn't listen."

"When did she get here?" he said.

"The Barracks' bubble brought her," said the steward. "They delivered her yesterday without a word of explanation. I have the invoice." She put her hands on her hips.

"Zed-ka, what possible use have we for a computer technician?"

Zed blinked at the total irrelevance of the question. Finally he said, "Cara, go away, please."

Cara opened her mouth, shut it with a snap like a door closing, and stalked from the room. Zed gazed at the woman on the terrace. He had not expected her to be here, not yet. He wondered what they had told her about him in the Barracks. He thought: Be human, damn it, Yago—be kind. Send her away.

He couldn't.

Softly, he said, "Tell me your name."

She said, "Darien Riis." She sounded fragile as glass.

Brusquely he said, "You don't have to be afraid of me."

She bowed her head.

"Do you know who I am?"

"You're Zed Yago. I remember you from the Net."

He had not seen her. There were plenty of prisoners he never saw; most, in fact. As chief medic, he checked the records, but the juniors only called him for certain cases. "I don't remember you," he said. "Were you sick? Did I come to your cell to treat you?"

She shook her head. "I saw you at the loading." She touched her hair. It was very lovely, long, red-gold, fine and flyaway. . . . "My hair was shorter then."

In the press of the loading he could easily have passed her without noticing her. "You're not on dorazine."

"No. They stopped the dosage two days ago."

"We don't keep house slaves on dorazine."

"Am I yours?" she asked.

"No," he said. "You belong to my sister Rhani. I don't own slaves."

"What do I call you?" she said.

"Call me by my name."

"Zed," she said. He caught his breath. Her voice was husky with nervousness; it made her sound like Rhani.

"Come to the garden with me," he said. She followed him downstairs and into the kitchen. Immeld was cleaning a countertop. She looked up at them, lips tight. At the southern bank of flower beds, Timithos knelt, adjusting a water sprinkler. He waved.

Darien said, "It's lovely here."

After the Net and the Barracks, Zed guessed that the estate came close to her memories of freedom. She was looking at the dimensions of the place. He hoped with genuine fervor that she had not started looking for ways to escape. "Where are you from?" he asked.

"Enchanter."

"Does this remind you of home?"

"Not at all," she said. "I just like it." She gestured with an upturned palm. "Has it been here long?"

"About a hundred years. My grandmother built it. Her name was Orrin Yago."

"Is that the one who went to Nexus?"

"Yes. That's the one."

"We learned about her studying sector history."

They walked beneath a bitter-pear. Darien reached up to pluck a dangling fruit. Zed caught her fingers. "Don't," he said.

"I'm sorry."

"It's nothing to be sorry for," he said. "The fruit looks good but it isn't edible. I'm sparing you an awful taste."

She stared upward at the tree. "Aren't they pears?"

"Certainly. But Chabad's soil is extraordinarily alkaline, and all the fruits and vegetables we grow are affected by the alkalinity. We can breed them to grow, but we can't make them taste good."

"That seems unfair," she said.

"Nothing here is fair," said Zed. Her fingers, in his own bigger hand, were trembling. He let them go, and sat on the grass. She copied him. "Tell me about yourself," he said.

She drew her knees to her chin. "I've always lived on Enchanter. I lived in a family-group till I was twelve, and in a peer-group from twelve to fourteen. I studied to be a computer technician because I like fixing things. The last job I held was in the Enchanter lab."

"What did you do that put you in prison?"

"I was stupid," she said angrily. She rubbed her hand over her face as if to hide the fact that she was blushing. "I skopped with another technician. He wouldn't leave me alone. I just wanted to distract him. He took me to his home and I gimmicked his cooking unit. He ended up with a bad burn. I ended up in prison." She half-smiled. "I tried to claim it was a practical joke, but the tribunal wouldn't believe me."

"Was it?"

"No," she said. "I wanted him to be burned."

Zed said, "We have a saying on Chabad: *'The past is past.'* I won't ask you again."

She bowed her head. The gesture was terrifying; it shrieked of vulnerability. "What did they tell you about me in Abanat?" he said.

She hesitated before she looked up. Her voice flattened. "They told me that you are a medic, and a pilot."

"Is that all?"

"No." She drew a breath; released it. "They told me that you're a sadist; that you like to hurt people."

"Is that the worst they told you?" He leaned toward her.

"Yes," she said. He wondered if she were telling the truth. Even he had overheard the stories they told about him and Rhani. His own hands were shaking. He touched the ground, seeking stability. Grass stems curled around his wrists. She flinched back.

"Don't be afraid," he said. "Please don't be afraid."

"How can I help it?"

"Say my name."

"Zed."

His hands curled like claws in the dirt. She still sounded like Rhani. "You look like my sister, do you know that?" he said.

Darien said, "I saw a holo of her."

"You don't agree?"

"I don't see it."

"Wait till you meet her." He glanced at the house. "Your hair's redder than hers, and your eyes are brown. Hers are the color of topaz. But they're the same shape." Darien rubbed her chin. A lock of hair, like a copper coil, fell across her cheek. You *don't* look like her, he thought. You look like what she was, at a time when you were huddling with your family in the snow of an Enchanter winter, when the future seemed as promising as a ripening fruit on a nearby tree, when I was fifteen.

He had wanted to touch her from the first moment he'd seen her. The impulse was frightening. Her jumpsuit was green, glittering with silver reflective threads; it made him think of seasons that Chabad did not have, it made her seem new, virginal. . . . He did not dare touch her. In that soft, husky voice, she said, "Why did you buy me?" They faced each other like distorted mirror images, under the shadows of the bitter-pear.

She spoke in Rhani's voice. Zed answered her truthfully. "I had to."

"Because I look like your sister?" He nodded. "Then why ask me questions? It doesn't matter who I am. Put me back on dorazine; I'll be anything you want me to be."

"No!" said Zed, with such intensity that Darien flinched away. "Oh, don't," he said, and reached with desperate, tense care to touch her cheek. "That *isn't* what I need."

"What do you need?"

He could not tell her. He could not say: I need you to love me and not be afraid of me. He could not say: I need you to help me destroy nineteen years of careful conditioning. All his barriers were coming apart. He was frightened. He should not have talked to Yianni. "If I had wanted a doll, I could have had one made," he said.

She tossed her hair back, in a gesture that had been Rhani's, when Rhani was seventeen. The uncanny resemblance made his heart leap in his chest. "I don't understand," she said.

"Don't try," said Zed. He stood, and held out a hand to help her to her feet. "Let's go back to the house," he said.

"Whatever you wish," she said quietly. Ignoring his hand, she stood, brushing bits of grass from her jumpsuit.

It crossed his mind that it was uncanny, almost frightening, how quickly she had adapted to him, almost as if she had been made for him. Somewhere inside me is a romantic fool trying to get out, he thought, I can hear him screaming. It's just an accident that she looks and sounds—and moves, a little—the way Rhani did. It must be an accident. Nothing in nature accounts for it.

Timidly she touched his right arm. "Do you want me to be your companion?"

It was as good a word as any. "You might think of it that way."

She persisted. "Is that my work?"

"Does that trouble you?"

"It's not my skill," she said. "I'm a computer tech."

"I'm sure my sister can make use of your skill. She may need a computer tech. She's going to be training a new secretary."

"Why?" Darien asked. Zed explained briefly. She rubbed her chin. "I have some experience as a secretary."

"Perhaps Rhani will want you to take the job on temporarily."

"I'd like that."

She faced him, in the kitchen. The house machinery sighed. She touched her upper left arm. "What about this?" she said.

"Even if I wanted to," Zed said, "I couldn't free you. I don't own slaves."

She caught her lower lip between her teeth. "I'll try," she said, shaking back the hair that fell loose and glowing like a sunset down her back. Zed couldn't tell if she spoke to herself or to him.

"Thank you," he said. "I'm going to my room now. It's the third door from the end on the left upstairs. I'll see you later, Darien." It was the first time he'd said her name. She smiled at him.

He went back to his bedroom. Never had it seemed more of a refuge. He put his palms flat against the cold glass of the terrace door. There were religions on the Living Worlds, but none thrived on Chabad, and though Zed had heard of several of them, he shared none of their beliefs. But he wished, with the vehemence of prayer, for patience with which to circumvent the danger in his own reactions.

She's such an innocent, he thought. I don't want to hurt her. He flexed his fingers. His left hand stung. Let me not hurt her. Let her trust my good will and not be disappointed.

Let her want *me*.

He ate a meal alone, in his room. Immeld, still obviously furious at him (probably for cutting Cara off), brought it to him. He looked idly through his booktapes, remembering Darien's questions about the estate and Orrin Yago. He was amused to find among them an old tape of Nakamura's *History*. In the later afternoon, he went to the hangar to repair the bubble. During the flight he had noticed a flaw, a flicker-effect in the opaqueing mechanism of the skin. He had a general idea what might be wrong but he was not an engineer. Still, it was something to work on. . . . He had to take the entire mechanism out of the craft and put it under a light on his workbench. It took him several hours to locate the weak spot on the microchip. He could not replace it himself; a new chip would have to be ordered from the Landingport, and that would take several days. Oh, well. He put the craft back together. The hangar was cool but not cool enough; by the time he was finished, his shirt was off and he was streaming sweat.

Darien was sitting on a sawhorse, watching him.

He had no idea how long she'd been there. "I didn't hear you come in," he said. He was not entirely pleased to see her. All afternoon the conviction had been burgeoning in him: Yago, you're crazy. He had almost decided to send her back.

She held out a towel. "Here," she said. "You need it." It was true: taking it from her, he scrubbed his face and hair until his eyes stopped stinging, and draped the cloth around his neck. She had brought him a pitcher of fruit drink. She filled a glass and handed it to him.

The drink was precisely to his taste, not too sweet.

"Have some," he said.

She filled a second glass. She was still wearing green, but she had pulled her hair back. She patted the sawhorse, and, gingerly, he seated himself beside her. "What are you doing?" she asked.

"Fixing a flicker in the bubble's skin. Trying to fix it," he amended. He found his shirt and put it back on.

"I thought you were a medic and a pilot," she said.

"I am. But I've watched engineers. I used to think someday I'd go back to Nexus, maybe pick up engineer's training."

She said, "I've never been to Nexus. I've seen holos of it, though. I'd like to go someday."

"Do you like cities?" he asked.

"Not especially."

"Then you won't like Nexus. Except for the Flight Field, Nexus is all city, and the parts that aren't city are flat and covered with grain. No mountains. There's an ocean or two, but even the oceans have been turned into kelp and fish farms. Imagine a city covering half a continent—that's Nexus. And only a small portion of that is Port City."

"Nexus Compcenter, where the starships are," she said. "I'd like to see them."

"The Net's a starship."

"That's not the same. Tell me about them?"

Pleased, he described Port City, the bubbles on their cables, the movalongs, the Bridge—Nexus' aerial walkways for foot traffic—casting shadows on the tree-lined streets. He described the Flight Field, which stretched for kilometers into the continent's interior. She sat with her hands in her lap and her head canted slightly to one side, listening. They finished the fruit drink. Leaving the hangar, they went outside and walked in the dusk. A dragoncat slinked to stroll beside them. "Thoth," said Zed. The great cat permitted Zed to scratch the ruff of his neck. But when Darien touched his flank, the cat sidled from her fingers.

"They all do that," she said. "They just don't seem to like me."

"Undiscriminating beasts," Zed said.

The dragoncat's tail twitched. He leaped away, offended.

The sweat on Zed's chest and clothes dried as they walked beneath the shadows of the trees. He took his shirt off again and left it, with a grin of mischief, hanging on a tree branch. Timithos would find it and bring it in. He reached behind for a middle-of-the-back itch. "I'll do it," said Darien, without subservience. "Hold still." They stood beside the bitter-pear as she scratched his back.

She laid her finger on his left shoulder. "What's this?"

"The mark?" It was arrow-shaped, two centimeters wide. "I was born with it."

"On Enchanter," she murmured, "we get such imperfections fixed."

Her fingers were cool in his skin. Turning around, he reached for her hand, held it. "On Chabad," he said, "we are not so neat." They walked slowly along the slate paths, linked hands swaying between them. Darien was silent. He wondered: Was she waiting for him to speak? The silence might have been uncomfortable; it wasn't. He watched her, marveling at her composure. She didn't look nervously at him, or fidget, or pull away from his touch, or stride ahead of him, or pace.

In bed that night he pictured her lying in her room in the slaves' hall. It would take no effort to call her through the intercom and summon her to him. But—that wasn't how he wanted it to happen. He kept seeing her in his imagination, laughing, smiling at him, touching him—and running. He tossed. He did not expect to get much sleep.

But in the morning, he awoke to morning sunlight and knew that he had slept, and slept well. He watched the sun pour over the skeleton's cranium. He felt light-hearted. It seemed almost disloyal. A clinking sound from the kitchens captured his attention, and he showered and dressed and hurried downstairs. Darien was arranging egg tarts in a pattern on a tray.

"You don't have to do that," he said.

Immeld, fussing at a drawer, straightened and glared at Darien, a resentful, puzzled stare. Already, he realized, he had stopped thinking of the girl as a slave. It was bound to create friction in the household. He didn't care. Picking up four tarts, two in each hand, he said, "Forget the tray, I don't want to eat indoors anyway. Come outside."

Timithos had set the sprinklers going, but they found a dry place in the grass. The arcs of water surrounded them with rainbows. They ate. "These are good," Darien said.

"Have you never eaten egg tarts before?" he said, licking his fingers clean of the thick sweet filling. A dragoncat poked its head out of the bushes, more than willing to help. But when it scented Darien, it sniffed and glided away.

"No," she said, watching the cat vanish into the shrubbery. "Are they native to Chabad?"

"The cats? No. They're a product of the Enchanter labs." As he said it, he realized how stupid it was of him to mention her homeworld. Her face had gone stiff. He had not wanted to cause her pain. "I'm sorry," he said.

She shook her head. "Talk to me."

"About what?"

"Anything."

"All right." He talked about the Clinic. Remembering her profession, he described the surgical computers—those marvelous machines which enabled the parameters of an injury to be mapped out even before the surgeons saw it—and discovered that she had programmed clinical computers on Enchanter but had never seen the results of her work. "That's ridiculous," Zed said, indignant. "They should at least have invited you to attend an operation."

"I've seen holos."

"It's not the same," he said. "Would you like to fly with me to Abanat sometime, come to the surgery, as my guest?"

Her face lit with pleasure. "Yes. I would like that."

This time, when they rose to return to the house, she did not shy away from his touch when he offered to help her to her feet.

In the afternoon he took her for a ride in the defective bubble. As she drank in the terrible aridity of Chabad's hills, her eyes grew bright with wonder. He flew northward to show the nearest green spot, which was Family Levos' estate. The opaqueing mechanism's failure finally made the interior of the bubble too hot for the cooling unit to cope with, and they headed back. They ate dinner in the kitchen together. He wanted her to sit with him in the evening, but there did not seem to be a place—he did not want her in his bedroom. Finally he told Cara to have Timithos remove the table and chairs from the dining alcove and fill it with cushions and two big armchairs.

He sat in one chair; Darien in the other. She read Nakamura's *History*. Zed read a book he had forgotten he owned, about ice climbing—the more traditional sort—on Ley. Immeld left food and drink where they could get it, and she and Cara retired. Zed had no doubt they would spend the rest of the evening discussing him. He was getting a little tired of Immeld's sour faces. Darien sat cross-legged in the big blue chair, soft red hair hiding her features as she read. Zed found himself looking up from the viewer to watch her. Every once in a while she asked a question about Nakamura's assertions. She kept checking the index.

"What are you looking for?" he asked.

She blushed. "I was reading the parts about your Family," she confessed.

Zed laughed. "Nakamura doesn't think much of us."

She said, "It's interesting—what he says."

He was midway through an account of a Class 5 climb

on Ley's Karhide Glacier, when the intercom began to spout a regular *beep-beep-beep*. Cara came to the alcove. "That's the com-unit," she said. "Do you want me to answer it, Zed-ka?"

"No." Turning off the viewer, he rose, beckoning to Darien. "I'll go." He walked to the stairs. Darien followed him.

Timidly she said, "What do you think it is?"

He smiled at her. "Nothing too disturbing," he said. "It's almost certainly my sister. Now you can see how much you look like her."

At the half-open door he stopped, suddenly apprehensive. The shadowed empty room seemed terrible, redolent of mystery. Irritated with himself, he jerked the door aside and stepped in, flicking on the light. It was Rhani's room, it smelled of her, that was all. . . . And before that, it had been his mother's room. Darien turned in a circle, looking with admiration at the richly textured curtains, the thick kerit skin rug, the blue walls. Against one wall the com-unit beeped plaintively.

Zed went to it and touched the keys. The display screen glowed: CALL FROM RHANI YAGO TO COMMANDER ZED YAGO, it said.

Zed pressed the accept key. Rhani's face appeared on the screen. She was smiling. She looked very severe; her hair was tied so tightly that he could see strain lines about her eyes. "Good evening, Rhani-ka," he said.

"Good evening, Zed-ka," she answered. "How was your trip? Are you well?"

"My trip was fine," he said, "and I am very well."

"Is the estate intact?"

"It is," he said gravely. He saw Dana at her elbow, a dark blue shadow, and behind him a smaller figure whom he took to be Imre. He wondered if she could see Darien. He stole a quick look behind him. Darien had retreated several meters back, well away from the reach of the camera. She was staring at the screen.

"Are you well?" he asked.

"Fine. I will be coming home soon, I think. Within three or four days. I am still waiting to be contacted by our Enchantean visitor."

Loras U-Ellen, he thought. He wondered if Dana had indeed made the connection he claimed. But that was not what his lie had covered. Zed was sure of that. Uneasily he thought: Maybe I should have forced him to tell me. . . . "And how is Ferris Dur, Rhani-ka?" he said.

A frown skating across her face for a moment warned him that she did not want to talk about Ferris Dur, probably because Imre was present. "As far as I can tell, he is well," she said. "Zed, Imre has received some interesting news, which we both desired to share with you. It seems that Michel A-Rae's replacement has been chosen. She's on her way here from Dickson's World. Her name is Cat Graeme. Do you know anything about her?"

Zed drew a breath. "Dickson's World? You're sure?"

"That is what Imre's informant says."

"Dickson's World," he said, "is a mercenary planet. Its citizens—a high percentage of them anyway—hire out to other worlds as bodyguards, police officials, and leaders of government forces. You remember the civil war on China III about a decade ago? The government hired a small group of folk from Dickson's World to put it down. They did, in six weeks. But I've never heard of one of them working for the Federation before."

Rhani was nodding. "And Cat Graeme?"

He shrugged. "I don't know her, but the Graeme clan is a powerful and respected one."

"Hmm. I see," she said. "Have you seen the PINsheets, Zed-ka?"

"No," he said. "Why, what's happened?"

"Referendum Momentum Diminished!" she declaimed. "The PINsheeters spread the news of A-Rae's criminal behavior all over the headlines, and now no one wants to sign the petitions."

"Then there may be no referendum at all," Zed said.

"Exactly. Perhaps a certain proposition which you and I have discussed—" she paused, and he nodded, knowing she was talking about the possible legalization of dorazine traffic by the Federation, "will never have to be made."

He scowled, thinking of what he knew of the folk of Dickson's World. "Rhani-ka," he said, "the mercenaries of Dickson's World are damnably efficient. If one of them has been named to head the drug detail, she won't do a halfway job. She may even finish what A-Rae, in his fanaticism, began."

"Another fanatic?" Rhani said.

"No. They aren't fanatics. But they do what they're hired for."

Rhani was scowling. "I see," she said. "Yes. That changes things."

Reluctantly, Zed said, "Rhani-ka, do you want me to come to Abanat?" He heard Darien move at his back. He glanced at her; she was shaking her head.

"No," Rhani said. Darien sighed. "You look rested. Stay there, and I will join you as soon as my business here is done. If Cat Graeme arrives, perhaps we can meet, and reach some kind of understanding." She smiled. "Good night, Zed-ka. I miss you."

"I will see you soon," he said. The screen blanked. Zed stared at it a moment. Darien glided to his side. He smelled the scent of her, unforgettable as the bitter-pear. . . . Reaching out, he rubbed the screen with one finger.

"What do you think?" he said.

Darien's shoulders hunched as she put her hands in her pockets. "Yes," she said. "I see what you mean."

They separated on the landing. Darien, without a word, went down the stairway to the slaves' hall. Zed went to his room. Seeing Rhani had brought the tension back. He stripped. The hanging skeleton cast a web of shadows across the room. He had left the city stupidly forgetting to replace his medikit; he would have to raid the supplies in the cellar storeroom if he needed a drug to help him sleep.

Someone tapped on the door. He called, "Come in."

He supposed it was Cara. But when the door slid back, he saw that it was Darien. Before he could stop her, she came inside the room and slid the door closed. She wore a long gold gown. Her hair crackled. She stepped toward the bed, one hand reaching toward him. "Please don't tell me to go away."

"What are you doing here?" he said.

She looked around for a chair, saw none, and sat delicately at the foot of the wide bed. She laced her hands together in her lap, unlaced them, smoothed her hair, touched her cheeks with both hands as if testing to see if they were hot. . . . "Yesterday you said I might think of myself as a companion."

"Yes."

She leaned forward with that too-direct look again. "Then I would like to sleep with you," she said.

His heart began to beat double-time. He felt flushed. He touched his cheek with his hand, her gesture. His mouth dried with the adrenalin rush. Detachedly he wondered why his body perceived the request as a threat. "No."

He expected her to say, "Why not?" She didn't. She rested her open hands in her lap and looked at him. Then she said, "They're true: the stories they tell in the Barracks."

"I don't know which ones they told you."

"I expect they're all the same."

"They're true."

She bit her lip, and then her mouth relaxed. She said, "I don't believe it."

He said, "Then you're a fool."

"I'm not a fool. I've been with you for two days, long days. I haven't seen you do one cruel thing."

"You should talk to Cara."

"Cara won't talk to me. But that's not the point." Her fingers began to clench. She relaxed them. "I'm doing this badly. The stories may be true. But they aren't true to me. They can't be. The Zed Yago I perceive is—a gentle being."

"You don't know what you're saying," he whispered.

"I know what I'm saying. Those stories are like that book I've been reading: one version of something that happened in the past, to other people. Isn't that a definition of history?" He understood. She was seeking a way to offer him the thing he most desired, and with all his strength he knew he could not take it.

"I'm a fool," he said bitterly. He threw the bed covers aside and got out of the bed. He put his hands on her shoulders, feeling the soft curve of bone and vein, muscle and nerve. . . . He wanted to tell her to leave, get away, get out of the room—it was too soon, too quick, too dangerous. His searching fingers found without thought the hollow in her shoulder where his thumb could go. He lifted his hands and locked them together. "God, woman, get away from me. I don't *want* to hurt you."

She had not moved. She said, "I don't think you will."

Her confidence was terrifying. Zed walked to the terrace doors and laid one shaking hand on the cool glass. "You don't know."

She didn't answer. He turned around and saw that she had stepped out of the gown. He saw a flat, smooth stomach, breasts with dark nipples, a ruddy triangle of hair. She beckoned to him. He moved like a stick away from the doors, frightened to touch her. Her mouth brushed his with the feel of flowers, wine, silk; a dense and sensual texture. The dark self, crouching, waited for the scent of helplessness.

She led him to the bed and tugged him to sit beside her.

She dimmed the light. Gently she began to touch him with her palms and fingertips, stroking his back and his sides. His muscles knotted. In the near-dark, he glimpsed her face. Her eyes frowned behind a curtain of hair. She concentrated, lower lip caught between her teeth.

He moaned, trapped in a private agony of anticipation, and tore himself from her touch. "Go away," he said, when he could speak. "You aren't safe."

She said nothing; she simply reached a hand to him. Like a wild thing coaxed from its lair, he moved slowly back to the bed. She pushed him into it. The dark room drugged his resistance. She loomed over him: Rhani, not-Rhani, lover, friend, sister, stranger, slave. . . . She rested her palms on his sternum, tracing circles on his chest, his belly, lower. Her hand encircled his sex, and it warmed and stiffened.

He lay frozen to the sheet.

She rested beside him, fingers flickering between his nipples and his groin. With painful care, he lifted one hand and laid it along the soft skin of her cheek. Maybe, he thought, as his body responded to stimulus older than he was, oh, god, maybe. . . . She lifted over him. Her body descended, closing, warm and seeking, and he cried out as they joined as if she had entered him.

The first time he was clumsy, still afraid to touch her, and his erection died before either of them attained completion. "I'm sorry," he said. "I'm sorry." Her fingers brushed his dry lips. She pulled him over her, long legs scissored over his. They rocked in slow time. As her hips against his own clenched and released, clenched and released, Zed saw, reflected in her eyes, a long-forgotten stranger, the image of a gentle, ardent lover who had once inhabited his room and his body: the boy he had once been.

Chapter Eighteen

Dana tapped on the bedroom door. "Rhani, are you ready?" he called.

Rhani said, "A minute!" She glanced once more at the letter from Loras U-Ellen before stuffing it in her pocket. It said, *"Domna Rhani: I agree with great pleasure to meet you. Please come tomorrow to Rad's Alley, number four, at the tenth hour of the morning. Please keep this message private."* It was signed, coyly, *"L. U-E."*

"I'm ready," Rhani said. She went to the door and opened it, feeling strange and self-conscious in her clothes. She'd never worn anything like them before—coarsely woven, almost webbed pants and a transparent purple tunic. Red glitterstick outlined her eyes; her skin felt sticky, as if she were wearing mud. Dana looked just as garish, in a vermillion jumpsuit with arrow-shaped earrings dangling from his lobes and a matching pendant around his neck. She scowled at him. "I'm ready, but I feel a fool!"

He grinned at her. "You look terrific," he said. "A little out of place in this house, that's all. But when we get out to the street, no one will look at you."

"That's ridiculous," Rhani said, but she left the room and headed for the stairs. "How can they not look?"

"Oh, they may look," Dana said, "but they've seen Hypers a thousand times on ten different worlds, and all Hypers look alike to them. It's costume. Hell—it's half of why we do it."

She caught his arm. "Do you mind?" she demanded.

His face grew still. "I don't know what you mean," he said.

She said, "Dana, you know. I'm not a Hyper. I have no right to these clothes."

He shrugged. From various doorways in the long downstairs hall, slaves, and Kyneths, were staring at them. "If there were another way to get you to the Hyper district without being recognized and without telling the

Abanat police, I'd prefer it," he said. "But there isn't—at least, you couldn't think of one."

It had posed an interesting dilemma: how to get her to the address on U-Ellen's letter—which had been hand-delivered in the middle of the night by someone whom even the night guard had not seen, he swore—without being noticed. Imre had suggested telling the Abanat police. But Rhani had little confidence in the Abanat police since they had failed to identify or control the "Free Folk of Chabad." Aliza, facetiously, had suggested disguise. It was Dana who had said, later, privately, in bed to her (she had smuggled him into the pink room)—"Why not be a Hyper, Rhani?" Her nose itched, and she scratched it carefully, so as not to smear the glitterstick.

Dana, watching her, laughed. "You know, you'd look more realistic if you didn't think you had to look perfect."

She scowled, and smeared glitter on her thumb. "All right." She reached out and streaked her thumb across his cheek. It left an attractive red smudge. "Now you're not perfect, either."

They walked out to the street. Rhani swung her legs and hips to try to copy Dana's walk, but it was no use, she could not move like that. It made her feel sullen, uncertain, out of her depth.

They took the movalong. It detoured at Auction Place, turning one block west. Another block, Rhani thought, and it would go right by what was my house. She had no desire to see it. Soon—she had not realized before how close the Yago house was to it—they entered the Hyper district. The small houses crowded together made her uneasy.

"Where does this movalong go?" she said.

"To Main Landingport," Dana said. "We get off in a block." He steered her to the left, and off. She was annoyed at his knowledge—after all, this was *her* city. But this was a part of the city to which she did not come.

On the movalong, surrounded by tourists, she had not felt particularly conspicuous. But here—she glanced around. It looked different (narrower, messier, older), and it smelled different. The streets were chipped, and the people strolling by looked dreamy and dangerous at the same time. . . . She heard her own thought, and shook herself.

It was dangerous to romanticize the Hypers, she told herself sternly. They did it themselves, of course, with the glitterstick and the traditions and the clothes. But she did not have to. "Now where?" she said to Dana.

He slowed. "Now here."

Here was an alley, dusty and dry, which ended in a wall with a door.

Dana scowled. "I don't like this," he said.

Rhani nodded. In a place like this, anyone would find it easy to corner them. She had a brief electric sense of what her brother would say to this escapade. Her brother—was Darien Riis at the estate? Was that why, when she called, he had seemed so cold?

Dana said, "Rhani-ka, wait here." Before she could protest, he slipped his arm from hers and strode into the alley. She watched him go to the door and then come out again.

He beckoned.

She joined him. "I think it's safe," he said softly. "There are no other doors here, it's all one building. Go to the door and knock. It's the right address. . . ." As she marched toward the door, Rhani thought: This is stupid. Suddenly she *knew* that Loras U-Ellen would not be behind that door. What if it's all a trick? she thought, and her heart pumped furiously, what if Michel A-Rae is behind that door; what if Dana is kidnapping me?

Oh, hell, she thought, and knocked. The door opened.

A person stood in the doorway. At first she was not sure what it was, or what sex it was: it wore a bright green gown, made of some light elegant cloth that shimmered, and its hair was glossy black. Its fingers, ears, and nostrils were elaborately jeweled. A hand extended out of the dazzle. "Domna Rhani," said a man's deep voice, "how nice." Suddenly Dana was at her side, one foot firmly in the door, holding it open.

"There are two of us," she said, focusing on the dark eyes. "I hope you don't mind."

He smiled. "I expected it. Please come in." She walked in. U-Ellen closed, but did not, as far as she could see, lock the door.

They had entered not a house but a courtyard. In the center of the space was a fountain: water arced up and outward from an abstract metal mouth. A colonnaded walk bordered the court. A lawn gleamed under the morning sun. In the middle of the lawn, near the fountain, accessible by red-flagged paths, were three chairs, a cabinet, and incongruously, a com-unit.

U-Ellen removed his outer robe, to display pale green pants and tunic of a somewhat more modest cut. He waved them toward the chairs. "Just like home," he said. Bending over the cabinet, he produced, like a conjurer, a glass of fruit punch for Rhani and for Dana a glass of what looked like red wine. He lit a cigarette. "Now we can be comfortable," he said, seating himself. Rhani sat, too. Dana prowled the courtyard.

Rhani focused on her host, noting that he had very white teeth, very thick dark eyebrows, and no hair, not even stubble, on his chin. She had heard that the men of Enchanter often removed their beards. "You are Loras U-Ellen," she said.

He smiled. "I am. Who else?"

"It would be nice to have proof."

His smile broadened. "Do you have a miniscanner? Would you like to see my I-disc?"

She said, "Who is Family Yago's drug dealer on Abanat?"

He looked at her, and then chuckled. "Sherrix Esbah. She *was* Family Yago's drug dealer in Abanat, Domna. She's on Ley, now, vacationing."

"How did you get her to do that?" Rhani asked, stretching her legs and sipping the punch. It was delicious.

"Bribed her."

"Did you ever meet her?" Rhani said, curious. He nodded. "What does she look like?"

He shrugged. "A dumpy woman. Bad teeth."

Rhani wrinkled her nose. She had forgotten that Enchantean penchant; they all believed the human form was plastic, to be molded according to fashion—it came from living with the labs, she thought. "Don't you care who my companion is?" she asked.

"Starcaptain Dana Ikoro," said U-Ellen. "Currently a slave. Picked up for smuggling—or attempting to smuggle—dorazine into the sector. One of your brother's, ah, acquisitions, I believe." His smooth voice was just barely contemptuous. Rhani felt her temper begin to rise. She thought: My friend, my enemy if that is what you make yourself, you would not say that *that* way if my brother were sitting in this chair.

Recognizing the anger, she damped it down. Dana came to stand beside her. "We're alone," he said.

"Thank you," she said, and gestured to the third seat.

They all knew that there could be six different kinds of recording equipment hidden around the courtyard, all of which could go undetected except to the most sophisticated instruments. But if U-Ellen wanted to record this meeting, he could. She watched the smoke curl lazily from U-Ellen's perfect mouth. "Tell me, citizen," she said, "according to my informants, you live in Palaua on Enchanter, are forty-seven years old, and play the Enchantean flute. You are also an executive of a major Enchantean corporation. What are you doing cavorting around with drug dealers on Chabad?"

He sucked the smoke up through his nostrils and beamed. "That is what I love about you Chabadese," he said, "so forthright. Do you know, on my world it is unutterably rude to come to the point unless you have first spent at least an hour involved in some terribly trivial gab!"

Indeed, Rhani thought. But you are on my world now, you superior, supercilious son-of-a-kerit. "Are you in exile?" she said.

He waved the cigarette. "Oh, no. I'm here on business."

Rhani said dryly. "So am I."

"Oh, dear," he said, "now I've offended you. I beg your pardon." He exhaled. Rhani's teeth ached, and she realized she was clenching them. "But you must have suspected, Domna, that one motive behind this rather elaborate charade was to attract and hold your attention."

"Charade?" she said.

He brandished his hand at the walls. "Well, as you point out, this is hardly where one would expect to find an officer of a major planetary corporation."

"One never knows," Rhani said. "People are so strange." She watched him begin to frown as he realized that he'd been insulted. "And I've never been to Enchanter."

"Nor I to Chabad," said U-Ellen. "I find it—charming, though a bit bleak."

"It can be, yes," Rhani said. She wondered how long it would take him to come to the point. "Of course, this is not a typical city district."

"I assumed not. But I'm afraid I haven't had a chance to see Abanat properly. Indeed, officially I am not here." U-Ellen smiled, and breathed smoke.

"How did you do that?" Rhani asked. I have a reputation to uphold, she thought, as a forthright Chabadese. Besides, he might actually be willing to tell me.

"Oh, I had help, Domna," U-Ellen said. "From The Pharmacy."

Rhani felt as if she had just been punched in the chest. She said, "I am astonished to learn that a respectable Enchantean businessman has any contact with The Pharmacy."

He nodded, pleased. "We are partners." He spread his hands. "You see, I trust you."

Rhani did not see at all. She wondered if U-Ellen were telling the truth. "Who is 'we'?" she asked.

"My company." His eyes gleamed from his smooth face. His physical perfection—even his hands were unmarred, delicate as glass—made her uncomfortable.

"I am flattered," she said gravely. "What you have just admitted would be of great interest to the Federation Police. How can you be sure I won't go to them?"

"Go to the Hype cops?" U-Ellen chuckled. "Domna, I'm not a fool. You would never go to them. Besides, they know it. Or rather, Michel A-Rae knows it. He's known it for years."

"Really?" Rhani said. "Then how is it that you are not in jail?"

U-Ellen choked, and coughed. His complexion darkened. Rhani glanced at Dana. His fingers were tapping on the arm of his chair. U-Ellen recovered sufficiently to say, "Domna, you have no idea how humorous that is."

"Enlighten me," Rhani said.

"Michel A-Rae is my cousin," U-Ellen said. "Michel U-Anasi that was. And even my fanatic cousin Michel is not about to hunt down and incarcerate the members of his own family."

Cousin? she thought. She looked for the resemblance—

but you could not trust physical correspondence when dealing with Enchanteans. They were all changelings. Michel U-Anasi, she thought. I'll remember that. "Do you ever see him?" she said.

"See Michel? Absolutely not!" said U-Ellen. "It's been years since he communicated with us. Indeed, his rather misplaced sense of duty is part of the reason I am here." Reaching to the cabinet, he lifted a straw fan and fanned himself with languid strokes. His nails were pale green.

Rhani wondered if he knew the value of the information he had just given her. He was so pompous. . . . But beneath his uxorious facade she sensed intelligence, caution, and malice. She would have to take care with him.

She said, hoping to hear more about Michel A-Rae, "He claims to be very moral. I assume he finds his family's connection with The Pharmacy repugnant?" As she said it, she remembered A-Rae describing how he had repudiated his family because they profited from the slave system. Her nerves began to vibrate.

U-Ellen said, "Moral is as moral does. He was an unpleasant child, very bossy and possessive. A charming bully. Perhaps you know the type?"

Domna Sam, Rhani thought. "Yes," she said.

"One man's morality," U-Ellen intoned, "is another's prison."

Rhani had heard the dictum before. She wondered if U-Ellen was feeding her a tissue of lies. She did not think so. She sipped the punch again. U-Ellen continued, "It's fascinating you know, how history alters according to who writes the books. Michel now claims he always hated the slave system. Yet at one time he wanted to be a medic, and to work on the Net. His ambition was quite vigorous, really." He smiled, and stretched his arms. "But I did not come to Chabad to talk about my cousin."

He seemed quite at home in the hot courtyard. Rhani's neck hurt. She wanted badly to shake him up, but could not see how to do it. Isobel would have known, she thought.

"I have a proposal to make," U-Ellen said. "More punch?"

"No."

"Then let me begin by acquainting you with a few

simple facts about the drug trade."

Rhani's muscles stiffened. "Citizen," she said tightly, "I doubt there is anything that you can tell a Yago about the drug trade."

He stubbed out his cigarette and looked at her. "Domna, please. I am not insulting you. There are facts that neither you nor any other Chabadese resident knows. Just listen."

Rhani said, "Go on." A sand lizard, impelled by curiosity or perhaps drawn by the smell of the smoke, wriggled through a crack in the stone by U-Ellen's ankle.

"You know the drug laws," U-Ellen said. The sunlight winked off the jewels on his hands as he brought the tips of his fingers together. "The Federation, in its wisdom, forbids the inter-sector sale of certain drugs, among them dorazine. Many decades ago, a criminal consortium known as The Pharmacy began to manufacture dorazine and transport it to this sector. The dorazine formula is a carefully guarded secret—so secret, in fact, that chemists working in the Enchantanter labs have been unable to analyze the drug or discover how it is made."

"I know this," Rhani said.

"Bear with me, Domna. More wine?" He lifted a decanter. Dana shook his head, declining. "Domna, more punch? No? Well, to continue—about fifty years ago, The Pharmacy approached us, Phamaceuticals, Inc., I mean. They were having manufacturing problems. They had started out as a transport network, and had no real idea of efficient production methods. You can imagine how they tried to run a plant! They asked us for advice. We agreed to sell it to them." He lit another cigarette.

Rhani watched the lizard. It had settled next to U-Ellen's discarded gown, and was tasting the green fabric with an orange tongue. Stay detached, she told herself. Don't get excited. Remember what Isobel said. . . . "That's very interesting."

U-Ellen was somewhat nettled. It pleased her that it showed. He sucked hard on the cigarette and blew the smoke out with force. "In exchange for this assistance, we bought a twenty percent interest in The Pharmacy."

"What?" Dana said.

"Yes," said U-Ellen. "We had hoped to buy the

dorazine formula from them, but they adamantly refused
to sell it. However, everything we could learn about
them convinced us that we would not regret our twenty
percent."

"And have you?" Rhani said.

"Our profits have been on the order of thirty million
credits per year."

Dana said, "Sweet mother." His lean face was awed.

Rhani scowled. "I would like some more punch,
please." She handed U-Ellen her glass; startled by the
movement, the lizard scurried to its hole. U-Ellen refilled
her glass with the sweet, cool liquid, and she sipped it.
"Thank you." She watched him over the rim of the glass.
"How has Michel A-Rae's behavior as captain of the drug
detail affected those profits?"

U-Ellen studied the fabric of his pants with great
interest. After a pause, he said, "Badly. The Pharmacy
now wishes to halt the manufacture of dorazine."

Rhani's nerves quivered. "That would be foolish."

"We think so, too," U-Ellen said. "Not that Pharmaceuticals, Inc., would not survive. We would probably
do quite well, since we hold the sector manufacturing
patent on pentathine." He coughed. "However, our
pentathine plant, while adequate for current manufacturing needs, is quite small, and in order to upgrade it we
would need to pour money into it, money which we will
not get if the present trade restrictions convince The
Pharmacy to cease manufacturing dorazine. . . ."

Rhani said, "You have, of course, offered to buy the
dorazine formula from them."

"Yes. And this time they agreed to do so." The words
should have been triumphant, but there was no joy in U-
Ellen's tone.

"And?" Rhani said.

U-Ellen stared at his cigarette tip. "They ask for
payment of thirty million credits."

"Fitting," Rhani said.

"You don't understand," U-Ellen muttered. "We don't
have it. They want the full amount, you see, and there's
no possible way we can liquidate that much capital.
Recently members of my family have undertaken certain
ventures which have not turned out as well as they

expected. A great deal of money was lost."

Rhani said, "I am sorry to hear that you have suffered such vicissitudes."

He scowled. "Therefore," he said, "Pharmaceuticals, Inc. would like to propose that Family Yago join us in purchasing the dorazine formula."

At last, Rhani thought, at last. . . . She drew a breath. "That's quite an offer, citizen," she said. "Tell me, why did you, in order to reach me, involve yourself and me in this—charade?" She looked pointedly at her own, and then at U-Ellen's clothes.

Affronted, he said, "Domna, I am wearing usual clothing for *my* world. What you are wearing—well, I assumed you dressed so by choice."

"I don't mean the clothing," Rhani said. "I mean why not approach me openly? You could have walked to my door and announced yourself. From whom are you hiding, your partners?"

U-Ellen winced. "No, Domna. Though we would rather that they remain unaware of this visit. No, the, uh, people I have been avoiding by living in this rather dispiriting and uncivilized part of town are my dreadful cousin and his henchmen-and-women."

"I see," Rhani said. She rolled the glass between her palms. U-Ellen picked up the straw fan and waved it. "But A-Rae is no longer powerful, and is being hunted by the Abanat police."

He said, "Until he is located and in custody, I feel I should maintain my current, uh, distance from him, Domna."

Rhani understood his desire to remain unnoticed by his cousin, as well as his unstated lack of confidence in the Abanat police. "I expect he will be in custody soon," she said. She saw Dana grimace, and grinned to herself. She wondered if U-Ellen had heard the rumor which Imre Kyneth had passed on to her, and decided to test it. "With A-Rae gone, what do you think will happen on the drug circuit?"

U-Ellen's brown hand whitened on the handle of his fan. "There are rumors that the next captain of the drug detail will be someone from Dickson's World. I don't know if you know what that means, Domna."

"I know what it means," Rhani said. Well, she thought,

if I hear it one more time, I'll know it's true. "So if The Pharmacy does not receive thirty million credits for the dorazine formula from us, they will either cease producing dorazine altogether or possibly sell it elsewhere."

"I doubt anyone would be fool enough to buy it," U-Ellen said. "One could always ask the Federation to legalize it. But the bureaucrats at Nexus Compcenter seem unenthusiastic about drugs now, and by the time the request is received and processed, the drug network will be in jail and there would probably be a major social upheaval on Chabad."

Rhani said, "We do not expect the referendum to take place, citizen, if that's what you mean."

"It isn't. By the time dorazine is made legally importable, Domna, you will have a slaves' revolution on your hands."

"Yes," Rhani said softly. This was the nightmare all Chabadese citizens lived with. U-Ellen was right; only if the manufacture of dorazine could be brought within the sector within the next six months could Chabad, under the current system, survive. *History has its own way of protecting the past*, she thought. *I wonder if Ramas I-Occad will be the revolution's first martyr.*

"How much money do you want from me, citizen?" she said.

"Fifteen million credits," he answered. "Fifty percent."

Rhani closed her eyes. Fifteen million credits in liquid assets: she tried to remember the figures Tak Rafael had shown her.

She might just have it. But to deliver it, without contract or guarantee, to the emissary of a criminal consortium. . . . She wondered what her mother would say to that. *"Do what you have to do."* That was one of Isobel's favorite sayings. But then there would be expenses of who knew how much for the plant, for workers, for slaves, for all the equipment. . . . "Citizen," she said, "you can hardly expect me to reply to this offer now."

He squirmed. "Domna, I will tell you what The Pharmacy told me. They expect an answer in the next four Standard weeks."

"That's not much time," she said. She rose. "Very well, citizen. I will get back to you. A private letter here will reach you?" He nodded. "Then you will hear from me."

She strode to the door. Gathering up his fallen gown, U-
Ellen followed her.

"You understand," he said anxiously, "that this offer
has not been made? That if anyone should check, they
will find that Loras U-Ellen is in Palaua?"

Rhani smiled sweetly at him. "I understand, citizen,"
she said. She laid her hand on the door's handle and
pulled. Dana stepped out first. He walked up the roadway
and back.

"It's clear," he said.

"Good day," Rhani said. She walked into the narrow,
dusty street. *Fifty percent of thirty million,* she thought
again. *I wonder if Family Yago can indeed come up with
fifteen million credits.*

Once out of the courtyard and the alley, Dana relaxed.
He glanced down the narrow roadway. Two Hypers
lounged on the corner, smoking a dopestick, and a woman
sat on the steps, but no one was looking at them. He
stretched, trying to loosen kinked muscles. Rhani was
muttering to herself, face intent. He caught her arm to
steer her around a hole. "Where to, Rhani-ka?" he said.

She looked at him. Her eyes were very bright. "You
heard nothing of that," she said.

"Nothing of what?" He grinned at her. "Hypers get
pretty good at keeping secrets."

As he said it, he thought how stupid it sounded, coming
from him. But she did not seem to care, she barely
seemed to have heard. "Damn, I wish I were home," she
said.

"You will be," he said. *Soon you'll be at the estate, and
I'll be gone.* He glanced over his right shoulder at the
bright shapes of the shuttlecraft, and a longing hit him for
his own ship, for *Zipper.* Resolutely, he shut his mind
against it, thinking that if he did not find a way to put a
message into the com-unit for Tori Lamonica, he would
lose his chance to leave the sector. But Nialle Hamish
guarded it like a dragoncat. "Where do you want to go
now?" he repeated.

"The Kyneth House," Rhani said. They angled toward
the movalong. Dana took her arm as they rode, fearful
that in her preoccupation she would lose her balance and
fall from the moving strip. He wondered what it would

feel like to spend fifteen million credits.

They disembarked the movalong on the Promenade. Suddenly, Rhani stopped dead in her tracks. Dana looked. Waddling toward them, with a dreadful, delighted smile on her face, was Charity Diamos.

"Cousin Rhani!" The squeal turned heads for ten meters in all directions. "Of course you got my letter so you know how I feel about the destruction of your house, it's a terrible thing, just terrible, and of course the entire city feels for you, such a wonderful house, truly a piece of history: do you know, people are saying the most interesting things? Because of that terrible A-Rae and what he did to you now there won't be a referendum, which I think is best although if we had a referendum I would vote to keep things the way they are, after all they've worked all these years and I always say the old ways are best—"

"Charity," Rhani said, "I have an appointment."

Charity Diamos looked from her to Dana, and giggled. "Oh my," she said. "Yes."

Later, sitting in Imre Kyneth's book-lined study, facing Christina Wu, Rhani wondered what Christina would say if she were asked: *"Should I spend fifteen million credits to buy the dorazine formula?"* But it was too soon to ask for legal advice. She needed to spend several evenings examining her corporate financial records. "Well," she said, "say I want to marry Ferris Dur, can I do it or can't I?"

Christina's good eye blinked. "You could," she said. "The Founders' Agreement stipulates only that if you do, you and Ferris must both put fifty percent of your Family capital into a trust for the child, or children, that trust to be handled by some third corporate entity."

So, Rhani thought, what Ferris told me is true. Rising, she strolled to the bookcase. She had to turn her head to one side to read the titles of the books. *The Time Machine,* said one. *Last and First Men,* said another. *The Dispossessed*—she wondered what that was about. "Would you like a drink?" she asked.

"Thank you, I would," Christina said.

Rhani tugged on the ornate, antique ribbon of tapestry that the Kyneths used to summon their slaves. A slave pushed open the round door. "Wine," she said. "Christina?"

"Wine would be lovely," said the lawyer. The slave
bowed and went away. In a moment he reappeared and
came at a crouch through the aperture. Setting it on the
desk, he poured wine from a carafe into two gilt-lined
glasses.

"Will that be all, Domna?" he said.

"Thank you, yes," Rhani said. She took one glass and
handed the second to Christina. "And this placing of
money in a trust, Christina, would it have to be done
immediately, or could it wait, for instance, until a child
actually appeared?"

Christina frowned. "I don't know. I would have to
examine the statutes."

"I see."

They drank in silence. Then Christina said, "Rhani,
how long have we known each other?"

Rhani ran her tongue over her lips. "Fifteen years?"
she said.

"About that. You returned from Sovka, and then
Domna Isobel died. I had only been practicing my
profession for a few years." Christina rose. She was truly
tiny, about one point three meters tall, and weighed
perhaps thirty kilograms. "I like this room; it's almost
small enough for me," she said. "I wonder who the
architect was. Perhaps I can have it copied, though not, of
course, with the books. Rhani, do you *want* to marry
Ferris Dur?"

"It's possible," Rhani said.

Christina said softly, "Despite the fact that while he is
Domni Ferris, he is not the chief financial officer of the
corporate entity that is his Family?"

"He—isn't?"

Christina shook her head. Her small hands caressed the
gilt-edged glass. Chabadese glass, Rhani thought. "No.
Family Dur is run by a committee which was formed,
before she died, by Domna Sam." She smiled. Her teeth
were almost as white as Loras U-Ellen's.

Rhani thought: I wish she had told *me*. She leaned back
in the chair. "You mean," she said, "that Ferris does not
control Family Dur's money?"

"That's correct," Christina said. "Oh, he has the
household accounts, and I believe a fairly extensive
private account to pay for his hobbies."

"But why?"

Christina said, "Because Ferris Dur is not quite an adult. Something in him never grew; he mimics maturity but he's not competent in those matters which you, sweetheart, manage by instinct. Why do you think Domna Sam disliked him so?"

"Does Ferris know?" Rhani said.

Christina said, "Who knows what Ferris knows? It appears so, sometimes. Other times, clearly not." As he did not seem to know, Rhani thought, when he first discussed this subject with me. . . . She sighed, and laid the glass down. She did not want any more wine. Why, she wondered, did that feel so long ago?

I could still marry, she thought. I could even marry Ferris Dur. Many corporate entities are run by committee; it does not make them less efficient. I probably know everyone on the committee, and Ferris wouldn't care as long as I was kind to him and let him pretend to be important.

Sweet mother, she thought, with fearful empathy, what does he do with his time? How does he fill his days? Dreaming up elaborate strategies which will fit him into a world in which he knows he doesn't belong? Rearranging furniture? Snapping his fingers at household slaves?

Inexplicably she found her eyes filling with tears. She rose.

"Rhani?" Christina leaped from her chair. "Rhani, I'm sorry, I had no idea this would distress you—Rhani, come sit, please."

"No, Christina, I don't want to sit." Rhani wiped her eyes with her knuckles. Christina was gazing at her, worried and disturbed.

"Rhani," she said slowly, "I—forgive me—are you *fond* of Ferris?"

Rhani laughed despite herself, and choked. She coughed, drank wine, and coughed again as the strong vintage burned her throat. "No, Christina, I'm not. I just feel sad for him. What the hell does he do all day?"

Christina said promptly, "He makes models."

"Models? Of what?" She had a bizarre vision of Ferris walking through a room filled with life-sized, lifeless dolls.

"Of houses," Christina said. "He makes them in the basement. I'm surprised he hasn't taken you to see them, but maybe he was saving it for a treat. He's very good at it; he puts them all together with his hands, and he tries to find original materials. His ambition, he told me once, is to have a model of all Abanat in the basement of that house. It *is* sad. You're not going to marry him, are you, Rhani?"

"No," Rhani said. She went to the chair and sat, wishing she were home on the estate, with Binkie sitting by the com-unit and Isis playing at her feet. . . . But Binkie was dead. "No, Christina, I'm not."

She saw Christina to the door. They embraced. The small woman's hands were steady on Rhani's cheeks. Kissing her, Christina said, "Get out of here, sweetheart. Abanat's bad for you." Rhani went to the windows to watch her. She looked fragile as a child on the broad street.

She went upstairs. As she got to the bedroom, the thought of Ferris made her want to weep again. Mercifully the room was empty; she slid the door closed and locked it. The clothes she had worn to the Hyper district and then stripped off lay scattered around the big pink bed. Desultorily she piled pants, shirt, sandals on a chair. Suddenly, her knees gave way—it felt as if the bones had jellied. She grabbed the chair arm and sat heavily on the heap of clothes. What the hell was wrong with her? She felt her head. Her hair was hot.

A touch of the sun. . . . She leaned back. In a few moments, she told herself, she could go downstairs and drink something cold. Not fruit punch. Ice water. She let her head droop against the chair's back, thinking about what Christina had said. Poor Ferris—and poor Domna Sam, realizing perhaps too late that her one and only son was not capable of succeeding her. Wearily, she plucked at the tie around her braid. It came loose, and she combed her hair out with her fingers. It wasn't fair, she thought. Our mothers had no luck with their sons. She felt disloyal, to think such a thing of Zed, but she knew—few knew better—how deeply wounded her brother was. Did my mother do that? she wondered. Or is there something in Chabad that transforms and destroys? Maybe A-Rae is right, maybe slavery is a moral disease, infecting us like that strange disease, that mutation they found at Sovka, what was its name—hemophilia. . . .

Not A-Rae. She rose from the chair and went to the com-unit. U-Ellen had told her A-Rae's true name: it was U-Anasi, or rather, had been U-Anasi until he turned eighteen. She punched in a request for Nialle to obtain all information possible on one Michel U-Anasi, who nine years back had been an Enchantean citizen. Most of the information, she knew, would have to come from Enchanter and obtaining it would take at least two Standard weeks.

Then she went to the washroom and ran cold water on her wrists until her heart subsided. I can't be sick, she thought. She checked her temperature with the gauge in the medikit. Normal. Because she was there, she felt in the medikit for the meter. She gazed into the bathroom's wall-sized mirror as she stuck the meter under her tongue. Dark crescents underscored her eyes, and she thought: Christina's right. Abanat is bad for me.

Her thoughts spiraled again. Maybe it isn't Abanat. Maybe it's Chabad. The heat saps our strength. . . . But she knew that was nonsense. There were other worlds among the Living Worlds whose conditions were inimical to human life, and they, too, had been colonized and settled. Dana—her Starcaptain, she thought with sudden tenderness—Dana would know their names, and what they looked, tasted, smelled like, and if their children had been hurt as Chabad's children were hurt. . . . She pulled the meter from her mouth and stared at it.

The indicator bulb had turned from a negative pink to a resplendent, positive orange.

Chapter Nineteen

Dropping into the estate hangar, Rhani thought, was like a bird homing to its nest, if the bubble could be said to be a bird, if Chabad had had birds. Dana cut the power. She swung from the bubble not even trying to conceal her grin of relief. It was good to be home. She stretched her arms to the sky. "I feel as if I've been gone months," she said to Dana. The hangar roof closed like two hands joining. They walked into the sunlight. Immeld, Cara, and Timithos stood on the front steps. Cara looked sour. Rhani thought of Amri, and of Binkie.

The steward stepped forward to kiss her cheek. She smelled of soap. "Welcome back, Rhani-ka." Immeld echoed the greeting. Timithos trotted toward the hangar to unload the luggage from the bubble. Three dragoncats swung around the corner of the house, tails waving, and she stood quite still and held out her hands for them to sniff. Recognizing her scent, they rubbed their heads against her hips. One of them—Thoth, she thought it was—licked her left palm.

"Where's my brother?" she said.

Cara looked at Immeld. "In the garden," Cara said, "with *her*."

Rhani bit her lip. She had deliberately put the image of the girl on the platform out of her mind. She wondered if she should wait, and let Zed come to find her—no. "Tell Dana to come find me when he is through in the hangar," she said. She went into the house. It was little changed, she thought—she amended that as she passed the dining alcove. The cushions on the floor looked comfortable. Resisting the impulse to go to her bedroom, she walked through the kitchen and out the back door to meet her brother and Darien Riis.

She found them under the bitter-pear. Zed lay with his head in the girl's lap. She stroked his forehead. He was saying something about the Net; his hands formed and reformed a circle in the air. His eyes were closed against the sunlight which came spattering through the bitter-pear's leaves.

The girl saw her first and said a soft, swift word to Zed. He turned his head and then rolled to his feet. "Rhani-ka," he said. Darien Riis rose, and he gripped her hand. Rhani waited for Zed to come to her, to hug her. He didn't move. The girl watched them, an expression of bland interest on her uncanny face.

"How did the meeting with U-Ellen go?" he said.

Rhani said, "It went well."

"You can speak in front of Darien," Zed said. He smiled at the girl, a loving, gentle look. "Was he of any use whatsoever?"

"Some," Rhani said.

"Good," Zed said. He smiled again. "Wonderful." His hair was loose and tangled; he ran his fingers through it. A dried leaf dropped to the grass.

Rhani said, "He wants to sell me a part interest in the dorazine trade."

"Are you going to buy?"

"I don't know." She waited for him to ask the questions she expected—what does U-Ellen know about the dorazine business? Who owns it? How much does he want? She waited for him to say: Have they found Michel A-Rae?

He asked none of these things; he said nothing. He was not even looking at her. As a starving man watches food, he was watching Darien.

Something had happened; she did not understand it. She felt as if the ground beneath her feet had turned to sand and was changing, shifting, blowing across the lawn. Dana called her name and she turned toward him with relief. "I'm here!" she called.

He appeared around a flower bed. He had put on a clean shirt; he looked sturdy, solid, unchanged. He came to stand beside her—and then Rhani saw his face whiten. She glanced at her brother. Zed's eyes were wide and smoky, and his free hand was curling, long fingers crooking into claws.

He took a step toward Dana, and was checked by Darien's grip on his wrist. Rhani whirled on Dana. "Go to the house," she commanded. Dana backed and ran. Zed relaxed. Darien disengaged her hand from his and flexed her fingers, smiling at nothing. He reached up and caressed her cheek, as if Dana had never appeared.

He said, "Rhani, I'm leaving Chabad."

Dry-mouthed, she answered, "Are you?"

"Yes. Darien and I are going to Nexus. Darien's never been there. You don't need me—Jo can command the Net for you. She'll make a better commander than I was. Nivas is easily competent to be the chief medic. We'll leave—" he shrugged, and touched the girl's red hair—"I don't know. In a while."

Rhani's legs felt unsteady, as if she had just climbed a mountain. She licked her lips. This isn't real, she thought, this is an illusion. . . . Summoning up her energies, she stretched her hand out. "Twin!" she said.

Zed was looking at Darien. He had not even heard her. The girl murmured to him, soft words that Rhani could not catch. She swallowed back sickness and left them together beneath the bitter-pear tree.

Dana was in her bedroom. He rose when she came in. Walking to him, she slid her hands beneath his shirt and they clung together. His heart thudded and finally steadied. Her own was racing. . . . She tugged at the shirt. "Take this off," she said. He drew it off and she held him, pressing herself into his warmth, fingers moving over his skin.

Finally she let him go. Dana pushed her into the wing chair. He pulled the footstool across the room and sat on it, holding her hands. "Do you want to talk?" he said.

She pressed his fingers to her forehead. "No. Yes." She drew a deep breath. "I don't know what to say. He's leaving Chabad, he and Darien. He's taking her to Nexus." She gazed around the room; it was smaller than her memory of it. "He said, *'You don't need me.'*"

Dana said, "He needs to believe that."

"Don't be glib!" she snapped. "How can you know what's happening in his mind?"

Dana's mouth crooked. "I know him pretty well," he said. "Not the way you do, though. Differently." He freed his hands from hers. Deliberately he rose and walked a few paces from her, toward the terrace doors. "I think he's crazy, Rhani."

"Don't say that." She clenched her fists on her thighs. "Insanity is a clinical, chemical disorder, detectable by blood test. Zed's a medic. They'd know if he were crazy."

"I'm no medic," Dana said, "but I know that blood chemistry changes in reaction to environmental conditions. The entropic imbalance between spacetime normal and the Hype drove the early hyperspace explorers nuts. Zed's been commander of the Net for how long? A long time. Test his blood. He's crazy."

Rhani said, "No. I won't accept that."

Dana shrugged. "There they are." Rhani went to him. Through the terrace doors, she saw Zed and Darien walking across the lawn. Their hands were linked, and they were laughing.

"No," she heard herself saying. Whirling from the sight, she sat in the wing chair, chin on her fists. Zed was not mad. Something—had changed in him, that was all. He had found a lover, for one thing, an event neither he nor she had thought was possible. She thought: I should be happy for him.

She said, "The sight of you seems to trigger him to violence."

Dana exhaled. "Yes. It has to go somewhere."

"What does that mean?"

Dana said, "He's a violent man. He's had years to create patterns for himself—" he hesitated, and then went on, "sadistic patterns around sexual acts. That girl looks so like you—and he would never hurt you, Rhani. He won't hurt her either. But the sadism is in him now, and it has to go somewhere."

Her breath jammed in her throat. "Could he know—"

"That we're lovers?" Dana finished. "I hope not. Oh, stars, I hope not, Rhani."

She heard footsteps on the stairs, and a woman's laughter echoed through the corridor. "I don't see how he could," she said. "All the same, you'd better keep well out of his way."

The house fissioned. Zed and Darien spent a lot of time in Zed's room. They ate in the dining alcove; they walked in the gardens. Except for momentary glimpses from the terrace, Rhani rarely saw them. She heard their laughter on the stairs, though, and sometimes in the night, through walls which had unaccountably thinned to paper, she heard their lovemaking. Finally, she admitted to herself that she was listening. She spent most of her time in her bedroom. She ate there. Though he slept in the slaves' hall, Dana stayed with her during the day. When he left her side, he went warily; he would stand at the door of the room, waiting, and she realized that he, too, was listening. He went to great trouble to avoid Zed. Once, he came into the bedroom trembling. She went to him. "Are you hurt?" He shook his head. "What happened?" He would not talk about it. She felt as if she were living in a puzzle, like the toys the Abanat street vendors hawked. She was the little ball scuttling and bouncing through the shaken plastic maze.

Dana spoke to Darien when they met on the stairs or in the kitchen, the rare times she appeared without Zed. Rhani asked what they said to each other. Dana shrugged. "Not much. She comments on the weather.

Sometimes she asks how you are, and doesn't seem very concerned with the answers."

"Can you tell what she's like?"

He spread his hands. "She looks like you. Sounds like you."

"Does she—does she care for him? Really?"

"How the hell do I know?" Dana said. "She seems to."

It makes no sense, Rhani thought, no sense. How can he care for her and shut me out? She listened, but they were in the garden, and she couldn't hear them.

She had intended, once she was settled in the estate, to call the proper agency and engage a secretary, maybe two. But she did not. The first few days in the house, she did nothing but sit at the com-unit. Her fingers regained their keyboard speed and skills. The load of work was soothing; it meant she did not have to think about anything else. Dana screened the mail for her. She read the PINsheets: the referendum seemed certain to fail, they said. The petitions were still gaining signatures only on Belle.

She spoke with Imre and with Theo Levos by com-line. In conference, they agreed that the Upper House of the Council could rest easy for a time. The dorazine shortage remained critical. Rhani wished that she could talk about Loras U-Ellen's offer with Zed. After several nights of pouring over her financial records, she ascertained that, assuming no emergency drain occurred on Family Yago funds, she could just come up with fifteen million credits. It was somewhat sobering to realize that The Pharmacy probably spent that much money every Standard month.

The fourth day, the mail bubble arrived at the estate. In the bag was a letter from Loras U-Ellen, reminding her that she had seventeen more days to make up her mind. Scowling, Rhani tossed it in the disposal. The knowledge that she was pregnant seemed to make every decision difficult. Rising to think, to pace, she heard laughter from the garden, and clapped her hands to her ears to shut out the sound.

She wondered, lying alone at night, if she should arrange to miscarry. She did not want to; she had gone to such trouble to conceive—and besides, in the small hours of the morning she would wake to see a small, heart-shaped face in the darkness, a face with wheat-colored hair and topaz eyes. Sometimes the child's eyes were black. She thought about Dana. She should free him now, she knew.

But if she freed him he would leave, and then she would be wholly alone.

She looked up Cat Graeme in the com-net. Catriona Graeme, born in Foralie on Dickson's World, age thirty-eight, trained as a soldier—which, Rhani discovered, was an ancient Terran word that seemed to mean both a mercenary and a police officer—took part in four major actions including the one on China III, three children, one grown and commanding his own unit—what, she wondered, was a unit? Reading about this woman, whose life was so different from her own, made her realize how many of the Living Worlds she had never heard of, dreamed of.

A second reminder from Loras U-Ellen drove her from her lethargy. She wrote a letter to Tak Rafael at the Yago Bank. In it she informed him that Family Yago was about to embark upon a new manufacturing endeavor, product unspecified, and that for it she would need investment capital of fifteen million credits. She sealed it and gave it to Dana to put in the mail bag.

Sitting at the com-unit, he was reading the PINsheets.

"What do they say?" she asked.

He shook his head, knowing what she wanted them to say. "Nothing about Cat Graeme."

"Nothing about Michel A-Rae?"

"Only that the Abanat police haven't located him yet."

"They're all fools," Rhani said. She rose, strolled to the terrace doors, and back again. Zed and Darien were in the garden, and Dana could see her trying to look elsewhere, anywhere but out. . . . She was rigid with tension—had been for over a Standard week. After eight days in close proximity to her, Dana felt as if the webbing of his nervous system had frayed.

In thirteen days, he knew, she would respond to Loras U-Ellen, one way or another. And in ten days, he would be off Chabad. He had put the message—directed to Russell O'Neill and in navigator's coding—into the com-unit two days back. His principal fear now was that Zed would catch him in the hall or in the garden and do something, Dana did not know what, which would keep him from ever getting off Chabad. He had begun to dream of the Net, which did not make the situation any easier. Once, he had walked into the kitchen and interrupted Zed and Darien with their arms around each other. The look Zed had turned on him—horrifying, feral anger—was like nothing he had experienced on this or any other earth.

Ten days, he told himself. You can stand ten more days of this. He wondered if Rhani could. It would pain her, he knew, when he left. But he had to go, he had to take the opportunity—what if she would not free him, as she had sworn she would? What if Zed and Darien did not leave for Nexus?

"File this under 'R,'" she told him, passing him a report. Automatically he glanced at it to see what it was. Its contents were none of his business but she did not seem to notice or, if she noticed, she didn't care. It was the report from the Barracks, detailing the number of slaves sold at Auction last year, the number sold after the Auction to dealers, money spent on drugs, food, and staff expenses, money taken in, profits made.

The bedroom door, which was open a crack, slid open all the way. Dana jumped like a thief, and then froze. Zed stood there.

Rhani said quickly, "Dana, go to the terrace." Dana laid the Barracks report aside. Rising, he stepped away from the chair, trying to go noiselessly. The terrace doors, swollen by heat, stuck. He jerked them open, back to the room, sweat coating his palms and rolling down his sides. As he stepped through them, he heard Rhani say, "Good morning, Zed-ka."

He watched them through the curtained glass. Zed's hair fell loose to his shoulders. He seemed younger, softer, as if something—someone, Dana thought—had peeled away time. Behind him, in the hall, stood Darien.

Zed said, "I don't need to come in. I just want to tell you that we're leaving. We're going to Abanat first; from Abanat, we'll locate Jo Leiakanawa and go up to the Net. From the Net we'll go to the moon, and from there take passage to Nexus. There's a letter on my desk for you, the official notice that I'm resigning my command."

Rhani's back was to the terrace, and Dana could not see her face. He heard her say, "How will you go?"

"We'll take the Yago shuttle."

She nodded. A dragoncat loped in. Ignoring both Rhani and Zed, it stood on the rug, meowing plaintively. Rhani said, "Isis, go away, please." The cat went out. Rhani put her hands on her hips. Dana felt tremendous pity for her. In a steady voice, she said, "I can see you've got it all planned."

"There is one thing," Zed said. He gestured toward the girl. "Darien must be freed."

"Of course," said Rhani. She went to the com-unit. Her fingers tapped the keys. In a few moments, a document emerged from the printer. She picked it up and held it toward her brother. "Do you want to see it?"

"No need," he said. His sudden smile was brilliant. "Would you be willing to take care of two trivialities?"

Rhani sat in the com-unit chair. "If I can," she said.

"I want to give my medical skeleton to Yianni Kyneth." She said, "I'll see that he gets it."

"Thank you. And would you say farewell to Davi, the youngest Kyneth child, for me?"

"Yes," she said. Dana could hear the exhaustion in her voice. He waited for Zed to walk to her, to hug her, to touch her face in that dreadful ambivalent gesture.

He lifted a hand to her from the doorway of the room. "Good-bye," he said.

Head rigid, she watched him out the doorway. Then she put her hands over her ears and her head on her knees.

Dana wrenched the terrace doors apart and went to her. He pried her fingers from her ears. "Rhani," he said. Her amber eyes were lightless with shock and grief. She looked blind. He lifted her from the chair like a child and laid her on the bed. "Rhani." In the distance, he heard the flat drone of a bubble. Her gaze touched his face, and then went elsewhere, inward. He sat on the side of the bed, holding her hand, talking to her softly, telling her nonsense stories, tales about Pellin, lies about his adventures in the Hype, anything to make her hear him. Her chest rose and fell with her steady breathing. Her pulse beat swiftly. Her eyes stayed open, looking into nothing. She didn't weep.

She brought herself out of it. Dana went to the cooler

for a drink of cold water, and when he returned to the bed, her eyes had focused. She reached for him across the rumpled sheet. She licked her lips. He went swiftly to the remains of breakfast and brought her a glass of juice. She swallowed avidly. "Dana," she whispered.

He stroked her face. The terrible pallor of her cheeks had lessened. "Yes, Rhani-ka. I'm here."

She struggled. "I want to sit."

Putting his arms around her shoulders, he brought her gently upright. She leaned into his chest. "Zed's gone."

He nodded.

"It wasn't just a dream."

"No, Rhani-ka, I'm sorry."

Her eyes blazed anger with unexpected force. "How can you say that? You hated him."

Did she expect him to deny it? Dana wondered. "I do hate him," he said. "I'm sorry for your pain."

She bowed her head to her lap, and he wondered if she were finally crying. He hoped so. But she lifted her head, and he saw that her eyes were dry. "I want to get up," she said. He helped her to the washroom. She called to him from it, "Tell Immeld I want some soup. And some wine."

"Are you certain it's good for you?" he said.

She scowled at him. "Am I a child? Bring it." He went down to the kitchen himself. Cara and Immeld were holding hands across the table.

"Rhani wants soup and some wine," he said.

Immeld got up. "Soup," she grumbled. "It's hot for soup. When will Zed and that woman come back?"

Never, I hope, Dana thought. "Ask Rhani," he said. He brought the tray upstairs. Rhani drank half a glass of wine, and sighed.

"I'm all right," she said.

He said, "Is there anything you want me to do?"

She gazed at him, and an odd smile flicked across her face. "Take me to bed," she said.

"You're in bed," he said.

"Fool." She reached for him and drew him to her. "Love me. I want you to love me." He shucked his clothes. It had been days since they'd been lovers. He slid beneath the covers with her. Her muscles were drumhead tight; he rubbed her back and shoulders until he felt the ridges melt. She sighed and fit herself to him, her body warm and pliant, and they paced each other into orgasm's dizzying surge.

A shrilling sound woke them. Dana was all the way out of bed before he realized where it came from. It was night. He rubbed his eyes and glanced at the chronometer. It was an hour before mignight. Stars, we slept like the dead, he thought. The com-unit message light was blinking; he shambled to it, pressed the keys which would accept the call and silence the alarm. Brilliant green letters stabbed at his gaze. CALL FROM CHIEF PILOT ORION TO DOMNA RHANI YAGO.

From the bed, Rhani called, "What is it?"

Dry-mouthed, Dana watched the words glitter on the screen. He heard the rustle of the sheet as she scrambled from the bed. "It's for you, from Tam Orion."

"The chief pilot? What's he doing? Sweet mother, it must be the middle of the night!" She walked to his side.

"It must be important," he said.

"It better be." She pushed the Accept key impatiently. The display didn't clear; instead, it flashed VERIFICATION. Scowling, Rhani splayed her thumb on the screen.

The words marched across the unit. TWENTY MINUTES AGO LANDINGPORT STATION REPORTED DISTRESS CALL FROM THE SARDONYX NET RECEIVED IN NAVIGATOR'S CODE CUT OFF MID-TRANSMISSION LANDINGPORT STATION UNABLE TO CONTACT NET REQUEST FOR ADVICE PASSED THROUGH ME. It was signed, TAMERLANE ORION, CHIEF PILOT. ABANAT MAIN LANDINGPORT.

Rhani said, "Turn the light on."

Dana obeyed.

"Zed is on the Net," she said.

Dana shrugged. "So? He's there, you're here. Nothing you can do."

She gazed at him. "You don't care," she said.

"Rhani, I just woke up!" He cycled the message through again. Even if there was trouble on the Net, what difference did it make? They had said good-bye. "Rhani, he's gone. Let him go."

She ignored him. Striding to her closet, she began to put on clothes. "I'm going to Abanat," she said.

Dana realized she was serious. He caught her arm. "What good will that do?"

"Something's wrong. I want to know what is it."

He said, "It could be something wrong with the com-link. Call Tam Orion and tell him to call LandingPort Station to send up a repair crew. Any Hyper engineer can fix it."

"It isn't that kind of wrong," she said.

"How do you know?"

She jerked her arm from his grasp. "Dana, use your mind! The Net's a starship, it's got every means of communication there is, radio, laser beam, com-link, message capsule, flare signals. Whatever's wrong isn't the kind of thing a repair crew can fix."

She was right. Dana stuck his knuckles in his eyes to rouse his dullard brain. Rhani wriggled into a shirt. Her head popped through the stretch-fiber neck. "Call Jo, the Skellian," he suggested. "Get her to go look."

"She's on the Net, with Zed."

"Oh." He watched her comb her hair with her hands. His unease grew. The distress call had been sent, he recalled, in navigator's code. Jo Leiakanawa was a navigator. It took a very distressing event indeed to bother a Skellian. He looked for his pants. Rhani put on her boots. "Rhani. Do you understand that this could be dangerous?"

Her mouth thinned with contempt. "Of course."

He considered all the things that could go wrong with the Drive Core of a starship. "You'll just be in the way."

She looked at him. He stepped back. The hairs on the nape of his neck lifted. Her face was stony; her eyes burned. She looked like Zed. "I have to know," she said. Dana stayed very still. The dark glare died. She tilted her head; her gaze suddenly coldly speculative. "You could go."

Dana nearly tripped on his own pair of pants. "What?"

"You can go to the Net. I'll give you the blueprints. You can get in. You're a Starcaptain: that means you're an engineer, too. You could help." She assessed him, the way an engineer might assess a tool. She was Domna Rhani Yago, who had once said to him: "You forget, *I own you.*"

She was serious. She looked at him as if he had suddenly become a stranger. She would send him to the Net, to the assistance of a man he deeply feared and more deeply hated, to a place that reeked in memory of tears and humiliation. He wondered what she would do if he refused to go. Perhaps she would feed him dorazine. . . .

She said, "You don't want to do it, do you." He shook his head. "I won't order you to." She walked to the com-unit. "I'll pay you to go." She pressed keys. The screen blinked. She thumbed the colored plastic. A sheet of paper glided from the slot to the shelf; she brought it to him. "Will this be a fair price, Starcaptain?"

He turned the flimsy piece of paper in his hands. It was his slave contract. At bottom, over the box with the Yago seal, the computer had printed in neat red letters, MANUMITTED. Beside it was the month and date. She had handed him his freedom.

He keyed the computer for a STATUS TRANSACTION: REPLACEMENT OF CREDIT DISC AND I-DISC. It requested his name: he punched DANA IKORO, STARCAPTAIN. It requested his I.D. code. He had to copy it from the abrogated contract. PELLIN NWC26R7P21-7669. He pressed his thumb to the cool sheet. The unit hummed loudly and spat one red and one black disc at him. He ran his fingertips across their surfaces, feeling the bumps and indentations that identified him.

He tapped the forearm tattoo. "How do I get rid of this?"

"There's a gel which does it. You have to get it at the Clinic."

"There isn't time for that." His mouth was stale. He went down to the room in the slaves' hall to get his boots. Rhani had put the agreement into the computer. He found the boots beneath the bed. It said (she had had to translate the legal language) that for services to be rendered in the form of assistance to the Yago Net, he, Dana Ikoro, pilot/slave of Family Yago, was free. He could not quite believe it. He laced the boots with stiff fingers. He could fly the bubble to Abanat, ride a shuttle to the Net—no, he couldn't. His tattoo would set off every alarm in the place, and as fast as he could drive the bubble, it would still take over an hour to get there. There had to be a solution. He couldn't think, and yet he felt that he was moving at top speed: the characteristic illusion of an interrupted sleep. He gazed out the window of the room. Moonlight made the lawn shimmer as brightly as a Flight Field under its bristle of lights. He struck himself lightly on the head. "Fool." Of course he didn't want a bubble or shuttle. What he needed was a starship.

He thought of *Zipper*. He yearned for *Zipper,* but *Zipper* was on the moon, and it would take as long to get there as to get to the Net. But he didn't need *Zipper*. He knew where he could get a ship. He went up the stairs quickly. Rhani was pacing, shoulders hunched, hands in her pockets. He went to the com-unit.

He called The Green Dancer. Amber's withered face wavered before him. Tightly he said, "Listen, Amber. This is an emergency. I need to get in touch with Starcaptain Lamonica."

Amber shrugged. "She isn't here."

"I know. But you know where she is, you're her mail drop. If you can't tell me so that I can call her directly, then send someone to tell her to call me."

"It's nearly midnight—"

"Damn it, I know what time it is! Tell her it's Starcaptain Dana Ikoro. Give her this line number." He read it.

Amber's eyebrows lifted to her hair. "Clear, Starcaptain," she said, and switched off.

"What are you doing?" demanded Rhani.

"Getting a ride to the Net, fast."

Lamonica called. Her voice rasped through the speaker, though the screen stayed free of picture: "Dana, what's going on? I thought we had an agreement."

"Canceled. I want to make a new one. Damn it, will you come online so I can see you!" She glared at him abruptly from the screen, hair standing on end, face bare of glitterstick. Dana put his hands in his pockets and held up the two discs. "Credit. I-disc. I'm free. But before that freedom goes into effect, I need a ride to the Yago Net. It'll mean a thousand credits for you if you can give it to me."

Greed and suspicion contended on her face. She frowned. "I don't like being rushed into things."

"This is an emergency."

"Two thousand credits."

Dana looked at Rhani. She nodded. "Done," he said.

"When do you want this ride?"

"Right now. How fast can your bubble do one hundred kilometers?"

She grinned. "Ask me something hard."

"See you when you get here."

It took her, as he had known it would, twenty minutes, a fifth of the time that it would have taken him in a sedately paced, planet-bound bubble. He heard the noise, a deeper sound than the city bubblecraft, before he saw it, skin opaqued and gleaming in the moonlight, falling out of the night sky like a meteorite to land at the estate gates. The dragoncats raced to the attack and then heeled to Timithos' whistle; Rhani had already warned him to keep them in. Lamonica swung from the bubble. Dana and Rhani went to meet her. She wore a silver-and-lavender jumpsuit. "Good evening," she said.

"Domna Rhani Yago, Starcaptain Tori Lamonica."

Lamonica nodded without ceremony. "If anyone's looking for me, they won't have any trouble finding me," she said. "All they'll need to do is follow the wind."

"No one'll look. Did you move *Lamia?*"

"I said I would."

Dana sighed. "Then we're in business. Otherwise, we'd have had to turn around to go right back to Abanat."

Rhani said, "Now what will you do?"

"Now we'll go to the Net. As soon as I know what's happening there, I'll get in touch with Tam Orion. I'll route the call through LandingPort Station."

"I see." Rhani looked at the blond Starcaptain. "Your payment's on record, Starcaptain Lamonica. All you have to do is spend it."

Lamonica said, "It's a pleasure doing business with you, ma'am."

Dana said, "We're in a hurry, let's move." He could not wait to be gone. He felt as if his blood was singeing his veins. Rhani was looking at him as if she wanted to tell him something. He touched her shoulder; she closed her hand over his. Tenderness, regret—he could not analyze the emotions that traveled like light between them."

Meaninglessly he said, "It'll be all right, Rhani-ka."

She smiled. The bubble door opened. Lamonica swung into the pilot's seat, hands on the ceiling bar. Dana followed her. He folded himself into the passenger's chair. Rhani waved. Then the bubble shivered and went up.

Lamia's skin was pewter-colored. As they dropped toward her, Dana saw her shining dully in the starlight. Lamonica had positioned her perfectly, between two hills twenty-five kilometers from the Yago estate.

Once in the ship, Lamonica moved to the pilot's chair. Dana took the navigator's seat. Events were happening very fast, and he made himself slow down, relax, breathe, damn it. He touched the control panel with his fingertips. He wanted to pinch himself hard to make sure that he, at least, was real.

Lamonica was rushing through the takeoff checkout. "What's going on?" she said. "Am I likely to be stopped?"

"No, Rhani made a shitload of calls. You're clear with LandingPort Station and at Abanat Landingport."

"And we're going to the Net. Are they expecting us?"

"No. That's why we're going out there. No one can reach them; they're not answering their lines. About an hour ago, they sent a distress signal in navigator's code, and it was cut off."

"So someone's on it."

"The Net commander and the chief navigator, and a passenger."

"What are we supposed to do?"

"*We* are supposed to do nothing. You're going to take me out to the Net, and I'm going to go in and look. There's a back-up repair crew waiting on the Moon. If I signal you, you'll call them."

"Right. Going under Drive," she said. The ship shivered. Dana closed his eyes. A hum filled the big round room, half-audible, half-subliminal. Gravity increased. Dana slumped in the contoured chair. He was not uncomfortable: he had done this so many times that his body adjusted automatically, not fighting the weight, waiting for it to pass. . . . It passed. His breathing slowed to its normal rhythm. He opened his eyes. In the vision screen in front of him he saw a swelling darkness, tinged with a red luminosity which, he knew, came from the heating of the outer shell of *Lamia* herself. The glow faded. On the surface of the swelling planet he saw distinctly one large and three small pinpoints of light. And then, as it always did, the view turned inside out. The swelling began to shrink. The planet's rim appeared in the screen, growing in arc and glowing with a purer and purer radiance. *Lamia* sped from shadow to sun. With reflex born of practice, Dana reached to cut in the light screens.

"Hey," Lamonica said. He looked at her, and realized that he was weeping. His eyes burned and his nose was thick. She handed him a cloth; he wiped his face clean of tears. Standing, he went to the water cooler and drew a cupful of water. He bounced a little; Lamonica had set the ship's gravity at two-thirds gee. The screen was dark now, with the edge of the moon in focus: they were going in the same direction but Lamonica had switched the camera readout on the vision screen.

"Thanks," he said, reseating himself.

She kept her eyes on the controls. "Bad time?"

"I've had better."

"It's over now," she said.

"Yeah." He dug his fingers into the chair's resilient foam. "Sol will freeze," he said, "before I come back to Sardonyx Sector."

She said, "Don't say that yet, you're still in it."

The words stung like salt on a wound. He could leave it behind, Dana thought, but it would never leave him. The pain and helplessness he had known was etched solidly into its own small corner of his brain.

"Explain this to me," Lamonica said.

"Explain what?"

"You were a slave when we met in the bar. Tonight you call me and you're free."

"This trip to the Net is the price of that freedom."

"Is it on a contract?" Lamonica said.

"Yes, of course."

"I wondered. . . ." Her forefinger made little circles on the arm of her seat. "Any contract involving slavery is only good in Sector Sardonyx, right?"

"Yes." His throat muscles tensed.

"So what are we doing here?" she said. "Say the word, and I'll change *Lamia*'s trajectory, shoot us past this big silver prison, and Jump. Two weeks in the Hype and we land on Nexus. You'll never have to hear the name Yago again."

He gazed at the moon. Already he thought he could see the Net, a spark of constant brilliance against the satellite's mottled surface. He imagined the screen changing, brightening to a rainbow nimbus, and then darkening to the stygian darkness of the Hype. . . . *Lamia* was Tori Lamonica's. Hers was the course choice, hers the responsibility. All he had to say was yes.

But Rhani Yago would know that he had broken a promise; left a contract unfulfilled. Tori Lamonica would know it. And he would know it himself. It would be, he reflected, supremely ironic if he freed himself from Sector Sardonyx by "rescuing" Zed Yago from the Net. Seen that way, this whole expedition turned into a joke, an expression of the universe's, or the luck's, cosmic and comic sense of justice.

The universe cared nothing for Dana Ikoro's pain, or for the memories that corded the muscles of his neck, dried his mouth to cotton, and gave him stomach cramps.

"Can't do it," he said.

Lamonica splayed a hand in the air. "It's up to you."

As they neared the starship, Dana dug the computer cube out of his pocket and held it up to Lamonica's view. She pointed at the console. "You do it." Dana turned the cube (blue, three-by-three-by-three centimeters' dimension) till he found the side with a small visual/tactile symbol. He matched the symbol to one on the console. That second symbol marked a sliding panel. He slid it aside and fit the cube, symbol-side first, into the opening there, and pulled the panel closed. The blue cube contained, as Rhani had promised, blueprints of the Net. "Let's see it," said Lamonica. Dana instructed the computer. Diagrams began to march across the compscreen.

Lamonica said, "That cube is worth a fortune."

Dana smiled. "It's not recordable, and it's programmed to self-erase."

"Too bad."

Dana leaned back in the chair to study the diagram. Despite the superstructure of cells, corridors, and storage spaces, the great wheel of the Net contained recognizable and familiar elements. The Drive Core and the ship's computer sat in the inner rim of the torus. Entrance locks were set at spaced intervals along the outer rim. The Bridge, with its observation windows, was located on what Dana arbitrarily (and temporarily) designated the Chabad-side of the wheel. Fusion thrusters decorated the opposite "side." The protruding jets gave the wheel, in diagram at least, a slightly lopsided appearance. He wondered why Isobel Yago had chosen to make her prison ship a torus, when a sphere would have been easier to construct and a more efficient use of space. Corridors traversed the doughnut. He asked for an enlargement of the section containing the Bridge. The computer obliged. The maps were detailed, labeled, and color-coded. Rhani had given him all the information she had.

He wondered where the emergency was, and what it was, and how much time he had to find it. He said, "Let's see if we can reach them."

"Right." Lamonica keyed a message. If the computer communications were alive on the Net, the message would be picked up and responded to automatically.

There was no response. "I'll call them," Lamonica said.

Dana caught her hand as she reached for the radio switch. "No. Wait."

"Why?"

"Moon Base has been calling them steadily since they got the distress signal. Call Moon Base."

Lamonica called. "LandingPort Station Communications, this is *Lamia,* Starcaptain Tori Lamonica, are you there?"

"Lamia, we hear you."

"Any sound out of the Sardonyx Net?"

"Zilch, Starcaptain. Do you want us to keep trying?"

"Yes," Dana said, interrupting. "Don't break."

"Understood. Will you engage?"

"Yes. I'm going in."

"Good luck, *Lamia* and captains."

The Net was very close. Lamonica said, "Where do you want to enter, Dana? We're in matching orbit now."

Dana grimaced. He stared at the computer's projection. If something were wrong with the Drive Core, it would be a waste of time for him to enter the ship on the lock nearest the computer. "Someone started to send a distress call." He tapped the plastic screen. "Maybe that someone's still trying. Engage at Hole Four. I have to start somewhere. I might as well try the Bridge." In the vision screen, the big wheel was no longer smooth. Knobs and strings and struts decorated its silver skin.

Lamonica tipped their seats. "Decelerating," she said. Gravity increased. *Lamia* sang, tail extending, thrusting, vision screen pointing outward once again to the brown and white and blue world they had just left.

Chapter Twenty

Dana suited up to go into the Net.

Most pressure suits were brightly colored, on the same principle that made mountaineers use fluorescent, orange gear. Lamonica's suits—she carried four of them in storage besides her own—were maroon-and-silver striped. They were one-piece suits, from crown to crotch to boot-soles; they contained an air supply and a moisture recycler. They were designed to withstand pressure and temperature extremes of both hot and cold, but you could not wear them for very long; once in one, you could neither piss, shit, nor eat.

Hole Four would not engage with *Lamia*'s extensible lock. Dana swam through and fastened it by hand. The lock walls stiffened as atmosphere hissed into it and it acquired gravity.

The outer lock door was jammed. Dana went back to *Lamia*. "I need tools." Tori pointed him at the tool locker; he took a variety, including a cutting laser, hooking them to the suit's magnetized patches. None of them were especially heavy. The outer air gauge appeared to be functional; at least, it claimed there was air in the inner lock. Dana unjammed the door. Whoever had jammed it had done a hasty job. It slid up. There *was* air in the inner lock. The inner lock door, luckily, was harder to damage and the vandal had left it alone. Dana closed it behind him but made sure before he moved that the outer lock door stayed up.

"I'm in," he said through the suit communicator.

"Clear, Dana. If you need anything, yell."

"You'll hear it," he said. He stepped into the Net. Gravity was normal. He was standing in an unadorned, white-walled corridor. He flipped through the pictures in his mind of the Bridge, fitting labels to spaces; this was

Transverse Corridor Four: the Bridge was reachable through the corridor which would be coming up to meet this one on the—left. The Net was very quiet. He remembered his first impression of it as a Möbius strip or a giant treadmill. Now he felt it to be something alive, sensing him as he moved, an interloper, through its gut; a metal-and-plastic intelligent worm. In the neutral confinement of the pressure suit, the hairs lifted at the back of his neck.

He damned his hyperactive imagination, kicked the wall, and went on.

At the entrance to the Bridge, he stopped, wary. The huge wraparound vision screens were blank. Shields covered them, the cameras were off. The room was just a big control room, filled with com-units, screens, computer panels, buttons, dials, gauges, and pilots' and navigators' chairs. It curved. Dana walked toward the communications units. Three meters from them, he saw what the partitions had hitherto concealed. The body of Jo the Skellian was lying on the floor. She was wearing a silver-and-blue uniform with the Yago "Y" on the shoulder. He started, with difficulty, to turn her over. She weighed, he guessed, one hundred thirty kilos, and dead weight she seemed to weigh a ton. She was limp and rubbery; finally he got her on her side and saw what had killed her. There was an odd-shaped hole under her left armpit; about fifteen centimeters long, and about two centimeters wide, it was horizontal, and as precise as if it had been cut with a surgical knife. Dana wondered how far it went. Far enough to touch something vital, lungs or heart. It had been made with a laser gun; he wondered if he should return to *Lamia* for a laser or stun pistol. He had been thinking in terms of an engineering emergency, not a human one.

Unsealing the seam of his pressure suit, he peeled it open, and let it fall down his back like a hood. He needed all his senses; and the pressure suit dimmed both taste and smell, though it left sight, hearing, and balance—the important ones. Now he could smell what his imagination had been trying to explain away: excrement, the death smell. He stood. Adrenalin speeded his heartbeat. He needed to find Zed Yago. He started once again toward the com-units, and again stopped. Assuming the ship's intercom was working, and it might not be, he still couldn't use it, not with someone with a laser pistol loose in the ship.

As he walked back to the doorway through the maze of partitions, he tripped over legs.

It was Zed, slumped in a contoured chair, head lolling, eyes closed, his breathing deep and even. He was out, not hurt, but drugged. The slackness of his facial muscles made his face look heavier. His big hands hung limp, nearly to the floor. The someone had a laser gun *and* a stun gun. Dana knelt and levered Zed's body across his back. As he pulled on the dangling arms, Zed shifted and muttered something. Dana almost dropped him. But the Net commander did not wake. Dana tried to estimate his weight. Eighty kilos? Eighty-five? He was heavy. The Starcaptain tensed his stomach muscles and straightened his legs, the unwieldy burden hoisted across his shoulder.

A cold voice said, "Put him down."

Dana turned his head. Stooped as he was, he could see very little by just turning his head. He saw a woman in a pale green jumpsuit, reddish hair, brown eyes, right hand holding a laser pistol pointing at him. . . . He let Zed's body slide back into the pilot's chair. Slowly he straightened, palms out and away from his body.

"Move away from him." The pistol moved a centimeter to the left. Dana stepped in that direction. He was out in the open now, directly in her line of fire, with neither chair nor partition to hide behind. His back ached and he wanted to piss.

"Which did you get first?" he asked.

"Zed," said Darien. "The Skellian hit the distress signal key. I couldn't risk the stun pistol on her; it might not have worked. Skellians metabolize drugs differently than other people. I had to kill her."

"Why?"

"Because she would have stopped me from completing my assignment. What are those implements on your suit?"

"Tools to open the lock."

"Take them off. Drop them on the floor."

Dana obeyed. He tossed them from him, not watching where they landed, but when he threw the cutting laser, it landed two-thirds of a meter from his foot.

Darien's hand did not relax.

"What was your assignment?" he asked, wanting to know, wanting to keep her talking because it would give him time to think. She didn't know what the cutting laser was, that was good, but she could cut him in two with her own pistol before he had time to get to it.

"To destroy the Yago Net." She leaned back against a bulkhead.

"How are you going to do that?"

"I'm a computer technician," she said. "That part's real. It took me two hours to program this monstrosity to blow itself up."

"What are you?"

She smiled. "I'm a cop." She still sounded like Rhani.

He snorted disbelief. "Since when do cops run around destroying sector property?"

Her eyes glittered anger. *"You* say that? You were *on* it. It's a symbol of power and of evil, it facilitates a vicious trade, it serves only to increase the profits of a slaver family—its very existence is immoral!" She glanced for a split second at the drugged man.

Dana said, "It's no worse than other prisons."

"No other prison is Zed Yago's private playground."

Dana edged a centimeter closer to the cutting laser. "I thought you loved him."

"You were supposed to think that. So was he. I didn't love him; I fucked him. It's different."

"Is your hair really that color?"

She laughed. "Of course not. Though it's close. My skin isn't this color, either, and I don't usually sound this husky. It takes a while for the dyes and the conditioning to wear off. I'm a weapon, Starcaptain. I'm an Enchantean, and I was a computer tech at Federation Headquarters till I was picked and primed and pointed at Zed Yago."

"Pointed by—"

"It was Michel's idea. He figured: to destroy the chain, break the strongest link. The weak ones will fall apart of their own accord. Rhani Yago is the strongest link in the slave trade, and the way to break her is to take Zed away for good. At first they were going to send a man to do it, but the psychologists decided that would be too dangerous. Zed hurts men, but he's never hurt a woman. The man, of course, would also have looked like Rhani Yago."

"Why not just assassinate him?"

"That wouldn't have done it. We considered it, but the psychologists said she would have remained only more determined to keep the slave system going." Dana edged two centimeters closer to the cutting laser. "If we'd assassinated *her, he'd* take over, and he would be worse, don't you think so?" Dana could not help agreeing. "Besides, killing is immoral."

"Too bad," Dana said. "If it weren't, you could have assassinated them both."

"You're right," she said, with evident regret. Her eyes narrowed. "If you feel like that, why are you here?"

"Rhani Yago sent me here to find out what was wrong."

"Oh. Then you're still a slave." She glanced at the wall behind his head. "This station's going to blow to pieces in twenty-five minutes," she said. "I'm shinnying on the shuttle. You want to come along? I'll take you. You can't have any loyalty to the Yagos."

Dana looked at Zed, still slumped in the chair. He hadn't stirred again. There was a trace more color in his cheeks than there had been before. "What about him?"

"He can stay here." Darien Riis' voice was very cold. "The Net blows, he blows with it."

"You don't care at all? You feel nothing for him?" As he asked it, Dana wondered why he cared to know. "He loved *you.*"

"No!" said Darien. She pushed her hair back with her left hand. "I feel bad about the Skellian. I didn't want to kill her. But him"—she looked at Zed for more than a second before fixing her eyes on Dana—"he didn't love me. He loved the image I was, he loved his sister in me."

"But wasn't that exactly what you wanted him to do? If they made you look like Rhani—"

"Yes. That's what we wanted. The Enchanter labs are good, aren't they?" She regained her pedantic tone. She tilted her head a little. "It worked perfectly, too. He was very easy to manipulate."

Dana wondered at the courage it must have taken to turn Zed Yago into a sexual tool. The thought of it—of willingly sharing the bed of a man you knew to be a practiced sadist—made his balls hurt and his skin crawl.

"Well," said Darien Riis, "are you coming with me or not?"

Dana smiled. "I don't have much of a choice," he said. "I don't want to be dead." When was she going to ask him how he had gotten to the Net? Maybe he could knock her out, carry her to *Lamia,* carry Zed to *Lamia,* get the fuck out of range in twenty minutes. . . . Part of him whispered: Never mind Zed. Leave him. Warn Tori and go. If you have to rescue someone, rescue the cop . . . .

Why? he wondered. Why this terrible hatred of the Yagos, of the Net, of Zed? Michel A-Rae had created it, fueled it—he wondered what had birthed it in *him.* Darien Riis wouldn't tell him if she knew, which he doubted . . .

Tori Lamonica's voice came clearly through his suit communicator. "Dana, are you still alive in there?"

Darien's pistol swung for him. Leaping at her, Dana grabbed for her wrist, pinned it. She fought him. He leaned close to yell in her ear, "That's just—" He gasped and leaned backward, almost losing his grip on her hand, as her elbow aimed for his throat.

"You son-of-a-bitch!"

"Listen to me," he said, starting to close with her. She stepped back and nearly took his head off with a sweeping side kick. He leaped backward and nearly tripped. She kicked him again. Sweet mother, she was fast! Tori was shouting at him through the suit mike. He moved in and trapped Darien's wrist again. She yielded, and her right arm relaxed. He heard a thud, as if something had fallen. Suddenly Darien's left hand blurred upward, laser in her fist, the pistol pointing not at him but out at the room. Dana saw Zed on the floor. He was aiming the cutting laser. Dana dived out of range. Light beams flashed, and Darien dropped. Zed Yago screamed and curled his body in agony, his head straining on his neck. He breathed in huge gasps, "Ah-hah, ah-hah."

"Shut up a minute!" Dana shouted into the suit mike. Tori shut up. He stood, rubbing his knee where it had hit the floor. He limped to Zed. The Net commander looked up, and Dana swallowed. The light beam had struck Zed's outstretched hands. They were claws, blackened and burned, bizarre skeletal things. The pain from them had to be unbelievable. He could not see why Zed was still conscious.

He knelt. "Zed, can you hear me?"

Amber eyes blazed into his. Zed croaked, "Get out."

"I've got a ship," said Dana lamely.

Zed's face twisted in spasm. "No."

"Damn it, this ship's going to blow in fifteen minutes! Tori Lamonica's at Hole Four, in *Lamia*. Let's—I'll carry you there."

"No."

"You want to die here?"

Zed's face spasmed again, not from pain; his mouth made a grotesque and terrible smile. "Yes." He looked past Dana to Darien's body.

"You're crazy," said Dana. "Rhani sent me here to get you and I'm going to do it, if I have to stun you with her stun gun and take you out over my shoulders."

Zed started to reach for him in reflex rage. He curled, sobbing at the pain. His face writhed. Dana watched. He was sweating terribly; the suit was having trouble keeping up with it. The same internal voice that had spoken before spoke again. It said: This is payment; this is right. Remember what he did to *you?*

But the sweat rolled down his sides like water over rock, and he kept having to swallow.

Before he could change his mind, he rose and went to Darien's corpse. Yanking the stun pistol from her belt, he returned to Zed and held it out. "I mean it." He checked the dial and turned it to a one-hour stun.

When he looked up, Zed was on his knees. "No," he said. Dana reached to help him. The Net commander snarled, and staggered, unassisted, to his feet. Keeping his hands in front of him, he walked toward Hole Four. Dana stayed behind him. At the closed door, Zed stood aside to let Dana open it.

"Tori, I'm bringing in an injured passenger. Get some anesthetic spray and get ready to cut loose. This station's going to blow to bits in ten minutes."

"Clear," said Tori.

Zed went ahead through the lock. Twice he stopped and leaned on the wall. Tori had *Lamia*'s door up; she was standing at the door, anesthetic spray in her hand. Her face paled as Zed walked in. "Sweet mother," she said, and aimed the spray. As it hit the charred flesh, Zed sobbed and nearly fell. Dana caught him under the armpits, and half dragged the Net commander to the lowest of a three-tiered bunk. He put Zed into it. He felt the jog as the lock tube coiled into place, and scrambled to the navigator's chair. "Five minutes," said Tori. "Damn it, if a hunk of that thing hits me it'll slice the hull like cheese. If only we could Jump—" But they couldn't Jump. Unlike some planets, Chabad was not in a hyperspace current. Dana had no idea what happened to ships that tried to use the Drive when not congruent to a current; nobody did. If anyone had tried it, they had not come back from wherever they had gone.

"Accelerating," Lamonica said. "Hold tight!" Dana took a deep breath. Tori flashed him a grin. He let it halfway out. The ship hummed. He was pressed into the seat, harder, harder, his muscles began to scream—Tori was pushing the ship to the limit. Ten gees. He watched the gauge climb. Twelve gees. Fifteen gees. The blood began to drain from his head and settled in his feet. If the thrust exceeded fifteen gees, he would certainly black out. He saw red: There goes a capillary, he thought.

The thrust stayed at fifteen gees for fifteen seconds, until the numbers on the compscreen said they were a quarter of the distance back to the planet. Then Tori slowed to one gee thrust. She used the compensator to reduce the gravity to three-fourths gee. Dana stretched as the pressure subsided. "Better check your patient," Tori warned.

"Stars." He hurried to Zed's bunk. The Net commander's eyes were open. Blood trickled from his mouth, but he was conscious. Grabbing a cloth, Dana wiped the blood away.

"Bad?" he said. "You want more anesthetic? A pill?"

"No," said Zed. He sat, very slowly. Dana marveled at his strength. "I. Just. Bit. My. Tongue."

Across the room, Tori said, "LandingPort Station, this is *Lamia*. Tell Chabad our mission's completed and we're on our way home."

"Clear, Starcaptain. Congratulations on your success. We'll notify—" The voice broke off into a muttered oath.

A second voice, thinned with awe and incredulity, said, "Jesus god."

Tori punched the unit to silence. She said, "I guess we know what that was."

Tori set course for the Abanat Main Landingport.

There was nothing for Dana to do. He went to the food unit for water and a food bar. Glancing at the silver-and-blue suited figure in the bottom bunk of the right-hand tier, he raised his voice. "Zed? Do you want a narcotic?" *Lamia's* medikit, like the kit of any MPL starship, was equipped with several different narcotics.

"No."

Dana walked to the bunk. Zed was paper-white. His facial muscles twitched. Fluid dripped from his hands. The sheet was damp. His pupils were pinpoints; pain lines like gullies ran from the corners of his mouth. It was easier to look at his face than at the fingers that stuck out from his wrists like sticks out of a fire, coated thickly with hardened spray. His eyes were dull. Suddenly his brows went up. He croaked. "Make. You. Feel. Good?"

"No!"

Zed's eyes closed. His body heaved. Eyes locked shut, he said, "Make. Call. For. Me."

"What call?"

"To Tam Orion. Message to—Sai Thomas. Medic. Main Clinic. Tell her—" he fought to breathe, sucked in air, continued, "bring burn trauma team. Get Ja. Narayan. Name's important. Narayan. Surgeon."

"Why?" asked Dana.

Zed said nothing.

"If you want me to call, tell me why."

The air hissed through Zed's teeth. His face contorted harshly. *Make you feel good?* The mocking question teased Dana's mind. The stench of burned flesh pervaded the cabin like the smell of some drug. He had hoped to see Zed Yago thwarted; he had not expected to see him helpless and hurting. It did not make him feel good. It made him want to be sick. He looked at the wall clock. Tam Orion could be home in bed. The clock was calibrated in Standard. He was tired. He walked to the navigator's chair, working it out: it was not quite dawn over Abanat.

Chabad bulged in the vision screen. He switched to

audio communications. "Abanat Flight Tower Control, this is *Lamia,* MPL48; home registry, Nexus; pilot and owner, Starcaptain Tori Lamonica; navigator, Starcaptain Dana Ikoro; passenger, Zed Yago. Permission to berth?"

"Permission granted, Starcaptains. We've been expecting you to call."

"Thank you, Flight Tower. Request for personal communication to be delivered to chief pilot Tam Orion from Zed Yago. This is urgent. Message to be relayed to medic Sai Thomas at the Abanat Main Clinic. Please bring a burn trauma team to the Landingport to meet us, and a surgeon named Ja Narayan. This communication's important, Control."

"Clear, Starcaptain. It will be delivered. Please keep your computer locked in."

"Bitchin' Control," said Tori.

Dana rubbed his eyes. His head felt thick. With longing, he thought about ten hours' sleep. He went back to Zed's bunk. The burned man had not moved. As Dana leaned over him, his eyes opened. "I made your call," Dana said.

Zed's mouth flickered in what might have been a smile.

Tori brought *Lamia* in like a snowflake on a breeze. As they settled into the black, powdery surface of the Flight Field, the com-unit said stridently, "*Lamia,* this is Port Administration. We understand you have a casualty in there. We have a medical team standing by. Please open up."

Dana answered, "Administration, we've called our own medical team. We're not opening up till it arrives."

"We have authority to examine your casualty!"

Tori said, "This is Starcaptain Lamonica. Stuff your authority up your nose."

Dana rubbed his arm. He had forgotten all about the slave mark. He walked to the bunk. "Zed?" he said.

"Uh."

"How do I get this tattoo off my arm?"

"Gel. Sai. Will. Know." He lifted his head to stare at Dana. "Need." His face spasmed. "Water."

Dana brought him a cup of water, and held it to Zed's lips so that the handless man could drink it.

A woman's voice said, "*Lamia,* this is Sai Thomas.

Sorry it took me so long; first they had to find me and then they had to wake me up. You have a patient for me?"

"Ja. Narayan," said Zed.

Dana said, "We do, Medic. Is Ja Narayan with you?"

"Ja's coming from home."

Dana looked at Zed, who nodded. "I guess we can open up."

Tori released the doorseal. People swarmed in. They were not familiar with starships. They climbed up awkwardly over the doorlip, not knowing what the ceiling bar was for. Tori Lamonica simply pointed toward the bunk. Zed said, "Hello, Sai." The woman saw his hands and drew her breath in sharply. Then she started giving orders. The team stuck a needle in Zed's arm and attached a tube and bottle to it. They coated his hands with white foam. They slapped gel ampules on his neck and both his arms. They brought in a stretcher and put him on it.

One medic left the ship and came back. She approached the Hypers. "One of you needs a slave tattoo removed?" she inquired.

Dana tried to roll up his sleeve and discovered that he still had the pressure suit on. He took it off. The medic spread gel from a tube over the tattoo. It was cool. She said, "Let it harden. In about six hours you can peel it off and the tattoo will be gone. With your skin pigmentation, there should be no scar."

A long hand reached over the doorlip. A rangy body leaped for the ceiling bar. Dana stared at the stranger who swung himself onto *Lamia* like a rope uncoiling. A voice said in his mind, *So you're Dana Ikoro. Thank you for taking care of my friend. I'm Chief Pilot Orion.* Dana opened his mouth and then closed it. He turned to Tori. "Chief Pilot Orion: this is Starcaptain Tori Lamonica." Tori held her hand out. The tall man did not take it, but suddenly she smiled. With quick steps, Orion went to Zed's bunk and loomed at the backs of the laboring medics.

The medics muttered at each other, and formed into a procession directed by Sai Thomas. They were taking Zed through the door. Tam Orion stopped them by standing in the doorway. "Please move," said Sai Thomas.

"Wait." Zed had opened his eyes. "Tam."

Orion folded his thighs until his face was on a level with Zed's head. "Hurt?"

Zed breathed out. "Not. Too. Bad."

"Help?"

"Nothing. You. Can. Do."

Sai Thomas said roughly, "The faster we get you to the Clinic, Zed the sooner Ja can get to work on your hands."

"Yes," said Zed. He glanced at Tori Lamonica. "Tools," he said. "Replace. Proper."

Tam Orion made a gesture of assent and stood aside. *Did you understand that?* he said. *Zed's asked me to replace the equipment you lost effecting his rescue.*

Damn him, Dana thought, we want nothing from him! But his answer did not seem to reach Orion at all, and Lamonica, predictably, was accepting the offer with delight.

Have a good trip home, Captains, the chief pilot said. He swung out of the ship. Dana watched the medics maneuver Zed's stretcher. The smell of the foam and of burned flesh lingered in the cabin. A Landingport mechanic delivered a heap of tools through the door, and went away. Dana munched on a food bar. His head was cotton. He returned to the navigator's chair and stared at the numbers bouncing on the compscreens. "I want to make a direct-line call."

Tori was watching the numbers. "Don't let it take too long. I want to get out of here."

He called Rhani. She answered instantly. "You look like I feel," he said. There was little color in her face; it was the white of dried bone.

He said, "Darien Riis was a cop, pointed at Zed by Michel A-Rae. He decided he could break you if he could take Zed away. Darien killed Jo Leiakanawa and blew up the Net. She had strong anti-slavery feelings. Zed shot her with a cutting laser. He's at the Abanat Clinic in the care of a medic named Sai Thomas and a surgeon named Narayan. I'm leaving on *Lamia.*"

She said, "They called from LandingPort Station. They told me he was alive." Her eyes were dark with exhaustion. "I'm grateful to you."

"We had an agreement."

She reached to him, touched the screen, and drew the
hand back. Her shoulders straightened. "Good-bye, Starcaptain."

Inexplicably, it hurt that she should choose to call him
that. He wondered what her waiting had been like.
LandingPort Station would have told her that the Net was
gone, blown to dust. Now she knew that she had Zed back
again; Dana wondered what she thought of the price.
"Rhani—"

Her voice wavered. "Starcaptain?"

"Please don't call me that."

Her face came a little closer to the screen; he could see
her weeping. "Good-bye, Dana. Go away now. Don't
come back to Chabad. I wish you good fortune. Live on a
green and pleasant world with a lover who treats you
better than this one." She switched off. Dana rested his
head against the chair back. He felt as if someone had just
punched him in the heart."

Tori shook him roughly. "Go lie down."

He pointed at the controls. "What about. . . ?"

"Sweet mother, you think I can't fly this ship by myself?
Get into a bunk."

"Where are we going?"

"To Nexus. Where else? Unless there's somewhere you
want me to stop."

Dana considered Pellin. It was a green and pleasant
world. His family would be pleased to see him. But he
was not ready to go world-bound. "Nexus."

"Go lie down."

He levered his head up. It weighed a ton. "No."

"As you please," said Tori. She talked to the Flight
Tower. The gel warmed on Dana's upper arm. Sleepily,
he realized that Lamonica was swearing into the com-
unit; that something, somewhere, had gone wrong.

"What is it?" he said.

"Fucking cops." Lamonica twirled the pilot's chair
around to face him. "We're grounded, man."

"Why?"

"Everybody's grounded, until they find that son-of-a-
bitch who started this, A-Rae." She mimicked the Flight
Tower's impersonal voice. *"All ve-hi-cles can-cel lift-off
pro-ce-dures."* She chuckled. "The shuttleship pilots are

going crazy. They've all got full passenger loads to deliver to the moon."

"When can we take off?" Dana said.

"Who knows?" She began to mutter the lift-off litany in reverse.

A voice from the com-line said, "*Lamia,* are you there? Stand by for boarding."

"What?" Tori slammed her hand on the chair arm. "Who's boarding my ship?"

"Drug Detail, Hyperspace Police," intoned the com-unit.

Dana sat fully up in the chair. His left arm had gone to sleep, and he shook it. A trickle of alarm raced through his nervous system. "Hey," he said. "Make sure you see a boarding pass."

The com-unit crackled with a different voice. "*Lamia,* this is the Hyperspace Police, Drug Detail, Captain Graeme. We request permission to board."

"Do I have a choice?" Tori said. She palmed the door switch. The starship's door shot up. A hand found the ceiling bar, another, another—bemused, Dana watched as four people in black-and-silver uniforms swung into the little starship.

"I want to see a pass," Tori said, advancing toward them.

A man with a communicator in his hand extended a sheet of paper toward her. The other three were standing at near-attention, close to the starship's door. Two hands gripped the ceiling bar and, with a smooth acrobatic heave, a fifth person entered the ship. The Hype cops stiffened. The newcomer glanced at each of them as she came upright and, stepping forward, extended a hand to Tori Lamonica. "Sorry for the delay, Starcaptain," she said. "Cat Graeme, Hyperspace Police."

At first glance, Dana thought she was the plainest woman he had ever seen. She wore the black uniform with no special grace. Her hair was dusky and coarse, her skin weathered, and her hands were lumpy and callused, as if she had once spent a long time doing heavy manual labor. She had a jagged scar on her right temple. Her eyes were blue. She was short and tough and, in the center of the MPL-class starship, she looked immovable.

"Starcaptain Dana Ikoro," she said.

Wearily Dana levered himself from his chair. "That's me," he said.

"The drug detail of the Hyperspace Police respectfully requests your cooperation."

Dana sighed. He wanted, very badly, to tell this woman to do something anatomically impossible with a black hole. "What kind of cooperation?" he said.

"Dull, boring work," she said. "We want you to sit in front of a machine and tell it what happened on the Sardonyx Net, before it blew up."

He leaned on the chair back. "What if I don't want to help?" he said.

She said, "Come on, Starcaptain. You're tired and you want to go home, but you're also not a child. We need that testimony. You're the only person who can give it."

"Ask Zed Yago," Dana said.

Graeme shook her head. Dana decided that her nose had been broken at least once. It leaned to the right. "Zed Yago's in Main Clinic, and can't talk to us. And might not, even if he were conscious."

Dana remembered, unwillingly, the sight and smell of Zed's seared hands. The memory made his stomach ache. "All right," he said. "Since I can't get out of here anyway." He yawned. "Tori—"

She nodded at him. "It's been fun," she said. "Let's do it again sometime." She slid into the pilot's chair.

"Let's not," Dana said. Cat Graeme gestured to the open door. Two of the cops preceded him; the others followed. The dark night was cold, but the lights over the Flight Field brightened it to day. Dana hesitated at the doorlip. *I thought I was going home. . . .* Leaning forward, he closed his palms around the cool metal of the ceiling bar.

In the Abanat Clinic, Zed Yago floated over a white bed in a silent room, gazing down at the form of a man with badly burned hands.

Until he realized that he was disembodied and invisible, it had disturbed him that the man in the bed could not or did not seem to see him. But then, no one else saw him either; not the medics or the guards in their blue-and-silver uniforms who stood near the bed. Two people entered the room, and he recognized them as Sai Thomas and Ja Narayan. They spoke to the man with the burned hands.

"I can do it," said the surgeon. "Medically it's simple; the light beam did most of the work for us. Your circulation below the elbow is fine. There's no infection. I can scrape the seared bone clean and graft new tissue in after I set the claw mechanism in place. CTD has an excellent tissue match."

Sai Thomas said, "Zed, are you sure you want this?"

"I'm sure," said the man on the bed. I'm sure, whispered Zed Yago.

He could see by the lines around her eyes that she wasn't happy. Don't worry, he said to reassure her, forgetting that he was disembodied and that she couldn't hear him. He wanted to tell her that he had been crazy, but also that he was sane again, as sane as he was ever going to get. In another time and on another world, they might say that he had been bewitched.

"Don't worry," said the man in the bed.

"I'll tell Yukiko," said Sai Thomas. The medics left. Zed Yago climbed back into his body. It took a certain effort to stay there. He could not feel anything. The slack body had no more hold on him than a shell. He wondered what Ja Narayan would think if he knew that he was not simply inserting fingerclaws into those hands, but that he was reattaching a soul.

They put him entirely out for the surgery. As he felt himself sink into chemical oblivion, Zed regretted that he could not float above the table to watch the repair. Then he slept. He woke in Recovery, woozy and dry-mouthed, but whole, himself. He tried to move the reconstructed fingers within the plaster of the healing gel. He couldn't tell if they obeyed him.

A woman came to stand at the edge of the bed. It was Rhani. They had dressed her in green but he knew her. He wondered if Rhani was angry at him. There was a reason why she might be, though he could not remember what it was. His throat hurt; he had to whisper. "Rhani-ka."

"Zed-ka," she said.

A second figure in green stepped forward with a cloth and held it for him to suck. Water trickled into his throat.

"The Net—" he said.

"I know," she said, "I know. Don't worry about it. I have other plans. I'll tell you about them when you're stronger."

He wanted to tell her that he was no longer crazy. "I'll come back tomorrow," she told him. "They don't want me to stay now. Get well, Zed-ka." She mimed a kiss as she went through the door. Intense joy, like a bright light, filled Zed's mind. He groaned.

The medic stepped forward, alarmed. "Are you in pain?"

"No. Oh, no. I'm happy," Zed Yago said.

Chapter Twenty-One

In the anteroom of Recovery, Rhani Yago spoke with Ja Narayan. "He knew me," she said. "He spoke to me."

The little surgeon was amused. His dark eyes glittered. "Certainly he knew you, Domna, there's nothing wrong with his brain. He'll be out of bed tomorrow; in four days you can take him home."

"Thank you," Rhani said. "Please send your bill to me at the Yago estate outside Abanat."

"As you wish," he said.

"I wish," said Rhani. She glanced at the pilot of the hired bubble, who had been waiting for her all this time. She had called Landingport East and rented his services just before she received Dana Ikoro's call. "Thank you," she said, "I appreciate your help."

The boy—he was gangling and awkward and seemed very young—smiled diffidently. "You're welcome, ma'am." He had a pleasant drawling voice. "I hope the commander's better soon."

Rhani said, "My brother is going to be all right."

"That's good. Do you want to go home now, ma'am?"

Yes, Rhani thought. "No," she said. "Thank you. If I need you again, I'll call Landingport East." She watched him walk away down the curving hall. In a little while she followed him along the route they had told her to take: Recovery to CTD, CTD to Outpatient, Outpatient to the street. Twice she passed people in blue-and-silver uniforms. The Clinic staff had told her that soon after Zed arrived they had begun to appear, and she wondered who had called them and how they had known.

In Outpatient she saw a PINsheet stand. "YAGO NET DESTROYED!" the headlines cried. A few of the people in the waiting room recognized her; she could tell by the way their eyes seemed to fasten on her face, and by the way they then looked quickly aside. No one spoke to her: she felt invisible, a ghost. Someone touched her shoulder; she turned, and found Ferris Dur beside her. The unexpectedness of it shocked her momentarily from her exhausted state. "Ferris, what are you doing here?" she said.

He flinched as if she had hit him. He was wearing red-and-gold and in the utilitarian Clinic he seemed completely out of place.

"I heard," he said. "About the Net, and your brother. I came to see if I could help."

"But it's dawn," Rhani said. Light stained the windows of the corridor.

"I know," he said. "Rhani—do you have a place to stay?"

Rhani blinked. She hadn't thought about it. She did not want to go to the Kyneths' again. "A hotel, I suppose," she said.

"Amid all those tourists?" he said, with one of his rare flashes of humor. "I thought—I hoped—I offered you my house." His fingers tugged at each other.

Rhani pictured Dur House: the heavy, stone walls, the odd melange of furnishings, half Domna Sam's tastes, half her son's. . . . She sighed. Her bones hurt. "Would I have to sleep in that damned gold bed?" she said.

Eagerly he said, "No! I have a room—I made it—" He stumbled over the words and stopped. "I won't touch you, if that's what you're thinking," he said in a low, miserable tone.

A medic walked by them, wheeling a tray filled with instruments. Well, Rhani thought, I can't sleep here. . . . "All right, Ferris. I accept your hospitality. Thank you," she said.

His heavy-boned face beamed. "I brought a bubble," he said. With infinite care, as if she were made of crystal or glass, something that might shiver apart at his touch, he cupped his hand beneath her arm.

They walked to the Clinic hangars. A bubble with the raised axe emblem on the door sat waiting. As they went toward it, a second bubble spiraled from the northwest toward the hangar. It landed, and six more uniformed Net crew members climbed from it. They looked grim. They strode toward the Outpatient entrance. "Wait," Rhani said over her shoulder to Ferris, and moved to intercept them.

They turned at her approach, and she saw one woman pull a small cylinder from a pocket. It looked suspiciously like the miniature stun gun her brother had brought her. But that, Rhani thought, was very long ago. She wondered where it was. *Gone with my house.* "Domna Rhani," said the woman. They closed in about her. They were all taller than she was and it was like being surrounded by steel columns. "How is the commander? Is he going to recover?"

"Yes," Rhani said. "Thank you."

"Can we help you?"

"No. No, I'm fine. I just wanted to know why you're here."

"We're guarding the commander," said the woman grimly.

"Why?"

"That cop—A-Rae," the woman said. "He's still somewhere in the city. They've grounded all flights from the Landingport until he's found. Except for us, of course." She jerked her thumb at the bubble they had come in. "We've got special clearance."

"From whom?" Rhani said. "How did you know?"

"Tam Orion," said one of the men. "He called us. Woke me from sleep."

The woman snorted. "*I* wasn't sleeping." She grinned, and patted Rhani's arm. "Don't worry, Domna. No one'll get to the commander while he's in this place."

"And if they try," the other woman said, "too bad. I'd like to get my hands on the people who killed Jo Leiakanawa."

"I see," Rhani said. "Thank you." She swallowed. They murmured reassuring noises at her as they walked away. She went back to Ferris, wondering how Tam Orion could have called them all when he never spoke,

and then remembering that he was a telepath. Odd, she
hadn't known that until Dana told her. Dana—was he still
on Chabad, then? Perhaps he had gotten away before
they grounded the flights.

She climbed into Ferris' bubble and closed her eyes. A
moment later he was shaking her awake. "Rhani, we're
here," he said. She rubbed her face and gazed at the
shadowy hangar. I wonder if I'm doing something stupid,
she thought. Maybe I should have gone to the Kyneths'.

But once within the walls of Dur House, she began to
feel, not less tired, but more awake, and she recognized
the artificial clarity of that state beyond sleep. Her eyes
burned, gritty with hours of wakefulness, and her clothes
were sticky with sweat. "I would like a wash," she said to
Ferris.

"This way," he said, guiding her along the upstairs
hallway. Noises drifted up from the kitchen below;
someone dropped a pot. He opened a door. "Here.
Look." He pushed her gently into the doorway. Rhani
gasped.

The room was like nothing she had ever seen in the
somber depths of Dur House. The walls were blue. The
bed, which was low and uncanopied, was covered with a
blue-and-white spread. A white kerit fur rug graced the
floor. One window looked south, another west, and
through its clear pane she saw the gleam of sunrise on the
Abanat ice. A wooden chair with curved runners at the
base of its legs stood beside the window. "What's that?"
she said.

"It's called a rocking chair. I thought you might like it,"
Ferris said.

Walking to it, Rhani pushed tentatively at the back.
The chair rocked slowly back and forth. It was a soothing
motion—good for the baby, she thought. Then the sense
of Ferris' words penetrated. She said, "You thought *I*
might like it? You brought it here, for me?"

He nodded, and his hands plucked at the gold buttons
on his robe. "Yes. When I first thought, maybe—about
the marriage, you know—I asked people what your room
at the estate was like, people who had been there, I mean.
I know you love the estate. I wanted to make you a place
where you would be comfortable."

Rhani said, "You made this room for me." He nodded

again. "How long ago?"

"A while. Since—since my mother got sick. She said you were more like a daughter to her than I was like a son. That's when I thought of asking you to marry me." He bit his lower lip, and said in a low voice, "Advocate Wu spoke to me. She told me I'd been stupid and unfair because I didn't tell you the truth about not being the head of the Family."

Rhani scowled. Christina had no business doing that, she thought, annoyed. "It wasn't stupid," she said. "After all, you are Ferris Dur, *Domni* Ferris Dur, and even if you don't make all the decisions for it, you are still head of your Family." For what it's worth, she thought. At least Domna Sam had the sense not to take that away from him. She gazed at the room, astonished at the care with which it had been furnished. The bed's coverlet was apton and silk, and the curtains were white gauze. The bed's headboard was white, wooden, with three sliding shelves.

Someone told him a great deal about my room, she thought. "Ferris, who did you ask to help you make this room?"

"Are you angry?" he asked.

Sweet mother. . . . "No," Rhani said, "I'm not angry. I think it's beautiful."

He licked his lips. "Clare helped."

"Clare Brion?"

He nodded. "And Aliza Kyneth, a little. Though she didn't understand why I wanted to know what your room was like. I was afraid to tell her. She probably thought me a nuisance. *Her* children are all clever."

Rhani said, "This is better than clever, Ferris. This is kind." Releasing her hold on the rocking chair, she walked to him, stretched to tiptoe, and kissed his cheek. "So kind that I think I'd like to stay here a little while, until Zed is out of the Clinic, at least. May I do that?"

Ferris' mouth went slack with astonishment. Then, straightening, he said, "Domna, I am honored."

"I am only Rhani," Rhani said. She glanced toward the closet, wondering if there were clothes in it. She was willing to bet there were, and that they were her size. She wondered if the washroom contained a blue-and-cream-tiled shower stall. "Is there a com-unit in this room?"

"I can have one installed," said Ferris. "Shall I?"

"Please," she said. She needed to talk to Christina Wu, and Loras U-Ellen if he would talk to her, she didn't know, he might be still hiding from Michel A-Rae, and, if Christina approved, she would then call Tak Rafael. . . .

She blinked as the door slid closed. Ferris had left with such uncharacteristic delicacy that she hadn't heard him. Kicking her shoes off, she curled her toes in the kerit fur. To her left, the metallic grate of the intercom gleamed in the azure wall. In the washroom, her favorite soap sat on the shelf beside a replica of the ivory brush Zed had brought her at the close of one Net circuit. It had come, she thought, from Sabado.

She did not want to think about the Net. As she took off her clothes, she admired the verisimilitude of the two chambers. So much time spent on fantasy. . . . She leaned close to the round mirror and saw that the stress of the last few weeks had bestowed upon her a legacy of threadlike lines.

I'm getting older, she thought. Soon I'll look like my mother.

The thought dismayed her. She didn't want to look like Isobel. I won't! she said to the doppelgänger in the mirror. Naked, she laid both hands on her abdomen. It didn't feel any different. I'm pregnant, she told the mirror, I'm going to bear a Starcaptain's child. . . . It was romantic nonsense, the kind that Isobel would have silenced at once, had she heard it. Gazing into the mirror, Rhani rubbed her arms. Remembering her mother gave her chills.

"*Whoever you are,*" she said to the unborn child in her womb, "*I promise you won't grow up as I did, loving and hating your mother as I loved and hated mine, tethered to one world with no chance to escape it. I promise you will have your chance.*"

And, nodding at the mirror—which contained, after all, no image more terrible than herself—she stepped into the blue-and-cream-tiled shower stall.

That night she went to visit Zed in his room in the Clinic, and found him on his feet.

The guards in their blue-and-silver uniforms were huddled together outside the room, speaking softly. They separated as she walked up to them. "Good evening," she said.

"Good evening, Domna," said one, a big man, almost as big as Jo the Skellian.

"How's my brother?" she said.

"Awake." He tilted his head. "And in a foul temper. That little man—the surgeon—won't let him shinny."

"Ah," Rhani said. She tapped on the door. "Zed-ka, it's me."

"Come in!" His eager voice reassured her. She palmed open the door. Zed was standing by the window. His arms and hands were bandaged from elbows to fingertips and beyond. "Rhani," he said. Lifting his swathed left hand, he laid the bandage against her cheek.

It smelled medicinal. Under the yards of gauze, she knew, was new tissue, and under it bone, and under it the intricate mechanics of the permanent claws, all of it layered with several different kinds of regenerative paint. Over the grotesque lump Zed's face looked leaner, warier. *What happened on the Net,* she wanted to ask him. *Darien Riis betrayed you, and you killed her, I know. What has it done to you?* Aloud, she asked, "How do you feel?"

"Impatient," he said. He walked to the bed and back again to her side. Through the window she glimpsed darkness broken by pools of lamplight and, beyond the dark, the shining interior of another wing of the Clinic building. She wondered which it was. "Ja won't let me out of here."

"What do you want to do?" she asked.

His face grew stony. "Find Michel A-Rae," he said.

It was on the tip of her tongue to say, *I know his birth name, Zed-ka.* But the ferocity behind that stony gaze held the words back.

Instead, she said, "I hope the Abanat police can find him, Zed-ka. It looks, by the way, as if the referendum most certainly will not take place."

"Ah." His shoulders hunched. "I'm glad."

"I saw Loras U-Ellen. Dana took me."

"Did you." His whole frame seemed to curve away from her. "We didn't talk about it, did we?"

"No."

"There's a lot we haven't talked about." He wrenched

himself around to face her, bracing his elbows on the bed. His arms dangled between them. He was waiting for her to speak, she realized, for her to question him as she had not been able to question Dana Ikoro, to ask him what Dana would not have known the answers to. . . . Did you love her? Would you truly have left Chabad? She closed her hands to fists and stared at the gleaming door. The tiles made a diamond pattern.

She was not Isobel; she would not punish him. She said, "You haven't asked me where I'm staying."

She heard him exhale. "Where are you staying?"

She looked up, smiling. "At Dur House."

His eyebrows lifted. "Isn't that a trifle premature?"

"Not really," she said. "I'm not going to marry him."

"Tell me."

Rhani explained.

She expected Zed to grow sardonic, to comment in that voice he reserved for emotions that he didn't share, or didn't want to share. Instead, compassion, or at least pity, moved in his eyes for a moment. "The poor bastard," he said. He let his bandaged arms, which had been sticking awkwardly out in front of him, fall to his sides. Rhani wondered how he slept, trussed like that.

"Do you want to keep on staying there?" he said.

"No!" she said, astonished. "No, of course not. The surgeon told me that you'd be released in four days. I thought I'd lease a house."

He smiled. "I'd like that, Rhani-ka."

She wondered what he did when he itched, or needed to sneeze. "Shall I tell you about Loras U-Ellen?" she asked.

"Please do."

She rubbed her chin. "You won't believe this, Zed-ka. He came to Chabad to sell me the dorazine formula."

"Has he got it?" Zed asked.

"No. But he knows someone who has." She explained the historic relationship between Pharmaceuticals, Inc. and The Pharmacy.

Zed was incredulous. "You mean a company based on Enchanter and a criminal consortium based wherever the hell they're based, Sector Vermillion or somewhere, is responsible for the dorazine trade?" He exhaled. "Has been, for fifty years?"

She nodded.

He said softly, "And our mother never knew."

"No," Rhani said.

"They want fifteen million credits—do we have it?"

He had said "we." Rhani smiled. "We have it, Zed-ka. Just." She hesitated, and then said, "Of course, our finances have been complicated by the destruction of the Net."

He said tonelessly, "It must have been insured. Isobel would never have neglected that."

"It was," Rhani said. "But insurance means nothing in the case of uncontrollable accident, malice, fraud, insurrection, or act of god, and the destruction of the Net is three and possibly all five of these."

"What will you do?" he said. "Rebuild the Net?"

"With what?" she said. "No. I have a factory in mind. What capital I can obtain will go to that."

His throat worked. "Rhani, I—"

She could not let him say it. "Zed-ka. . . . I will need your help."

"Help?" He glanced at his hands. "I don't know what use I can be to you, Rhani-ka. I've traded my medical skills for climbing."

She said, "You can only climb so many icebergs, Zed-ka. Our plant, our factory, or farm, is going to need a manager. I thought of you."

"To run a farm?"

"You have experience," she said. "You know how to handle problems. You can give orders. And you know a great deal about drugs."

He looked past her. She wondered what he was seeing. He said, "Will there be slaves at this factory?"

"Of course," she said.

He drew a breath that seemed to drag from the depths of his lungs. "I'll do it," he said.

Rhani wondered what he would have done if she had not offered him this refuge. Looked for victims elsewhere: in the streets, or at the Hyper bar, or in the Abanat houses where sex might be bought. Once she had hoped he would change, but if there had been any chance he might, Darien Riis had destroyed it. She pressed a hand on her abdomen. *I should tell him about the child. But not yet; not until I'm sure that Dana's gone.*

He said, "If we must pay The Pharmacy fifteen million credits, where will we get the capital to build this plant?"

Rhani grinned. "Guess," she said.

He frowned. "Borrow?"

She shook her head. "No. Try again."

He shook his head. "Tell me."

Rhani said, "From the Federation."

"What?"

"It was Christina's suggestion," she said. "She says that the Council should make a formal request of the Federation that it pay reparations to Family Yago for the destruction of the Net."

He half smiled. "That's clever."

"Christina's clever," she agreed. "She says there's legal precedent for it." She did not, she knew, have to underscore the irony inherent in the request. Instead, she said, "Have you heard, Zed-ka? All flights from Main Landingport have been canceled until Michel A-Rae is found."

"I heard," Zed said. "Stars, I wish I could leave," he said. "I hate this room. It's too much like a cell."

"The door opens," she said.

"Yes, but they won't let me leave the wing."

A silence fell. Rhani thought of Binkie, drugged and hating in the Abanat Police Station. She said, "Zed-ka, I never told you, I think, that when I still thought I was going to marry Ferris Dur, I planned to celebrate the occasion by freeing my house slaves."

"No," he said, "you never told me."

She gazed at her hands. "I never told Binkie, either. I told him so much else. If I had—"

"He might not have burned the house."

"Exactly."

Gently he said, "You can't know that, Rhani-ka. 'If you had done—if I had done'—it doesn't work."

And if Michel A-Rae had never been born, she thought, your hands might be whole. She said aloud, "I don't want to live at the estate any more. I think I'd like to stay in Abanat."

"I don't want to go back there," he said.

The door opened. A round man, wearing surgical green, came in. "Excuse me," he said, "but it's time for your medication, Senior, and the Clinic doors are about to be shut. Perhaps your visitor would be willing to come back tomorrow?"

Zed glared, and Rhani saw him transformed into Senior Zed Yago, dealing with an importunate subordinate. Gratingly he said, "This is my sister, Rhani Yago. Rhani, meet my orderly and keeper, Haldane Ku."

Ku inclined his head. "A pleasure to meet you, Domna." His face was cherubic. He seemed unfazed by Zed's tone. "Your brother heals faster than anyone I've ever seen, which is fortunate, because he is an utterly abominable patient."

Zed said, "You would be, too, if you couldn't even wipe your ass without help." He held his bandaged hands in front of him. "I hate being fed."

"I'm sure you do," Ku answered. Strolling to a cabinet, he opened it and began to remove pills from slots. "Domna—"

Rhani said, "I'll go." She went to Zed and leaned to kiss him. "Zed-ka, don't be a bully."

"Excellent advice, but too late," Ku said. He turned, holding water in a plastic cup. Rhani left, knowing that Zed would hate for her to see him helpless. In the cool bright hallway she hesitated. The big guard grinned at her.

"You can't get lost in this place," he said.

The woman on the other side of the door said, "Domna, you aren't walking through the city, are you?"

She had come to the Clinic in the Dur bubble. "No," she answered. "Why?"

The woman leaned toward her. One of her canine teeth was gold, and her face was pitted with tiny round scars. "Same reason we're here."

"Michel A-Rae?" Rhani said. "If he can't get off-planet, he'd be a fool to compound what he's done by attacking me."

The woman shrugged. "Hell, Domna, he is a fool."

The big man said, "You want an escort, you tell us."

"Thank you," Rhani said.

The two guards exchanged glances. The woman said, "Domna, what's going to happen, now that the Net is gone? You building another one?"

"Another Net?" Rhani said. "No." She smiled at them,

understanding their concern. "But don't worry. You haven't lost your jobs."

They both sighed. "Thanks," said the big guard. Inside the room Zed's voice lifted sharply. They both moved reflexively to either side of the door. "Can't help worrying—"

"Kids to feed," said the woman. "Family depends on all the income it can get, you know. Abanat's an expensive town."

"So live somewhere else, it's a big world," said her companion, grinning.

Walking down the corridor to the hub of the Clinic wheel, Rhani wondered if she had been right to refuse an escort. She was sick of being followed. But she knew the woman with the gold tooth had been right: Michel A-Rae was a fool, and therefore unpredictable. As she climbed into the waiting bubble, she said to the pilot, "Did anyone ask you who your passenger is tonight?"

"No, Domna."

"If anyone does, don't tell them."

He looked mildly affronted. "That's Dur business. I don't talk about it."

"If anyone asks you who I am, or who that visitor to Dur House is, tell me."

"Right." The bubble lifted from the ground. The walls were opaque, but through the window strip Rhani saw the city, brilliant with light, laid out decorously below them.

It was beautiful, so beautiful that she almost wanted to weep. The bubble spiraled, and the city seemed to open like a flower. From its center—Auction Place, now dark—ganglia of light flowed in all directions. In the northeast they halted at the foot of the Barrens; in the west at the edge of the bay; but elsewhere they flowed like shining ribbons, and it seemed to Rhani that they, the lights, were the city, not the buildings, which simply reflected the blazing lamps, or the people, whom she could not, at this height, even see. Only the icebergs glowed with a radiance which, though stolen from the city, seemed their own: she leaned into the bubble window to see them pass below her, and the pilot, at first she assumed by chance, banked the turning bubble directly west. She cried out in amazement and delight. Etched upon the southernmost berg was the image of the city. At first she saw no difference between the true city and the imaged one, and then she realized that the city in the ice was upside-down. Fantastic as a dream, the mirage flamed and shimmered and then vanished, leaving the ice swept clean, except for a few orange pockets of reflected light. "What was it?" she whispered.

"An optical illusion," said the pilot. "It only appears at night, and you have to be at just the right angle to see it. I was lucky to get it right away."

I want to see it again, Rhani thought. She almost said it, but the bubble was dropping swiftly, and they were almost to Dur House. "Thank you," she said. "That was wonderful."

"You're welcome, Domna," the pilot said. The bubble dropped into the hangar. The overhead doors came together like hands folding on each other. Rhani stepped from the bubble. Ferris was waiting for her.

"How was your flight? Is your brother better?"

She gazed at him, and, lightly, touched his lips with her hand. "Ssh," she said. "Don't talk." He swallowed, and was silent. Quietly she led the way into the house. As the dazzling memory faded, she sighed. "All right," she said.

"What was it?" he asked.

She shook her head. "An optical illusion," she said. The smells of food made her mouth water suddenly. "Ah, I'm hungry."

"Good. There's dinner waiting for you." He glanced diffidently at her. "And I thought maybe, after you eat, you might want to see my models."

"His ambition is to have a model of all Abanat in the basement of his house. . . ." Rhani smiled. "I'd be delighted, Ferris," she said.

And after I do that, she said to herself as they walked to the dining chamber, I must call Nialle Hamish and get from her the computer code for the file I asked her to establish on Michel U-Anasi.

The models were more interesting than she'd expected them to be.

They spread out across the great expanse of the Dur cellar, set waist-high on a sturdy table, lighted by concealed ceiling lamps, remarkably realistic in construction and materials. Proudly Ferris explained that the streets and buildings and even the tiny fences and the intricate bridges were made of the same materials from which the actual streets and houses and bridges had been made. The parks were green plastic, but the fountains spouted real water. The movalongs moved, and within the replica of Landingport East there was even a miniature bubble that flew. The table was twenty meters square. Vacancies marked the districts not yet finished: the Hyper district had streets but no buildings, and where Main Landingport should have been there was a hole. The center of the city, Auction Place, the Barracks, and the homes of the Families looked complete. "How did you manage the center portion?" Rhani asked.

Ferris said, "I did it first."

"But what if you have to change something?"

"The table comes apart." He touched a button on the wall; humming, the table separated into sections. He touched the button and they joined again.

Rhani squinted, trying to see her house. Looking west from Auction Place she walked two blocks in her mind. . . . There was Founders' Green. She gazed north. "My house?" she said.

He coughed. "I took it out."

Of course, that was why she had been unable to find it. She had not recognized the ruins because she had seen them only once, at night. . . . She took a deep breath. Sweet mother, she thought, this thing is seductive. The brown hill of the Barrens loomed in the northeast. There was a figure on it, the only human figure in the city, as far as she could tell—it was, she realized, a small boy. He held a kite string in his fist. The kite lay fixed above him, dragon head soaring, trapped in a nonexistent breeze.

"Look," Ferris said. He turned out the ceiling lights. Rhani gasped. The lights of the city sprang to fiery life. She gazed upon the city she had seen from the bubble, Abanat in flower, truncated, miniaturized. Only the Abanat ice was missing. "Look up," Ferris said. She gazed up. An illusion of stars drew gleaming whorls on the high ceiling.

Then the lights came back again, and the stars disappeared. "Do you like it?" Ferris said.

Rhani said, "Ferris, it's spectacular. You ought to show

everyone. Give a party, and let everyone see it."

"Oh, no," he said, alarmed. "No, I can't do that. Rhani, promise you won't tell anyone about it. It's private."

"I promise," she said. "But I mean it, Ferris, it's lovely. You did this all yourself, by hand?" He nodded. "I'm impressed."

He said, "My mother used to say it was all I could do, play with toys. I'm no good with real stuff, you see. People and money confuse me."

Rhani said, "I wish I were as good at dealing with people and money as you are at this." She watched as the movalongs moved and the fountain waters played. Bereft of people, the facsimile city appeared cleansed of the emotions that racked it in truth, cleansed of ambition and pain and lust and fear.

"Ferris," she said, knowing that she had to tell him but hating to have to make it plain, "you know I'm not going to marry you after all, don't you?"

"Yes," he said.

"Did Christina Wu tell you that, too?"

He shook his head. "I guessed. Sometimes my guesses are right." For once, his agitated hands remained still.

"I'm sorry," she said. "You've been kind to me. But I can't marry you to be kind back."

"I understand." He passed one hand across his face. "Now what are you going to do? You won't want to stay here."

"When Zed gets out of the Clinic I'll lease a house," she said.

He looked interested. "Really? Where?"

"I don't know yet." Rhani rubbed her chin. "Would you like to help me find a suitable home?"

"I'd be delighted."

"Thank you. I have a favor to ask you, if I may."

"Anything," he said.

"I'd like," Rhani said, "to be able to come and visit this city from time to time; maybe even watch you work on it, if that wouldn't disturb you."

He swallowed. "I'd like that very much," he said. His hand touched the light plate and the room darkened. They walked toward the elevator. At its door, Rhani glanced back. The adumbral city shimmered beneath imaginary starlight.

Alone in her room, Rhani placed a call to Nialle Hamish on her newly installed com-unit.

When she came online and realized who the caller was, the secretary was scandalized. "Domna, you don't want me, you want Domni Imre. Let me get him—"

"No," Rhani said quickly. "No, Nialle, I do want you. Give my love to Imre, if you will, and tell him that I will call him soon? Tell him I insisted on keeping the call short enough to obtain one small piece of information from you."

"Certainly, Dom—Rhani-ka," Nialle said. She smiled, rather shyly. "You see, I didn't forget."

"No one would ever dare accuse you of something so mundane as a memory lapse, Nialle," Rhani said gravely. "Do you recall a request I left for you on the com-unit, before I left Abanat, to obtain all the information you could gather on Michel U-Anasi, an Enchantean? Did you put that query through the network?"

"Of course, Domna," Nialle said.

"What is the code on the file?"

"File R5574. I assumed you would want it restricted—"

"I did. How did you guess that?" Nialle blushed. "You're remarkable. Thank you, Nialle. When you speak to Imre, please give him my love and tell him that I am well and that Zed is healing but should not be disturbed." She terminated the call and punched the file code in eagerly.

Before reading the green lines, she went to the intercom and asked the kitchen slaves to bring her a dish of fruit. When the slave entered, she carried a gold-bordered dish, in which sat three small pears. Rhani said, "Put them down." The slave smiled a dorazine-entranced smile and went away. Rhani touched one of the pears with a finger, remembering. Finally she picked up a pear and bit into it. It was juicy and sweet. She wiped a runnel of juice from her chin, and looked at the file. It seemed scanty, until she remembered that Michel U-Anasi had changed his name when he turned eighteen.

He had been born in the town of Loge, on South Continent on Enchanter; his I.D. number was

SC33L8Y32-9914. He had attended four schools. Rhani did not bother to read the names. At sixteen he entered the Yalow Clinic and began medic training; first course of study complete, he had applied for a position on the Yago Net. He was rejected for the job. Rhani bit hard on the pear. The reasons for the rejection had to do with the psychological evaluation made on all job applicants by the Net personnel. Could that have been it? she thought. But ridiculous—no one blows up a starship because nine years back he was refused a job. She nibbled another bit of pear and entered a request for the details of the psychological examination. Lines flashed on the screen. "DISASSOCIATIVE EROTIC REACTIONS TO OTHER-INFLICTED NEGATIVE STIMULI, TENDENCY TO NONCONSENSUAL VICTIMIZATION, RÉAGE'S TEST REACTIONS UNDER FOURTH PERCENTILE. . . ."

"What the hell is this?" she said.

But she had seen another such test result once, by accident. She laid the pear down. She had been scanning the psychological profiles of the high echelon Net staff when she had, unexpectedly, come upon her brother's. Some of the words were different, but the conclusions, she thought, the conclusions appeared to be the same. . . .

She rose. Michel U-Anasi, eighteen, a trained orderly, had probably been drawn to the Net because it presented him with certain sexual opportunities that he could find nowhere else. Cell interiors were monitored, but no one troubled to observe a medic on rounds. Most of the slaves he might choose for his particular attentions would probably be too drugged to feel very much. Certainly none of them would complain. But he had been rejected. Rhani could almost feel sorry for him. Had they told him why? He might not have believed it if they had. She thrust her hands into her pockets. Nine years ago Juichi Heika had been commander of the Net, and Zed Yago had been the newly appointed second-in-command to the senior medic.

How widespread had the rumors gotten then? she wondered. She didn't know. But it must have galled Michel U-Anasi beyond sanity when he heard, as he would, that Zed Yago, by all evidence, was a sadist, and of a particular unusual type.

And then the same Zed Yago had been promoted to be senior medic and commander of the Net.

It would have seemed—it was—horribly unfair. She admitted it to herself. If Zed had not been a Yago—but it was silly to speculate on might-have-beens. She wondered if U-Anasi—A-Rae, rather—knew what he was. His moral passions were an obvious screen. But she knew, because she had watched her brother, how hard it was to be a productive member of a society where your deepest erotic responses were judged to be violently antisocial. Of course A-Rae hated the Net. And his family, which owned a percentage of the illegal trade that supported the Net, he had to hate them, too. She swallowed. The taste of the pear was bitter in her throat. It made sense, now, that A-Rae had aimed his hatred at Zed. He wanted to be Zed, to have what Zed Yago had. Failing that, he would hate Zed. It was undoubtedly easier for him to despise Zed Yago than it was for him to despise himself.

Nevertheless—she shook her head, angry. None of this excused him. She thought of Amri, dying in a burning house, of Jo Leiakanawa, of the wanton destruction of the Net. Even *she,* Darien Riis, did not deserve being manipulated into a criminal act. What would A-Rae do when he realized that he could not get out of the city? Suicide? She didn't think so. Throw himself on the mercy of the family he'd rejected? She was sure they would want nothing to do with him. As a Federation official, he would probably demand to be sent to Nexus for trial. She scowled. That wasn't fair. What he'd done, he'd done on Chabad. Why should Federation officials be exempt from penalties that other citizens were subject to? Striding to the com-unit, she erased the file from the screen. Then, taking pen and paper from the headboard of the bed, she sat at the desk Ferris Dur had made her and began to draft a letter to the Federation, describing the damage done to Chabad and Family Yago by A-Rae's acts. Copies of the draft would go to Ferris, Imre, Theo Levos, and Christina.

And, as part of the reparations, she decided, she would ask that Michel A-Rae be remanded for trial and—assuming conviction—sentenced to the world whose inhabitants he had manipulated, lied to, and killed.

Chapter Twenty-Two

Dana Ikoro was drunk.

He could not remember the last time he'd been drunk, though he remembered, dimly, where—he'd been in Liathera's, or Rin's, anyway, in some Hyper bar on Nexus. Now he was on Chabad, in The Green Dancer, and he wanted very badly to be on Nexus. The Dancer was jammed, sweating bodies pushed against each other, and Rose and Amber were working so fast that he could not see their hands as they poured—but then, in his present state, everything seemed blurry to him. He wondered why his head hurt. It's the liquor, he thought, and giggled at the exquisitely crafted joke.

Two-thirds of the Hypers on Chabad were in the bar tonight, and another third roamed the streets outside, drinking, smoking, yelling to their friends, getting sick beneath the jeweled street lights. Tori Lamonica was sitting at the corner of the bar. She saw him watching her and raised her glass. Juno and Lyn were quarreling; Lyn's whispered comments could not be overheard, but Juno's bellows, few of them intelligible, echoed throughout the bar. You try talking, Dana told himself. I bet you're not so fucking intelligible.

He had spent two days—two entire days, it seemed to him now, though sober he knew that it had been about four hours each day—talking to a machine in the Abanat Police Station. For another hour each day he had been permitted to talk to a human. He had described to the machine everything that had happened to him on Chabad that had involved Michel A-Rae. Some of it was embarrassing, even humiliating. Some of it he had refused to talk about: he was not going to tell even a Chabadese computer that he had slept with Rhani Yago. The first night they had let him sleep in the police station and he had not been able to get drunk. But tonight he had insisted on leaving, though they'd made him promise to come back in the morning to answer whatever questions human or machine had managed to come up with during the night.

He was drunk because he wanted to leave Chabad so

badly that if he were not drunk, he would be weeping. You don't have to weep, you're a fucking hero, he reminded himself. You saved Zed Yago's life—tried to save Jo Leiakanawa's, but didn't get there in time. Nevertheless, for the attempt, the loaders from Abanat Landingport, many of whom were Skellians, had been buying him drinks by the score. He'd only downed a third of them and he still couldn't walk. He couldn't feel his ears, either. They seemed—he decided it was the noise—to have gone pleasantly numb.

Bare skin flashed beside him. He looked up: Rose, dressed in net pants and a glittering apton halter that looked as if it had been sewn of fish scales, held her tray in front of his nose.

"Do'wan'drink," he said.

"Look at the tray," she said. "You sot."

Stung at being called a sot, Dana stared at the tray. It steadied—or his vision steadied—enough for him to locate on it two small red pills. "Wazzat?"

"Sobitrex." she said. "Clear your head. Better take them. They're from Tori."

Dana's stomach heaved at the assumption that he could put anything more—even small red pills—inside it. But after a long, long time, his brain told him that it might not be such a bad idea to get sober. He reached for the pills and, after a hazy minute, managed to scoop them into his right palm.

"Thanks," he said.

She laughed at him and went away. The room swayed. The parts of his body seemed to be flying off in all directions and he was afraid he was about to be sick. . . . Cramming the pills in his mouth, he gulped them down without water. "Won't be sick," he muttered into his hands.

"Hey, man, how ya' doin'?" a voice boomed. At first he thought it was Juno come to feed him more drinks, but as he focused, more or less, on the face, he realized this was a stranger.

He said, trying to speak clearly, "Do I know you?"

"No," said the stranger. "Want a drink?"

"No."

"Want to take a walk? You look like you could use one."

Dana doubted he could stand. "Too cold," he objected.

"Hey, it's not cold at all out there," said the man. Somehow he had drawn his chair quite close to Dana's. Now he stood, and Dana felt an arm go around his shoulders and draw him irresistibly to his feet.

Blinking, he tried to see the man who was holding him, but all he could see was a swirling cloak, the kind that Zed Yago wore to parties. . . . The thought of Zed brought a rush of memories to his head—twisted, blackened hands and the smell of burned flesh—and with them a rush of blood. Dizzy, he leaned on his new friend's shoulders and was enveloped by the cloak. It smelled musty, as he tried to tell the man in the cloak how sick he was of Chabad, the heat, the smells, the people. He fumbled for a chair back to steady himself and found that he was holding a wall. Light puddled on the street beside him. His companion said, "Just a little bit more now."

Dana dug in his heels. The cold air burned his nostrils, but it also cleared his head—or maybe that was the Sobitrex. "I don't want to go to bed with you," he warned.

The man laughed. "I don't think I asked you."

"Where the hell are we going?" Dana said. He grabbed at the stranger's cloak. "Just stand still." The man stopped. Dana looked around. The Landingport, with its corona of light, was behind them. "This isn't where I'm staying," Dana said, though he had no idea where he was going to stay that night. He had hoped to sleep on some drinking companion's floor. But this sudden excursion was making him uneasy. He turned in a circle, trying to place himself. The street looked familiar. He thought perhaps the Abanat Police Station was nearby, two or three blocks to the north. "Are you a cop?" he said.

The man grinned. He wore a black pearl earring in his left ear. "You just said the password, Starcaptain." He clapped Dana on the side of the neck with one hand. It stung.

"Hey!" Dana took a step away from him. "You—" The street reeled. His breath streamed away in front of him in a plume of smoke, infinitely long. . . . I'm falling, he thought. The stranger caught him and slung him over his back with contemptuous ease.

"Relax, man, and don't skop it, it'll wear off soon." His

steps jolted Dana's belt against his stomach. He spoke to the air. "One fish, caught. No trouble. It'd be nice if someone could meet me at the corner and help me bring him in."

They carried Dana into a house and dumped him on a bed. They strapped him to it: he fought them, feeling the drug they had given him fading and the Sobitrex taking hold. He got in several effective strikes before the big man who'd carried him to the house punched him in the stomach. As he was struggling not to be sick, they pulled the straps tight, opened the window over his head, and left him alone. As he sobered, Dana realized that he did know the man who'd carried him in—he had been wearing a black-and-silver uniform, and had been standing at Michel A-Rae's right shoulder the day of the Auction.

That told him where he was. A sour taste filled his throat; without volition, he leaned as far as he could over the side of the bed—it was a cot, really—and vomited. What the hell did they want from him? he thought. That they had deliberately sought him out in the bar, he had no doubt. Information? Revenge? He had saved Zed Yago's life; he wondered if they knew that he had killed Darien Riis. He had not, really—Zed's hand had held the laser—but it was his laser. The wind blew through the window, chilling him so that he shook, and the foul scent of the mess he'd made filled the little space.

It was near dawn when they finally returned to the room. The wind had lessened, and though it was still cold, the night had paled to a deep, hard-edged blue. The door banged open and two men and a woman walked in. Dana knew the woman at once; he had kicked a broken bottle out of her hand. She was carrying a stun gun. The two men were the man who had tricked him in the bar and Michel A-Rae. The big man—he was very dark, with hair that stood out from his head in great coiled springs—yanked the straps loose and pulled Dana to his feet in one fluid motion. "Pig," he said.

"Pig yourself," Dana answered. The dark man hit him, a slap that reeled him off his feet. He landed in a heap against the opposite wall.

"Get that out of here," A-Rae said, pointing his chin toward the cot. The big man walked to it, folded the soiled mattress in two, and carried it through the door. When he returned he held a mop. He pointed the mop at the crusted vomit and turned it on: it coughed and then sucked the dried stuff up, leaving no trace except a stain. The big man held the mop in one hand and the cot frame in the other and edged out.

Michel A-Rae sauntered to Dana's corner. His black-and-silver uniform was soiled, and his eyes looked wild. Dana tensed. "Better not," the woman with the gun said tersely. Dana glanced at her; she was pointing the gun directly at him. "It's set on lethal," she warned.

Dana opened his hands. Slowly he tried to ease himself to a more comfortable position on the floor.

"Look at me," said Michel A-Rae.

Startled, Dana looked. A-Rae took a step forward, swung his right foot, and kicked Dana hard in the side.

Dana gasped and bent over. "What the hell was that for?" he said. He breathed shallowly. His ribs ached with each breath. He tried to gather his feet together.

"Better not," said the woman with the gun. She was watching him, lips parted, and there was no mercy in her eyes.

"Every move I made on this world," A-Rae said, "you've been in my way."

"Bullshit," Dana said. And twisted, not soon enough. A-Rae's kick slammed into his ribs. He bent over, hugging himself. Damn it, he thought, that's the wrong answer, it's always the wrong answer, you fool. . . . He wondered if any answer was the right answer. He had the terrible feeling that what Michel A-Rae most wanted to do in the world was to kick him slowly to death.

Maybe not. If he does it again I'll go for him, gun or no gun, Dana thought. "Why do you say that?" he whispered, because his ribs ached too much for him to speak normally.

"The bomb," said A-Rae. "You were there. The attack in the street, you were there. The house—" he paused. "You had nothing to do with that," he said grudgingly. "But on the Net—" his eyes gleamed hotly. "You killed Darien. I could kill you, just for that."

"Don't kill me," Dana whispered.

It was begging, of course. But honor no longer troubled him: if it seemed expedient, he would beg. He watched A-

Rae's righteous fury increase, like fuel-fed fire. "You're disgusting," he said.

Fine, Dana thought, lecture me. Don't kick me.

"Tell me what happened on the Net."

Dana said, "I didn't kill Darien Riis. I didn't know she was a cop until she told me, after I boarded the Net. Rhani Yago sent me there to find out what was wrong. When I arrived, Jo Leiakanawa was dead and Zed Yago was out cold. Darien told me that the Net was going to blow up. I thought she was going to kill me and I grappled with her. Zed Yago woke from stun and shot her with my cutting laser, which she had told me to throw to the floor."

"You carried him out of there," Michel A-Rae said.

"That's right."

"Why?"

Dana did not know what to answer. He didn't know. "I just couldn't leave him," he said finally.

"That's because you're a moral cretin," said A-Rae, with sacerdotal satisfaction, and kicked him a third time.

Dana moved just swiftly enough to catch most of it on his shoulder. Then he rose, despite the flare of pain from his side, and put his thumbs into A-Rae's throat. The woman with the stunner swore and shouted, and the big man came through the open door and pulled him off.

A-Rae was breathing hard. "You son-of-a-bitch," he said, and behind his anger Dana saw a look that he knew very well on another face, a look of pleasure at a victim's helplessness.

"You bastard," he said, "you're like him, that's why you hate him!"

A-Rae ignored the comment. He said to the big man, "He hurt me, Elon. Make him feel it."

"Sure," said the man genially, and thrust his thumbs into Dana's neck. Suddenly, Dana could not breathe. He tried to clap at Elon's ears; a knee slammed into the small of his back. Then he was dropped to the concrete floor. A-Rae gave the order to tie him, and the big man knelt and trussed him with his hands behind his back and a slip-knot around his neck.

A-Rae prodded him with one foot. "There," he said. "That's tamed you." Dana shook his head and tried to stand. A-Rae grinned and tripped him. Dana twisted so that he would land on his side, not his head. "Tie his feet, too." Elon obeyed, lashing the cords tightly around Dana's ankles. A-Rae hunkered down beside him and passed a hand lightly over his face. Suddenly he seized a lock of hair and yanked. Tears came to Dana's eyes. He jerked his head free.

"He's lively," said the big man admiringly.

"Yes," said A-Rae. "Tell me, Dana Ikoro, where is Rhani Yago?"

"What?" Dana said. "What d'you mean, where is she? When I left, she was at the estate."

"She isn't there now."

"Then I don't know where she is."

"Guess," said A-Rae. Dana swallowed. All three were watching him avidly. Cold sweat began to run down his sides.

"Wherever Zed is," he suggested.

A-Rae sighed. "Zed Yago's in the Clinic, being guarded by the Net crew as if he were a gold mine. Try again." He put a thumb on Dana's closed left eyelid.

"I don't know," Dana said. He tried to keep his voice steady, decided it didn't matter and that he couldn't control it anyway, and let it shake. The Kyneth House, he thought, and did not say it. His bladder hurt. . . . A-Rae took the thumb away.

Through the thud of his heartbeat Dana heard A-Rae say to the others, "She could be in the Clinic under another name. Can we check that?"

The woman said, "Fallon is checking the hotel registers. Maybe Sindic can do it. What about him?" She gestured toward Dana with the stun gun.

The big man said, "*I* think he knows." He put a great, spatulate thumb on Dana's right eyelid, pressing hard. . . . Dana leaned away from it until he touched the wall and could go no further. The pressure made yellow moiré patterns behind the lid, and it hurt.

"Enough!" A-Rae said. The thumb lifted.

Dana blinked. Through a clearing haze he saw A-Rae stand, circle the small room, and come to stand beside him, over him, like a magistrate to judgment. His eyes no longer looked wild. "He'll tell us," he said. "We've got days before they find us. Days." The big man nodded as if he had heard a pronouncement of some subtle wisdom.

"What'll I do with him?" he said.

"Keep him tied. And give him a blanket. We've got other things to do; we can deal with him later." The woman holstered the stun gun. Elon sighed and walked out, to return a moment later with a blanket which he tossed over Dana's helpless form.

"Days," he said. He and the woman marched out. She went first. A-Rae hesitated. He licked his lips.

"Days," A-Rae said. He did not sound pleased. He sounded frightened. He went out. Curling his wrists upward behind his back, Dana rolled and wriggled until he was sitting. There was a way to get out of this cord configuration, he knew, but it only worked if you were double-jointed in both shoulders, and he was not. The cords, he guessed, were probably apton and nylon and would not break or fray. But they could be cut, if the angle was right and the edge was sharp. . . . Slowly, Dana began to crawl over the floor, looking for a sharp implement. He did not expect to find one but it was better than waiting to discover what A-Rae had in store for him next.

He did not find one, and when he stopped moving, his throat was raw from the rasp of the cord.

The fourth afternoon after the destruction of the Yago Net, Ja Narayan wandered into Zed Yago's room at the Clinic. He was jaunty. "Bored?" he said to Zed. "Want your hands back? Silly of you to burn them in the first place, you know."

"I know," Zed said. He left the chair by the window and moved to the bed.

"How are you feeling?"

"I've been better." He was tired. It was difficult to sleep with his hands always either propped in front of him, lying by his sides, or extended over his head.

"Should read," said Ja. He sauntered around the room, in no special hurry, and as if by accident ended up at Zed's side. "Play games."

"I've tried," Zed said. He had invited the Net crew in for endless rounds of the six or seven varieties of dice games they knew. . . . But he loathed games, and loathed more not being able to hold the dice. It enraged him not to be able to use his hands to do even the simplest thing.

The water dispenser and the bookviewer could be connected to foot controls, but some things he could not do with his feet. That morning, a letter from Rhani had arrived, telling him that she had left Dur House and where she was. He had had to ask Hal Ku to open it.

And he itched, as if sand had gotten under his skin. Boredom and confinement were infuriating but the itch was torment, the more so because he knew it to be imaginary. He was bathed every morning. He hated that too, being handled like a child. Hal had learned after the first day to do it quickly and without saying anything.

Ja sent a technician for a sterile instrument tray. "How do they feel?" he said.

Zed said, "They don't feel like anything."

"Good." The technician returned. "Put it down, open it, and go away," Ja said. The technician obeyed, clearly disappointed. The wrists of the sterile gloves sat open in the dispenser: Ja fit his fingers into them and pushed. The gloves squeezed over his hands. He withdrew them from the dispenser and wiggled his fingers. . . . "Perfect fit," he said, though the extruded gloves were always a perfect fit, that was how they were made. "Right hand, please," the surgeon said, lifting forceps from the tray. Zed braced his right elbow against his knee. His right hand bobbed in the air like a layered white balloon. "Hold it still." The forceps plucked the bandages off and dropped them in the disposal. Beneath the gauze were more layers of regenerative gel.

"If you hadn't shown up," Zed murmured, "I was getting ready to take this stuff off with my teeth."

Narayan chuckled. "Very poor technique," he said. He picked at the edge of the hardened gel with the forceps. "There's one," he said, peeling a strip of gel away, "there's two—" He chanted the count. When he was done, the strips of gel dangled from Zed's wrist like the rind of a peeled fruit.

The hand still looked like a construct, something made, not flesh, and it still had no fingers. Reparative paint, a thick, membranous substance, covered the ungainly lump. The paint gleamed like tarnished silver. Ja picked up a sponge from the tray and dabbed at the crusted paint. Slowly the paint dissolved, dripped, and fell off. Fingers began to emerge from the lump. They looked red, grotesque, ugly. . . . "Looks good," Ja said. He sponged off the last flake of paint. "Waggle your fingers," he commanded.

Zed tried. He felt a tingling in the wrist. Then the fingers moved. "Response time one point three seconds," Ja said. "That's quite common. Left hand, please."

As Ja picked away at the left-hand bandages, Zed tried moving his right hand. He had seen the effect before in cases of limb replacement or tissue match: no matter how expert the surgeon—and Ja Narayan was very good, indeed—it took a certain time before the original and the new neural pathways synched. The response lag would lessen and finally disappear, he knew. He was more concerned about the numbness. He wiggled the fingers, turned the hand at the wrist, searching for a way to waken feeling in the restored digits.

Ja finally freed the left hand from its wrappings. "Move it," he said. Zed moved the fingers. "The synaptic lag appears less, don't you agree?"

"What do you think?" Zed asked.

"I think you should stop taking up a bed," said Ja.

"How much can I use them?"

"It depends what you plan to do with them," said the surgeon. "Don't lift anything heavy, and don't try to do anything precise. Get some gloves without tips to protect them."

"That's a good idea," said Zed. He closed his eyes and tried to pour his senses into his hands, to reawaken the nerves. Nothing happened. He opened his eyes.

Ja said, "Try the claws." Zed licked his lips. The claws would not extend unless the fingers were slightly crooked: he curved them. Ja prompted him. "Keep the hand extended and make a fist."

"I remember." The instructions sounded contradictory but were not. Zed imagined as he tensed that he could feel the neural impulse traveling down his arms.

The claws slid out.

They were impressive: about two and a half centimeters long, metal, gleaming, sharp as a scalpel. Zed turned his hands in the air, admiring them. He relaxed the tension; they retracted. "Thanks, Ja," he said. "They're exactly what I wanted."

Ja gazed at his handiwork as if he had never seen it

before. "Not bad," he said. "What're you going to do with them?"

"Climb mountains," Zed said. "And—other things."

"Put a gel layer on them before you go out," Ja advised.

"When can I. . . ?"

"Climb mountains? Come back here in three weeks. It'll be at least that long before the meld takes, maybe longer."

"Can I scratch?" Zed said. "Can I bathe?"

"You can scratch anything you like," Ja said. "As for bathing, they won't rust, if that's what you mean." Dutifully, Zed smiled. "And they won't extend by accident. The fingertips may feel a little sore."

Zed nodded. "Got it," he said. "Ja, many thanks."

"Wait'll you see my bill," said the surgeon. He took his gloves off, dumped them into the disposal, and left. Zed sighed, and, cautiously, scratched his left arm with his right hand. He could not feel the texture of the skin, nor—he moved his hand—the texture of hair, or the fabric of his clothes. No matter, he told himself, discernment would come. Quickly he hunted around the room for his belongings, and found only clothes and Rhani's letter. Everything else—bookviewer, booktapes, old PINsheets—belonged to the Clinic.

Haldane Ku walked in. "How do they feel?" he said.

Zed held the lumpy hands for him to see. "It's nice to have the bandages off."

"I'll bet," said the rotund orderly. "You want to leave now, I suppose."

"Yes. I need some protective gel."

Ku went to the supplies cabinet and brought out a tube. Zed extended his hands. Carefully Ku covered them with a thin layer of paint. "How's that?" he said.

Zed flexed the hands, feeling the slight coolness of the gel through the new skin. The sensation delighted him. "Good. Now gloves."

Ku rummaged in the cabinet for a pair of gloves. "Hmm," he said, holding them up, "large enough? No, I think not." He found the next larger size. "Better let me do this." Zed submitted—for the last time, he told himself—to the indignity of having someone else assist him in donning an article of clothing.

"The tips have to come off," he warned.

"Right," said Ku. He procured a pair of shears from the cabinet and nipped the ends of the fingers from the gloves. "Now—" he tugged the gloves on the rest of the way. The extra layer seemed to increase the anesthetic effect, but Zed told himself that this would not last, that soon the sense of discriminate feeling would come back.

"Thanks," he said to Ku.

The orderly smiled. "Glad you're going home," he said.

"Sorry I was such a bad patient."

"No, you're not," said Ku calmly. "Sorry, I mean. I don't think you could be anything else."

Taken aback, Zed glared at him. But the truth of what the orderly said penetrated and unwillingly, he laughed. "You're right."

"I know. Good day, Senior. Have a pleasant life." Ku smiled, turned his back, and began to strip the bed.

Zed walked into the corridor.

The lounging guards came to attention automatically, and then relaxed. He recognized them vaguely: they were both members of the Net Communications unit. "How's it going, Commander?" said one of them, the shorter of them. She wore a stun gun on her hip. Zed was surprised that the Clinic had let her display the weapon so openly. She followed his glance and grinned. "It isn't loaded," she said. A stun cylinder flickered between the fingers of her left hand, and vanished. "But this is."

Zed said casually, "Let me see that." She held it out to him, and he gripped it in his right hand. After a moment of stupefaction, she laughed.

"Hey," she said, "the bandages—gone! You gettin' out of here?"

"I am," said Zed. He dropped the silver cylinder into her left hand.

"Hey, Raeka, tell the others," she said to her companion. The tall woman with the communicator on her belt lifted it to her lips. She thumbed the stud and spoke softly. Zed heard his own name. "Where to, Commander?"

"Home—or, at least, where my sister is," he said.

"Right. We're ready." Raeka thumbed the communicator stud to off and put the device back in her belt.

Zed frowned. He did not want to be escorted around the city as if he were an incompetent or a tourist. "I didn't ask for company," he said.

The two women looked at each other, and then the short one—whose name, he remembered suddenly, was Barbara—said, "We know that, Commander. But when we decided to do this, we decided to keep at it until the fucker A-Rae's caught. You want not to see us, we can do that, I think, but we're not shinnyin'. Sorry."

Despite himself, Zed's fingers began to curl. He recognized the gesture and, alarmed, halted it. What the woman said was fair—indeed, with the Net gone, the crew was free to do what it liked and technically they were all on leave, certainly not subject to his orders. . . . After a while his breathing steadied. Neither of the women had moved, but Barbara's little stun pistol glinted in her hand. He wondered if she would have used it. His throat hurt.

He shrugged. "I won't argue," he said. They walked from Recovery to CTD, CTD to Outpatient, Outpatient to the street. At the door of Outpatient, Zed halted. The waiting room, as usual, was filled with people punching computer keyboards, baring their arms to technicians, holding urine samples, reading booktapes or listening to auditors while they waited for someone else to appear from the bowels of the building. . . . He wondered if he should go back to Surgery and say farewell to the people he had worked with.

But the only people he wanted to see again were Sai Thomas and Yukiko.

He gasped as he walked onto the street. The Clinic was temperature-controlled; even in four days, he had forgotten what Abanat's heat was like. He fumbled Rhani's letter from his pocket and read the address again. Forty-seven Cabell Street. He stopped in front of a pressure map. He found Cabell Street: it was two blocks long, in the southwest quadrant of the city, equidistant from the Clinic and Landingport East. He wondered why she had chosen to live in so unfashionable a district. The homes were very different from those in the western section of Abanat—maybe that was why. A vendor swerved toward him; Zed saw Raeka, on his left side, glide toward the unsuspecting man. He waved her away. "Chobi seeds," he said.

The vendor tossed them to him underhand. "You're welcome, Commander," he called as Zed dug for his credit disc.

Forty-seven Cabell Street was a corner house. It was all on one story, and so surrounded by vines that he could barely see the configuration of the roof. As he knocked on the front door he saw Barbara and Raeka vanish into the garden. The door opened; a thin, brown man with no tattoo nodded to him and stepped back to let him enter. "Welcome, Commander."

"Thank you," Zed said. He gazed at the house's interior. He had stepped not into a hall but into a room. Soft green light filled it; sunlight, shining through leaf-covered windows. The rug on the floor was woven straw. Some of the interior walls were latticelike, not solid, and through them he could see the shadowy figures of other people. "Rhani?" he said.

"Zed-ka." He turned. One of the latticed walls had grown a door. She stood framed in it, wearing Yago blue. Her hair was braided and the braids fastened to her head with a silver comb. "Thank you, Cole," she said, and the dark man effaced himself. Zed's pulse was suddenly beating hard and fast. He wanted to run away. Memory moved in him, and behind it lay an agony that he did not want to remember, did not dare remember. . . . He held out his reconstructed hands, and she gripped them. She said, "You told me to give your skeleton to Yianni Kyneth, Zed-ka, but I couldn't. It's in your room."

His room was opposite hers and looked directly into the garden. She brought him to it, kissed his cheek, and left him there. The skeleton was there: he rubbed its bald head as he passed it, feeling hardness but no other sensation through the deadening layers of gel and glove. Sitting on the bed, he flexed his arms. The muscles did not seem weak. He pushed against the wall with both hands. They trembled. He needed to exercise, he thought, to rebuild the strength which had been seared from the old muscle tissue by . . . by . . . . Warned by his racing pulse, he slammed his fist against the wall. He would *not* remember. Pain like a cold wind shot through his punished hand and arm.

A terrible, gelatinous darkness seemed to hover just outside his field of vision, poised to descend. He clamped his lips and waited for the throbbing to stop. When it ceased, he extended the hand and, curving the fingers, willed a fist. The claws slid out. He marveled at the interior sheathing that Ja had devised to keep the edges from ripping open his fingertips.

He would get another pair of gloves—silver, he thought, with blue trim. He would have to have them made. He relaxed his hand; the claws retracted, he did not even have to look at them. A noise made him start; he glanced outside to see Raeka prowling through the shrubbery. Rhani called him; he went to the hall and looked through the lattices to find her. A woman in dark clothing directed him to one of the solid-walled rooms, calling it "the library."

Zed found it. It had shelves for booktapes, but the shelves were bare. In one corner stood an empty, old-fashioned viewer on a metal stand. Rhani stood beside it, reading a letter. She gave it to him. He scanned it briefly, and saw that it was in fact one letter repeated four times. It was from Family Yago, to the Federation. The first sheet had the initials "FD" in the margin. The second and third sheets had comments down the sides. The fourth sheet had a page of comments attached to it, signed "C. Wu."

Rhani said, "Christina wants me to cite legal references. Theo's changes are trivial. Imre sends his love and agreement. Ferris had the sense just to sign his name."

"How much money are you asking for, Rhani-ka?"

She grinned. "Sixteen million credits. That's what it would cost Family Yago to replace the Net."

"I see," he said. "And with that money—"

"We will build a dorazine plant."

"What will the other sector worlds do for prison transport, without a ship?"

She shrugged. "They'll do what they did before the Net was built. Each of the worlds will be responsible for shipping its own prisoners to Chabad. Family Yago will supply the dorazine and the technicians necessary to staff the ships." She held out another piece of paper. It was a contract, stating Family Yago's intention to pay Narcosis Enterprises the sum of fifteen million credits.

"Narcosis Enterprises?" he said.

"That's the trust Christina set up for the money which

will be paid to The Pharmacy."

He nodded. He did not care, not really. All that had become unimportant, though it would always matter to him because it mattered to her. Rhani was watching him. He said, "It's a tremendous achievement, Rhani-ka. Worthy of Isobel."

She smiled. "Loras U-Ellen will be coming here tomorrow for a celebratory drink."

"Do you want me?"

She said, "You won't like him, Zed-ka. He's a fop. But you're welcome to stay, if you like." She took the contract from his hand. "Have you met my staff yet?" she asked. "The tall man is my new secretary. His name is Cole Arajian. Our steward is Denya I-Chanu—housekeeper's the word she prefers—and Merrill Lune is the cook. She makes excellent egg tarts."

He had to turn away from her. The darkness threatened to overtake him. He fought it off. "No pilot?" he managed to say.

"No," she said. She rubbed her chin. "I wonder if Dana managed to get offplanet before the ships were grounded."

Zed did not want to think about Dana Ikoro. Dana was part of the darkness. "Rhani-ka," he said, "is there a room in this house that I can equip as a gym?"

"A gym?" She frowned. "You can have this room, Zed-ka. I'm putting a com-unit at the front of the house. Why a gym?"

"For my arms and hands," he said.

"Oh."

"By the way," he said, "I hope you haven't been disturbed by the people sneaking through the shrubbery."

"No." She smiled. "I think it's rather sweet of them to be there at all. They seem to believe that Michel A-Rae is out there, plotting terrible things. Myself, I think Michel A-Rae is plotting how to get offplanet and save his own worthless skin."

I want him, Zed thought. His fingers, within gel and gloves, began to curve. Every nerve in his body seemed to rouse and twitch. "I want him," he whispered, and was ashamed, because he had meant not to speak that need aloud in Rhani's presence.

She pointed to the paper he still held in his right hand.

"Look at it, Zed-ka," she said quietly. "Read clause seven."

Zed read clause seven. It was two paragraphs of tightly plotted legal reasoning explaining precisely why, when Michel A-Rae and his cohorts were caught, they should be tried, not by a Federation court, but by the courts of Chabad.

Chapter Twenty-Three

Loras U-Ellen was ecstatic. He patted the pocket of his gown, into which he had put the agreement which said that Family Yago and Pharmaceuticals, Inc., would both pay Narcosis Enterprises the sum of fifteen million credits. "Domna, I am delighted that we have concluded our business so fruitfully," he said.

Rhani smiled. She had smiled so often in the last hour that she felt as if her cheeks were about to crack.

"Within a month, I'm sure, we should receive the first packet of information from The Pharmacy. And within three months—" he chortled, exhibiting perfect teeth— "we can be well on our way to the erection of a functioning dorazine plant."

"I commend your enthusiasm," Rhani said. She, too, was pleased with the agreement they had signed. Pharmaceuticals, Inc., would build the plant, but Family Yago would staff it, and ultimately would be able to buy Pharmaceuticals, Inc., out of its share of the profits. She wondered how much Pharmaceuticals, Inc., would seek to pad their accounts. It did not worry her unduly. She had great faith in Tak Rafael's accountants. She gazed at the litter of food and drink around them. She had spent three hours with U-Ellen, listening to him tell her about Enchanter, and then about Chabad and how different it was.

"All that remains to make my joy complete," U-Ellen said, "is for the Abanat Police to locate and arrest my stupid relative."

"We all hope that," Rhani said.

"I'm so glad," U-Ellen said, "that I let you coax me here today. I'm sorry that the commander is occupied. I had hoped to meet him." He gazed at her with limpid eyes. What he really wanted, Rhani knew, was to question Zed about what had happened on the Net. Perhaps, she thought, I *should* ask Zed to join us for a few minutes. U-Ellen would say something unforgivable, and Zed would strangle him. I wish I could do it myself.

She rose from her chair. "Citizen," she said, "it has been wonderful to visit with you, but surely it's time for you to prepare for your departure? I recall you said The Pharmacy was providing transport for you this evening. I regret that the ship traffic has not been released, so that you could make the trip in comfort, on Family Yago's private shuttle."

"Oh, the day is young yet," U-Ellen said. But he, too, stood. He was wearing a fantastic orange kaftan, all folds, with an extraordinary tasseled hood. "Oh, I wish you could see Enchanter, Domna. You would really appreciate the beauty of it after spending your life on this bleak world. You could visit the labs—" But I don't want to visit the labs, Rhani thought. The Enchanter labs produced Darien Riis. She paced to the door; U-Ellen followed her, still talking. Rhani opened the door; outside stood Sid Arioca, one of the larger members of their volunteer guard. He grinned at Rhani.

"Citizen, should you return to Chabad, make certain you visit me again," Rhani said, wishing that before U-Ellen could visit Chabad again, ever, he and all his progeny would drop dead.

"I certainly will, Domna," U-Ellen promised. He wafted onto the street. Sid stalked at his back. Rhani walked into the house, sighing with relief, to find Denya sweeping plates onto a tray.

"Is he gone?" the dark woman demanded. The tight curls around her head quivered indignation.

"All gone."

"Is he coming back?"

"Sweet mother," Rhani said, "I hope not!" Nevertheless, as she walked to the com-unit, on which she had put her copies of their mutual agreement, she smiled. She had done it—she had purchased the formula for dorazine from The Pharmacy!

Lightly she whirled around the room in a private dance of joy, and stopped as Zed came through the doorway.

"Is he gone?" Zed said.

Denya, her arms laden with plates and bowls, chuckled.

Rhani said, "Yes, Zed-ka, he's gone." Sunlight sifting through the leaves patterned his bare chest with light and dark. She watched his muscles lift and fall with his breathing. His hands gleamed; to cover them he had devised tipless silver gloves made of flexible apton mesh. "You can stop hiding."

"I'll shower," he said, "and join you." He left. Rhani walked across the room to her new acquisition, a rocking chair. Ferris had ordered it for her. He had wanted to pay for it, too, and call it a Founders' Day gift, but Rhani had refused to permit that, knowing how easy it would be for him to grow unhealthily attached to her.

Sitting, she pressed the button on the chair arm which signalled Cole Arajian. He came from his own room, which was toward the north side of the house.

"You called me, Domna?"

"Yes, Cole, thank you. I wanted to see those PINsheet handouts. Do you have them finished?"

"Not quite, Domna. I'll show you what I have." He went to the com-unit and tapped the keyboard; the printer whirred. "Here." He handed her the printouts. She leafed through them. They were a marvelous tissue of historical reference and non-fact, designed to explain to the Chabadese public how an Enchanter corporation, Pharmaceuticals, Inc., had "discovered" the dorazine formula after years of patient research, and how Family Yago and Pharmaceuticals, Inc., were going to build a plant so that, for the first time ever since the founding of Chabad, dorazine could be manufactured intra-sector.

"They're wonderful," she said. "Let my brother see them, finish them, and send them out."

"Certainly, Domna." Cole went away. He preferred to work in his room, and she had placed a small com-unit there for his use. Neither Cole, Denya, nor Merril ever called her anything but "Domna." Following the lead of the Net crew, they called Zed "Commander."

She rocked in the chair, pleased and peaceful with herself. The agreement with Pharmaceuticals, Inc., meant that for the first time in Chabad's history, the planet would not have to depend on criminals, drug runners, for the substance it needed so badly. There would be no more smuggling on Chabad. The Hype cops would go to other sectors, looking for smugglers carrying other drugs, drugs she did not know the names for, and the Federation laws against traffic in dorazine would lie unused, unapplied—except in cases where people tried to smuggle dorazine out of Sardonyx Sector to some other sector.

Merril walked in with a dish of sourballs. Rhani had recently developed a craving for sour things, surely an effect of the pregnancy, though her belly was still flat as ever. "Thank you, Merril," Rhani said, taking the dish on her lap. Zed strolled out of the lattice-walled hall and, bending over her shoulder, took two of the crunchy candies from the dish.

"When did you start eating these?" he said. "They're good."

"I got sick of chobi seeds."

"Hmm." He took a third, and sat in the basket chair which swung from the ceiling. "I read Cole's article for the PINsheets. He ought to write fiction, he's got the knack. If I didn't know better, I'd believe it myself."

"I'll tell him," Rhani said. She had not understood, at first, why Zed avoided Cole. After a while, she had asked him.

"Because," her brother had answered, "he's like Binkie. Physically, I mean, not in any other way." And, looking at Cole, Rhani agreed that he was thin and tall and reticent in the way Ramas I-Occad has been reticent. But the resemblance did not bother her the way it seemed to bother Zed.

The com-unit beeped, telling her there was a call online. Rising, she went to answer it.

The caller was Aliza Kyneth. "Hello, darling," she said. She was wearing orange, which reminded Rhani of Loras U-Ellen's gown, but while U-Ellen had looked like a butterfly, Aliza looked like a flame, "You seem happy. Are you?"

"Yes, Aliza, I am."

"Good. You must tell me all about it sometime. I am calling to invite you to a party, you and Zed."

Rhani said, cautiously, "You know we have not been going out recently, Aliza—"

"It's a small party," Aliza Kyneth said ruthlessly, "in fact, it is a birthday party for Imre. He is seventy-eight."

Rhani sighed. "I was supposed to help you plan that party, as I recall."

"You were. But I forgive you," Aliza said.

"How magnanimous of you."

"Yes. There will only be forty people, and Charity Diamos has not been invited."

"That doesn't mean she won't come," Rhani warned.

"If she comes, she won't get in. I don't have to be nice to her, she isn't *my* relative. Now, you will come, won't you?"

"Of course. When is it, and what time?"

"I'll send you an invitation, my dear. Make sure you bring Zed. Oh, and don't tell Imre when you talk with him. It's supposed to be a surprise." Aliza waved and terminated the call.

Rhani said, "Zed-ka, will you come to Imre Kyneth's seventy-eighth birthday party with me?"

He looked up. There was a viewer on his lap. "Hmm?" Rhani repeated the question. She saw him begin to frown, and then shrug. "If you want me to."

"I want you to." She went back to the rocking chair. "Stop eating my sourballs, Zed-ka. What are you reading?"

"An old book," he said. "It's called *Climbing Ice*. It's a classic."

"Oh," Rhani said. "Would music disturb you?" Lately, she had gotten into the habit of listening to musictapes from the computer network's music library, trying different kinds of sounds. She told herself it was for the baby. Zed shook his head. He had already gone back to the book. Rhani rose and walked to the unit. Idly she glanced through the *R*s, the *S*s—Shostakovich, who was that? and halted at a familiar name. STRATTA, VITTORIO, the entry read. MELODY FOR MELLOPHONE.

She was sitting in the same place, after dinner, listening to a second Stratta piece ("Concerto in D, for Ella") when the distrubance began in the garden.

She did not hear the words at first, only a subliminal discontinuity in the flow of the music. Then she saw Zed, in the hanging chair, look up and turn toward the front door. He gestured to her to lower the sound. She switched the auditor off. "What is it?" she asked.

"Listen," he said.

Rhani frowned. "I don't—" she began, and then halted the sentence as she heard a thud. A woman spoke, outside the house.

"Take your hands off me, you fucker!"

Zed strode to the front door. Cole Arajian peered through the wooden lattice of the wall. "Did you hear something?" he said.

Rhani stood, as Sid Arioca's fluted tenor answered, "Man, don't skop with me. You want to go in, fine, we take you in, otherwise you don't *get* in."

"The hell," said the first voice. Someone yelled. Zed opened the door. A woman in a maroon-and-gray jumpsuit walked through it. She had one green and one white eyebrow, and her hair was dirty gold. Sid loomed behind her, his hands spread apologetically.

"Sorry, Commander, Domna," he said. "She just cut through. Hit Barbara a good crack; she's behind a bush, whoopin' her guts out."

Tori Lamonica, hands on hips, advanced into the room without requesting entrance. "I don't like being questioned," she said tightly. "By anyone."

Zed said. "Never mind, Sid. You tried." The big man shrugged and stepped back. Zed closed the door. "Good evening, Starcaptain," he said.

Rhani rose. "Starcaptain Lamonica," she said. "I'm sorry you had to fight your way to the door."

Lamonica shrugged. Her pearl-gray jumpsuit shimmered like the mottled iridescent layering on a mollusk's shell. "I don't mind a good scrap," she said. She nodded at Zed. "You look better than you did when I last saw you." She turned in a circle. "How many houses you folks got?"

"Two," Rhani said.

"Nice," Lamonica said. She glanced at the carved walls, the woven straw rugs, the mirror sculpture Rhani had placed beside her chair; "Yeah, nice." Her medallion shone on her chest. She stroked the chain with one hand. "I come to ask *you* a question." She took a breath. "I'm lookin' for someone you know. Dana Ikoro. You seen him?"

Rhani said, "Not since the night you landed a bubble-craft on the Yago estate lawn." She could not see her brother's face, but she watched his shoulders hunch. . . .

He turned around. His hands were in his pockets, and his mouth was rigid as stone. "Why?"

"Because no one else has either, since four nights ago, when he walked out of The Dancer drunk out of his mind with some big stud wearing a cloak. Also wearing one black earring, you know, the kind with a remote?" She was talking to Zed. He nodded. "Dana's mostly hetero, so there's damn little reason I can think of for him to nest with some man for four days, and no one's seen *him* again, either."

Zed said, "Are you Dana Ikoro's keeper, Starcaptain?"

She put her hands on her hips and glared at him. "No. But ten years I've been riding the red dust, and I've learned to listen to feeling. Something's wrong with him. He's a nice kid and he got a raw deal from you, Commander, and a hard deal from you, Domna. So if I'm right and he's in trouble somewhere in this damn town, I figure you owe him. Tell me I'm wrong." Her eyes flickered from Zed to Rhani.

What kind of trouble could Dana be in? Rhani thought. "No," she said to the angry Hyper. "You're not wrong."

Suddenly, Tori Lamonica deflated, became a diffident woman in a gray suit. "Sorry to come blazing at you," she said. "But I went to the A.P. Talked to the Hype cops. They don't care. Two days he spent yipping his throat hoarse to their damn computer."

Merril appeared at an archway in the lattice. "Would you like something to drink, Domna?" she said.

"Starcaptain?" Rhani said. She reseated herself in the rocker.

"No, thanks," Lamonica said. "I mean, nothing for me. I've been drinking all evening, how else do you think I worked up the snap to come here?"

Rhani grinned. She liked this woman, who could be rude and still disarm by her very rudeness. "Please sit, Starcaptain," she said, pointing to the second hanging chair.

Lamonica shook her head. "I'm not going to stay."

Zed said, "You've tried the usual ways to reach him?"

"I sent out a com-call, yes. Set it to key whenever he used his I-disc or his credit disc. No result. That was three days ago. Told folks to keep an eye out for him—told your crew, even. Nothin'. Checked the Clinic, even. He's not there; he wasn't there."

"What do you expect me to do?" Rhani said.

Lamonica scowled. "Hell, I don't know. You're a Yago, they say you run this fucking planet. Tell me you can't find someone if you want him?"

Rhani thought: We haven't found Michel A-Rae. But then, he doesn't want us to find him.

Zed echoed the thought. "Maybe Dana doesn't want to be found." He picked up the viewer and was switching it off and on.

"I'm no telepath," Lamonica said. "I don't know. I'll shinny now, I've said what I came to say. I'm at NW724-07 if you want to reach me." She opened the front door. A cold wind licked slowly in from the garden before she could close it.

Rhani said to Zed, "What do you think?"

He was still holding the viewer, but she did not think he saw either it or her.

He said, "I'm going to bed." He walked through the arch in the lattice, and Rhani saw his shadowy form retreat down the hall. She heard the door close. Well, she thought, sleep is one way to handle a problem you can't solve. Instead of reading about ice climbing, I wish he'd *go* ice climbing. . . . But she knew it would be another two weeks at least before his hands would be strong enough. Meanwhile, he would withdraw, grow moody, walk around the house and the city like a kerit in a cage, and watch the PINsheets, with malignant intensity, for news of Michel A-Rae.

As she fell asleep that night, she thought about Dana, remembering their loving, and the tenderness with which he had touched her. He was decent, gentle—in a way that she was not—and it troubled her that he had dropped out of sight in such a way that it worried someone with experience, someone like Tori Lamonica. A black earring. . . . She snapped awake. How had Lamonica described Dana's companion? ". . . *Some big stud wearing a cloak and one black earring. . . .*" Rhani remembered—and her skin crawled at the memory—that Michel A-Rae liked to wear one black earring. He had worn it the afternoon of the Auction.

No, she told herelf, really, *really* that's coincidence, you cannot build on it, it means nothing—but as she thought it she was out of the bed and hurrying through the darkened hall to the common room, to the com-unit. As she reached it, she thought—Rhani, don't do this, they'll laugh at you, they'll think you're crazy—but her hands, working without direction, had already made connection with the Abanat police. The wall clock told her that it was not even midnight, not late, and if she were wrong, it wouldn't matter whether it was day or night, she would still be wrong, and if she were right. . . . "This is Domna Rhani Yago," she said to the face on the screen. "Can you connect me with Captain Catriona Graeme of the Hyperspace Police?"

"One moment, Domna," said the duty officer. The screen blanked, and lit again, with a different face.

"Domna, I'm Captain Graeme. What can I do for you?"

Rhani hesitated. She had not expected this conventional-seeming woman with a crooked nose whose face, on the display screen at least, appeared as homely as her PINsheet pictures. "Captain Graeme, I hope I haven't disturbed you."

Cat Graeme smiled. She had a singularly pleasant smile. "You haven't, Domna. Tell me how I can help you."

Rhani sat in the com-unit chair. Behind her, something creaked in the darkness, and then a light came on and a robe fell over her shoulders. She glanced up at her brother.

"Captain Graeme," she said, "I'm worried about a friend. I think he may be in trouble, perhaps in danger, and I think Michel A-Rae has something to do with it.

Nothing changed on Cat Graeme's face, but shadows moved behind her, and suddenly a board at her back winked into life. Beside her, Rhani heard Zed's breath hiss through his teeth. "Go on, Domna," said Graeme.

Rhani took a breath. "Do you know who Dana Ikoro is, Captain?"

"Certainly," said Graeme. "A very cooperative young man. He spent two days here, telling us everything he could remember about Michel A-Rae and his cohorts."

"Starcaptain Tori Lamonica"—Graeme nodded—

"came to my house tonight, a few hours ago, to inform me that Dana Ikoro disappeared four days ago, accompanied by a total stranger, and hasn't been seen since."

Graeme's face remained polite, but her voice was tinged with weariness as she said, "Dana Ikoro's a Hyper, Domna Rhani, and Hypers tend toward odd friendships and adventures. When he left here, as I recall, he expressed a strong ambition to be very drunk."

"He was drunk, Lamonica said so. But she also said—" Rhani licked her lips. "Captain Graeme, this may not make much sense, but please try to take it seriously. Dana Ikoro went off with a man no one seems to know, a man wearing a black pearl earring, with, she said, 'a remote.'"

"A transmitter-receiver unit, yes. They're quite common pieces of equipment, Domna, you can buy them anywhere."

"Michel A-Rae wore a black pearl earring the day of the Abanat Auction," Rhani said.

A thin line appeared between Cat Graeme's eyebrows. "Domna, that's one hell of a speculative jump. Do you think Dana Ikoro was kidnapped by Michel A-Rae? What for? As a hostage toward escape? Surely, we would have heard from him by now if that were his intention."

Rhani said, "I don't know what his intention is. I do know that Dana Ikoro has vanished, that he is not in the Clinic or in jail, that he has not used his credit nor his I-disc in four days, and that—"

"Three days," said Zed softly.

"—Three days," Rhani said, "and that I don't believe he left with a lover." Not a male lover, she thought.

"I'm sorry, Domna," said Catriona Graeme, "but though these speculations are interesting, they aren't evidence. Starcaptain Lamonica proffered no suggestions as to what might have happened to Ikoro, but she did refer frequently to her intuition. He seems to have been rather a popular young man, as well as a cooperative one."

For a moment, Rhani wondered if they were still speaking the same language. "I beg your pardon," she said.

"I think you know what I mean well enough, Domna," Cat Graeme said.

Not, Rhani thought, if you mean what you seem to be

implying. . . . A wave of heat passed from her heart to her head and back down to the soles of her feet. She felt as if the nerves of her skin had begun to crackle, and that her hands might be letting off sparks. "Captain Graeme," she said, in as measured a tone as she could achieve, "do you have pictures of Michel A-Rae's male cohorts?"

"Yes, we do," said Graeme, clearly puzzled.

"Then I suggest you call Tori Lamonica at NW724-07, show them to her, and ask if she recognizes them. I also suggest you discuss with the Abanat police the best way to locate two people, both male, one large and wearing a cloak, one slender and drunk, who left The Green Dancer at whatever time they left it five nights ago. If you have any problems with cooperation, I hope you'll mention my name."

Cat Graeme looked as if she had swallowed something which stung her. "Domna, you don't appreciate the—" she paused. "Might I submit that you don't entirely understand police work?"

"I don't care what you submit," Rhani said. "Nor do I care, Captain Graeme, if you or the Abanat police get credit for Michel A-Rae's arrest. I can easily repeat this entire conversation with the Abanat chief of police and receive a more appropriate response. You are not dealing with a hostile force, Captain Graeme, you are dealing with an intelligent planetary community that needs to be neither manipulated nor subdued. No, let me amend that. You *were* not dealing with a hostile force." She turned off the com-unit. She was no longer hot. She drew the robe around her shoulders, savoring the feel of the silk.

Beside and over her, Zed said. "What made you so angry, Rhani-ka? Her intimation that you and Dana Ikoro were lovers?"

"No!" Rhani said. She swung around in the chair. "No. But she assumed that my judgment would be less reliable because of it, and decided that she could, with impunity, be rude about it. I don't mind being told that I'm wrong, Zed-ka, but I *despise* being told I am wrong as if the teller's opinion itself was proof." She gazed at the com-unit. Suddenly, it began to *beep-beep* with anxious regularity. She turned the alarm's audio off. A green light blinked. Pulling the two halves of the robe's front seam together, Rhani sealed them with her thumb, and stood.

Light glowed through the lattice walls from the direction of the kitchen; Merril, too, was up. Rhani swallowed. Vehemence had parched her mouth, and she wished for some sweet lemonade or some fruit punch—Corrios' fruit punch. Or even, since it was night, some sweet chocolate, a taste from her childhood, remarkable because it was one of the few childhood memories for which she felt a true nostalgia. . . .

"Were you, Rhani-ka? Lovers?"

Rhani was shocked. Zed never asked about her lovers. And because he had never asked before, she knew that she had to answer it. Fingers clenched together, she said, "Yes, Zed, we were."

She heard his in-drawn breath. She could only see his face in profile against the lamplight. At the very edge of her vision, the green light went off and on, off and on. Better tell him the rest, too. "Not only that, but I'm pregnant," she said. "Dana doesn't know. I never told him."

He did not move. In the single light, he appeared ghostly, an eidolon. Then he walked, slowly, to one of the hanging chairs. It creaked. Released to response by the sound, Rhani took a step toward him. "Zed?"

"No," he said.

Had he wept, she would have ignored all words and gone to him. But the exigency of his isolation was too extreme for comfort. She knew; she remembered. So she extinguished the light and left him to his grief.

In the morning, Zed did not appear for breakfast.

Rhani lingered in the dining space off the kitchen, hoping that he would come from his room and join her. When it was clear that he would not, she went into the common room to wait. Cole Arajian was sitting reading a PINsheet. He passed it to her and she looked the front page over: it contained the first of his creations, and a quotation from Imre Kyneth. . . . "Once more a Yago has found a solution to a problem of such complex dimensions that many of us believed it was insoluble. . . ." There was a bad picture of her on the second page.

As she returned the sheet to Cole, someone knocked at the front door. Cole opened it. John Salambo, one of the

Net crewmen, was standing just outside. Behind him were three strangers. One of them was Catriona Graeme.

"Domna, these folks want to speak with you." Salambo was studiously casual. Cole looked at Rhani.

"Thank you. Let them through, please." They walked in: Graeme, a burly-shouldered man in black, a tall woman holding a communicator. The morning sunlight touched the gray strands in Graeme's dark hair.

"Domna," she said, hands at her sides, shoulders square in an unconsciously military stance. "I came to apologize." The jagged scar at her right temple pulsed. "I made some stupid assumptions last night. I was wrong." She swallowed. "Starcaptain Lamonica confirms identification of the man she saw leave with Dana Ikoro was one Elon Liddell, ex-member of the Hyperspace Police, who disappeared with Michel A-Rae the day after the Auction. We have ascertained the route they took and the district they went to, on the other side of the Boulevard, just south of the Barrens. I am hopeful that, within a few hours, we will have located the very house."

Rhani thought: it took courage to come and say that to me in front of my entire household and her own subordinates. . . . "Captain Graeme, I appreciate your choosing to tell me this in person," she said. "I have complete confidence that you will indeed find what you're looking for. Last night was an unfortunate misunderstanding."

The tall woman murmured into the communicator. "Clear," she said. "Captain, we've got it! One-oh-nine West Cooley. A big man with a black cloak has been seen by the neighbors going in and out of the house. Three of them recognized a holo of Liddell."

An electric current seemed to shimmer suddenly through the latticed walls of the house. "Good," said Graeme. "Notify the A.P. and ask them to set up backup, just in case. Seal off the block, tell city services to cut the power on the northeast slideway, call Moa Li at Base and tell her to move Group B to within a block of the house and set up a perimeter, and to wait. Domna, we have to go—as you've gathered, we may have found our target." She turned toward the door, which the burly man had already opened.

"Captain Graeme," said Zed from the archway.

She turned impatiently. "Yes?"

"May I join your forces?" His voice was very steady. His skin looked stretched across cheekbones and jaw, and it was flushed to a clear, even rose. His clothes were drab, except for the silver mesh of his gloves.

"Who the hell are you?"

"Zed Yago, ex-commander of the Yago Net."

"Can you take my orders?"

"Try me," he said.

She frowned. "I don't need amateurs in the middle of this. They get hurt, or hurt someone else."

Zed said nothing.

Graeme flicked a look at Rhani. "All right, Commander," she said. "You come with us. Malachi—" she jerked a thumb at the man by the door—"will tell you where to go." She strode out of the house. The others followed her like the tail on a comet.

"Zed-ka," Rhani said, "what. . . ?"

He smiled, and brushed her cheek with one hand as he passed her. "I love you," he said, and then the door closed.

In Auction Place, the heat shimmered upward from the pavement, distorting vision. The air thickened, and it smelled of burning. Overhead, the city flags flapped fitfully on their poles. Malachi, twenty meters to Zed's left, was walking throught the square with disinterest, a busy man with somewhere specific to go. He swerved right. Zed counted to ten and followed him. Behind them, irritated tourists milled around the stationary movalong. Zed counted the streets in his head. Four more to go to West Cooley. One-oh-nine was a corner house. B Group was already in position, cutting off possible escape routes. Zed reached up to rub his left ear, caught the motion, stopped it. He was not used to wearing a remote. It spoke suddenly. "A Team, positions in eight minutes." Zed lengthened his stride. Malachi had vanished, but twenty meters to Zed's right strode a figure in cream-colored pants and a brown, webbed shirt, ordinary garments, except for the stunner in the boot holster.

In the quiet sunlight, Zed held his hands in front of him and worked his claws.

Graeme had refused to give him a weapon; he was a spectator at the feast this day, not a celebrant. He crossed an intersection. "Five minutes," said the voice at his ear. He breathed easily, feeling the film of sweat casing his body like a caressing hand. Another intersection. "Three minutes." He wondered if the people in the houses had noticed the strangers hurrying through their streets and speculated on what was going on. A muscle cramped in his left thigh and he snarled, unable to halt and flex it. He kept moving and after a while the knot went away. The houses were small, set close together on crooked streets. "One minute," said the voice at his ear.

He crossed the last intersection and turned right toward the corner of Cooley and Thaine. Malachi beckoned him. Zed went to him and dropped to his knees beside the brawny, dark cop. He was holding a communicator in one hand. There was a water gauge on a pole beside him; Zed pretended to examine it. "Now what?" he said.

"We go in," said Malachi. "You stay here. Move when you're told to."

Zed nodded. He had hoped that Graeme would let him join the first attack team but it had been an unlikely hope. He did not want to get in anyone's way. "They're still inside?" he said.

"As far as I know." A tone sounded in Zed's ear. "That's it. See you later." Rising, Malachi sauntered away from the pole. A second tone sounded in Zed's ear. Sweat curled his hair and plastered his shirt to his body. Malachi was running now toward the corner house. It had white walls, a slanted roof with solar panels turned toward the sun, a gravel path. . . . He watched running figures converge in all directions. The side windows of the house fell inward. The sound of shattering glass brought saliva to his mouth; he swallowed. Human shadows flowed through the windows. Smoke puffed from one window and dissipated on a warm slow breeze.

"All units move in," said Cat Graeme's voice in the remote. Zed stood. The muscle in his thigh cramped again. He loped toward the house. The front door eased slowly open. Cat Graeme stood framed in the doorway. She was holding a stun gun.

"You mount an impressive operation, Captain," Zed said.

She grinned. "Thanks."

"Have you got them all?"

"Every one."

The blood roared in Zed's ears like the sea. He walked into the house, noting a huge, motley pile of things against a wall, tools, clothes, electronic components, stun charge casings, rope, blankets. . . . He almost stumbled over the first body: a woman, holding a stunner in one hand. He glanced at the charge; it was set at lethal, but the casing gauge showed it to be empty. She was breathing stertorously. He moved on. A second room held two three-tiered bunks like the bunks on a starship. A second man lay slumped on one of the bunks. His head and upper torso on the bunk, his hips, legs, and feet trailing on the floor. He, too, was snoring. A fourth man lay on the hall floor with a laser burn through his shoulder. He was moaning. Zed closed his nostrils against the smell of burned flesh and walked to the rear of the house. He heard voices and angled toward them. "Can you cut that—yeah, right, now get him on his feet. Did they even feed him, I wonder?"

"Took you long enough," said Dana Ikoro.

He was standing, one hand on the wall to steady himself. As Zed entered the little room, he wavered, and one of the members of the attack team caught him and eased him to the cot. The room stank of feces and urine. Dana's mouth was bruised. But his voice was steady as he swore—in Pellish—and tried to lift himself again. Zed walked to him and levered him away from the soiled bunk. "Need a hand, Starcaptain?"

"Thanks," Dana said, and then all his muscles went rigid. "Zed?"

"Can you walk?" Zed said.

"My legs shake," Dana said.

"Then hold still," Zed said. Wrapping an arm around Dana's waist, he picked the slighter man off the floor. It was only a few meters down the hall to the kitchen. Dana put both hands out rather blindly, and Zed set him down beside a wall. "Here's a chair." He guided Dana to it and lowered him to the seat before he fell. Dana steadied himself.

"Thank you," he said. He breathed arhythmically, and Zed guessed that his ribs were bruised and maybe broken. His clothing was filthy, and there was a blotch of what looked like dried blood in his unkempt hair.

"Bad?" Zed said.

Dana looked up. His mouth quivered. But he straightened in the chair. "Not too bad," he said. "It was mostly the big man, Elon. A-Rae—" he paused—"he left me alone after the first two days. It frightened him too much to watch." He rubbed his face with one hand. His cheeks were stubbled with beard. "May—may I have some water?"

Zed walked to the cooler and brought him water in a plastic cup. Dana took the cup. He had it halfway to his mouth before his hand began to shake. Zed steadied it for him and helped him drink. Dana put the cup on the table and wiped his mouth with the back of his hand. "I kept telling myself it could never be as bad as the Net," he said. "I even told Elon. He didn't like that."

"Was it?" Zed said.

Dana tried to smile. "No. Oh, no."

"*Did* they feed you?"

"Off and on. No baths, though. I must stink."

"You do," Zed said. The darkness was seeping into him, but he held it back. "Think you can remember an address?"

Dana nodded.

"Forty-seven Cabell Street. Rhani's there. She has something important to tell you. I suspect she'd even let you take a bath."

"Cabell Street, forty-seven," Dana repeated. "Got it."

"Good," said Zed. Then, before the dark rage moved to snare him, and Dana with him, in its embrace, he walked from the kitchen and began, with methodical diligence, to check the faces of the fallen.

He found the ex-chief of the drug detail in the smallest room in the house, really a closet. Someone had bound his hands behind his back. An attack team member in a tattered shirt and pants said, "Hey, maybe you—" but Zed was already past him. The windowless concrete room reminded him of a Net cell. A-Rae lay on his side. Stunned, his face was slack with sleep; he seemed harmless, and very young.

Zed wound one hand in the dark hair and lifted the slumping head. His other hand reached to stroke A-Rae's cheek. The claws extended. With tremendous effort, Zed checked the motion. He rose. "Don't move him," he said to the man standing guard at the door. "Has this place got a medikit?"

The man shrugged. "We brought one with us." Zed went back down the hallway. He found Cat Graeme in the cottage's front room, talking into a communicator. Shards of glass littered the floor.

He waited for her to notice him. "What is it?" she said finally, letting the communicator crackle into silence.

"You brought a medikit with you."

"That way." She pointed. "The kitchen." Zed went to the kitchen. Dana had vanished. The man with the laser burn was sitting groggily on the floor, being treated by a puzzled young medic. Zed rummaged through the open medikit beside her, picked out a stimulant ampule, and returned to the closet where Michel A-Rae lay asleep. Kneeling, he pulled up A-Rae's collar and laid the ampule against the carotid artery.

The guard said, "What are you doing?"

Zed said, "Bringing him out of stun." He watched A-Rae's eyelids flutter. "I'm a senior medic attached to the Abanat Clinic. Would you close that door, please? You can leave it ajar if you like. This won't take long."

"Well—don't take those cords off," the guard warned. He shut the door. The latch clicked. As the room blackened, Zed palmed the light switch. He did not need or desire light but he wanted Michel A-Rae to be able to see. The darkness, freed of the constraints he had bound it with, devoured him, creeping through bloodstream and nervous system and into his hands. He extended the claws, and waited.

In about twenty seconds, Michel A-Rae blinked. He squirmed weakly. "Where—" His dark eyes focused on Zed's face. he worked his lips, tried to swallow, couldn't.

Zed smiled lovingly at him. "You know who I am," he said, in a conversational tone.

A-Rae's shoulders spasmed as he struggled against the cords. Zed caught his head by the hair. He held it still, and let A-Rae see the claws.

"You can't—"

"I can," Zed said. "Anything. I. Want to do. I can." Lightly he drew the claws of the right hand from the corner of A-Rae's left eye to the lower line of his jaw, stopping short of the artery. "Greetings from Darien," he said, and lifted the hand to let A-Rae see the talons touched with blood.

At the last minute, the Hype cops stopped Dana as he tried to leave the house.

"Hey," said one of them whose name, he thought, was Malachi, "why don't you come with us? You look pretty bad, maybe you ought to see a medic. Hey, Captain!" This shout down the corridor brought Cat Graeme out of the front room.

"What?"

"I'm taking the Starcaptain to the cop shop." He closed his hand around Dana's wrist.

"Don't hold me," Dana said wearily. "I've been tied up for four days."

"Sorry." Malachi let go of the wrist. Dana thought, I don't want to go to the police station, really I don't. . . .

"Wait a minute," Graeme called. Malachi sighed and walked to her. "Don't leave," he said warningly to Dana.

"I'm just going out for a breath of air," Dana said. He opened the door. Forty-seven Cabell Street, forty-seven Cabell Street. . . . The glare of sunlight nearly knocked him down. He basked in the cleansing light for a moment, and then turned north. Five steps from the house and Malachi caught up with him.

"Thought you'd sneak away, huh," he said. "That was silly."

Dana stopped walking. His knees wobbled. "Look," he said, "I've been locked in a room, I've been beaten, I haven't had much food—the last thing I need is to be pried at and pushed around. I need a bath and about forty hours' sleep. Once I've had that, I'll be glad to come to the police station and talk to your damn computer for hours—" He swayed. "Forty-seven Cabell Street. That's where I want to go."

"The Yago house," said Malachi. "Who told you to go there? The commander?" Dana nodded. "Well—" the burly man hesitated, and then said, "Oh, why not. You're out on your feet anyway. Come on, they'll have the slideway running again by now. Can you walk by yourself? I'm not real enthusiastic about carrying you.

You smell rotten."

"I'll walk," Dana said. "Thanks." Just put one foot in front of the other, preferably in a straight line, he told himself. Malachi chattered beside him, needing no response, it seemed, as he discussed Chabad's weather— "I'm from Samarkand, myself"—Catriona Graeme, Rhani Yago, whom he admired though he had only met her for five minutes—"Hey, that's one high-powered lady"—and Chabad's markets. Every so often he would say, "You still with me?"

"Still with you," Dana said.

On the movalong, the passengers took one look at Dana and edged away, until around him and Malachi was a clear space. Malachi said politely, "You don't mind if I stand upwind?" Dana didn't mind. Near the movalong exit they passed a fountain and Dana was tempted to wade into it. "Better not." Malachi said.

Dana had almost decided that walking was easy when Malachi said, "Here we are." Dana looked up. They stood in front of a house. It was low and covered with green vines that grew over the roof and down the sides of the house and against the windows. It reminded Dana very strongly of a house he had lived in on Pellin.

"You're sure?" he said, because it did not look like either of the houses he associated with the Yagos. It was almost plebeian.

"I'm sure." Malachi said, knocking on the door. A tall, very thin man opened it. Dana frowned. For a minute he could not think why the man seemed so familiar, and then he realized that he looked like—not in feature but in manner—Binkie, only he was brown, and Binkie had been white. . . .

He smelled the scent Rhani used on her hair.

"Dana!" She was standing in front of him. "Sweet mother." He fended off her outstretched hands.

"Better not," he said. "I haven't had a bath in days."

"Then you shall have one," she said. Turning, she gave a multitude of orders to people who came and quickly went. The man who looked like Binkie vanished and returned with a glass of what smelled like fruit punch. Dana clasped it in both hands.

It was fruit punch.

"Where's my brother?" Rhani asked Malachi.

"I don't know, ma'am. He stayed behind—I suppose he had something to do."

Something—Dana held the glass out and someone took it from him—yes, you could say that, Dana thought. He remembered Zed moving from body to fallen body like an avalanche hunting for a place to spill. God help Michel A-Rae, he thought. Rhani was thanking Malachi, and he gathered the strength to turn and add his own grateful words.

Malachi was diffident. "Don't worry about it, man. Take care of yourself." He backed out of the house. Dana felt Rhani's cool, strong fingers close around his wrist.

"Bath," she said, and led him through her bedroom to a washroom. "Take off those clothes." He stripped. As he bared his left side, he heard her suck breath sharply. She stepped close to him and touched the purple-black bruise with her right palm.

"Now we match," he said.

"Only mine was on the other side."

A tub of water stood steaming at his back. He lowered himself into it, trying not to cry out at the sharp pain. The surface of the water turned dark as dirt floated off his skin.

"Here," Rhani said, handing him a sponge. He sponged himself. It was luxury to be clean. "I'll do your back," she offered. He let her take the sponge from his hand.

"This is a nice house," he said, as the soft, thick sponge moved up and down his spine. The touch was mildly rousing; he felt his genitals stir.

When he climbed from the tub, he tried to hide his erection with the towel. Rhani saw, and grinned. "Hey, I've seen it before," she said. Suddenly she pressed herself against him, ignoring the water that ran down him, soaking her clothes. "Damn it, Dana," she said, "why did you come back? I wanted you to leave."

It was an odd thing for her to be saying as she hugged him, he thought. "I tried to leave," he explained. "The ships were grounded, and then I got drunk—"

"I know," she said. She handed him a thick plush blue robe. He put it on. "Tori Lamonica told us you disappeared. I called the Abanat police but Captain Graeme didn't want to have anything to do with me." She grinned, not pleasantly. "I changed her mind."

Dana thought for a moment that he would have liked to have seen Cat Graeme and Rhani Yago skopping it. But of course, Rhani had won. This was her world. "Zed— looks well," he said.

She nodded, and brought him into the bedroom. Instantly he was ravenous. A tray of food waited on a table. He scooped up a meat roll and bit into it. The crisp taste almost made him weep. "Oh, that's good," he said.

"He is well," Rhani said. Who, he thought, were we talking about? Oh, Zed. yes. "He has a gym in the back of the house, he exercises a lot. He doesn't go to the Clinic any more, of course. He reads—" She sat on the bed, hands between her knees. Her gaze sharpened. "You spoke with him?"

Dana nodded. "He gave me something to drink. We talked for a few minutes. Rhani, why?" Her intense stare alarmed him.

She licked her lips, and reached for a piece of fruit. "Because he knows we were lovers," she said. "He found out last night,"

It was too late to be frightened, but Dana's nerves reacted anyway, drying his mouth and racing his heart. "Oh," he said. "That must be—he said you had something to tell me."

"No," she said, "that isn't it."

Her tone warned him. He sat on a straw chair. "What is it?"

She said, "I'm pregnant."

He blinked, and looked to see.

"It won't show for a while yet."

"Is it mine?" he said, incredulous.

"Half," she said, smiling, head tilted to one side. He remembered the evening they met. She had worn a red shirt, and black silk pants. . . . She was wearing them now. It had to be coincidence.

"And you want me to *leave* Chabad?" he said.

She frowned. "I didn't want to tell you. I would have, after the baby was born. I would have written to you, 'grammed a message care of your family, to Pellin. I—it's complicated, Dana. I was going to marry Ferris Dur. But

I didn't want to go to bed with him, and you were here, and I liked you—"

"How can you have a child and not tell the father?" he said.

She stared at him, her amber eyes unashamed. "I told you," she said, "that's Yago custom."

He stood, because he couldn't sit any longer. "Yago custom," he repeated. "And I suppose you plan to shut the kid up on the estate, with just slaves and her mother and her damned crazy uncle for company. She'll never see a starship, or a mountain, except those icebergs, she'll never see a horse or a dog or even a tree in its natural habitat, she'll grow up thinking slavery is humane and dorazine is a wonderful drug and hating her mother the way you and Zed both hate your mother—" He drew a breath and found that he had run out of words. Rhani's face was very white. Her hands were clasped in her lap, the knuckles icy. He wondered if she wanted to hit him.

She said, very calmly, "What would you want me to do, then? Would you stay?"

"Stay—" He hadn't thought of it. No, he could not stay on Chabad. Nor would she leave, of course. His anger drained from him. He sat again, not too close to her. He wondered what the child would look like, would it—she— he—whatever—have black eyes or amber eyes? Red hair or dark hair? "No, I couldn't stay." He bit his lip. "Rhani, I'm sorry."

"No," she said, "You're right. It isn't fair to you."

"Nor to the child," he said.

She rose. "You wouldn't consider coming back, I suppose," she said.

"Coming back?"

"Yes." She walked to the headboard of the bed. It had shelves in it. She took something from one of the shelves. It was an auditor. She turned it on, and music filled the sunlit bedroom, well-remembered music; Stratta, Dana thought. "Concerto in D, for Ella—" She snapped the pellet from the auditor and tossed it into his lap. "There are two more downstairs," she said. "I found them in the com-net's music library." She leaned over him, hands on his shoulders. He felt their grip through the supple cloth. "Come back." Her fingers tightened. "I don't want my child to grow up hating me, Dana. She—or he—

is not going to grow up alone on the estate with only
slaves and her mother and crazy uncle for company. We'll
live in the city. I'll bring her to the LandingPort, and even
to the moon. I'll show her holos of other worlds. I'll let
her read Nakamura's *History,* and then, when she's
fourteen Standard, I'll give her the choice I was never
given: to leave Chabad, to leave me, and Family Yago."

"You'd do that?" Dana said. She nodded. "I don't believe you."

"Come and see," she challenged. "Come back to
Chabad! Take her to Pellin with you. Let her meet your
family, join your wagon journey to the mountains, eat
goats and ride horses and live however people live on
other worlds."

Dana thought: I never want to see this world again. . . .
He laid his hands over hers. Stratta's melody mocked him
in lifting tones. Well, Starcaptain, it said, so much for fine
words and rages. What will you do?

"All right," he said. "I'll come back."

They stood on the shuttleship platform of the Abanat
Landingport. Chabad's sky burned about them, a harsh,
stark blaze of blue. Porters with the "Y" insignia on their
shirtsleeves jostled each other, jockeying around them.
The air smelled of sweat and heated metal.

Dana's medallion gleamed gold against his cream-
colored suit. He touched it; he had thought it lost in the
debris of Michel A-Rae's house. Rhani smiled at the
gesture. She was wearing blue-and-silver, Yago colors.
She slipped her arm through his. "Are you so glad to be
leaving, Starcaptain?"

"Yes, Domna, I am," he said. "After all, I've wanted
to leave since I got here."

"Will you go home, to Pellin?"

He shrugged. "I don't know. Maybe I'll go to Nexus."

"So that you can meet Tori Lamonica, and run more
drugs?" she teased.

"Oh, no," he said. "Not that. Never again." He smiled.
"Hell, I'm going to look for legal work." Rhani mimed
shock. He slipped his arm around her shoulders. Her hip
kissed his. Once that delicate contact had been enough to
make him stumble, but no longer. . . . He found himself
glancing at her waist. She chuckled.

"Impatient man," she said. Sliding from his grasp, she stretched her fists to the light. "Ah, I almost wish I were going with you."

"No, you don't," he said. "You can't leave Chabad now. Your work is just beginning."

"True." She dropped her arms to her sides. A bubble circled overhead in a lazy spiral, awaiting permission to land. She said, "I have a dorazine factory to find a site for, a resolution to shepherd through the Council, and a party to go to. It's Imre Kyneth's seventy-eighth birthday."

Dana remembered Immeld saying, *"They don't celebrate birthdays at all, on Chabad!"* "I thought Chabadese didn't celebrate birthdays," he said.

Rhani smiled. "True. But the Kyneths do."

Stars, he thought: I know so little about this world, and here I am leaving it. For the twentieth time, he nudged the bag at his foot. In it were an auditor, three tapes Rhani had given him of Vittorio Stratta's music, a few bits of clothing, and a certificate which returned the ownership of one MPL starship from Family Yago to Starcaptain Dana Ikoro. *Zipper* was his. In a short time—a very short time—he would ride a shuttle to the moon where she waited for him, fueled, tested, rebuilt, and ready to go.

"I would send best wishes if I thought he would remember me," Dana said.

"Imre might," Rhani said seriously. "He remembers people."

"Even slaves?"

"Even slaves." She stroked his arm. "You have no scar. I'm glad."

Bleakly he said, "There are other scars."

She flinched, and he was sorry. "I didn't say it," he said.

"You didn't say it," she agreed. But he had. He was not thinking of himself, but Michel A-Rae. The former Hype cop lay in the Abanat Clinic, under heavy guard. Dana no longer hated the Enchantean. It was hard to hate someone when you knew that he had spent ten minutes being torn to bloody strips by Zed Yago's merciless hands.

Catriona Graeme, on finding A-Rae, had wanted to charge Zed with assault. Rhani had had to do some clever talking to get her brother out of that. She had pointed out to the mercenary that although A-Rae was under the jurisdiction of the Hype cops at the time of the incident, he was still an Enchantean citizen and thus the "assault" could technically only be tried in a Chabadese court. Even Catriona Graeme agreed that it would be hard to get a Chabadese court to prosecute the case. Dana glanced behind them—Zed was standing in a pillar's shade, watching the shuttleship land. He wondered what would happen to A-Rae. If Rhani's resolution failed he would be returned to Nexus for trial; if it passed, he'd be tried on Chabad. Poor bastard, Dana thought.

The signal chimed two notes: *bing-bong!* "That's the call to the shuttle," he said. "I have to go."

"Yes," said Rhani. Dana picked up the bag. The sun made Rhani's hair seem waxed. Turning toward the pillar, Dana lifted a hand. Zed's left sleeve moved; it might have been a wave. I'm free now, Dana thought, for the hundredth time. You can't touch me. And he wondered—also for the hundredth time—why he had promised Rhani that he would come back.

He would, though. Not soon; but in six years, or ten—a long time, anyway.

"Good-bye," Rhani said. "I'll write to you."

"Yes. Send me a picture."

"I will," she said. "More than one."

"Send one of yourself, too."

She grinned. "You think you'll want one, once you're off my world?"

"I'll want one," he said, wondering what his child would look like, wondering what Rhani would look like, in two or three or six or ten years.

The signal belled a second time, and third. She pushed him. "Go!" Bag in hand, he loped toward the shuttleship. A crew member waved both arms from the top of the ramp. Dana broke into a run toward the tall ship that would take him to the moon, to his starship, home—to the irresistible clouds and the surging carmine currents of the Hype.